The first [...] enough to r[...] But it was [...] engulfed the Subrano chamber as the members of the expedition froze in mid-stride, breath held, eyes wide.

Then it came; a growling, tearing thunder that seemed to rise from the very bowels of the earth beneath their feet. The second tremor, violent spawn of the first and a hundred times stronger . . .

Like an actor in a nightmare play Anton Vlasek looked up at the roof of the cave to find himself staring into the eyes of Khan's chained bear, the painted orbs burning with a hideous fire. And the bear spoke to him with a rending, grinding scream as the roof split open, tearing the beast in half, the crack extending the length of the chamber like the grin of a massive death's head. A wedge of stone twice the size of a man knifed down, sheared from the broadening fissure, and struck Vlasek, burying him beneath its ten-ton weight, a fraction of a second after the doctor's heart exploded in his chest, saving him from the ultimate horror that followed as the lights went out and the Subrano Cave was thrown into sudden, total and absolute darkness.

STYX

Christopher Hyde

Hamlyn Paperbacks

STYX
ISBN 0 600 20662 9

First published in Great Britain 1982
by Severn House Publishers
This Hamlyn Paperbacks edition 1982
Copyright ©1982 by Christopher Hyde

Hamlyn Paperbacks are published by
The Hamlyn Publishing Group Ltd.,
Astronaut House,
Feltham, Middlesex, England.

Reproduced, printed and bound in Great Britain by
Hazell Watson & Viney Ltd, Aylesbury, Bucks

This book is dedicated to Andrew Bell and the Royal Bank of Canada, with many thanks.

'The greatest mystery of all is man himself. Finding a solution to the riddle he presents is the endless work of world history.'
Novalis

PART ONE
THE CAVE

CHAPTER ONE

1

The two Japanese had travelled up from the village, climbing through the pre-dawn mist beyond the vineyards and steeply sloped fields of stunted corn. They went higher still through bleak stands of oleander and pine, coming at last to the barren karst plateau.

They stood silently on the edge of the tumbled limestone plain, the valley below still drowned in darkness. Ahead, the rotted landscape was cut with shadows cast like shrouds from the massive blocks of soft crumbling stone that had been scattered across the scarred land tens of thousands of years before. There was no pattern to the fall of rock, no symmetry to soothe the eye. It was as though this Yugoslavian plain had been used as a dumping ground for some mad sculptor and the shattered stone was his ancient midden, desolate witness to his monumental labours. A dead place.

Beyond the karst, miles to the east, were the mountains, source of the stone, hump-backed and bald, long since stripped of the thick enfolding blankets of forest and thick layers of earth and cool moss that had covered them. The bitter mounds were touched now with light from the rising sun, but the light would bring no life to the land; that time had gone forever.

'*Fukitsu,*' said the shorter of the two men. His larger companion shook his head slowly, dark eyes watching the land ahead.

'*Fukitsu nai. Utsukushi.* Not sinister. Beautiful,' he said quietly.

'You are much too religious about these things, Izo Harada,' smiled the younger man. 'We are searching for interesting pot-holes to explore, not the way of Zen.'

'Sometimes they are one and the same,' murmured

9

Harada. Kenji Takashima, his friend, laughed, the sound brittle as it echoed from the ruined stone ahead of them.

'*Toshitotte, ira-san,*' he scoffed. 'You are an old man. You philosophize even before breakfast.' He shifted his heavy pack, anxious to be moving. Harada waited for a moment longer, watching the sun burn the edges of the distant mountains. Then he moved off, a soft smile on his broad impassive face as he led the way into the karst.

Harada knew the science of it well, knew even that the term karst was a distortion of the local word "kras", referring to an area of the country several hundred miles away, just east of Trieste. He knew the term was applied to any area of limestone outcropping which had been developed by water solution of the rocks. As a geologist he understood how the soft stone was eaten away by the water, carrying off soil, then the stone itself, until the land was riddled with cracks and fissures that in their turn aided the quick absorption of water, eventually resulting in caverns and underground rivers and leaving behind a land where nothing grew or lived, a deceptive shell above a complex midnight world below. Harada knew the science, and understood it, but the knowledge and the understanding did nothing to exorcise the deep, primal sense that filled him as he and Takashima picked their way across the tortured stone. A sense of trespass that went beyond being oriental in a Caucasion land. It was a trespass in time that he felt, a violation of the past, increased with every step into the surreal landscape, each shadowed boulder and crack-faced block a brooding tombstone erected above the bones of a world forgotten in the inexorable march of ten thousand generations. Takashima had called it sinister, but Harada felt sadness, and the beauty in it.

They walked until the sun was well over the mountains and the cool air of dawn had been replaced by sweltering heat. They stopped every few minutes to examine a fissure or a doline that looked promising. The dolines, small saucer-shaped depressions that varied in size from a foot to several yards in diameter, were the most likely places to find access to lower cave systems. They paused just after nine and drank Thermos-warm soup in the shade of a large boulder. They rested beside a high-cliffed gorge that might once have held the flow of a major river.

'This place is cursed,' groaned Takashima, leaning back against the rock. 'We have been walking for five hours and we have found nothing.'

'We have been on the karst for less than three of those hours, Kenji, it takes time. You know that,' replied Harada.

'Perhaps there are no caves at all,' said Takashima. 'And that would be something to tell them back at the university. Their renowned geologist and his assistant take a year's leave of absence to travel in foreign lands and come back with nothing. We should have stayed at home, Izo.'

'There are no karst areas in Japan,' said Harada. 'Which is why we are in Yugoslavia. To study the karst you must go to the karst, and once there you will find caves. Always.'

'Is that a guarantee, esteemed Isha?' asked Takashima, using the word for doctor with a satrical edge. Harada smiled.

'Yes, *boi-san,*' he said, using the word for student with an equal bite. 'It is always so.'

'So!' grunted Takashima, rising and slipping on his pack again. 'Let us go in search of these caves you guarantee.' Harada put on his own pack and let Takashima lead the way.

They followed the crumbling edge of the ancient river course for another hour, searching for a place to cross easily to the far side. Takashima, a hundred yards ahead, disappeared for a moment behind a tall outcropping and then Harada heard his excited call.

'*Harada san! Koko ni kite kudasai. Hayaku!*' Harada followed the voice and found Takashima on his stomach, peering down a doline some five or six feet across.

'*Hayaku?*' asked Harada. 'Why do you call for haste? This hole has been here ten thousand years. Would it have disappeared?'

'Not for ten thousand years, Izo. Look!' Takashima pointed to the rough-edged mouth of the pothole. Its surface was uneroded. 'This is new. There has been no time for water to smooth the rock.'

'Possible,' said Harada, squatting. Takashima was right and Harada felt a small surge of excitement himself. He stood and stripped off his pack.

'Seismic?' asked Takashima, looking up from the hole. Harada shrugged.

'Perhaps,' he said. 'Yugoslavia is known for its earthquakes.'

'An entrance?' asked Takashima. Harada laughed.

'There is only one way to find out,' he said. Takashima grinned and they began unpacking their equipment.

Within half an hour they were ready. They had completely changed their clothing, donning steel-toed miners' boots, gaiters, woollen underclothes and heavy denim overalls topped by bright red sailing jackets. Each wore a miner's hard hat complete with light. Takashima had a fifty-foot length of rope looped like a bandolier across his chest while Harada carried two of them. They both wore wide belts with a variety of picks, hammers and pitons. The full load of their equipment added twenty pounds to each man's weight.

Harada unrolled a 25-foot length of aluminium and nylon ladder, playing it out over the edge of the hole after first securing it to a small spur of rock. The ladder met no obstructions as it unrolled down the hole. The sink was clear, at least for the first few yards.

There was no question about who should go down first. Harada had been spelunking for twenty years, almost half his lifetime. Takashima, with only five years of caving experience, was a novice by comparison although he was classified as an expert. Harada eased himself over the side, the thick rubber soles of his boots gripping the swaying ladder, while Takashima made sure the ladder held firm at the top.

Harada descended slowly, one step at a time. His nostrils flared as he drew in the damp bitter scent of the rock and he grinned in the engulfing darkness. Each time he went below the land he had the same memory, the turning point in his life when he had decided to become a geologist. The smell, the first tang of cool rock in a seaside cavern close to the village, where he and his family had once spent a holiday. The odour had been overwhelming; so strong that he had caressed the hard rippled surface, then tasted it with his tongue. The taste had never left his mouth and from then on he had used any excuse to recapture that moment, descending into the earth to be swallowed by the darkness, to be surrounded by the infinite rock, wandering through the tunnels and caverns of the massive womb. It was only here, below, that he felt at one with himself and the world, as though by the act of touching the earth and trusting it so completely he could touch and trust all others.

The hole widened quickly and even in the dark Harada could sense the space around him. He reached the end of the ladder and unclipped a flashlight from his belt. He turned it on and swung the beam from side to side. The chimney was a dozen feet across, the rock knobbed and cracked with dozens of natural hand and foot holds. He shone the light downward. A few feet below the chimney narrowed again until it was barely wide enough for a man to squeeze through. The bottleneck had left a narrow ring of ledge. Harada replaced the flashlight on his belt and let himself down, dangling off the ladder. His toe touched the ledge and he let go, bringing out his arms to brace himself. He turned on the lamp on his helmet and peered down the hole.

It wasn't really a chimney at all, more like a fissure between two large blocks of limestone. The walls were smooth but it would be easy enough to descend, using his back and knees as brakes while he slipped down. Climbing back up, however, might be difficult. He called up to Takashima, telling him it was safe to come down, then took off one of the rope lengths. He hammered a ring-ended piton into the rock and looped the rope through it, letting the rest drop down the fissure. He took a coil of the rope and pulled it between his legs and over his shoulder, using it as a safety line, then dropped down the crack, bracing himself firmly against the rock walls.

He went down foot by foot, the pressure of the rock firm against his knees and back, one arm extended, hand splayed against the stone, the thick sensitive fingers judging every slight feature like a blind man reading someone's face, trying to judge his character by touch alone. He could have used his light but Harada had long ago learned that to depend on light in a place where darkness ruled could be fatal. To live with the rock you had to accept the dark, and *know* each tiny knob and crack and fracture.

13

Thirty feet below the bottleneck the fissure ended, narrowing to a razor-thin crack. Wedged firmly, the rope still slung around him, Harada turned on his light again. The face of the rock was within a few inches of his face. He turned his head, his eyes following the light, looking for some way to move downward. Far above he could hear the faint sounds of Takashima's descent.

There was another fissure, wider than the one he had come down. This crack was horizontal, running away at right angles from the first. Harada nodded to himself. He had reached the corner joint of two major blocks of stone. Sometime in the recent past seismic activity had jolted the blocks, separating them. He frowned. The chances were good that the horizontal fracture would dead end when it reached the next block. The fault was too new and there was little chance that the passage would lead to a cave. Takashima, he knew, would be disappointed.

Rather than wait for the young man and listen to his outraged comments, Harada decided to keep on. It would be foolish to take the fissure for granted. He would keep on until there was nowhere else to go.

The crack was wide enough to stand in, but there was no footing at its base so Harada went down it crabwise, keeping his feet against the far wall, and leaning against the rock at his back. He worked his way forward, concentrating on each step, but with part of his mind keeping track of distances and angles, storing the information until he could get to his survey note-book and begin a rough mapping of the fault. By now he knew he was travelling roughly parallel to the river gorge, about fifty feet below the surface. If the crack extended far enough it might eventually cut across an old cave dating back to the time when water had actually flowed down the gorge.

Suddenly the fissure ended and Harada's outstretched arm met empty air. He let his fingers trace the edge of the crack. It was more than just a widening of the fault, it was an opening of some kind. He went forward, sliding his booted feet carefully until he reached the end of the passage. Keeping one hand on the rock wall and both feet firmly planted he turned on his light again, poking his head out of the opening.

14

It was a cave, not just a widening of the fissure. He played the light slowly down. There was a smoothly-worn slope that met the floor of the cave fifteen feet below. The bottom of the cave was granular, like dried clay. Harada frowned. The geology was wrong. By rights the cave floor should have been made up of smooth flowstone built up by limestone deposits. He squirmed around until he was facing back down the fissure.

'Kenji?' he called, his voice rebounding dully from the rock.

'*Hai*,' came the young man's voice, still far away.

'There is a cave,' shouted Harada. 'Follow the horizontal fault. Use your light after you have gone about one hundred feet. I'm going in.'

'*Hai*,' responded Takashima in the distance, his voice muffled. Harada turned again and began his descent into the cave, dropping down to the floor easily. He stood and took out his flashlight again, shining the narrow beam around the cavern. The far wall was at least sixty feet away, rising steeply to the uneven corrugations of the dark, arched roof. Harada swung the flash-light to the left and right, trying to establish the cavern's depth. To the left the floor went on for a little less than a hundred feet, stopping abruptly at a sloped barrier of rubble that reached the ceiling. If his calculations were correct the rubble wall had probably once been the original cave mouth, blocked hundreds or thousands of years before as the roof of the cave collapsed close to the opening. To the right, the cave narrowed quickly, the roof sloping down to the floor. There was an area of depression there, perhaps a passage to another cave lower down. For the moment Harada ignored it, his interest piqued by the floor. He squatted and trained the flashlight on the dark grey substance. He reached between his knees and dug into the substance, bringing his cupped hand into the light. Dried mud, but once it had been soil. Still squatting, he played the light across the floor. The surface was almost perfectly smooth with the exception of a few irregularly placed depressions making puddles of shadow in the glare. Harada shook his head, trying to unravel the mystery. The soil simply should not have existed in the cave; it would have to have been brought in. He looked up.

Takashima's light was casting its long beam down the fissure passage to the cave. A moment later the young man appeared in the mouth of the passage, starkly lit by Harada's flashlight.

'Izo! A real cave!' excalimed the young man. Harada smiled and snapped off the light, letting Takashima's helmet lamp illuminate the cavern.

'Am I not the esteemed Isha who promised you such a place?' he grinned. Takashima repeated the sequence of movements that had taken Harada out of the fissure and reached the cave floor, panting for breath.

'I am almost twice your age,' chided Harada, 'and yet it is you who fights for air.'

'Do not whip me with your religion, Izo. It is like a scourge,' wheezed Takashima.

'Rightly so,' smiled Harada, enjoying the familiar banter. 'For your skin is so thick it needs regular lashing to allow penetration of even a small amount of knowledge. And even you must admit, *bio-san*, that my religion as you call it, leaves my lungs cleaner than yours.' He clapped the young man on the back. 'Anyway, Kenji, you have your cave, and a strange one at that. Look.' He lifted a handful of dirt from the cave floor and let it shift into Takashima's palm.

'Clay,' said the young man, examining it under his helmet lamp.

'No,' said Harada. 'Mud. Dried, sodden, dried again, countless times. It is soil, Kenji – or it was, thousands of years ago.'

'But that is impossible,' said Takashima, letting the small grains fall through his fingers.

'Not impossible,' murmured Harada. 'Simply difficult to understand.'

'Do you understand?' asked Takashima. Harada shook his head.

'Not yet. We must examine the cave more completely. We will do a survey.'

'*Hai*,' agreed Takashima.

They got out their equipment and began taking accurate measurements. Takashima paced out the dimensions of the cave while Harada logged them in the survey notebook, taking specific points as benchmarks for a map which he sketched quickly. Harada's earlier estimation proved almost perfectly accurate. The cave was one hundred and forty-five feet long and seventy-nine feet across at its widest point.

'Shall we follow the sink at the rear of the cave?' asked Takashima, completing the measurements. Harada jotted down the last of the figures in his book.

'I think not,' he said thoughtfully. 'This cave is obviously flooded regularly, you can see that by the fine grain of the floor. To excavate the sink would be too dangerous. We might even find ourselves in a mud-filled chimney which we couldn't get out of. No, it is too dangerous. Even a slight rainfall while we were below could prove fatal.'

'There were no clouds when we came down,' argued Takashima. 'It is mid-summer; there is little rain here at this time of year.'

'Prudence,' said Harada. 'This is a country and a geology unfamiliar to us. I would prefer a somewhat less risk-filled cavern to practise on.' He caught Takashima's raised eyebrow and laughed heartily. 'And do not call me an old woman for my decision, Kenji,' he said. 'We will take some photographs and then return to the surface. There is nothing more to be learned here.'

Takashima grunted his disapproval and unpacked the Leica from his small knapsack, fitting it with a powerful sun-gun flash unit.

'Which positions?' asked the younger man. Harada thought for a moment and then spoke.

'Rear, looking forward; front looking to the rear, and several of the floor. Those depressions interest me.'

Takashima nodded and walked to the rubble wall at the front of the cave, the lamp on his helmet sending a bobbing puddle of light ahead. Harada waited expectantly. Because the lights they used were focussed in narrow beams he almost never saw an entire cave fully lit; the use of the sun-gun gave him that opportuunity, for a split second bringing the sun below the surface, peeling back the impenetrable dark for a fleeting instant. Takashima reached the far end of the cave and turned, his lamp piercing the blackness.

'Here?' he called.

'*Hai,*' agreed Harada. There was a brief pause and then the flash unit exploded silently, filling the chamber with brilliant light.

Later Harada wondered what would have happened had his face not been tilted upward at that moment. Would they have left the cave, ignorant of what it held, its secret lost forever? But he *was* looking at the ceiling when the flash went off and he had a moment of perfect clarity. Then the darkness dropped again, the flash leaving a burning after-image on his retinas. The moment had been enough. Harada felt his heart begin to pound, and he blinked again and again, not trusting what his eyes had seen was true. He stood, stunned, unable to speak. He was vaguely aware of Takashima's light approaching.

'*Desu ne kyoi*,' he whispered.

'Excuse me?' asked Takashima, stopping. Harada shook his head, trying to clear it.

'Did you see, Kenji?' asked Harada slowly.

'See what?' asked Takashima.

'Flares,' muttered Harada. 'Do we have flares?'

'Yes, we have flares,' said Takashima, puzzled. 'Why? The flash unit is more than enough to light the photographs.'

'Light a flare, Kenji, quickly,' said Harada.

'I don't understand,' said Takashima. Harada waved a hand.

'Light one,' said Harada softly, still not believing what he had seen in that instant, almost afraid to find that his eyes had lied.

'*Hai, Isha-san*,' said Takashima. He pulled a flare from his belt and tore off the magnesium igniter strip. The flare went off, a blazing sceptre in the young man's hand.

'Hold it up, Kenji,' said Harada. 'Hold it up high and look at the roof.' Takashima did as he was told. Harada stared upward and knew that he had not been deceived.

The ceiling of the cavern pulsed with life. Colour, form and texture danced up from the mists of time as ridgeback bison, black and ochre, reared, strongly muscled haunches worked into protrusions of rock. Ibex, scores of them, fled in bent-leg flight, horns swept back along the roof, gleaming eyes wide with fear as a dozen stick figures, codpieced and waving spears, ran after them. A bear, life-size, loomed, head

18

peering down at Harada and Takashima, mouth yawning in a fanged grimace, its spreadeagled legs pinned down to the rock by thinly painted lines of black that might have been ropes or vines. Yellow, green and red, tan, black and ochre, flowing muscle and fine-wrought bone, animals, men, creatures that were both and neither, hundreds of them, herds of them, armies of them, all danced, ran, galloped and writhed above the two awe-stricken men below. It was a masterpiece of colour and line, the whole of it a monumental fresco depicting a life and time long dead. It was the past, fleeting moments of it, preserved forever, locked in the darkness for eternity, suddenly revealed to humankind again.

Harada knew that theirs were the first eyes to have seen the painting in millenia, and he felt a shudder pass through him as he was touched by the ghosts of those who must have lived here once. Even the air was alive, and he could smell the dank sweat, the cold ice-age wind, the cooking odours. Soft rhythmic singing filled his ears with ancient cadences, and he heard the welcome cries as the hunters returned. Images filled his brain, one on another, as time stood still and he was almost overcome. He had an overwhelming urge to leave, and seal the cave behind him, to hold the knowledge to himself so that man would never violate this sacred place again. The cave was a tomb, the paintings a transcendant elegy beyond any words. But Harada knew that all things had to be revealed in their time, and that the secret was not his to keep.

'We must tell them,' he said, his voice rising strongly, somehow sensing that the man who had painted this rock would have wanted it so. 'We must give this to the world.'

2

Dr Anton Vlasek, general practitioner in the Dalmatian village of Subrano, sipped his late afternoon demitasse of Kaj, enjoying the thick bitter coffee as he stared myopically out at his garden. The double glass doors leading out from his study gave him an excellent view of the densely-bedded flowers and herbs and it was a sight that never ceased to please him. The sun was sinking, casting long shadows across the colourful square of rich soil, the imported earth protected by a high stone wall enclosing it, keeping the somewhat less pleasant realities of Subrano at bay.

He had been back five years now, after almost two decades of practice in Belgrade. At first he had been enthusiastic about his return to the house where he was born, glad to be rid of the pressures of city life. Now, after five years of tending to the minor aches and pains of the Subrano villagers, most of them geriatric, he wasn't so sure. For Vlasek, medicine was a profession, a job, nothing more. His passion lay elsewhere.

Vlasek's first and, indeed, only love had always been history, the endless search for past truths, but historians make little money and on his father's orders he had taken the scholarship from the university in Sarajevo to become a doctor of medicine. He studied hard and well, bringing honour to his village and his parents, but it was never enough. Throughout his student years, and later as a practising physician, he had always found time to haunt the Rejik Musima and the libraries, forever reading and dreaming about discoveries he would never make, and archaeological digs he would never be a part of.

So, for Anton Vlasek, archaeology and anthropology became a hobby, and he an amateur. He hated the term, but he had learned to live with it. Lately though he had found his hobby consuming more and more of his time, and the amateurishness of his endeavours grated. He was not yet sixty, but here he was puttering about with flint knives and shards of bone, cataloguing books instead of artifacts. The quality of his medical practice made him only half a doctor and the limits of his education made him less than half a historian. He knew now, at his age, he would never make his mark in either field, and the knowledge saddened and depressed him. He smiled wanly and drained the last of the Kaj. It was childish, but he wanted to be more than Anton Vlasek. He wanted to be *the* Anton Vlasek.

He turned in his ancient swivel chair and placed the cup

down on the scarred leather surface of his desk. Reaching into the pocket of his worn blue serge jacket, he brought out a crumpled packet of cigarettes and lit one with a match. He dragged deeply, savouring the acrid bite of the foul-smelling "Ljuti duvan" as it seared his lungs. He looked around the room, a furrowed, brooding expression on his tanned face.

It was a gloomy room, full of memories. Three walls were lined with an uneven collection of bookcases filled to overflowing with treasured volumes collected over the years. The fourth wall, behind him on either side of the glass doors to the garden, was whitewashed and hung with photographs from his past. Teresa, his wife, killed in the last days of the war, his parents, stiff and uncomfortable, their peasant faces staring nervously into the camera eye. Bruno, his best friend at medical school, gone now as well. They were all dead, his wife, parents, friends. A wave of sadness engulfed him and he turned to look out into his garden once again, his eyes wet with unfallen tears. There was a harsh rapping at the door leading into the hall outside the room.

'Come,' he said, without turning. The door creaked open and he felt an accusatory presence: Stasha, the fat old Montenegran housekeeper he had imported from the hills on his return to Subrano. He sighed and slid around in his chair, knowing that the old harridan wouldn't speak until he was facing her.

She stood, nearly filling the doorway, her close to three hundred pounds fitted into a shapeless brown dress that served to camouflage the worst of her body's features.

'What is it?' he asked. The small mouth centred in her drooping, fleshy face pursed even more tightly.

'The two oriental people have come back,' she said. 'They want to talk to you. The older one with the very slanted eyes says that it is important. Shall I send them away, Doctor?'

'Certainly not!' replied Vlasek. The two men, geologists from the University of Osaka, had been a bright spot in his week, having arrived the previous day, looking for likely cave areas. Krejiin, the mayor, had referred them to him as the resident expert on such things.

'You want me to send them in?' asked Stasha, obviously displeased.

'Immediately, and bring us some pivo. They are probably thirsty.' The old woman waddled away, returning a few moments later with Harada and Takashima and carrying a tray with several bottles of the local beer, and glasses. She gave the two Japanese a slow suspicious look and then left, leaving the door slightly open as she went out.

'You must excuse me,' said Vlasek to Harada in English, the only language common to them. He went to the door and closed it lightly. From beyond it he could hear the fat woman's irritated footsteps march away. He turned, smiling, and indicated two chairs in front of his desk.

'You will have some beer, perhaps?' he asked, pointing to the tray on the desk. Both men nodded gratefully. Vlasek poured out three glasses and handed them around, taking his own behind the desk to his chair. He stared curiously at the two; both seemed excited, their eyes glistening, but neither spoke. They sampled the beer and then nodded approvingly.

'It is very welcome on such a hot day,' said Harada, bowing his head slightly. Vlasek inclined his own head, not quite sure of the accepted protocol. He took a sip of his own beer and then the two men drank in earnest, draining their glasses within a few seconds.

'It appears that your journey was a succesful one,' said Vlasek politely. He had little interest in geology, but he was pleased to have been of help. Harada nodded.

'More successful than we could have imagined,' the older Japanese replied. He looked at Vlasek carefully. 'You mentioned yesterday that you held an interest for archaeology.'

Vlasek nodded. 'In a small way,' he said, taking another sip of beer. 'It has long been an interest of mine.'

'Have there been a great number of finds made nearby?' asked Harada.

Vlasek shook his head. 'Almost none. Some late Mousterian flints at the end of the river valley. Once a carved piece of bone. Nothing else.'

'Late Mousterian,' said Takashima. 'You mean Neander-thal?'

Vlasek shrugged. 'I am not sufficiently educated to judge. I think so, but they could be Cro-Magnon. The finds were of insufficient interest to attract the staff of the University of Belgrade.'

'*Jiki*,' admonished Harada softly. He smiled at Vlasek. 'You must excuse my young colleague's impatience. He wants me to tell you of our find without any delay.'

'You arouse my curiosity,' replied Vlasek. 'What exactly have you found?' He found himself subjected to the older man's searching look again.

'We have found a cave,' said Harada finally.

Vlasek smiled. 'For you that may cause excitement, sir, but caves are common in this part of the world. There are dozens of known ones in this valley alone.'

'Not one such as this,' said Harada. 'I felt that its discovery should be brought to your attention immediately.'

'You found this cave on the karst?' asked Vlasek.

Harada nodded. 'Yes,' he said. 'By the banks of what must once have been a major river.'

'The Mostari Gorge,' nodded Vlasek. 'It exits at the head of the valley here at the River Subrano. Why do you think this cave would be of interest to me?'

'Not just to you, Doctor. To everyone. It is, I think, a major archaeological find.'

'I understood you were a geologist,' said Vlasek, frowning.

'I am,' nodded Harada. 'But I think I know enough of anthropology to recognize something important.' He paused. 'Doctor, I believe I have with my friend discovered a cave to equal those at Lascaux or Font de Gaume. Do you appreciate what it is I am saying?'

Vlasek felt his heart almost stop in his chest. His eyes widened and he replaced his half-empty glass on the desk.

'This cave is painted?' he whispered, unbelieving.

'Yes, Doctor. Incredibly painted. Scenes of hunting, of battle. Animals, men, weapons. Sealed, hidden for many thousands of years. It is my opinion that some recent seismic activity opened up a small doline on the surface. In times past there was a rock-fall closing the river opening of the cave.'

'My God!' breathed Vlasek.

Harada went on. 'Has there been any recent activity to open up such a pothole?'

Vlasek nodded distractedly. 'Yes, yes,' he murmured. 'Several months ago there were some tremors. Nothing large.' He looked at Harada. 'The cave is truly painted?'

'Yes, Doctor. And more. There is evidence on the floor of some kind of human activity. Regular shaped depressions.'

'Fires,' said Vlasek, nodding. 'Perhaps a bear ritual tomb.' The doctor stood and began pacing behind the desk. He stopped, facing the lowering light of the garden. 'I will cable to Penfold at the University in Paris,' he said to himself, nodding. He turned to Harada and Takashima. 'You must take me to the cave!'

3

Dr David Alexander Penfold Senior left the apartment on the Boulevard Haussmann after what he considered to be a most unsatisfactory lunch with his son. The tall, distinguished man climbed into the large Maserati Citroën provided by the University and jerked out into the heavy early-afternoon traffic. He bullied his way into the centre lane, piloting the shark-nosed automobile southward, heading in the direction of the Henri IV bridge across the Seine.

His son, David Junior, was intractable. The elder Penfold had connived and virtually bribed his way into a position where David could be made assistant during the two years' tenure at the University of Paris Archaeology Faculty, and after nine months David had come to the conclusion that he was bored.

Bored! He'd kept on using the word all through lunch. At thirty his son felt he should be moving out from under his father's wing, making some headway on his own. It was ridiculous. No, it was ludicrous, thought Penfold, cutting in front of a rusted Saviem van to make a sweeping turn on to Boulevard de Sébastopol. He himself had been in his early forties before he'd won any acclaim with his research on aspects of Neanderthal culture. Yet David thought it was time to get out on his own. Didn't he realize what a priveleged situation he was in? As the son of one of the foremost archaeologists in the world he had access to people and places any other struggling archaeologist would give his left arm for. When his latest book, *The Birth of Man,* had been published a year ago, David was listed as a contributing editor. What more did the boy want?

'Ungrateful little bastard!' muttered Penfold. He slid to the left, circling the monument at Place de Châtelet and geared down, jerking the car on to the Quai de Gesvres. Out of the corner of his eye he could see the spires of Notre Dame rising out of the trees on the Ile de la Cité. He ignored the classic postcard view and stepped down on the accelerator.

If David decided to make good his threat and leave his position as assistant it would be terribly embarrassing. Penfold had been brought to the university with a fanfare, taking the chair as Director of Archaeology in a wave of publicity about joint US - French scientific cooperation. It looked good on paper, but the reality was that he'd been shoehorned into the post politically, over the objections of the faculty – most especially Alain Bouchard, the man primed for the position when old Dulac-LaBarre died suddenly in the late summer of the previous year. David's resignation as assistant was precisely the kind of thing that Bouchard could use as a rallying flag – see, even the cuckoo's child deserts him! He had less than eighteen months to run in his term, with the chance of a Nobel at the end of it if the Istrian dig turned out well. He'd been fighting Bouchard on that score for months now. Bouchard, a conservative by anyone's standards, wanted to work at a site in the south of France that had been originally found before the second world war. Nothing new would be found there, but according to Bouchard the dig was a necessary one, even if it wasn't glamorous.

Glamour, thought Penfold, turning the car on to the bridge across the Seine, that was the key to Bouchard's personality. He loathed anyone who had the faintest odour of popular success, but he craved it himself. His hatred of fame came directly out of his envy of it. Bouchard knew perfectly well that the preliminary investigation on the Adriatic coast site was promising. But it wasn't his choice and it wasn't in France. Penfold on the other hand couldn't have cared less where it was. You dig where there is something to dig for, not in a mined-out quarry like the French site.

As Director, Penfold knew that he could veto Bouchard at

any time, but in his own way Bouchard *was* famous, at least within the tight circle of archaeologists and anthropologists. He was a member of at least a dozen societies, national and international, and he could do a lot to cut Penfold's chances at the brass ring of the Nobel. In some ways, Penfold knew Bouchard was right; he *was* a usurper. To be an archaeologist in the United States meant a lifetime deciding which Indian kitchen midden to dig. The human history of North America was only fractionally as large as Europe's, and Bouchard played upon that constantly, making oblique references at faculty dinners and meetings about their interim director's search for a mother-lode. The parallels he drew to Carter's raping of the Tutankhamun site on behalf of himself and the then fledgling Metropolitan Museum in New York were common and far from flattering. The concept of the Ugly American was still strong, at least in Bouchard's mind.

To top it all off there was David's relationship with Bouchard's daughter, Irene. The little bitch had been on her way in to the apartment as he had left. At least he had to congratulate his son on his taste. She was quite beautiful, short, slim and small-breasted, her face almost classic, huge-eyed and high-cheekboned, topped by a boyish thatch of blond hair. The friendship between the two had begun within days of their arrival, and seemed to be getting more and more serious as time went on. It irritated Penfold that his son would take up with the child of his adversary, but there was a certain satisfaction in knowing that the relationship went beyond irritation in Bouchard's case — it infuriated him. As Penfold turned in through the gates of the Science Faculty off Rue Cuvier on the Left Bank he found himself wondering if David had bedded her yet. It was unlikely; Penfold doubted if his son had it in him. The boy bore more than a physical resemblance to his mother, Penfold's ex-wife: both were wallflowers. He parked the car in his spot and went up to his office.

Bouchard was waiting for him. The dapper grey-haired Frenchman was seated in the outer office flipping rapidly through a copy of *Archaeology Today*, his small eyes flashing behind the thick lenses of his wire-rim glasses. He tossed the magazine down on the coffee table in front of him as Penfold entered.

'Dr Penfold,' he said, standing. Penfold looked at him, trying to summon up at least the semblance of a smile. As always Bouchard was dressed immaculately. Dark grey suit, crisp white shirt and plain tie. He wore an Académie Française pin conspicuously on his lapel.

'Bouchard,' nodded Penfold. He lifted a hand, directing the sullen man ahead of him into the inner office. Penfold followed, going around the massive carved oak desk and seating himself in the modern leather office chair. Bouchard sat across from him, his hands folded neatly in his lap, the fingers twined together.

'We must discuss the choosing of a site,' said Bouchard without preamble. 'It is already late June. If we are to utilize the funds at hand we must begin work before the end of July.' The man was breathing quickly, a worm-like ridge of vein pulsing high on his forehead. 'The staff has been chosen already as you know. Months ago in fact.'

Penfold knew Bouchard meant that the expedition members had all been chosen before his assumption of the faculty chair. It was another sore point between them.

'That staffing was done based on the Marbeaux site,' said Penfold, sitting forward and placing his hands flat on the desk.

Bouchard nodded. 'Correct,' he said.

'A *fait accompli*, to use your language.'

'I would not say that, Doctor. I would say merely that the Marbeaux site was scheduled for further investigation several years ago. Your predecessor was the one who authorized the disbursement of funds for the project.'

'I am not Dulac-LaBarre,' replied Penfold.

'I am quite aware of that fact, Dr Penfold, I assure you. Nevertheless, the funds were allocated for that project specifically.'

'I already have permits from the Yugoslav government, Bouchard. They are eager to have such prestigious institutions as the University of Paris and the National Museum of France backing the dig in Istria.'

'Not to mention the illustrious Dr Penfold,' put in Bouchard, his lip curling. Penfold resisted an urge to slam his fist down on the desk, taking a deep breath instead. He let it out slowly.

'Bouchard, I am trying to do my job. I am the head of this faculty . . .'

'For the moment,' interrupted Bouchard. Penfold ignored him.

' . . . and as the head of this faculty it is my responsibility to choose sites. The Marbeaux location will add nothing to our knowledge of the past. You know as well as I do that the site was worked over years ago.'

'There is much important work that remains to be done,' interjected Bouchard. His fingers worked in his lap, knuckles whitening. Penfold sat back in his chair, sighing.

'Shards,' he said. 'Nothing but a few remaining pieces of the flint workings. Dr Bouchard, if it is one thing we know well by this point it is how Neanderthal and his relatives worked flint. The Istrian dig is different. For one thing the site is on the coast; that in itself is interesting. We know almost nothing of prehistoric maritime culture. I spent much of last year travelling through Yugoslavia, Doctor, and I can assure you that I found more speculative evidence of Neanderthal in six months than you could get out of Marbeaux in twenty years.'

'Yes,' said Bouchard, his voice almost a hiss. 'And that is the point, Dr Penfold. *You* travelled in Yugoslavia for six months, *you* located this coastal site. The Istrian dig is *your* project, not this University's. You may wish to travel the world like a wandering gypsy, digging where you will, but I for one am interested in the history of *this* country.'

'I am afraid the Ministry of Science disagrees with you,' said Penfold heavily, playing his trump card. 'I spoke with Marais last week; his office is willing to take on all the transportation costs of the Istrian dig.'

'So you have decided, then,' said Bouchard, his voice cold.

Penfold nodded. 'I am afraid so, Doctor. We will dig at the Istrian site,' he said flatly.

'Then there is nothing more to be said,' muttered Bouchard, standing.

'I'm sorry, Doctor,' said Penfold.

Bouchard's eyes, enlarged behind the thick glass of his lenses, flared angrily. 'I don't think you are,' he said, then turned on his heel and left the office. Penfold watched him go, breathing a sigh of relief as the door closed behind him. When the man had gone he leaned wearily back in his chair, squeezing the bridge of his nose in the pinch of a thumb and forefinger. Then he sat forward, pulling a bulky file from the centre drawer of the desk. He had at least an hour's work to do on budgets before his meeting with the Yugoslav MD who had sent the intriguing telegram a few days before. He found himself thinking about Bouchard's daughter, fantasizing what he would do to her if she was his mistress. He frowned, annoyed with himself, and brushed the thought from his mind, settling down to work.

4

'I often wonder why you spend the money on rent here when your father has the house the University rented for him,' said Irene Bouchard, standing by the tall window of David Penfold's apartment on the Boulevard Haussmann. Her English was Swiss finishing school smooth, aided by a further three years at Oxford.

'Can you actually imagine my father and I living in the same house?' said David, lying on the platform bed at the other end of the small, high-ceilinged room. '2500 francs a month is cheap to avoid that, let me tell you.'

'Do you really hate him as much as you say?' she asked, looking at him. He shrugged, his smooth almost adolescent features tightening.

'It's not hatred,' he said. 'It's what in highschool they used to call a personality conflict. He just can't seem to get it into his head that I'm thirty years old and not four and a half. And anyway, who are you to talk, you don't get on so well with your own father.' She smiled and came across the room to the bed, the soft fabric of her shirt moving against her small breasts.

'That's different,' she said, sitting down on the edge of the bed. 'I am the daughter of a Frenchman. A very French Frenchman. In English you would call him a doting parent. It

29

becomes a little claustrophobic at times and I react, that's all. He is a man brought up from the traditions of Teilhard de Chardin and Rousseau. History is very strong in him, among other things. He wants me to be a classic child. The fact that we disagree on major social and moral issues doesn't change the fact that I love him very much, David.' She reached for the package of Disque Bleu on the bedside table, lit one of the short, fat cigarettes and dragged in the smoke, letting it dribble slowly from her nostrils.

'And what about me?' he asked. 'Do you love me?' He brought one hand from behind his head and began stroking her arm.

'*De temps en temps,*' she said, smiling. 'When you are strong I love you but when you fight with your father you are a little like the child he sees in you. And it hurts you stupidly, David. This thing about you quitting at the University is a political thing between you, it has nothing to do with your work.'

'It's not political,' said David. 'I'm just not getting anywhere working under him, that's all. I have to get out from under his shadow.'

'Where would you go?' she asked pointedly. 'No one could ask for a better position than yours.' David grimaced; it was a question that had been on his mind a lot recently.

'I don't know,' he said finally. 'All I do know is that I'm tired of sweeping up after my old man. I didn't get a doctorate in archaeology to become his office-boy, you know.'

'And your doctorate was on Neanderthal and his historical position in relation to Cro-Magnon,' she said. 'The same area as your father's work. You compete, David.'

'So what can I do?' he said. 'I really am interested in Neanderthal. I think my father's basic theories about the anomaly of Neanderthal suddenly vanishing and Cro-Magnon's instant emergence are true. Am I supposed to avoid the subject simply because it puts me behind him?'

'Perhaps,' said Irene. 'This thing between you is a sickness.'

'Sure,' muttered David. 'Throw in the towel, just like I always do. Give in because he was there first.'

'You're being childish, David. The field is a large one. You can work with Neanderthal without copying your father, or being in direct competition with him. There is room for both of you. Look at the Leakeys and Olduvai Gorge,' she suggested.

'Richard Leakey didn't come into any kind of prominence until his father died,' countered David.

'I'm not talking about prominence,' said Irene. 'Richard Leakey had a respectable career completely separate from his father's. He made finds of his own, anyway, at Lake Rudolf in Kenya as well as Olduvai. They worked together, David.'

'My father isn't Louis Leakey and I'm not Richard,' said David bitterly. 'My father is a domineering son-of-a-bitch who would sell his soul for a spot on the *New York Times* best-seller list, and ten minutes on the CBS Evening News. He's a glory hound and he's arrogant. He told my mother he divorced her because she wasn't stimulating enough. I think he'd like to divorce me as well. Fine. I'm just speeding up the process by getting out of his way, that's all. I've been offered a position on the Mayan dig I told you about for next summer. I'm going to take it.'

'You don't have the slightest interest in Mayan culture,' said Irene.

'I'll cultivate one,' said David. He reached out and took the cigarette from her and puffed on it angrily. Irene sighed, watching him silently.

She studied his face and body, feeling a growing tension in the pit of her stomach. He was handsome, more so than his father, almost like a Michelangelo sculpture. If it hadn't been for the flash of his dark brown eyes that burned under the thick fall of dark blond hair he would be almost too perfect. And the eyes were the windows to the soul, she reminded herself. He was a man, but troubled with the anger and fears of a child.

'David,' she whispered. *'Reste calme, petit.'* She let her hand fall on the hard muscle of his thigh, shrouded beneath the tight-fitting denim of his jeans.

'Don't call me that!' He snapped, and stubbed out the cigarette in a scarred Cinzano ashtray on the table. He reached for her, pulling her down on top of him. She accepted the first hard, thrusting kiss, then gently pushed herself away.

'I'm not ready yet,' she said, sitting up. She stood and then walked to the bathroom, picking up her bag along the way. She went into the tiny cubicle at the rear of his apartment and closed the door firmly. Going to the chipped enamel sink she studied her face in the mirror. Tense. She stuck out her tongue at the reflection and rummaged around in her bag, pulling out the blue oyster of her diaphragm case. She popped it open and stared at the dome of pale rubber it contained, feeling a familiar twinge of guilt. At twenty-four she was a long way from virginity but all the same the years of convent schooling had left their mark. For a moment she paused, wondering if she should put the device inside her. The thought of having David's child sent a glow through her, but a short-lived one. She loved him and wanted him, but it was too soon, and should not happen that way. She picked up the diaphragm and began spreading cream on it, thinking about the hundreds of times she had performed the ritual before and wondering which was the greatest defiance to her upbringing: using a birth control device and contravening the laws of the church, or not using it and having an illegitimate child. She smiled to herself as she went about the business of inserting the thing; it wasn't birth control that was a sin, sex was the ultimate transgression, married or not. She giggled, remembering a frail, white-haired nun who'd taught her, named Sister Benedict, trying to imagine her in the throes of orgasm.

'Irene Bouchard,' she whispered, 'you are a blasphemer.' She slipped out of the rest of her clothes and went back to the bedroom.

5

'It is a great pleasure to meet you once again,' said Vlasek, shaking Penfold's hand enthusiastically. Penfold ushered him to a chair, trying vainly to place the man. He'd spent half the previous year in Yugoslavia and met hundreds of people, but the man wasn't unfamiliar. He sat down behind his desk and watched as Vlasek gingerly set down his wide, worn briefcase on the floor between his legs. He reached into it and took out a manila envelope, keeping it on his lap.

'We met last summer,' supplied Vlasek, sensing Penfold's confusion. 'You were on your way through our village, which is Subrano, and you had a flat tyre. While it was being fixed I showed you our flint workings near the river.'

Penfold nodded, remembering vaguely. He had a misty recollection of a dusty little hamlet in an interior valley, two days across the Greek border. The flint workings had been Neanderthal all right, but of no particular interest. A rest stop for a band of hunters on their way home perhaps, but nothing more. He looked over Vlasek's shoulder and out through the opened door of his office, hoping for an interruption. He hadn't made a dent in the budgets so far.

'I will take little of your time,' said Vlasek, noticing the look and understanding what it meant. 'I would have taken my discovery to the Museum in Belgrade but since we had already met, and knowing of your great importance in the field Neanderthal . . .'

'Yes, yes,' said Penfold. 'I understand.' Vlasek would not be deterred and kept on with his little speech. Penfold sighed. Vlasek was an amateur, and they were invariably the ones who talked the most and had the least to say. Verbosity disguising banality.

'I have travelled all the way from Subrano to tell you of what has been found. I wished to bring it to you personally because it is my feeling that you are the greatest man in the field of Neanderthal and that only you can do justice to this great discovery.'

'You flatter me,' said Penfold. What was it, he thought, a flint axe to go with ten thousand others in the basement here?

'It is not flattery,' replied Vlasek. 'It is truth. This is a find on the level of Schliemann's Troy.' Another amateur, groaned Penfold to himself. The Troy he'd discovered had eventually turned out to be the wrong one. He watched without eagerness as Vlasek opened the manila envelope on his lap and withdrew a sheaf of eight-by-ten photographs. He handed the pictures across and Penfold leafed through them, and then a second time, a look of growing irritation on his face. He finished his inspection and then laid the photographs down on the desk.

'Interesting,' he said, looking at the Yugoslavian. 'A question?'

'Certainly,' said Vlasek, beaming.

'The cave, these photographs were taken in — you discovered it yourself?' Vlasek shook his head.

'No. It was found by two men: foreigners.' Penfold nodded, relieved, at least the man hadn't been trying to pull a hoax, he'd just been caught in the middle.

'Did these men know of your interest in archaeology?' asked Penfold. Vlasek nodded.

'Yes, they are geologists. They came to me for information about where to find caves. I directed them to the karst in our area.' Penfold let out a long breath, trying to think of a way to let the man down easily. There wasn't one.

'These are fake,' he said. 'Phoney.' Vlasek stared at him, confused.

'Pardon me.'

'Forgeries,' explained Penfold. 'You were set up by these two men who discovered the cave.'

'*Ne razumen,*' said Vlasek, agitated. 'I don't understand.' Penfold sat forward and fanned out the pictures in front of Vlasek.

'It's happened often enough before,' said Penfold, trying to soften the blow. 'Forgeries are an occupational hazard for archaeologists. These happen to be quite poor. The men didn't know what they were doing.' He tapped the photographs with his forefinger. 'These are supposed to be Cro-Magnon cave paintings, yet they occur in a region where Cro-Magnon never settled.'

'But . . .' said Vlasek.

'Let me finish,' said Penfold. 'Not only that, but no Cro-Magnon would be caught dead painting like it. The quality simply isn't good enough. They were a talented race, Doctor, and these paintings are second rate in comparison to the ones at Lascaux for instance. The lines are wrong, sketchy and simplified, and this overlapping is out of the question. Cro-Magnon had a fair grasp of linear perspective and these paintings show none of that knowledge. Your two geologists underrated the men they were copying and you wound up making a trip to Paris for nothing. I'm sorry, Vlasek.'

'Excuse me, Dr Penfold, you refer to Cro-Magnon. I came to you because you are the world's expert on Neanderthal,' said Vlasek quietly.

'I don't see what you're getting at,' said Penfold.

'It is simple, Doctor. These are not Cro-Magnon, nor an attempt to forge Cro-Magnon style.'

'If they aren't supposed to be Cro-Magnon, what are they?' asked Penfold wearily. He was beginning to tire of the man.

'Neanderthal,' said Vlasek simply. Penfold sat back in his chair.

'Rubbish,' he said. 'There is no such thing as Neanderthal cave art.'

'Yes there is,' said Vlasek. 'And I have here proof.' He bent down and opened the briefcase between his feet, taking out a large newspaper-wrapped bundle. He laid it reverently on the desk and removed the several layers of covering, revealing a human skull, almost completely intact except for the lower jaw. The bone was dark with age, the nasal sinus cavities plugged with dirt from its recent exhumation. The empty brooding sockets of the eyes stared up at Penfold blindly, the gaping holes topped by a faintly protruding brow ridge. Vlasek spoke.

'I am not a professional like yourself, Dr Penfold. I have been on no major digs, and have little practical experience with Neanderthal excepting the flint workings near my village. But I have read many books, Dr Penfold, and been to many museums. The two men who discovered the cave and myself decided to dig a small test hole close to one of the hearth depressions we found. We came upon this skull only a metre down, within what I think you would call the first level. That means that this man was one of the cave's last occupants and does not date from an early period after which the cave might have been used by a Cro-Magnon group.' Vlasek's voice was confident and intense. Penfold kept his eyes on the skull. 'You will notice I am sure, Doctor, that this skull does not fit into the "Classic" Neanderthal type. The braincase is too high and too rounded, the face too small. The skull is also long enough and narrow enough to prevent it from being placed in the "General" category. It is neither one nor the other, Dr Penfold. It has the aspects of both Neanderthal and Cro-Magnon, but the shape and the large brow ridge indicate Neanderthal strongly. I read your last book with interest, Doctor. You hypothesize a Transitional Neanderthal Race, as the Swanscombe and the Steinheim skulls were transitional from Homo Erectus to Neanderthal. A lost people, Dr Penfold, of which we know nothing. I believe this race has been found, Doctor. The skull is clearly transitional, and so are the paintings.'

Penfold was thunderstruck. It fitted. If Vlasek was right and the cave held more evidence . . . Vlasek finished the thought for him.

'If a major investigation proves this to be correct, Dr Penfold, then the Subrano Cave is the archaeological discovery of the century.'

CHAPTER TWO

1

Franklin Gaynor Speers adjusted the Tekna mouthpiece and went a little lower, his heavily-muscled legs driving him easily downwards with slow, even kicks. The air bubbles from the regulator atop the big twin US Divers tanks rolled leisurely to the surface, twenty-five feet above his head, the gentle intermittent stream flurrying in tune with Speers's steady breathing.

The water was crystal clear and warm, not Speers's usual diving environment. He felt more at home in the dark places his work took him to; the depths below floating oil-rigs, or even better, the icy waters of a submerged cavern. For him, the sparkling waters of the Adriatic were almost boring, completely without challenge or excitement. Still, he thought, it made sense to test some of the new equipment before the work began. He brought his arm up in front of his mask and checked the time lapse on his heavy, military-looking Chronosport UDT. He'd been down almost an hour; another ten minutes or so and he'd go back up. He'd wanted to try out the new Henderson dry-suit for comfort, but it was designed for cold-water diving and he was beginning to sweat.

He kicked down until he was within a few feet of the mottled pebble bottom, then turned parallel to it, legs beating slowly, arms limp along his sides. In his left hand he grasped the butt of a black Scubapro Panther. The fat little man in the Dubrovnik Internal Affairs office had informed him that the use of a speargun was prohibited, but he was goddamned if he was going to let a tubby bureaucrat with an accent tell him what to do. He stared through the AMF mask, his eyes wide behind the Plexiglass as he watched for fish. As he swam his mind kept on imagining what the job was going to be like.

The only thing he really knew was that the Subrano Cave was in all the newspapers. The article he'd read in *Time* magazine said they'd found some kind of prehistoric paintings that were "pivotal", whatever they meant by that. The call he'd taken in Orlando the week before had been a little more specific but not much. They wanted a diver because there was evidence of a water-filled cave close to the one they'd found. They'd chosen him not only because he was a qualified professional cave diver, but also because he'd been involved in underwater archaeology before; once in the Gulf of Mexico and another time in the Bahamas. He frowned behind the mouthpiece. Archaeology hell, it was nothing more than putting down big metal grids and then mapping it all.

He'd warned this Penfold kid that he'd have to cover the loss on the contract from Walt Disney World but the guy didn't seem to care. Not only did he match the Disney contract, he went over it by a good twenty per cent, travel and accommodation thrown in. According to Penfold, they wanted the best and Frank Speers was it.

And that was fine by him. He didn't care a whole hell of a lot about paintings done by some ape-man a million years ago, but the Subrano thing was getting a lot of publicity; the job would be good for business. He'd even accepted the fact that he wasn't going to get laid for a couple of months. He knew there were going to be a few broads involved in the dig, but if the Tarvanin chick was any example of what to expect he was in for a hard time. The red-head was good-looking enough – average height, small tits, good legs and a sexy mouth – but when he'd put the make on her the night before in the hotel it turned out she had a temper like a box of rusty nails. The bitch had almost chewed his head off. According to the list the young Penfold character had given him she was the team artist. Terrific; he'd make damn sure she never painted *him*. The only other women were locals and you could write them off for sure. All ten pounts overweight and speaking English like they had ball bearings in their mouths.

Speers rolled over on his back and looked up at the surface, still swimming. The water above was like broken glass, a maze of tiny glittering particles, prismed by the sun. Beautiful, but boring. He rolled face down again, and scanned the ocean floor. He spotted a big red mullet, just like the one he'd had for supper the night before in the hotel dining room. He stopped, letting his legs drop below him, and brought up the Panther. He placed the flat stockplate against his chest and dragged back the quadruple lengths of hard rubber, fitting the thin wire loop over the trigger release. The sixteen-inch stainless steel spear was already in the guides, the spring-loaded tines and needle-sharp point gleaming in the refracted sun from above. The speargun loaded, he began to track the mullet, keeping overhead and several yards behind, following its erratic, nervous course as it forged along the bottom.

Keeping his shadow from alerting the fish to his presence, Speers dropped to the left, increasing his speed by a few strokes. He was still above the flat-sided creature, but flanking it now. Less than six feet separated them, man and quarry. The fish, still unaware of Speers, continued to move slowly, its large pink gills working in time to the pursings of its mouth. Speers kept pace with it, looking for a shot. He raised the long weapon, holding it in one hand, and brought it to bear on the fish. He lined up the point with the creature and squeezed the trigger.

There was a faint sucking sound as the gleaming rod sped away from the grooved guide along the top of the gun, the thin blue nylon retrieving line snaking out from below. The point caught the fish right where he had been aiming for: dead centre in the eye. The razor-sharp point sliced through the delicate organ, the V of the tines tearing into the soft flesh on either side, thrusting all the way through the head and out the other side, taking out the right eye as it exited. The blinded fish began to twist and turn spasmodically, the strong tail twitching back and forth as the gills pumped futilely, trying to feed oxygen to a minuscule brain that no longer existed. Speers watched the fish die, feeling the tug on the retrieval line as it went through its final agony. He grinned, teeth clutching the mouthpiece. A good shot.

He waited for a few moments, watching the fish, then pulled on the line, drawing in his catch. He got his hand around the flailing tail and pulled, removed the shaft, ripping the head half off in the process. He fitted the shaft back into the Panther, letting the fish glide down to the sea-floor where it lay, ravaged and twitching. Ignoring his kill, Speers headed back to the surface. It was almost lunchtime.

2

St Blaise wasn't coming right, she decided, rubbing out the sketch using a fat artist's rubber. She dropped the sketchbook on to her lap and peered up at the grey statue set into its niche above the Pila Gate. She began again, trying to capture the spirit of the gaunt man in granite robes who had supposedly had a vision that staved off a Venetian attack on Dubrovnik in the seventh century.

Sitting on a low stone wall, Mariea Tarvanin worked at her drawing, ignoring the crowds of tourists moving through the low arched gate into the old city. She drew rapidly, the soft pencil seeming to be almost an extension of her large, muscular hand. After fifteen minutes she had completed a detailed study and sat back against a parapet, satisfied. She lit an American cigarette from a pack in her bag and relaxed, occasionally running her hand through the mass of dark red hair that fell across her shoulders.

Well, she thought, it sure wasn't Carmel. The ancient city, with its walled old town and dark stone buildings was a strange, if welcome, change from the California atmosphere she was used to. She smiled wistfully, thinking about the small weatherbeaten bungalow on the beach where she lived and wondered what Auni and Garth were up to. The twins were twelve, easily old enough to be left in the care of her mother, but she still worried. The dig was slated to last until mid-September and two and a half months was a long time to be away.

Not that she had hesitated when the offer came through. A chance to work on the Subrano Cave was just the boost her career needed. There wasn't much call for specialist illustrators in Southern California and she'd been making do working for a maniac animator who had made a fortune on pornographic cartoon take-offs on classic stories. The last one, *Bambi Girl,* had taken the cake; the only reason she'd stuck to it was the money.

But this was different, she thought, elated. It was what she'd been trained for, and what she'd always longed to do. The fact that it was David making the offer was even better. They'd taken classes together at UCLA and until Bill came along they'd had quite a little thing going. Lots of dope, lots of good times and lots of down-to-earth, tie-me-down horniness.

She grinned at the memories. The sixties; what a time to come of age. She almost hadn't, she thought wryly. Bill had appeared, all beard, beads and slogans, ready, willing and able to die for the cause as long as it meant he didn't go to Vietnam. She'd dropped David and hooked herself on to Bill like a limpet, willing to do anything for him, including taking on a succession of demeaning jobs to keep them alive. She almost hadn't graduated because of it, and thankfully the pregnancy had come close to the end of her final year. When Bill discovered she was going to have a child he was overjoyed; until he came face to face with the realities: diapers, depression, toys underfoot, and a sex-life scheduled around her breast feeding. All of a sudden the cause needed him elsewhere, and he was gone. She put the twins in day care, moved into a welfare apartment and started looking for work. Her parents helped out a little, but it took them a long time to accept the fact that their two grandchildren were bastards. She had to make it on her own. And she did. There were lots of nights when she wondered if she was going to be able to keep on going, but somehow she managed it. The dreams of working at Mexican temple sites and delving into the mysteries of the Inca vanished, replaced by the hard, cold truths of having to earn a living.

But the jobs came, slowly. A bit of ad work here, the occasional commission, regular if poorly paid work at the university doing artifact sketches for the catalogues. It all added up and somehow she pulled through. And now this, with David to thank for it. They'd only talked once or twice since her arrival and she wasn't sure if he was still interested in her as a woman. The spark was there, but there was also a hint of something else. Embarrassment? She shrugged; it didn't matter, she hadn't taken the job to get laid. She looked down at her sketch of St Blaise and smiled. It was good – really good.

'Hungry-looking sort, isn't he?' asked a voice at her side, the accent British. She looked up. It was Tony Grace, the only journalist attached to the dig. He looked faintly ridiculous, knobby knees poking out of Bermuda shorts, his shirt five years out of date and the muddle of brown hair on top of his pale, sharp-chinned face uncombed. But there was something about him, a schoolboy innocence, that kept him from being offensive. He was funny too, the sparkle in his dark brown eyes bubbling up regularly as he poked fun at everyone, including himself.

'Have a seat,' offered Mariea, patting the stone beside her. He frowned theatrically.

'Good Lord, my haemorrhoids.' He tested the stone with the flat of one hand and then sat down gingerly, crossing his legs and grasping one ankle in time-honoured British tradition.

'How's it going, Tony?' she asked, flipping a page of her sketchbook and picking up her pencil again. She began

41

roughing in a large oleander on the far side of the narrow walkway.

'Picking up local colour,' he said, watching her, fascinated, as the tree took shape on the paper. 'Sidebar material. Good for the book.'

'Book?' asked Mariea. Grace arched an eyebrow.

'Certainly,' he said. 'I intend to make my fortune with it. *With Penfold at Subrano* perhaps. Or better, *Penfold's Man*. Can't go wrong. Everyone's up on archaeology these days. I shall make a pile and retire to Jersey in the Channel Islands.'

'There's a zoo there, right?' asked Mariea. Grace nodded.

'Umm. Run by a chap named Durrell. Writes funny books about animals, and does work with endangered species. Interviewed him a couple of times. Marvellous fellow. Reminds me of myself actually. I think I'll buy a cottage next to his zoo and watch him scamper about after escaped wombats and things. He's always doing it in his books. Should be entertaining.'

'Sounds like fun,' agreed Mariea. She finished the tree and began adding bodies, caricatures of the people walking by. Grace frowned, watching her.

'You shouldn't do that, you know,' he said quietly. She looked up at him.

'Pardon?'

'The caricatures,' he said, motioning with a bony finger. 'You had a perfectly good tree, the real thing, then you added those funny bits.'

'I thought you liked funny bits,' she said. He shrugged.

'Because I'm good at it,' he said. 'And you're good at trees. It's rather like slinging mud at your talent.' He blushed, then began a stuttering apology. 'Look, I'm terribly sorry. I shouldn't have said . . .'

'Sure you should,' said Mariea, closing the sketchbook. 'You're right. It's a bad habit I got into working for a freak in LA. He put Snow White in rubber brassieres and that kind of thing. I guess a bit of it wore off on me.'

Grace looked confused at her explanation but he didn't follow it up. They sat silently for a few moments and then she spoke.

'How did you manage to get involved in this?' she asked.

Grace shrugged, his narrow shoulders rising under the shirt.

'Luck, I suppose,' he said. 'And a series of articles I did on Dr Penfold a year ago. I was impressed with the man, and I flattered him a bit. It must have stuck in his mind. And I'm qualified. I'm the only science writer about who's up on his theories, as far as I know.'

'What's he like? I know his son quite well, but I've never met Penfold Senior.'

'Hard to say, really,' answered Grace thoughtfully. Mariea offered him a cigarette and he took it gratefully. 'Brilliant,' he continued, puffing. 'No doubt about that, certainly. He's done more for modern archaeology than anyone else in the past twenty years. Bit of a radical with his Neanderthal Superiority study, but fascinating.'

'I don't mean his brain,' said Mariea. 'I mean what's he going to be like to work with?'

'Hard, I should think,' said Grace. 'He doesn't get on well with people, as far as I know. Bit of a leadership complex.'

'Leadership complex?' asked Mariea.

Grace nodded, thrusting one hand under his shirt, elbow crooked, and beetling his eyebrows. 'Napoleon. Touch of egomania as a child. Festered in his youth. Came to full flower as an adult. He wants the Nobel badly. This will get it for him, too.' He added soberly, 'He'll rule that dig with an iron hand. Make a mistake and he'll have you served up on toast for breakfast.'

'Lovely,' said Mariea. 'Does he have horns and a tail, too?' Grace laughed and waved a hand.

'He's not that bad. It's my journalistic nature. We tend to overstate now and then. It won't be a pleasure trip, but the dig will be fascinating. They're not kidding when they call it the greatest single historical event in the past hundred years. If it proves his basic theories, it's bound to upset the entire applecart. Heads will roll over this.'

'Don't tell me any more,' smiled Mariea. 'I just want to have a crack at drawing the pictures. I had my fill of politics long ago.'

'Pictures! Hah!' scoffed Grace. 'You'll never see them again after the crusty Alice Braden gets her hands on them. A fiend for filing, you know. All propriety and efficiency.

Freud would have had a field-day with that one. Yesterday she came at me with that clipboard of hers and started asking questions about insurance coverage.'

'Oh, come on,' chided Mariea. 'Leave Alice alone. She's just trying to do her job. Maybe under that crust she's nice.'

'Don't look at me to find out!' said Grace in mock horror. He stood up.

'Going?' asked Mariea. He nodded.

'Back to the wonderful Villa Dubrovnik,' he grinned. 'Home of the only concrete beach in the world. I must prepare for the briefing tonight. Are you going to be there? Penfold is coming back from the site, you know.'

'Don't worry,' said Mariea, opening her sketchbook again. 'I wouldn't miss it for the world.'

3

Alice Braden stood on the balcony of her hotel room and looked across the narrow sound to the island of Lokrum. She blinked in the hot sun and felt a trickle of perspiration making its way down between her large breasts, hidden by the high-collared dress she wore. She reached up absently and patted the thick club of auburn hair she always kept firmly pinned to the nape of her neck.

Lokrum, she thought — what do I know about Lokrum? Almost without effort the facts came spilling into her mind. Lokrum, one of approximately one-thousand Adriatic islands. Lying a mile and a half off the city of Dubrovnik, the large pine-covered island is legendarily associated with Richard the Lion Heart, who, it is said, stopped there on his way back from the Third Crusade, AD 1191. Correction, she thought, shipwrecked. The island contains an abandoned Benedictine monastery built in the eleventh century, the residence of Archduke Maxmilian of Austria, constructed in the 1800s, and a classically designed star-shaped fort built during the French occupation at the beginning of the nineteenth century. The fort is in ruins, but the Archduke's residence is used as a natural history museum, a botanical garden, and a small museum dedicated to the Dubrovnik mathematician and astronomer Rudjer Boskovic.

Alice sighed. The information was accurate, but it was dry and without substance. Who cared about Lokrum? Or Dubrovnik for that matter? None of the facts, figures and dates she kept stored in her head really meant anything at all. She didn't mean anything at all; a useful tool, used when necessary, then forgotten. It had been that way ever since she could remember.

She'd never been pretty, not even as a child. But she had been bright. The teachers all applauded her quiet nature and her dedication to learning, but it hadn't earned her much status with her classmates. Bookworm, suck, gook — that's what they called her. Highschool was even worse. While the other kids smoked pot, fumbled with each others' bodies and raved about the Beatles and the Rolling Stones, Alice worked on chess problems and proof-read the *Yearbook*. The closest she ever got to the Senior Prom was running the soft drink concession for the Student Council Fund.

The anonymity of University had been a welcome relief, but the higher concentration of intelligence came as a shock. She wasn't as smart as her proud parents had always boasted. She was intelligent, but no more than a thousand other people there. But she *was* methodical, completing assignments accurately, if unimaginatively — always typed, always properly organized. Several of her professors told her to take a business administration major after her first year, but she refused, and went into Anthropology instead, augmenting it with a course in Statistics and another in Library Science. She had recognized her limitations and decided to capitalize on her assets. She graduated in the middle of her Anthropology class, and close to the top in Statistics and Library Science. No museum or university wanted her as an anthropologist, but she was snapped up within a week of graduation by the Smithsonian, working as an administrative assistant. By the age of twenty-five she had added a Master's degree to her curriculum vitae, and had established a reasonable reputation as an efficient First Assistant on several digs in the United States and South America. By thirty she was the best to be found, and spent more time away from the Smithsonian on loan than she did in Washington. She had worked with Dr Penfold a number of times over the years, and they maintained a good working relationship. She had been on a site in Brazil when she heard about the Subrano find, and she had immediately begun to make travel arrangements, knowing that Penfold would be calling on her. She was correct, as always.

So now she was in Dubrovnik, waiting for his return from the site. She felt a tremble ripple through her at the thought of seeing Penfold again, and quelled it immediately. She'd given up all those fantasies a long time ago. Work was everything. She turned away from the view and went back into her room, stripping off her clothes and going into the bathroom. She had been in the sun too long and felt in need of a shower.

She adjusted the water temperature, put on a looselyfitting shower cap and collected her soap and face-cloth from the small case on the toilet tank. She stepped into the shower, pulling the curtain across, and turned on the spray, giving herself up to the tepid water. As with everything else, her bathing habits were methodical to a fault. She lathered herself carefully, scrubbing at every niche, paying particular attention to her face and underarms, then rinsed under the spray and lathered again, repeating the process, her eyes closed, head back under the gushing jet of water.

Dr Penfold. His eyes were dark and penetrating, seeming to ask for more than she could give, his wide smile softening the demand. The face-cloth dropped to the floor of the shower, and she began using the soap with her bare hand, the palm straying to her breast of its own accord. She rubbed softly, teasing the nipple erect, dulling her thoughts. The dunning sound of the water filled the small enclosure with a rhythmic echo, and Penfold's face shimmered in her mind's eye — and then his body, lithe and strong, the muscles of his back corded as he bent over an artifact, the fashionably full head of salt-and-pepper hair falling across his forehead and over his eyes.

She shivered under the spray and banished the vision. It was foolishness. She knew herself for what she was, a woman in her early thirties, plain and unassuming. Love was not part of her life, nor would it ever be. Her feelings for Dr Penfold

46

could not go beyond loyalty and dedication to her work. He was handsome; she was not. He was famous; she was not. There was no relationship between them beyond that of employer and employee, and that was as it should be. She wanted nothing more, because, in her heart, she knew that anything else was impossible. And, above all other things, Alice Braden prided herself on her good common sense.

She turned off the shower and stepped out of the enclosure. As she began to dry herself roughly with a towel she thought about Lokrum again, using the island's statistics to keep the welling pain in her chest at bay and the tears in her eyes from falling.

4

David Penfold Junior leaned against the railing on the observation deck of the Cilipi Airport, waiting for the arrival of the JAT flight from Rome. Once again he was playing busboy while his father did the real work. This time he didn't mind so much. He'd been gone from Paris for almost three weeks, arranging the logistics of the dig from Dubrovnik, and he was eagerly looking forward to seeing Irene again. The fact that she was travelling with her father and the remaining members of the staff took the romantic edge off it, but he was happy nonetheless. He shook his head appreciatively, trying to figure out how Irene had managed to get her father to agree to her coming. And not just for a visit either; she'd got herself on the staff list as an assistant, which meant they were going to be together for the duration of the expedition.

But when he really thought about it, her position made a certain amount of political sense. When the old man had announced the find, he'd called for an international staff, oozing all sorts of platitudes about co-operation and the family of man. What it meant was that he wouldn't have to use the staff Bouchard had lined up for the other dig, which was entirely French.

His father's choice was anything but that. Most of the ten actual staff members were Americans. The exceptions were staff, but they gave the dig the "global effort" effect his father wanted. So in the numbers game Irene was important. Her father was obviously willing to swallow his paternal jealousy if it meant he was going to have someone in his camp.

David grimaced. The inhabitants of the Subrano Cave had been dead for at least 40,000 years, but their bones were enough to cause internecine warfare in the present. It was crazy, but David had been working in the field long enough to know that it wasn't confined to his father and Bouchard. Archaeologists and the museums and universities they worked for had been clawing at each other from the beginning. Politics, and the playing of politics, were an integral part of the game — the foundation on which grants and allocations were built. It was an art, and one his father practised extremely well.

Art. He thought about Mariea Tarvanin and frowned, wondering if there was going to be a problem there. It hadn't really occurred to him when he'd come up with her name when his father requested an on-site illustrator and draughtsman. It was only after he'd found out Irene was going to be on site that it hit him. They'd had good times together, and it was obvious Mariea hadn't forgotten about them. The fire was still between them, and it wasn't entirely one-sided. He was pretty sure Mariea didn't know it, but she had been his first, and it was a connection that had never faded. He also knew Irene was perceptive enough to spot that. The two were like flip sides of the same coin — radically different, but in some ways very much the same. And he didn't want to hurt either of them. It was a problem he didn't have much experience with — trying to separate the concepts of sex and love. He hadn't known enough of either to be able to make a judgement.

And he didn't have time to make one now. It had been hard enough to go along with his father and take the job as Site Supervisor. Somehow he felt he'd lost a battle, giving in to him once again. He really had been going to leave Paris, no matter what the old man said, but the Subrano find was too immense to pass up. It would be the last time though. They'd only be able to do a preliminary dig now; the full-scale dig wouldn't really begin for at least another year. He'd be able to get enough clout for a grant from the short season's work; and if he kept his nose to the grindstone he could get a book out of it by the start of the next year, beating his father to the punch. David had come to the conclusion that the only way to get out from under his father's heel was to operate the way he did. By definition, the book would be superficial, but it would give him a headstart and a stepping stone somewhere else, and that was all he really wanted.

There was an incomprehensible crackle from the loud-speaker a few yards away, and in the distance David could see the rapidly growing shape of the red and white Tupolev jetliner. He checked his watch; it was right on time. He left the observation deck and went down to the arrivals gate. A few minutes later the Tupolev taxied up and began to disgorge its passengers.

The crowd began funnelling through customs, and David squinted, trying to pick out the Subrano staff. He spotted Richter first; the six-foot four-inch photographer was hard to miss, even without the bushy beard he wore and the mass of curling black hair on his head. Jason had worked on his father's last book, and David liked him. Richter was closer in age to his father than to him, but he had a boisterous sense of humour and a fund of highly improbable anecdotes that made him fun to be with. David waved and Jason saw him, returning the wave and turning to talk to someone behind him. The bear-like man stepped aside and pointed down with a huge ham-hand. It was Irene. David lifted his hand again, a grin spreading over his face, and then stopped. Irene's father was right beside her, and even from that distance he could see the angry expression on the man's face. He stuck his hands in the pockets of his Levis and waited, scanning the last of the passengers for Merrill and trying hard not to keep his eyes on Irene.

The conservator finally hove into view, deep in an argument with someone in uniform. The short, barrel-chested Canadian was festooned with dozens of canisters and bags, and from the look of it the paraphernalia was the centre of the argument. David knew why. Conservators use a range of chemicals and tools that would make a terrorist envious. The bags and containers undoubtedly held everything from hydrochloric acid to ice-picks. It was a wonder the gruff, iron-faced man had managed to get as far as this without being stopped. He settled the argument eventually and went to join the others at the carousel. The baggage began coming down the chute and a few minutes later the group emerged into the small concourse. David greeted them, giving Irene a quick smile, then led them out to the waiting mini-bus provided by the Villa Dubrovnik. They loaded their luggage in the side compartments and then climbed on, David choosing a seat in the front. Discreetly, Irene sat at the rear of the bus beside her father. The bus left the airport and swung on to the E27, Yugoslavia's main highway, running along the coast for the entire length of the country. With mountains on the right and the Adriatic below them on the left they headed north towards Dubrovnik. David turned in his seat. Merrill was behind him, clutching his equipment jealously.

'How was the trip?' asked David. Merrill grunted, his already angry expression darkening even further.

'Terrible,' he said, biting off the word. 'These people don't have the slightest idea of what manners are all about.'

'Well,' soothed David, 'you can relax now, you're among friends.'

'I have no friends,' snapped Merrill. 'And I don't want any.' The conversation ended. As David turned to the front he caught Richter's eye. The big man on the seat across the aisle gave him a slow wink and bared his teeth fiercely. David suppressed a laugh and watched the road unwind in front of him, strongly aware of Irene's eyes on him from the rear of the bus.

Twenty minutes later they arrived at the hotel and David helped carry luggage down the steep steps leading to the main entrance. The hotel was built below the road, terraced on several levels of the steep embankment leading down to the water. Once inside the group headed for the front desk. While her father checked in David managed to snatch a few seconds alone with Irene. She looked tired and more than a little worried.

'I've missed you,' he said urgently, touching her arm. She froze and pulled away slightly, checking over her shoulder to make sure that her father was still occupied.

'*Moi aussi,*' she murmured.

'I want to talk to you,' whispered David. Irene shook her head.

'There is no time,' she said.

'Not now. Later. In my room. It's 420. After the briefing.' She shook her head again.

'I can't, David, please,' she pleaded.

'Why not? Papa Bouchard have a bed check or something?'

'It's not that. It, it just wouldn't be right.'

'Right? It's been three weeks, Irene!'

'Please, David, you're making it worse. We'll talk, but not tonight. My father is very upset by the dig, and about us. He said some terrible things before we left Paris. I must have time to think.'

'What kind of things?' prodded David. It was too late. Bouchard completed the check in and Irene joined him. David watched as the two headed for the lift. He frowned angrily and was turning away when he felt a massive hand clamp down on his shoulder. It was Richter.

'Come on, Davey boy,' he boomed. 'Take me to the nearest bar and I'll tell you about this girl I knew in Zaïre.' David looked over his shoulder and caught a final glimpse of Irene as the lift doors slid shut. Then she was gone. He turned back to Richter.

'Yeah,' he muttered, 'I could use a drink about now.'

5

David Penfold sat at the back of the small dining room in the Villa Dubrovnik, nursing a snifter of Vinjak, the local brandy. It was faintly reminiscent of French brandy but David was far more interested in its effects than its taste. It was his fifth since his abortive conversation with Irene and his brain was numb. He peered into the gloom and watched as his father began his briefing at the lectern placed in front of the head table. The room was filled, not only with the assembled staff for the dig, but also with members of the local and international press. This would be their last chance before the group headed for the cave the following day. David recognized the oratorical stance his father had taken and knew he was playing to the media. There would be lots of quotable quotes.

'Ladies and gentlemen,' he began, 'I have just returned from the Subrano Cave.' Patton in from the front, thought David. 'What I have seen there exceeds my wildest expectations. I have no doubt that we are on the verge of a major breakthrough in the study of man.' He leaned forward, hands gripping the edge of the lectern. He was still in his standard navy sweater and workpants uniform and David wondered if he'd left the clothes on to project a common-man image. The only thing missing was a smear of dirt on his forehead. His father began again, the tone more intimate.

'As many of you know, I have long held the theory that the leap from Neanderthal to Cro-Magnon was too vast. There had to be an intermediary step. Cro-Magnon is nothing more than a rather scruffy version of Modern man, and they are both termed Homo Sapiens. Neanderthal has never been given that honour, and has been relegated to the position of Homo Neanderthalis, a separate species that didn't quite make it. I believe that the lost race I presupposed has been found at Subrano.

'But Subrano Man is more than simply an interesting piece of the puzzle of history. In the short time I have been at the site two things have become apparent. One is the chemical composition of the cave floor itself. If the evidence I have found so far proves correct, then investigation of lower levels may well reveal materials in a state of previously unheard-of preservation. The acidity of the cave floor is such that it may have acted in the same way as it did in Denmark for Tollund Man, the famous Body in the Bog. If that is so, then the possibility of finding a Subrano Neanderthal with body organs and tissue intact is excellent. This, as I am sure you are aware, would be of incredible importance. For the first time we would know what Neanderthal really looked like,

52

and beyond that we would have a marvellous opportunity to fill in the gaps in our knowledge concerning the diseases these people were prey to, and perhaps even their diets. This could have far-reaching medical implications.'

David sat forward, fighting the alcoholic fog that shrouded his brain. He knew his father. He wouldn't make a statement like that without being absolutely sure of himself. If he was talking about the possibility of finding preserved organs and tissue, then he had already done so, saving the actual announcement until he could bleed every ounce of drama from it. He peered past his father to the head table, looking at Bouchard. The man was sitting rigidly, staring at his father's back, a look of malevolent hatred on his face. The announcement was obviously a shock. Irene was sitting next to him, listening intently.

'The second thing that has come to light,' went on Penfold, 'is the obviously high intellectual curiosity of Subrano Man. He was inventive to an incredible degree. Several of the drawings on the lower portions of the cave walls seem to be diagrams of weapons and schematics for hunting methods. This is unheard of even in Cro-Magnon, and it has led me to a startling conclusion.

'Not only was Subrano Man, undeniably a Neanderthal, exceptionally intelligent, he was more intelligent than the men who followed. For years archaeologists and anthropologists have discussed the question of Neanderthal's brain size. Unquestionably it is larger than Cro-Mangnon's, and larger than ours. Most have denied that it has any relation to intelligence, offering the face size to cranial capacity theory as proof. I am now of the opinion that they, all of us, were in error. Neanderthal, or at least Subrano Neanderthal, was genetically superior. He had to be, for as a transition from those who had gone before him, he had to make tremendous strides in a relatively short span of time in evolutionary times. Subrano Neanderthal, to my mind, was a race of geniuses.'

The room dissolved in an uproar as the implications sank in. David took a long pull at his brandy and shook his head unbelievingly. God, he thought, race superiority; the deadliest snake in the anthropological pit. The arguments would go on forever. His father had done it again.

6

Izo Harada sat on the hotel room balcony in the darkness, letting the cool breeze off the Adriatic wash gently over him. His room faced the sea and during the day gave a view of glittering water and the anchored fleet of nomadic yachts in the bay; at night there was only the star-covered vault of the purple sky and, in weak imitation, a few scattered flickers of light from the boats that bobbed unseen in the dark water.

Izo leaned back in the comfortable balcony chair and stared up at the stars overhead. He was confused, and it was a sensation he didn't like. He tried to empty his mind, concentrating on the limitless sky, forcing himself to deal with his conflicting thoughts in order, carefully, one by one.

As a scientist, and as a geologist in particular, his interest in Subrano should have ended when he found the water-filled cave at the second level. The paintings, and the archaeological and palaeontological discoveries, while exciting, were outside of his discipline.

Yet he found himself drawn to the caves almost against his will. The paintings, the artifacts, seemingly the very air of the cavern were magical, giving him a deep inner peace whenever he was in the cave. He knew the feeling well, and that was even more confusing, because the sensations he felt while in the presence of the Subrano paintings was almost identical to the feeling he had when he visited the shrine that held the ashes of his family. It was a sense of communion and of communication that seemed to span the millenia, bonding him to the unknown people who had once lived and died in that cavern.

But there was something else. Each time he made the voyage through that narrow slit, ending in the ancient cavern, he also had an overwhelming sense of some wraithlike sinister spirit that still haunted the cave after forty thousand years. Even now, secure within the twentieth-century walls of the hotel, he could visualize the terrible snarling figure of the bear that loomed over the cave like some timeless god. According to Dr Penfold the cave bear had been a kind of god and to find pictures or even clay models was not uncommon.

No one seemed even slightly worried about the figure on the ceiling, and of course there was no reason why they should be; it was, after all, nothing but a painting.

Suddenly the dark sea and the cool breeze were gone and Izo's nostrils were filled with the thick smell of wet wood smoke and the tang of freshly-killed meat. He could see the others, crouched on the far side of the fire, watching the flames, their eyes moving from side to side, their heads held alertly, waiting for any sound that might herald danger.

He glanced upward, knowing what he would see, and he felt a surge of pride as the flames from the dying fire brought life to the masterpiece above him. He and the bear were one and it was through their united strength that his tribe had come so far while others had perished. He grinned up at the dark and terrible figure. Tonight he would take the woman to his secret place, the cave he had hewn with his own hands from the living rock, and the place where no one came except the woman. He would have to hurry because soon she would not be able to move through the narrow crack that led to his hiding place, for her belly was filling quickly. He stared up at the giant beast and whispered a prayer to the god. An instant later his eyes widened as the god answered with a thundering roar, and then, like an opening wound, split in two, letting the million eyes of the stars fall through.

Izo shook his head slightly and found himself looking up at the sky. Faintly he could make out the blinking red and blue of an evening jet. He took a deep breath and let it out slowly, his hands unclenching from the arms of the chair. He willed himself to relax, and after a few moments the wild beating of his heart had slowed and he could think clearly again.

It had been a dream, of course, a terribly vivid dream, but no more than that; a product of his imagination, fuelled by the memory of the snarling painted bear on the roof of the cave. Every cell of his brain told him that it was no more than that, but he could still almost smell the fire and hear the thunder as the great bear spoke.

So, if not a dream, then what? Unbidden, a thought came to him, a thought that sent a shiver down his spine. Was it an omen, a race memory of the ancient past, or was it another kind of vision, perhaps a premonition?

CHAPTER THREE

1

David Penfold stood on the raised wooden platform that took up the entire rear half of the Subrano Cave and surveyed the site. He nodded with satisfaction. Only seventy-two hours had passed since his father's press conference at the Villa Dubrovnik, but the dig was already well underway. Most of the necessary equipment had been brought down into the cave before their arrival by a team of Yugoslav army sappers. The military engineers had also constructed the platform, erected the half-dozen plastic and tube-steel bivouacs the group would use for living accommodation and strung a series of high-powered flood-lights connected to a generator on the surface.

David craned his neck and stared up at the roof of the cave for the hundredth time that day. The harsh glare of the carbon arc floodlights served only to intensify the theatrical aura of the gigantic mural, bringing out each colour and line so brilliantly that it seemed the fresco has been painted yesterday rather than thirty or forty thousand years before. Ironically, almost no one was paying any attention to the paintings now — it was the floor of the cave that held the expedition's interest. David looked down at his clipboard and checked the daily schedule his father had prepared. Everything was in order. At the far end of the cave, dwarfed by the piled mass of rubble that had blocked the original entrance, his father, Merrill the conservator, and Vlasek were huddled over the test hole that had produced the Subrano Skull.

Since the area had already been disturbed by the amateur work done by Vlasek and Harada, his father and Bouchard had decided to keep on working at it, deepening and widening the hole to expose the perimeter of the grave site.

The rest of the dig would be done using the more efficient "stripping" method, where each layer of the site was peeled off over its entire area. The geometric string-grid had been laid out by Alice Braden and himself the first day and now the rest of the group was working the whole front half of the cave, inch by inch, grid square by grid square. When the front half of the cave had been excavated down to an uninhabited stratum the living platform would be dismantled and moved over to the back half of the cave, so work could start on the rear, but that was months, perhaps years away. From the depth of the test hole dug by Vlasek, David's father estimated that the inhabited strata went down for at least ten feet — and that was a lot of digging. There was enough work at Subrano to keep the expedition working for a long time.

David looked down. Directly below him Irene Bouchard and her father were working at the artifact table, checking each item as it was brought to them by other members of the group, and logging the finds on a grid map. When the artifacts had been logged they were tagged, numbered and packed away by Alice Braden. David frowned, watching Irene's long, slim fingers as they delicately handled a small flint tool. Since their arrival at the cave there had been no chance to see her alone, and from the look in her eyes it seemed as though she intended to keep it that way. His frown deepened; they were going to be down in the cave for a minimum of two months, their only breaks brief climbs to the surface now and again for a look at the outside world. The descent had taken almost an hour for each member of the expedition, even with a permanent metal ladder installed down the pothole, and ascent would take at least that much time. Visits to the surface were going to be few and far between, and they wouldn't offer much privacy anyway. David sighed.

'So near, yet so far,' he whispered to himself.

'Pardon?' said a voice behind him. David turned. It was Jason Richter, the bear-like photographer. He was working with a Hasselblad on a tall tripod, shooting up at the ceiling.

'Nothing,' said David, flushing. 'How's it going?' The bearded man shrugged and moved the tripod a measured foot. He leaned over the square viewfinder and clicked off another exposure with a cable release.

'I'm getting there,' he said, looking up, his big teeth shining in the forest of hair around his lips. 'I've done about two hundred frames so far. Another day or two and I'll have the rear half done. You'll be able to assemble a reconstruction of the whole roof. It's not going to be so easy when I do the front half though — lot of uneven ground.' He paused and gave a discontented grunt. 'Not to mention the fact that I don't have any idea of what I'm getting. I'd like to be able to process some of this stuff.'

'You could send it out,' grinned David. Richter rose to the bait.

'Don't make me laugh!' he growled. 'I can just imagine what the chemicals in a Yugoslavian photo lab are like. No way. I'll do it myself when we get back to the States.'

'But think of it,' teased David, 'you could shoot for a couple of months, get back home and then find out your light-meter had been off the whole time. Ten thousand under-exposed frames. The suspense must be killing you.'

'The suspense isn't, but this cave might,' grunted Richter, glancing up at the roof, frowning slightly.

'Claustrophobic?' asked David lightly. The big man shook his head.

'Naw. Not really. Cabin fever maybe. I'm used to a horizon, you know. Down here your eyes keep coming up short all the time. Nothing but rock no matter where you look. It gets to you after a while.'

'Think what it would be like if the lights went out,' smiled David.

'Don't even mention things like that,' muttered Richter, looking up at the cave roof again. He went back to work and David turned his attention to the dig once more. He spotted Mariea Tarvanin, perched high on the rockfall at the front of the cave. She had her sketchbook out and was transcribing one of the paintings. He smiled to himself. She hadn't changed a bit. She was down on the schedule for today to work with Alice doing schematics of some of the flint tools that had surfaced, but the woman had a mind of her own. He shook his head ruefully. It had been like that back at school too. If he wanted to go to a movie, she wanted to take a hike in the woods. The only place they ever met eye to eye was in bed. He felt a surge of feeling for her, remembering the times they'd had together. Good times. At least she'd picked up the situation between him and Irene. There had been no big hugs and kisses when they met. She was keeping her distance. He let out a long breath. Here he was with the two women who really meant something to him and he couldn't do more than pass the time of day with either of them. Someone up there had it in for him, he was sure. He walked to the far side of the platform close to the curved rock wall of the cave and went down the sloping ramp to the cave floor. Ahead of him Alice Braden was instructing Kenji Takashima in the proper way of stripping a grid square, demonstrating with a small trowel and a broad bristled paint brush. He stepped around them, careful not to disturb the precisely laid-out squares of string that had transformed the cave floor into a huge chequerboard. He went over to where his father and the other two men were working on the test hole. His father looked up as he approached.

'Anything interesting?' asked David, squatting down beside the narrow trench. His father was standing hip deep in the hole, a dentist's pick in his hand.

'It's all interesting,' his father said shortly.

'We think we have found the rest of the skeleton,' said Vlasek excitedly, sitting at the edge of the hole. Merrill, busy with his box of tricks, was coating a long piece of bone with polyvinyl acetate, or PVA. The PVA was used to impregnate the bone so that it could be moved without damage; later it would be removed with a solvent. He raised a bushy eyebrow at the Slav's eager comment.

'We may have found the rest of the skeleton,' corrected David's father tersely. 'However, I'm much more interested in this.' He motioned to Merrill who handed him a small square of glass, like an outsize laboratory slide. He squatted down in the shadows of the pit and reappeared a moment later. He handed the square of glass up to David.

'I see what you mean,' said David, looking at the specimen. It was a minute piece of leather, deep brown with a few coarse hairs still attached.

'It's from the sixth level,' said Dr Penfold. 'Three down

from where Vlasek here discovered the skull. It fits with the seed pods I found on the fourth and fifth. There's enough acid in the lower-level soil to preserve organic material.'

David handed the specimen to Merrill. 'Animal?' he asked his father. The older man shook his head.

'I don't think so. Dr Vlasek found the skull on the third level. The levels show no appreciable lapse of time between them, perhaps a hundred years or so, no more. The sixth level is contemporary. They wouldn't bury a member of the tribe over an area used as an offal pit. I think it's another grave. That specimen could be a portion of scalp.'

'You think we might find a mummified figure?' asked David. His father looked at him sourly.

'There is that possibility,' he said. 'But I wouldn't go off half-cocked.' The archaeologist glanced at Vlasek pointedly. David reddened, catching the reference to his amateurishness. He stood up.

'Well, I'll leave you to it,' he said stiffly. His father nodded and went back to his work. Swallowing hard David turned and walked back to the platform. As he went up the ramp, heading for the tent he shared with Richter and Speers, Irene Bouchard looked up from the artifact table and for a moment their eyes locked. There was anguish in her glance, combined with a distance David knew was impossible to bridge. Their love would have to wait. He looked away, his fingers gripping the clipboard tightly. He went up the ramp quickly, suddenly aware of the oppressive weight of the rock looming high above him. He wondered if he was going to be able to make it through the next few months, trapped with her in the echoing crypt of Subrano.

2

Tony Grace watched David Penfold disappear into his bivouac and grimaced. It looked like the old man had taken another strip off the lad. It hadn't taken the journalist long to pick off the undercurrent of tension between the two men, and the romance between the younger Penfold and Bouchard's daughter had been equally obvious. The spindly science writer pursed his lips thoughtfully. Given the time and the talent he could have turned the whole thing into a cracking good series for BBC2. He grinned at the thought. He had neither the talent nor the time. His editors paled at the thought of human interest. Grace caught a flicker of movement out of the corner of his eye and turned to the rear of the cave. He was just in time to see Speers heading down the recently opened hole at the extreme rear of the cavern. Harada was watching too, squatting like a modern Buddha at the edge of the platform. The older Japanese and his friend Takashima had gone down the flue the day before and come back to report that it was full of water, almost to the ceiling. Apparently Speers was off to do a bit of exploring. Grace padded over to Harada and sat down beside him, his long legs dangling over the edge.

'Going on a hike, is he?' asked Grace. Harada lifted his shoulders.

'It would seem so,' he murmured. 'A foolish man.'

'Why do you say that?' asked Grace.

'Because he is alone,' said Harada. Grace gave a braying laugh, the sound echoing dully from the sloping roof of the cave ten feet above them.

'Bloody right, he's alone,' said Grace. 'I've known the man less than a week and I've grown to loathe the fellow. He's the John Wayne of the scuba set – all macho and International Communist Conspiracy. I mean really, Izo, would you want to go down that hole with him?'

'If he had asked,' said Harada. 'His politics are not my concern. I have no affection for the man but I would not like to see him die.'

'No, I suppose not,' said Grace. 'You really think he might get into trouble? According to his biog he's the best cave diver in the business.'

'Accidents happen to us all,' said Harada. 'The earth does not play by a rule book. She is unpredictable.'

'So go after him,' suggested Grace. Harada turned to him and smiled.

'I think not,' he said. 'My presence would not be

appreciated. I think he finds the shape of my eyes offensive.'

'Umm,' said Grace. There was a long silence. Grace noticed that the geologist was no longer looking at the mouth of the flue; instead he was staring up at the far wall of the cave. The lighting there was dim, the shadows impenetrable. At one time or another there had been a collapse of the cave roof, leaving a miniature version of the rockfall at the other end of the cavern.

'Interesting,' said Harada eventually, keeping his eyes on the darkened portion of the cave wall. Grace followed his glance but couldn't see anything.

'Lovely,' he said. 'Limestone. Fascinating stuff.'

'There is a split,' said Harada, pointing at a block of shadow cast by the V-shaped slide of small boulders just to the right of the flue entrance leading down to the water cave.

'Can't see it,' said Grace, peering.

'It is there,' said Harada.

'A fissure?' asked Grace. 'Like the entrance?'

'I do not know,' said Harada.

'Going to take a look?' asked Grace. Harada nodded.

'Yes,' he said. 'It might prove worthwhile.'

'I'll get some lights,' said Grace. A few minutes later, equipped with safety helmets, lights and ropes, the two men were clambering over the small rockfall and up into the gloom that lay beyond the reach of the carbon-arcs. They reached the top of the rubble mound and paused, heads ducked under the seamed slope of the cave roof. Grace peered into the darkness on the far side of the rockfall but he still was unable to spot the fissure Harada had seen.

'You must have eyes like a hawk,' said the journalist, breathing hard. 'I can't see anything.'

'I do not have eyes like a hawk, Tony. I have just been down more caves than you. I know what to expect.'

'That's comforting,' said Grace. 'Since this is the first cave I've ever been in. I'm afraid my subterranean experience is limited to knowing which line on the London Underground will take me to the British Museum.'

'You have done no climbing?' asked Harada. Grace shook his head.

'I stood on a chair and changed a light bulb once, but that's about it, unless you include the trip down here.'

'There's nothing to worry about,' smiled Harada. 'I will move slowly, and we are roped together. Are you afraid of small places?'

'Not really. As long as my curiosity is being satisfied I can usually manage to keep my cowardice at bay. Lead on, Izo.'

The Japanese moved off the rockfall, following a narrow ledge less than a foot wide, bracing his hands against the pitch of the cave roof to keep his balance, feeling his way along. The light on his helmet cut into the shadows, revealing the complex corrugations and pits of the rock surface. Grace followed, placing his feet carefully and keeping his eyes on Harada. The floor of the cave was less than twenty feet below them, but even that short a fall could be painful.

As they reached the limits of the cave the ledge widened into a relatively broad fold. The cave roof was so steeply sloped now as it arched down to the floor that they were forced down on to their hands and knees. Harada stopped and turned to Grace.

'There,' he said, and turned the light on his helmet to the rock wall. The beam illuminated a narrow slit in the rock. At its widest point it was no more than eighteen inches across.

'You're joking,' said Grace. 'You expect to get into *that?*'

'Why not?' asked Harada. 'Since someone has done so before us.' He moved his head slightly and the light fell across the smooth surface of the limestone wall beside the narrow opening. There, fixed in the strong light, was the imprint of a splay-fingered hand, outlined by a dusty circle of brick-coloured pigment. Grace stared, feeling his heart begin to pound.

'Good Lord!' he whispered. 'It's just like Robinson Crusoe and Friday's footprint in the sand.'

'I beg your pardon?' said Harada.

'Forget it,' murmured Grace, his eyes glued to the ancient handprint. 'Who do you think could have done that?'

'The artist who painted the cave roof, perhaps,' said Harada. 'I talked to the young Dr Penfold about the paintings. He told me they were sometimes "signed" by handprints such as this. He said he was surprised that they had found none, in fact.'

'But why here?' asked the journalist. 'It's a bit out of the way, don't you think?'

'According to Dr Penfold the paintings usually have a religious significance. The artist was something of a priest. To place the print here was perhaps part of his magic.'

'Or a warning,' said Grace thoughtfully. 'To make sure no one went into that hole.' He stared at the opening. 'Do you think that might lead to some secret hiding-place?' he asked. Harada shrugged.

'It could be,' he said slowly. There was a long silence as the two men studied the knife-edged wound in the rock.

'So do we violate the curse, tempt fate and all that?' asked Grace. Harada smiled.

'If it was a curse then it was laid by someone who wanted to keep away only those who would not understand the magic,' said the Japanese.

'And do you?' asked Grace.

'Perhaps,' said Harada. He shuffled forward and turned on his side, squeezing into the narrow crack.

'Well, that's one of us who does, at least,' muttered Grace, following.

3

Frank Speers crept headfirst down the gently sloping flue, the quadruple beams of the heavy-duty, waterproof flashlights clamped to his mask guiding the way. He pushed the aluminium canister containing his tanks and the small inflatable raft ahead of him, grunting with the effort. The passage had been smoothed by centuries of seasonal water flow and he met few obstacles. It was his third trip down the flue that day. Each time he had brought down more equipment: a battery-powered compressor, extra tanks, spare batteries, a large inflatable raft to use as a floating base and two small ones in case he discovered a side passage. This was the last load — finally he was going to be able to dive.

The flue opened on to a fan-shaped expanse of smooth rock, scalloped into shallow pans of limestone. He pushed the canister out on to the top row of basins and eased himself from the flue, standing erect and flexing his arms and legs after the cramped journey down the 200-foot-long tunnel. He searched the ground at his feet, found the large pressure lamp he'd brought down on the previous trip, and lit it. Instantly the darkness vanished, replaced by a flood of light from the gas lantern. Speers reached up and switched off the flashlights on his headgear and looked around the cavern.

It was at least twice as large as the cave above and almost perfectly circular, the ceiling etched with smooth ripples that moved in concentric rings away from the flue. The ripples were caused by the rapid movement of spring water through the cave and were proof that it was completely filled during the rainy season. As such Subrano 2 would be of no interest to the archaeologists, but Speers knew the ripples in the cave roof also meant that the water had to flow out somewhere into yet another cave. It was also more than likely that Subrano 2 hadn't always been totally submerged on a seasonal basis either; the floor, or bedding plane of the flue wasn't deeply cut enough to be the carrier of a major stream, so it was probable that the flooding was a fairly recent phenomenon. The only way to find out for sure was to dive down and bring up a few cores from the bottom of the cave. If the cores showed evidence that the cave had once been occupied it could either be drained, or excavated using a vacuum pump and a set of graded screens.

Speers began unloading the canister, whistling to himself happily, enjoying the duet he was playing with his own echo. It was a pleasure to be away from the turkeys upstairs, that was for sure, especially Harada. There was something about the man's broad passive face that irritated him constantly; he always had the nagging feeling that the son-of-a-bitch was laughing at him. The others weren't much better. The Penfold kid was a wimp, and Grace got on his nerves with those stupid jokes. The rest of them were dry as dust, even the women. Except for Tarvanin. A bitch, yes, but she had something he liked. At least she didn't talk in sentences a mile long like the old man Penfold or Bouchard.

He strapped on his tanks, slipped into a pair of thick-soled rubber shoes and stepped down into the inky pool, using the flowstone scallops as a set of stairs. When he was up to his waist he bit down on his mouth-piece, lowered his mask and turned on his flashlights once again. He dropped forward in a half roll and submerged, his vision momentarily obscured by a welter of bubbles. He moved away from the wall of the cave, arms pumping in a slow breaststroke. He looked down.

The water, like that of most cave pools, was crystal clear and free of any kind of sediment. The floor of the cave was about thirty feet down and pebbled with cave pearls, the perfectly-rounded stones made from hundreds of layers of calcite built up around a grain of sand. Here and there the strong motion of the water had whirled the pebbles, creating rock hills in the bottom. More evidence that the height of water in the cave was temporary — holes like that were only created when there was a fast, but relatively shallow flow.

Speers tucked in his legs and pushed down, moving towards the bottom. He reached it and gathered up a few of the pearls, shoving them into the snap pocket on the leg of his dry-suit. He continued along, keeping a few feet above the bottom, heading for the far side of the cave. A few moments later the striated rock wall loomed in the beams of his flashlights and he rose to the surface. He spat out the mouthpiece and turned, looking back the way he'd come. Seventy yards away across the mirror-smooth expanse of water he could see the bright ball of light cast by the gas lantern. He was almost directly across from it. He replaced the mouthpiece and dived again, keeping his lights on the rock as he swam around the perimeter of the cave looking for the outlet he was sure he'd find.

Twenty minutes later he surfaced again, having returned to the flowstone pools below the flue entrance. He'd seen nothing of interest except the clean-picked skeletons of a pair of bats, another link in the chain of evidence proving that Subrano 2 wasn't always water-filled. He rested briefly, sitting on the rim of the pool, enjoying the silence, then went down again, working his way back to the half-way mark on the opposite side of the cave. Within a few yards he discovered an underwater ledge four or five feet below the surface, the product of some ancient seismic intrusion that had pushed a block of limestone laterally. Fifty yards further along he found what he was looking for.

The ledge ended at the base of a broad underwater fissure at least six feet across. He stuck his head into the hole and shone his light down but he couldn't see an exit point. He checked for a current, dangling a length of cord from his weight belt in front of the crack. There was no movement. It was a sump, a passage flooded with water that led to another cave on approximately the same level. He checked the elapsed time ring on his chronometer; he'd used almost an hour's air, and even with the thermal suit he was beginning to feel the cold. He was tempted to make a fast run through the passage but he knew it would be foolish. It was time to go back.

4

'Bloody hell!' groaned Tony Grace, cracking his elbow on a sharp-edged ridge of rock in the narrow passageway. 'That's the tenth time so far,' he added, looking ahead at the bottoms of Harada's boots. They had been moving forward, inch by inch, for almost an hour, going steadily upward at a very slight angle. 'How much farther, do you think?' asked Grace. He was barely able to catch Harada's muffled reply.

'There is no way to know,' said the geologist. Grace blinked the sweat out of his eyes and watched as the boot toes dug in, propelling Harada onward. He concentrated on his elbow, using the pain to distract himself. For the past twenty minutes he had been fighting a steadily rising fear that verged on panic. Harada had explained that in caving terminology the crack they were travelling along was called a "letterbox", and the term was an apt one; there wasn't an inch of free space. The roof brushed his hard hat and the walls scraped his arms and thighs with each movement.

'Christ, no wonder they call it birth "trauma",' he whispered to himself. He gritted his teeth and kept on, trying not to think about the tons of rock pressing in on all sides. Ahead of him, Harada stopped and Grace followed suit, feeling the panic welling up. As long as they were moving it wasn't too bad, but when they stopped it was as though he could feel the weight of the entire world above him, threatening to collapse and crush him into nothingness at any moment. He wondered what would happen if they came to the end of the crack without it widening; there was no way in the world that they'd be able to turn around.

'What's wrong?' asked Grace sharply, fearing the worst. On top of everything else he was sure that the battery in his helmet light was fading. He knew it was paranoia, but the thought of having to go back in the dark was enough to make his stomach roll with nausea. 'Why have we stopped?' he urged, hearing the fear-born break in his voice.

'The fissure is narrowing,' replied Harada. Grace groaned aloud.

'It can't be!'

'I am afraid it can, and does,' said Harada. 'But it appears to open up a few metres beyond. Turn on your side when you see me do so. Use your fingers on the rock to pull yourself forward.' Grace did as he was told, shifting himself around. Harada began to move ahead and the journalist followed, his face pressed up to the wall of the crack, his nostrils taking in the sour smell of the rock. He closed his eyes and began hauling himself forward, wincing as he felt the wall at his back pulling at his sweater. He began humming to himself, keeping the demons at bay.

'Incy wincy spider, climbed up the water spout, down came the rain and washed the spider out . . .'

Grace's hard hat slammed into something solid and he bit back a yell as he realized he'd run into Harada's feet. The geologist had stopped again.

'Trouble?' asked Grace.

'No. A small cave. Remain where you are for a moment.'

'Hallelujah!' sighed the journalist. There was a grating noise as Harada pulled himself forward again. A moment later there was a dull clatter. Grace craned his neck and saw Harada's light shining back down the fissure.

'Come ahead. There is a sharp protrusion. Arch your back as you come out,' instructed the man. Grace did as he was told. He felt Harada's strong hands grasp him under the arms and he arched his back and pushed with his toes. Harada kept a firm grip as the journalist worked frantically to release himself from the confines of the fissure. A few seconds later Grace found himself able to stand upright for the first time since they had entered the narrow crack in the wall of the Subrano Cave.

'This is not a natural cave,' said Harada, shining his lamp on the rock wall. Grace saw what he meant. There were well defined grooves in the soft stone, as though someone had worked it with an adze or a chisel.

'I don't get it,' said Grace, looking around. The cave was seven or eight feet across, a narrow oval with a sharply peaked roof. It was little more than a broadening of the fissure they had crawled through.

'Look there,' said Harada. Grace followed the beam of the geologist's lamp. A bench had been hacked out of the limestone and on it Grace could see a jumble of stone implements, roughly made, but recognizable. Half a dozen small bowls made from hollowed flint cores, scrapers of bone, their ends sharpened to a fine point, and something that looked vaguely like a mortar and pestle.

'My God!' whispered Grace. 'An artist's studio!'

'Or a magician's den,' said Harada. 'Look.' He lifted his head slightly, the pool of light from his lamp moving up the wall. Assembled above the low stone bench were dozens of small designs etched into the rock, some coloured, others merely roughly-drawn lines. Grace could see the outlines of creatures more accurately drawn in the main cave: ibex, bear, bison, mammoth. In the centre of the jumble of sketches was a single completed figure. A woman. The journalist had seen photographs of cave art depicting human figures before, but he'd never seen anything to match this. She was magnificent, an anatomically-perfect rendition of a female figure, the drawing centred on a carefully-smoothed oval on which a face had been etched. If this was Neanderthal woman, then all the reconstructions made by scientists over the years were monumentally wrong. The face was strong, the mouth full below a wide-nostriled nose and heavy brow ridges, but the eyes, the line of the jaw, the whole expression denoted an intelligence and humanity that was almost frightening. By any critic's standards it was a masterpiece, and the model had

69

been a woman of extraordinary beauty. The softly-rounded shoulders, the swell of the full breasts, and the broad sweep of the belly had been drawn with care. It was obvious that the woman was pregnant. A fertility symbol? thought Grace, or something more personal, perhaps the artist's mate, heavy with his child.

'I know what they'll call her,' he murmured. 'The Venus of Subrano.' He turned to Harada and found the Japanese lost in thought as he stared at the figure. 'You knew this place would be here, didn't you?' said the journalist, knowing he was right.

'I didn't know,' said Harada softly. 'Only hoped.' He looked at Grace and smiled. 'Art is a private thing, for the artist at least. In my country it is that way. There was nothing personal in the main cave. No place for the artist to think his drawings, to see them in his mind. It is a gallery of his work. This place was where he dreamed.'

'For a geologist you're quite the poet,' said Grace. Harada laughed gently.

'You sound like Kenji.' He grinned. 'He chides me endlessly whenever I veer from the textbook. Is there something wrong with a geologist liking things other than cold stone?'

'Not at all,' said Grace, returning Harada's smile. 'In fact, I find it quite refreshing.' He turned away and let the light from his lamp move slowly around the tiny grotto, but inexorably his gaze returned to the Venus. The two men stood motionless, hypnotized by the ancient goddess the artist had somehow managed to bring to life from the rock.

'We should get back,' said Grace after a few minutes. 'The others should know about this.'

5

The food which had been brought down into Subrano 1 was almost all tinned, but Alice and Jason Richter, the duty cooks for that day, had managed to put together a reasonably palatable meal of steamed ham, potatoes and peas. The food was augmented by several bottles of Yugoslavian wine brought in by Vlasek. Everyone had worked hard and there was little conversation around the long table in the mess enclosure as the staff ate.

When the meal was over and a round of coffee served, Dr David Penfold, seated at one end of the table, rapped with his spoon on the side of his mug, calling for attention.

'Well,' he began, 'I think we can all agree that it has been a most successful day.' There was a chorus of nods and murmured words of agreement from around the table. David Penfold, seated on his father's left, lit a cigarette and leaned back in his folding chair. The old man's after dinner "talks" were infamous. They tended to be long monologues that drifted rapidly into obscure nooks and crannies of archaeological process. He tried to think up a reasonable excuse for getting up from the table but couldn't find one. He watched Grace, seated directly across from him, scribbling away in a small notebook. The man was probably high as a kite, thought David enviously. To be in on a discovery like the finding of the artist's grotto was a once in a lifetime event, the kind that he himself had often dreamed about. He released a twin trail of smoke from his nostrils and turned his attention back to his father.

'There have been two notable discoveries made today,' said David's father, continuing. 'We now *know* that the acid content of Subrano's lower levels is adequate to preserve organic materials. According to a general field examination by Dr Merrill the operative chemical in the soil would seem to be tannin, although we will have no absolute proof of this until we have run a proper series of lab tests.'

Merrill, seated between Mariea Tarvanin and Frank Speers, halfway down the table, kept his eyes on the cup of coffee in front of him. Penfold went on.

'The second discovery is of course that of the artist's cave by Dr Harada and Mr Grace.' Tony Grace looked up at the mention of his name, smiled, and then bent over his notebook again. 'Dr Harada described the cave and its contents to myself and Dr Bouchard. As you know, such hiding-places were common among Cro-Magnon tribal groups, and were usually reserved for the tribe's shaman, or witch-doctor. This would also appear to be the case with our proto-

71

Neanderthal. Tomorrow Dr Harada and Jason will return to the cave for a photographic session. Thankfully Jason has a full Polaroid set-up with him, so we will be able to share in the discovery without having to make the journey to the cave. According to Mr Grace it is quite arduous.'

'I don't mind going,' said the tall photographer, working his way around the table retrieving dishes, 'just so long as Doc Harada here can give me a guarantee I won't get stuck halfway.'

Harada, sitting between Kenji Takashima and David, smiled broadly.

'I can give you no guarantees, Mr Richter, except to say that although in height you are a veritable mountain in comparison to me, our breadth is much the same. It is enough to shame me into dieting.'

'At any rate,' broke in David's father, 'tomorrow we shall all be able to see the so-called Venus of Subrano.'

'I think the artist should have a name as well,' said Grace, looking up from his notebook. 'After all, he's the whole reason we're down here, isn't he?'

'He's bones now,' said Speers, leaning forward and looking down the table. 'What does it matter who he was?'

'I think it matters much,' said Vlasek, from the far end of the table beside Alain Bouchard. 'It is too easy to think of the occupants of this place as just "bones". He was a man, and a great artist.' Speers snorted.

'Breuil,' said Bouchard. 'He was one of the first to discover cave paintings and to bring them to public attention.'

'Too obscure,' replied David's father. 'The good Abbé is well known among people such as ourselves, Doctor, but the general public wouldn't know who you were talking about.'

'A Yugoslavian name?' suggested Vlasek, timidly.

'I think my readers might find it a trifle hard to pronounce,' said Grace gently.

'Khan,' said Mariea Tarvanin, doodling with a felt pen on her napkin.

'I beg your pardon?' said Dr Penfold. 'I'm afraid I don't quite see the connection. Genghis Khan was hardly what I would call an artist.' The red-haired woman looked up from her sketch and raised an eyebrow. David grinned, watching her. He knew that expression well. His father was about to get some of his own medicine.

'Wrong Khan,' said Mariea, smiling. 'I mean Coleridge's.'

'I still don't see . . .' began Dr Penfold.

'I think she means the Xanadu fellow,' put in Grace. Mariea nodded.

'That's him,' she agreed. She looked up at the curved plastic ceiling of the mess tent and closed her eyes. She began to recite.

'In Xanadu did Kubla Khan
A stately pleasure-dome decree:
Where Alph, the sacred river, ran
Through caverns measureless to man
Down to a sunless sea.'

'Bloody good,' said Grace beaming. 'We've got the pleasure dome, complete with frescoes, and Speers tells us there's water down below, which should do for Alph. If we forget about the sunless sea it's bang on. I agree with the young lady from California, Khan.' He looked across the table at Harada. 'What do you think, Izo? You've got veto on this I should think, since you discovered the fellow's hideout.' The geologist nodded thoughtfully.

'It is a good name,' he said slowly. 'Strong. I think the man who painted here was a strong man. Yes. Call him Khan, if there are no objections.' Grace looked around the table. No one voiced an opinion one way or the other, except for Speers, whose lip curled.

'Right then!' said Grace, banging his hand on the table. 'Khan it is.'

6

There was no sun to make the passage of time in the depths of Subrano 1, so to maintain a normal schedule Dr Penfold had the lights dimmed at nine, mimicking the sunset high above them on the surface. He made the decision based on Harada's advice. The geologist told him about an experiment done by two French cavers in 1969. The men, Jacques Chambert and Philippe Englander, spent five months in the Olivier Cave near Nice carrying out experiments to test the possible effects on body and mind of a prolonged underground existence. They rapidly discovered that without the passage of day and night to guide them, their internal clocks soon began to operate independently of real time. Minutes and hours dissolved together until neither of the men had any real sense of the passage of time. They also found that their tempers were much shorter than usual and they were unable to maintain high levels of co-ordination and judgement after a few weeks below the ground. All were things which Penfold wanted to avoid; sound judgement and even tempers were a necessity on an archaeological dig if anything was to be accomplished.

The lights dimming seemed to work. The staff, tired from their day's work, welcomed the semi-darkness and by ten, no lamps were showing in the sleeping tents and the vault of the cavern was silent except for the occasional snore or rustle of a sleeping bag.

David Penfold stared up at the translucent plastic ceiling of his tent, hands cupped under his head, listening to the breathing of Speers and Jason Richter; by the sound of it, both men were deeply asleep. He let out a long breath and tried to relax, but he knew it wasn't going to happen. His brain was working at full steam, his mind filled with conflicting thoughts that refused to put themselves in order.

He'd felt this way almost from the instant he'd first arrived at the Subrano Cave. He'd put it down to the growing tension between himself and his father, but he knew it was more than that now. He'd never got on well with the old man, it was something he was used to. There was even a grudging sort of familiarity about it that was strangely comforting. No, he mused, it was more than just his father.

Distance. That was the only word to describe it. A feeling of separation from the whole world and everyone in it. The cave and the members of the dig had all somehow become unreal, like ghosts. Or maybe he was the ghost, trapped inside the confines of his own head, unable to reach out for help, or, when you got right down to it, not really wanting help at all.

The situation with Irene was a good example. He loved her, but it was as though he could watch himself loving her and knew that the love was false and hollow. He sighed again. It was enough to make Freud do back flips. How could he love Irene when he didn't have the slightest notion of who he was, let alone her. Maybe the cave was acting on him like some sort of Gestalt device; by removing himself from the world he was seeing himself for the first time. He scowled up at the roof of the tent.

'Horseshit,' he whispered. He rolled over and unzipped his sleeping bag. He dressed quickly, goosebumps erupting in the constant cool air of the cave. He slipped on a sweater, pushed his feet into his sneakers and tiptoed out of the tent.

He crossed the platform, shivering, and sat down on a wooden crate. He lit a cigarette and stared out across the gloom of the cavern. The only light still on was behind him, a floodlamp over the mess tent. The rest of the chamber was thick with shadow. He let his eyes roam the cave wall to his left until he spotted the entrance fissure. For a moment he felt an almost overwhelming urge to escape the cave and get to the surface as fast as he could. He puffed angrily on the cigarette and waited for the feeling to pass. Whether he liked it or not, he belonged here, even if it was like living in a tomb.

He grunted softly. It wasn't just *like* living in a tomb, it *was* living in one. There were bodies here, long dead, only a few feet below the surface, waiting to be revealed. But of course that was the essence of archaeology − digging up the past, grave robbing in the name of science and of history, disinterring secrets laid to rest millenia before, stripping them of dignity and putting them on display. To die was to give up all rights to your humanity.

Had it ever crossed Khan's mind? he wondered. This phantom artist who'd turned bare rock into a miracle of design? David gazed out across the high-ceilinged cavern and tried to picture it. Hearths, fires low, banked for the night. There would be sleeping figures, huddled under furs, clustered around the fires, well back from the yawning mouth of the cave. There would be soft moans as one of the men copulated with his mate. But Khan would not be sleeping. Somewhere, far back in the cave, or maybe in the tiny

75

grotto discovered by Harada and Grace, Khan would be thinking. Not about food, or lust, but of ideas. Sticks of charcoal in his hands would work at the stone, bringing his world to life with each stroke, and his mind would be on fire, dreaming of things never dreamt before. How did he see the passage of time? Did he think in terms of past, present and future, or did he live for each moment, forgetting what was gone, unable to conceive of what was to come?

David took a last drag on his cigarette and crushed it under his shoe. No. Khan knew about time. He knew that his art was meant for more than the simple act of creation. It was to endure, to live on. That was its magic. It existed outside of life, and because of that it was immortal.

'Hi.' David jumped up, startled, and turned. It was Mariea Tarvanin.

'Jesus, you scared the hell out of me,' said David, sitting down again.

She sat down in front of him, cross-legged on the platform. She was still dressed in jeans and her inevitable T-shirt, this one with a UCLA crest on it.

'I couldn't sleep,' she offered, keeping her voice low. David nodded.

'Neither could I.'

'Everyone else is out like a light,' said Mariea, smiling. He looked down at her and grimaced.

'Things never change, do they?' he said. 'Remember the Midnight Ramblers?'

'Sure,' said Mariea, dreamily. It was the way they'd met. Both had been out, walking the streets at two in the morning, trying to shake off their insomnia. After a quick check to make sure that he wasn't a rapist and she wasn't a drag queen, they'd begun talking. The conversation had come to a close as dawn crept in through the windows of her apartment, covering their intertwined bodies with a wash of silver and sleep.

'I don't know . . .' he began, the words trailing off.

'Don't know what?' asked Mariea, her voice as soft as the shadows obscuring her face. David shrugged.

'This place,' he said slowly. 'It's like one of those sensory deprivation chambers. It makes me think too much.'

'Baloney,' said Mariea. 'You'd be an introspective son-of-a-bitch in downtown New York.' She chuckled. 'And for all your navel-gazing you always seem to wind up blaming where you are for what's happening to your life. You used to talk about the east when you were in the west, and I bet you talked about the west when you were in the east. You've got a severe case of the grass is always greener on the other side of the hill.'

'Isn't it?' said David.

'Probably,' said Mariea, smiling, her eyes crinkling. 'But that's no excuse for self pity. Give me a cigarette and Momma Tarvanin will solve all your problems.'

He handed her one and lit it for her. She dragged, the glow lighting up her face briefly.

'So what's my problem,' he challenged.

'Love,' replied Mariea, puffing. 'Same as everyone else. You're in love with Irene Bouchard and you don't know what to do with it.'

'Her father hates my guts,' said David.

'Nuts,' said Mariea. 'From what I can tell her old man hates your old man, and vice-versa. That doesn't have anything to do with the two of you.'

'It tends to get in the way,' replied David. 'Especially since Irene won't do anything to offend her father.'

'So because you can't make with her, you can't love her, is that it?' said Mariea. David winced.

'No, it's not that,' he said defensively. 'I just think she should be honest with him.'

'Just the way you're honest with your old man?' asked Mariea.

'Screw you,' muttered David. Mariea laughed.

'All right, if that's what you want.'

'I wasn't speaking literally,' said David. He felt a growing tension in his chest as memories of their lovemaking together flooded into his mind.

'Relax,' said Mariea. 'I'm not going to make a pass at you.' She took another drag on the cigarette, tapping the ash into her palm. 'As I recall, it was that kind of thing that broke us up, way back when.'

'We broke up because we couldn't agree on a lot of things,'

said David.

'Like possessiveness,' said Mariea, 'and that's what's biting your ass right now. You don't like Irene's father exerting any power over her. You want her all for yourself, like a kid with a new toy. Remember that time you went off on a field trip and you came back and found out I'd been to bed with another guy while you were away? You threw a fit. Someone else had been at your own personal pussy. You never considered me at all. You never once said to yourself, okay, she had some guy in her bed, I hope she had some nice orgasms and a good time. You only thought about yourself. You make love into a funeral, David — you don't give a shit for the dead person, you only care about your own grief — something's been taken from you and it hurts.'

'Can I ask you a question?' said David.

'Sure,' said Mariea.

'Tell me why you're being such a bitch,' he grinned. She smiled up at him.

'Because I still love you, idiot, and I want to see you happy. You're smart, sensitive, good-looking, and an ace in the sack. You also have an old man who makes Macchiavelli look like a piker, and a guilt complex as long as Hollywood Boulevard.'

'And what about you. Turnabout is fair play,' said David. She shrugged.

'I've got two kids, a shack on the beach and no one to keep me warm at night because I have this habit of talking too much, too soon, and too seriously. I'm someone who hates bullshit above all things and I live in a world that's full of it. I guess you could say I'm lonely a lot.'

'Maybe we should make love,' said David, not really meaning it. She stood up, dropping the ash over the edge of the platform and stubbing out the cigarette on the plank floor. She looked down at him and put a hand on his shoulder.

'We just did, stupid,' she said. She turned and went back to her tent. David watched her go, a faint smile on his lips. Then he got up and went back to his own tent. A few minutes later he was asleep.

CHAPTER FOUR

1

Tony Grace sat at a small table he had set up close to the edge of the platform and let his fingers play across the keys of his portable typewriter. The notes he'd made on the discovery of Khan's hideaway had been transcribed into a nice piece of journalistic prose for his editors, but it wasn't enough. There seemed to be no way to get the feeling of being inside the cave across in words, or at least in the kind of words you used in a science magazine. He glanced down at what he'd just written and shook his head sadly; it wouldn't do for his readers at all.

'There is a complex atmosphere of tension among us all that seems almost suffocating in its intensity. Each of us puts on a bold front and continues working, but there is always a feeling of time running out, as though we must do all we can before the shades of the past become so strong that we are bound to them forever, doomed to sleep, like modern Jonahs in the belly of this stone-age whale.

'Working so closely together in such a confined space has intensified the personalities of every one of us, and given time I wouldn't be surprised to see us at each other's throats as our civilized façades are stripped away and we become more savage than Khan or his kind ever were. Maybe we *have* invoked some prehistoric curse by venturing underground, bringing the bright lights of our science to this place where time had drawn a midnight curtain so long ago.'

He scratched the stubble on his chin and frowned. Another paragraph or two and he'd be quoting from Edgar Allan Poe. He sat back on the wooden crate he was using as a chair and stifled a yawn. His sleep had been full of dark echoing dreams and he had awakened feeling as though he hadn't slept at all. He looked at his watch. Not even noon yet, and it felt like evening already. He looked out across the cave and wondered if there was any point in trying to do inverviews with Penfold and Bouchard today. Both men were working at the grave site below the rockfall and had been since breakfast. Grace sat forward, cupping his chin in one hand and wondered about the two scientists. Each of them was working as though the other wasn't there, Bouchard with his back to the hole, examining some small object, while Penfold and Merrill worked in the pit itself, occasionally bobbing up to retrieve some instrument from the litter of brushes, dental picks and trowels scattered at the lip of the grave.

The journalist grimaced. It was idiotic. Both men were experts, and working together they could do more than either one could singly, yet their professional jealousies kept them apart. Neither one seemed willing to give an inch. At dinner the night before, after Khan had been named he'd watched the conversation around the table develop into a battle between the two men. Penfold would postulate, Bouchard would rebut, then Penfold would pick away at Bouchard's rebuttal. The two elder archaeologists had turned the Subrano site into some adolescent playing field, competing with each other endlessly. On top of the animosity between the men, Grace could also see the withering effect of the battle on their children. During the conversation Penfold had relentlessly asked for corroboration from his son, and Bouchard had done the same with his daughter, Irene, forcing the two to join in a battle they didn't want to fight. More than once Irene Bouchard had been on the verge of tears. Grace had a sinking feeling that it was all going to end in disaster. Everyone was already walking on a razor edge after only a few days in the cave. Tempers would begin to flare pretty soon, and things would be said that couldn't be retracted. It was a waste and a bloody shame.

Still, he thought philosophically, it made for an interesting time. He looked down at the page in his typewriter again and smiled. It was no good for the magazine, but it pleased him. He nodded to himself happily. He'd keep on with it, a personal journal maybe, as well as the slightly more academic stuff his editors required. He knew perfectly well it would come to nothing, but it would pass the time down here in the dungeons. He shivered suddenly, and looked up at the crusted roof of the cavern high above, the burning eyes of the spread-eagled cave bear seeming to bore into him. A quotation popped into his head and for a moment he couldn't identify it: 'I am going out. I may be some time.' Grace frowned, trying to place the line; they were somebody's last words. Then he had it — Oates, the wounded man who had been with Scott on his last fatal expedition to the Pole. Oates had known that there wasn't food enough to keep the survivors going so he had left the wretched tent in the middle of a blizzard, knowing that he was going to certain death. The journalist scratched his chin again, wondering why it had come to mind. Maybe it was the thought of keeping a diary; things like that were always found after you died heroically in the midst of some magnificent adventure, usually ending in mid-sentence just as you were going out to fight off the attack of the man-eating pygmies.

'No such luck,' muttered Grace. Any adventures in Subrano 1 were going to come from his imagination. He grinned. Maybe he could tear off an Edgar Rice Burroughs in his spare time. Khan. King of the Cave-Men. He shook his head and pulled the sheet out of his typewriter, crumpling it into a ball. It was time to get back to his real work. He picked up his notebook and headed down to the cave floor.

2

David Penfold moved slowly along the string grid, checking each person's progress. The entire staff except for his father, Bouchard and Merrill was working on the floor today, finishing off the preliminary stripping of the first layer. Jason Richter, taking time off from his photography of the paintings, was busy shooting artifacts *in situ* before they were removed for tagging, cataloguing and packing. A few minutes before he'd checked the square Irene was working on, but the conversation had been brief and strained. She kept her face from his the entire time, responding to his questions stiffly. He reached Harada's square and squatted down beside the muscular geologist. He watched as the broad, spatulate hands held the brush, sweeping infinitesimal specks of soil away from the fluted edge of a flint burin, a chisel-like tool used to manufacture other implements. Harada's grip was firm, but the sweep of the bristles was almost a caress.

'You have the touch,' said David admiringly. The geologist looked up and shrugged, a smile on his face.

'It is a question of respect,' he answered. 'The Japanese are raised to respect their ancestors. It is pounded into us almost from birth.'

'Still,' said David, 'I'd have thought you'd be more at home with a rock hammer or a core sampler.'

Harada laughed.

'I spend more time with a microscope than I do with a hammer,' he said. 'I think scientists become too specialized. Until becoming part of this dig I had always assumed archaeologists simply dug holes in the ground; the detailed way in which things progress has been a revelation to me. I am learning a great deal.'

'And maybe I can learn some things from you as well, Doctor. Here I am digging away in a cave, and I really don't know much about the way in which it was formed.'

'Perhaps we can talk this evening,' replied Harada. David nodded, pleased. There was a quiet strength in the Japanese man's personality that he liked. He exuded a sense of peace that somehow managed to put his own problems into perspective. David stood up and bumped into Tony Grace, who had come up behind him.

'Got a minute?' asked the lanky journalist. 'A few words for your legions of fans, perhaps?'

'Talk to my father,' said David. 'I'm second string.' Grace lifted his narrow shoulders.

'So maybe I'd like the second string's opinion. We can't all be stars, you know.'

'I suppose not,' said David. 'Sure, we can talk.'

'There's a pot of coffee in the mess tent. I'll pour us a

couple of mugs and we can chat there,' said Grace. David nodded.

'Okay,' he said. 'As long as it doesn't take too long. I've got a lot to do.'

Five minutes later the two men were alone in the mess tent, sipping their coffee. David lit a cigarette and looked across the table at Grace, who already had his notebook out.

'What would you like to know?' asked David.

'I'm looking for an informed hunch,' said Grace, smiling, twiddling his pencil between two fingers. 'Which is why I wanted to talk to you and not your father or Dr Bouchard. They tend to be a bit highbrow, lots of talk about stratification and things but not much about people.'

'So give me a for instance,' said David.

'The tribe that lived here,' said Grace. 'What kind of people do you think they were?' David dragged on his cigarette and stared thoughtfully into space.

'Hunters, obviously,' began David. 'You can see that from the cave paintings. Most Neanderthals found before this seem to have been migratory, following herds, but it's hard to say about the group that lived here. The cave seems to have been in use for a long time, and it's doubtful if they would have gone to such trouble decorating it if it was only a temporary stop. This was just about the limit of the last ice-age, so maybe it was a permanent camp.'

'You're not saying anything about them as people,' interrupted Grace. 'I can find out about their habits from books, or from your father. I want to know what they were like as human beings.'

'It's an impossible request,' said David, frowning. 'All we have to go on are a few scattered bones and some paintings.'

'Intuition,' suggested Grace. David laughed wryly.

'Archaeologists don't have any,' he said. 'Ask my father. If you show the slightest sign of it they bounce you from the high order. It's a no-no in the business.'

'Bollocks,' said Grace. 'You can't tell me you haven't daydreamed about what this place was like when Khan and his tribe lived here.' David looked at him sharply. The writer wasn't the court jester he sometimes made himself out to be. He'd picked up on something David had felt from the beginning; a haunting feeling that he could look over his shoulder at any moment and *see* Khan, or his people. He leaned back in his chair and shut his eyes.

'More than anything else it smelled,' he said softly, seeing the cave in his mind's eye. 'Cooking smells, charcoal, rotting meat. There were women, waiting in the shade of the cave mouth, scraping flesh from skins they'd use for clothes. An old man, seated by himself, working at a flint core, shaving off wafers of stone for blades. Old by their standards anyway, maybe forty, not much more. He'd have a deeply-lined face and a lot of scars from hunts gone by. Arthritis too, enough to cripple him, swell his joints and keep him from going off with the other men.

'There would be children, small by our standards, playing games with old bones cast from the hearths, or wrestling together. There would be no one father or mother to a child, they were members of the tribe, and cared for by everyone.'

'What about Khan?' asked Grace, his voice almost a whisper. 'What was he like?'

'Khan was their leader,' murmured David, caught in a trance. 'Taller than any of the other men, almost as tall as a modern man. Because he was their leader he would only take part in the great hunts, the ones that were used as omens. He hunted the cave bear, and he hunted it alone. When he was successful and had another head to add to the pile of skulls beneath the centre stone of the cave, the tribe would know that the winter would be kind, and that there would be live births instead of stillborn or deformed ones. When he wasn't hunting the cave bear he would spend his time painting the cave, working the magic that gave the other members of the tribe their courage and skill. He would spend his nights in the grotto you found, tracing the lines of the ibex and the antelope, capturing their strength and their speed on the rock walls, forcing them to obey the dream hunts he saw, making them fall before the spears by his magic. Late in the darkness he would come back to the main cave. Everyone would be asleep and the fires would be low. He would choose a mate then, because he had *droit de seigneur*, and could take any man's woman to his bed. It was he who was the only member of the tribe to touch a woman during her menses, and only he was allowed the right to copulate first with the daughters of the tribe. His seed was the magic that brought forth children, even though the tribe knew nothing of the mechanics of reproduction. The history of the tribe was invested in him, and so was its future. All of them knew that without him and his magic they would die.' David stopped, his head falling forward and his eyes snapping open. He gave an embarrassed grin.

'Marvellous!' said Grace, writing furiously. 'And you said you had no intuition!'

'Fantasy,' said David, lighting another cigarette. 'Based on nothing. Khan was probably a squat little brute who just happened to know how to draw. The tribe members spotted it early, and made him into a demi-god. He was as mortal as you or I.'

'It makes a great story though,' said Grace. 'I prefer the dignity of your daydream to the overgrown ape that facts give.'

'He was no ape,' said David firmly. 'That much I am sure of. He was a man.' Suddenly he tensed, then looked up at the roof of the mess tent.

'What?' asked Grace. David shook his head.

'Nothing,' said David. 'I thought I felt something. It must be the platform supports settling.' He looked down at his half-empty mug. Tiny concentric ripples moved out across the circular pool of black, steaming coffee, rebounding off the rim of the mug.

3

'There's no doubt that it's another grave,' said Dr Penfold, kneeling over the mound of rubble at the rear of the cave behind the platform. Returning from Khan's grotto in the middle of the afternoon, Jason Richter had stumbled on his way down from the rocky ledge and had knocked aside some of the stones at the base of the small rockfall, revealing an obviously man-made mound of the clay-like soil that covered the floor of the cave. He and Izo Harada had shown their

85

discovery to Penfold and Bouchard. The two archaeologists, intrigued by the odd placement of the low hammock, had dug down a few inches, unveiling the tumbled skeletons of three people, one of them, by its size, a child.

'It is very odd,' said Bouchard, adjusting his wire-rimmed glasses and peering down into the shallow trench. 'There appears to have been no attempt at ceremony, and the grave is so shallow.'

'Disease?' asked David Penfold, standing beside his father. The older man looked up at his son and shook his head.

'No. If these three had been sick they wouldn't have been buried in the cave at all.' He looked down at the skeletons again, still firmly wedded to the bed of soil. Daniel Merrill, the grim-faced conservator, squatted beside the grave, frowning.

'I'm no palaeontologist,' he murmured, 'but it looks as though these people had a lot of broken bones.' He gently prodded the skull of the child's skeleton. 'Looks like the whole back of the head was shoved in.'

'You're a medical man, Vlasek, what's your opinion?' asked Dr Penfold. Vlasek beamed, more than happy to offer his assistance. He got down on his hands and knees, examining the skeletons where they lay.

'Dr Merrill is most correct,' he said after a few minutes. 'The small skeleton has a fractured skull and the entire rib cage is depressed. From what I can see it would appear as well that the pelvis was shattered. The two adult skeletons show similar trauma. They could have been killed by this very fall of rock, yes?' He looked up at Penfold. The archaeologist shook his head.

'I'm afraid not, Dr Vlasek. They were buried formally, if hastily. This rockfall came later, covering the mound.'

'So someone took the time actually to inter these three, yet without a ritual burial,' mused Bouchard.

'Some danger, perhaps?' asked Merrill, his forehead wrinkling.

'If there was a danger, then why were they buried at the back of the cave?' said Penfold. He shrugged and rose to his feet, brushing dirt from his trousers. 'I suppose it is one of those mysteries we shall never unravel.' He smiled at Jason Richter. 'Interesting though.' He turned to Bouchard. 'I suggest we leave this until later, Dr Bouchard. We still have more work to do at the first grave-site.' The short, bespectacled Frenchman nodded. The two men clambered back up on to the wooden platform, followed by Vlasek and Merrill, leaving David and Jason Richter alone in the shadowed rear of the cavern.

'What does Harada think?' asked David.

'He didn't say,' said the photographer, eyeing the sepia-tinted bones at his feet. 'He seemed a little upset, actually. I don't think he likes the idea of digging people up. Bit of a mystic, Izo is. He got this glazed faraway look in his eye while we were in that little rat trap at the end of the tunnel. It was like he was seeing things. Bit spooky.'

'He just thinks differently than we do,' said David.

'So what do you think happened here?' asked Richter, changing the subject. David Penfold chewed thoughtfully on his lower lip, studying the fall of rock above the huddled bones in the grave.

'I think Merrill came close,' he said after a few minutes. 'They were buried fast because whoever was doing the burying was in danger. He wanted to do what he could, but he was working quickly.'

'Your father made sense though,' said Richter. 'Why the back of the cave? And what kind of danger?' David shrugged.

'Fire maybe. Or an attack by a rival tribe.'

'Not fire,' said Richter. 'The kid there had his head bashed in. An attack makes more sense.'

'It was neither,' said a voice from above them. David and the photographer looked up. Harada was standing on the platform a few feet away, looking down at the grave. His expression was dark and remote. He bent his knees and dropped lightly down to the floor of the cave.

'You sound pretty sure of yourself,' said Richter, frowning. Harada approached the grave and glanced down at the remains of the three people it contained.

'I have been thinking about it,' said the broad-shouldered Japanese. 'I think these people died in the main rockfall that sealed the front entrance to the cave.'

'That would account for the broken bones,' nodded David. Richter shook his head.

'It doesn't make sense,' he said. 'If the cave was sealed what happened to the others, the ones who buried these three, for instance?' He nodded down at the grave. 'They didn't just spirit themselves away.'

'What would you do if you suddenly found yourself trapped in a cave such as this?' asked Harada. The tall, bearded man laughed.

'Piss my pants!' he grinned.

'And afterwards?' said Harada. 'After the initial fear had passed?'

'Look for a way to get out, I guess,' shrugged Richter. 'But there was no way out after the big rockfall at the front of the cave, you know that. Christ, you were the one who discovered the pothole that got us down here. Unless you're saying that fissure was there in the first place.'

'No,' said Harada. 'The pothole and the fissure came much later, that is quite plain.'

'So where did they go?' asked Richter.

'You think they went down?' said David, seeing what Harada was getting at. 'Down to the lower cave?' Harada nodded.

'They would have had no choice,' he said slowly. David looked down to the end of the cave and the gaping throat of the tunnel that led down to the half-submerged chamber below them.

'Fairy tales,' scoffed Richter. 'I've got better things to do.' He boosted himself up on to the platform and disappeared, shaking his head.

'You really think that's what happened?' said David. Harada nodded, looking down at the grave.

'Yes,' he murmured. 'It would be the only way. It tells us something of these people, that even in their fear they would take the time to bury their dead.'

'But what happened to them?' said David, staring at the tunnel a dozen yards away, the opening lost in shadow.

'Who knows,' said Harada. 'Perhaps they did find another way out, or died looking, without light, or food.'

'My God!' whispered David. 'What a terrible way to die!' He felt a surge of pity for the long-departed travellers who had gone down that dark yawning hole, almost certainly knowing that they would never feel the warmth of the sun on their faces again. Doomed to wander endlessly in pitch-black catacombs until hunger or madness defeated them. He glanced down at the gravesite, feeling a breath of horror set the hairs at the nape of his neck on end. The three people in the grave had been lucky if Harada's scenario was right, and somehow David knew that it was.

4

Dr Antonin Vlasek stood in the small toilet cubicle, head bent over the collapsible aluminium sink, splashing his face with cold water, trying to remain calm. He dried himself with a sheet of paper towelling, then reached into the pocket of his overalls for his pills. He grimaced, reading the label, his own name printed on it as the prescribing doctor.

'Physician, heal thyself,' he muttered to himself. He opened the small medicine bottle and downed two of the white pellets, wincing at the bitter taste of them on his tongue. He stood for a moment, staring at the bare plastic wall above the sink, massaging his chest with his right hand, waiting for the pain to recede. Even without a mirror he knew that his face was the colour of cold ashes. The pains had been coming more and more often, the attacks becoming stronger with each day he spent in the cave.

Simple fear, that's all it was, he told himself. He had diagnosed his own heart condition several years before, and until the dig it had seemed to be in control. But he had lied to himself, told himself that it was worth anything to be a part of the expedition, even if it meant confronting his life-long fear of enclosed spaces. Standing there he shuddered, remembering the terror he'd felt as a child when one of his friends locked him in a tool-shed behind the school. When he was released, sobbing, his clothes soiled, the teacher who found him had been appalled by the boy's bleeding fingers and the splintered gouges in the wood of the door, mutely testifying to the horrors undergone by the near catatonic child.

His excitement at the discovery of the Subrano Cave had carried him through the first descent, and he had managed to endure the second passage with the rest of the expedition by strength of will alone. But now it was getting worse, almost by the hour. The enclosing walls of the cave seemed to be moving in on him and the vaulted roof above his head was a constant threat. At least once every five minutes he found himself searching out the narrow slot of the fissure entrance to the cave, every muscle in his body taut with anxiety. He could see himself rushing at the wound in the rock wall, clambering into the orifice, clawing his way along the terrible breach, finally arriving at the foot of the pothole, his mouth dry as alum with clotting fear. And then the climb, up, up to the mote of light above, staring down at him, beckoning like some god's eye in the heavens.

But he was trapped. There was nothing on earth that could make him take that hideous journey, and nothing that could make him stay a moment longer in the cave. His fear was like a cold knife thrust deeply into his chest, a frozen blade that filled him with humming waves of pain.

And it was his own fault, his own stupid pride that had put him here. He turned away from the sink, knowing that if he remained much longer he would be sick. He let himself out of the cubicle and took a deep breath. As long as he had the pills he would be all right.

But what happens when they run out? He asked himself. What will you do then, good doctor? Scream aloud? Tell the world of your childish phobia. Make a fool of yourself in front of all these people. He straightened his spine and walked stiffly to the ramp. According to the afternoon's schedule he was supposed to be helping the young Japanese man finish another of the grid squares.

He stood at the head of the ramp, looking down across the brightly lit expanse of the cave, the first rush of the tranquillizers' balm hitting him, dulling the edge of his fear. He blinked, focussing. Everyone was hard at work, it was time to join them. He started down the ramp, his legs still slightly rubbery.

The first tremor was mild, barely enough to raise dust on the cavern floor. But it was noticeable. Total silence engulfed the Subrano chamber as the members of the expedition froze in mid-stride, breath held, eyes wide.

Then it came; a growling, tearing thunder that seemed to rise from the very bowels of the earth beneath their feet. The second tremor, violent spawn of the first and a hundred times stronger. The ground shivered like some prehistoric behemoth rising at last from its long hibernation.

Like an actor in a nightmare play Anton Vlasek looked up at the roof of the cave to find himself staring into the eyes of Khan's chained bear, the painted orbs burning with a hideous fire. And the bear spoke to him with a rending, grinding scream as the roof split open, tearing the beast in half, the crack extending the length of the chamber like the grin of a massive death's head. A wedge of stone twice the size of a man knifed down, sheared from the broadening fissure, and struck Vlasek, burying him beneath its ten-ton weight, a fraction of a second after the doctor's heart exploded in his chest, saving him from the ultimate horror that followed as the lights went out and the Subrano Cave was thrown into sudden, total and absolute darkness.

Blindly the sounds continued as the ceiling collapsed, sending down a rain of boulders that pounded into the earth and those standing on it like gigantic hammers, filling the cave with a boiling, unseen cloud of choking dust. Then the tremor passed and faded, leaving eyeless chaos in its wake. Slowly the dust began to settle and the cavern was still.

CHAPTER FIVE

1

David Penfold was blind. He lay on the floor of the cave, blinking, seeing nothing. He felt a sharp pain in his back and shifted his weight, groaning, his voice coming to him hollowly. He lifted his arm and held it in front of his face. Nothing. He moved his arm until his fingers touched his cheek. He could feel the grit that covered him, but he could still see nothing. He felt a scream of fear rising in his throat as his fingers scrabbled upwards to his eyes and then it died stillborn as the realization of what had happened sunk in. There had been an earthquake and the lights had gone out. Without the lights the cave would be dark, completely without illumination.

He struggled into a sitting position, hearing the soft clatter made by the small stones that covered him. He managed to get his feet beneath him and stood, swaying, his arms held out for balance. He swallowed, tasting bitter dust, trying to keep down the bile of terror welling up in him. He stood, rooted to the spot, too terrified to take a step. Moments ago the cave had been a familiar place; now in the total darkness it was a potential death trap. He moved his head in a slow circle, squinting, trying to find some faint light anywhere, but there was nothing. Gagging, he cleared his throat.

'Hey!' he called. He cocked an ear and listened, praying for some response. There was a long silence and then from somewhere almost directly ahead of him, a distant groaning reply. David felt a surge of relief. He wasn't alone.

'Who's there?' he called again. A rattling cough echoed in the chamber, followed by the sound of retching. David bit his lip, feeling the copper tang of blood on his tongue. A voice, words, anything!

'It's me, Merrill,' came the voice weakly. There was a dull

groan and the sound of movement. 'Good Christ! What happened?'

'There's been an earthquake, I think,' shouted David. 'Where are you exactly?'

'David?' The sound came from behind him. It was Irene's voice. 'Is that you, David?'

'Irene?' he said, turning to the voice. 'Don't move. Just stay still for a minute!' He turned back again. 'Merrill! Tell me where you are!'

'I was at the front of the cave, by the rockfall. Oh God! My arm! I think it's broken!'

'Irene! Where are you?' called David.

'I was at the artifact table,' she called back. David's mind worked furiously, trying to pinpoint his own location from the sounds of the two voices. He had been on the floor of the cave, about halfway between the platform and the main rockfall, checking work on the grid close to the wall opposite the entrance fissure. He took a single shuffling step forward and almost tripped over a large boulder. He reached out with his arms blindly and moved to the left, trying to get around it. He stopped. Another voice. Irene's father.

'Irene. *Mon dieu, ça va? ça va?*'

'Papa! *Oui, ça va. Toi?*'

'*Oui, oui, ma chère!*'

David moved forward again, checking the floor ahead cautiously with the toes of his boots. If he could reach the far wall of the cave he knew he could work his way back to the platform and find one of the emergency lanterns. He concentrated on each step, desperately trying to still his panic, preventing himself from breaking into a run.

His left foot struck something soft and he stopped again, bending down carefully. He squatted, one hand out for balance, and reached out. His fingers touched fabric; cloth, a man's shirt.

'Are you all right?' he said softly, speaking to the unseen figure. There was no reply. David's fingers moved across the arm of the figure and on to the chest. A man. He recoiled as his hand slid into a warm wet cavity and touched splintered bone. There was something else there too — hard and un-yielding. A shard of rock that jutted up out of the body.

David slid to his knees and found the man's arm again, feeling for the pulse he knew wouldn't be there. There was nothing. The man was dead. He ran a hand up to the man's face, trying to trace the contours for some clue to his identity. No beard. It wasn't Jason Richter then. The right side of the face gave too easily under David's hands and he could feel the grotesque slide of flesh that meant the cheekbone had been shattered. Forcing himself, he kept on. No glasses, that meant it wasn't Tony Grace, and Bouchard had been accounted for.

With a horrible intuition David traced down the right arm, partially trapped beneath the body. He pulled it out and felt the hand, searching for the little finger. He felt the hard band of gold and then the raised oval of the stone. There was a series of small protrusions around the bezel, and even blind David knew what the raised letters around the stone said: *Per Ardua Ad Astra*. The motto of the United States Air Force, the only piece of jewellery his father ever wore, a momento of his wartime work as a liaison officer in Washington. The young man's ears filled with a high cicada buzzing and he reeled back, both hands clammy and slick with blood. He looked down unseeing at his father's corpse. A howl of anguish was torn from him and he collapsed over the body, hugging the mangled flesh in his arms, rocking back and forth, weeping with grief and fear.

2

Izo Harada had been in the rear of the cave when the earthquake struck. Even before the first mild tremor had passed he knew what was going to happen and, acting instinctively, he had thrown himself under the narrow ledge that led up to the entrance to Khan's hideaway. Had he not moved, the second, more powerful tremor would have killed him. The main quake dislodged the high pile of rubble from the secondary rockfall, sending a hail of boulders down into the back of the cavern. As it was the newly formed rockfall raised a wall in front of the ledge, sealing the Japanese geologist behind it.

Harada, arms raised protectively over his head, waited until the tremor passed, and then, keeping his eyes firmly closed, he began to dig his way out. He had been in caves where the lights had suddenly failed before and he knew that the only way of knowing where he was in relation to the cave was by keeping his eyes closed, maintaining a memory of his location rather than reacting to the instinctive fear of suddenly being without light.

The geologist worked methodically, pulling chunks of rock away, thrusting them into the cavity behind him, using the sensation of gravity on his body to keep him heading in the right direction. He had heard of cavers trapped by falls or mudslides who, in their panic, dug their way in even deeper. Harada knew that panic and fear were his enemies, not the inanimate rock, and he breathed in a slow, steady rhythm, letting his mind fill with the touch of the stone in his mind, denying any other thoughts.

Finally he was free, and there were no more obstacles within reach of his outstretched arms. He squirmed up out of the hole he had made, still keeping his eyes closed, visualizing his location. He realized that standing upright would immediately give him vertigo, so he stayed on his hands and knees, moving across the rock-strewn floor of the cavern, heading for the platform. He reached one of the support posts and let his hand travel up it. If his memory was accurate he was at the edge of the raised wooden floor, close to the cave wall. He stood slowly, keeping his hand on the support post. There were voices coming from beyond the platform in the front section of the chamber but he ignored them, intent on his work.

Harada felt with both hands, letting them move across the rough wooden surface. It sloped away from him, and he guessed that the front supports had given way during the quake. The wood beneath his hands seemed firm, however, and he boosted himself up. He rested for a moment, his eyes still firmly shut, then put out a probing leg and tested the slope. It was steep, falling away quickly. The centre supports had failed as well. He formed a picture of the platform in his mind, and then collapsed it, watching the tents and equipment slide into a jumbled wreckage. He nodded to himself. The auxiliary lighting equipment had been stored in metal crates placed behind the toilet cubicle. If the platform had fallen the way he'd visualized the crates would be close to the top of the pile. He eased away from the relatively level portion of the platform he'd been resting on and slid downward, digging in his heels and putting both arms out, letting them slow his descent.

He stopped suddenly as a terrible scream echoed around him, his head jerking up, listening. Then he moved on, more quickly now, urged on by the sound of the pain-racked voice. A few seconds later the soles of his boots struck something solid and he stopped again. He crouched forward, letting his full weight slowly come to bear on the object. It held. He reached down and felt its contours with one hand. His fingers touched wood and then a section of metal. One of the collapsible sawhorses used to hold up a work table. He shifted to his right and almost immediately his boots met another object. This time it was made entirely of metal. He felt around the edge of the cool, smooth container and found a hasp. He grasped it and tugged, opening the box. He squatted down beside it, bracing himself against the sawhorse to his left, and reached into the crate's interior. His fingers closed around the handle of one of the big six-volt sealed beam units and Harada allowed himself a smile of satisfaction. He pulled the lamp out, and then checked it over, making sure all the connections were still in place. When he was satisfied he fumbled for the switch on top of the handle and turned on the lamp.

'I can see a light!' the voice came from the head of the cave. Harada opened his eyes.

The powerful beam of the lamp revealed a scene of utter chaos that shocked the normally calm geologist. His eyes widened as he moved the probing cone of light across the floor of the cave.

The chamber had been utterly transformed; where there had once been smooth floor there was now a litter of gigantic cleavings from the demolished roof above, boulder leaning on boulder in wild disarray, the blocks of limestone splintered and heaving in every direction. Here and there Harada could pick out the pale features of survivors and the tumbled wreckage of equipment. It looked as though the entire midline of the cave roof had opened up, spilling a lethal barrage of stone on the people below. He swung the light up and checked the ceiling of the cavern. There was no trace of the paintings, nothing but the clean scars of newly sundered rock, free of the wrinkles and seams that had marked the old roof. He squinted; there was a narrow cleft that ran from one end of the cave to the other, with smaller fissures leading off it like veins on a leaf. He frowned; the new roof contour hadn't barrel vaulted, providing support for itself. The earthquake had changed the Subrano Cave, but the transformation was still incomplete; Harada knew that it wouldn't take much to bring down another rockfall.

He ran the light across the remains of the platform, tracing out the pattern of damage around him; several massive blocks had struck within feet of where he crouched. The platform had been completely demolished, the bivouacs, equipment cases, crates of artifacts, food and supplies thrown into an impossible tangle at the base of the sharply-sloping wooden floor, splintered now with large gaping holes where sections of the ceiling had plummeted through. Harada was sure that anyone on the platform when the tremor began was now dead; no one could have survived such a deadly cascade of stone.

The geologist wedged the lamp into the crosspiece of the sawhorse, aiming the light up at the ceiling as a beacon for the others. He then grasped the metal handle of the box and began manhandling it down to the floor of the cave, working his way carefully through the wreckage.

3

The survivors sprawled in a loose semicircle around the lighting box on the cavern floor, staring hungrily into the harsh yellow glare, as though the steady upward-tilted beam could somehow give them the answer to their dilemma. Five people were missing from the group; Dr Penfold, Kenji Takashima, Jason Richter and Anton Vlasek had been killed during the collapse. David Penfold sat outside the circle, refusing the comfort of the light and staring into the darkness beyond its range, his eyes glazed and unseeing, his father's ring held tightly in his fist. It had been an hour since the tremor.

'We have rested long enough, I think,' said Alain Bouchard firmly, breaking the long silence, his voice ringing in the stillness. 'We must gather together what we can and make our way out of this place.' He looked at the others, a tight frown tugging his thin lips downward. 'With Dr Penfold gone I must assume responsibility for the expedition.' This last was as much a question as a statement and he checked the faces of the survivors for any disagreement. He saw nothing but the expressionless apathy of shock. He turned to Harada, who was squatting on the far side of the box, squinting thoughtfully into the light. 'We can send others down at some later time to, um, retrieve the bodies,' he added, his voice trailing off. Harada shook his head slowly.

'I am afraid that will be impossible,' said the geologist quietly.

'Christ, you don't mean you want to take the corpses with us, do you?' grunted Speers, still dressed in his diving suit. He had been on his way into the lower cave when the ceiling fell and it was his position in the flue which had saved him. He had dug himself out in much the same way as Harada.

'I do not mean the bodies,' said Harada. 'I meant that our way out is no longer available. The fissure is closed.'

'That is absurd!' snapped Bouchard. 'We must uncover it. There are enough of us to accomplish the task.'

'No,' said Harada simply. He picked the lamp up off the box and trained the beam on the far wall of the cave; all except David Penfold followed the moving light. The geologist shone it on the place where the fissure had once been, a four-foot-wide slit in the furrowed face of the limestone. There was nothing now except a narrow shadowed scar, less than six inches across. 'The fissure lay between two blocks of bedrock. The tremor moved them together. It is likely that the pothole itself no longer exists beyond it.' The others stared into the circle of light, stunned. Harada placed the lamp back on the box.

'Then we must wait for rescue,' said Bouchard, covering his fear with a shrug. 'The authorities know we are here, it is simply a matter of time, yes?'

'Right!' said Tony Grace, his tousled mat of hair thick with dust. His eyes gleamed with frantic humour. 'The Yugoslavian lads will dig us out in no time. We'll be heroes on the Belgrade Evening News. Archaeological expedition saved from certain death.'

'Shut the fuck up!' snarled Speers, angrily, his face twisted into a frightened sneer.

'We *can* wait, can't we?' asked Mariea Tarvanin, looking toward Harada and pausing in her work. Both she and Alice Braden were binding a make-shift splint to Daniel Merrill's shattered right arm. The thick-set conservator sat stoically, his gritted teeth the only indication of his pain.

'Of course we can,' said Irene Bouchard, sitting beside her father. 'Papa is right, I think, it is only a matter of time before we are found.'

'Sure,' muttered Speers, 'just like it rains wooden nickels in Nebraska. How the hell are they going to get to us if the fissure is closed and the pothole is gone. Stupid broad,' he added.

'*Cochon*!' she snapped. 'They can dig in through the old rockfall at the face of the cave. With heavy equipment it would not take more than a few days I think. It was intended to open up the original entrance on the next season's dig.' She looked at Harada expectantly. The geologist ran a hand through his hair and closed his eyes, wondering how he could explain the situation without panicking the group. He didn't have to; a new voice echoed from beyond the circle of light.

'It's not a question of digging us out,' said David Penfold, standing at the edge of the circle. Tears still stained his grime-encrusted face but he had his grief under control now. He crouched down between Tony Grace and Mariea Tarvanin, who shifted slightly to give him room. A few feet away Irene Bouchard smiled at him, her eyes filled with the sympathy she felt, but she said nothing. Penfold glanced at her briefly, managing a pale ghost of a smile in reply, then turned to Harada. 'You're thinking about aftershocks, aren't you, Izo?' Harada nodded.

'Yes, I am afraid so,' he answered. He reached out and picked up the lamp again, running it over the newly-formed roof of the cave high above them, following the tracery of cracks. 'There is never a single tremor in an earthquake, and the first is rarely the most severe. The next shock will bring down even more of the roof.'

'God!' moaned Grace. 'You mean it's going to happen again!' Harada nodded.

'Yes.'

'You cannot be sure,' interjected Bouchard stiffly. 'Even with a new tremor the roof could hold.'

'No,' said Harada, turning to the French archaeologist. 'I come from a country where earthquakes are well known. I took my doctorate in the subject. In some cases the cave will remain intact after a series of aftershocks, but not here. To remain stable the first tremor would have had to create a barrel vault in the roof, the arch distributing the pressure evenly. As you can see, this is not the case here. The roof has sheared, splitting along old faults, leaving a relatively flat plane. The next tremor will disturb the bedding layers above us and the joints will fail, bringing down more rock. The cave will be filled completely.'

'You are absolutely sure?' asked Bouchard in a whisper. Harada nodded.

'Yes. To do the damage that has already been done the first tremor must have been at least 7 on the Richter scale of intensity. The next one will be even stronger, 8, or more. A 7.9 intensity is enough to destroy a modern city. Beyond anything else that is enough to ensure that we will not be rescued. I am sure the Yugoslavian authorities have more serious things to consider now than the rescue of a small group of foreign scientists.'

'How long until the next big shock?' asked David Penfold.

'A few hours at most, I would think,' said Harada.

'Then there is no hope!' moaned Bouchard. 'We are doomed.'

'Perhaps not,' said Harada after a long moment. All eyes

turned to him.

'What?' asked Speers, grimacing. 'You got some magic wand you're going to wave to get us out of here? You don't look like any fucking Tinkerbell to me.'

'Please be quiet, Mr Speers,' said Alice Braden calmly. 'And I would appreciate it if you would control your language.' Harada looked at the plain-faced woman with respect, suddenly realizing that he knew almost nothing about her. Since the beginning of the expedition she had been little more than a fixture, a nonentity. She looked at Harada and nodded. 'Please go on, Dr Harada.'

'Obviously we cannot stay here,' he began. 'If we remain, we are, as Dr Bouchard put it, doomed. But there is an alternative. We can go further down. Into the lower cave.'

'What good will that do?' asked David Penfold.

'I am not sure,' said Harada. 'But it is better than waiting here for the roof to come down upon us again.'

'It is idiotic,' said Bouchard. 'It serves no purpose. At least by remaining here we have some chance of rescue if your estimation of the roof's strength is inaccurate.'

'Isn't it just delaying the inevitable, Izo?' asked David. The Japanese man shrugged.

'Nothing is inevitable,' he said, smiling. 'As long as you are alive to make choices. Mr Speers maintains that there is a siphon at the far end of the lower cave; perhaps it leads somewhere else. In any cave system there is usually more than one way out or in.'

'That's a point,' grunted Speers, nodding. 'The siphon could lead to an air cave beyond.'

'Or it could lead nowhere,' said Bouchard. 'I still maintain that we should remain here and wait for help.'

'Wait a second,' put in Mariea Tarvanin. 'Let's have a few more facts before we come to any decision. This siphon thing you're talking about, what exactly is it?'

'A water-filled passageway,' said Harada. 'The lower cave is partially submerged; the siphon is below the waterline. If there is a third cave beyond, which is quite likely, it might be on the same level as the second, or perhaps slightly higher. If that is the case, the third cave will be filled with air.'

'And if this third cave is at a lower level?' said Bouchard.

'What then?'

'It will be completely submerged,' answered Speers. 'No air.'

'Madness!' said Bouchard. Harada ignored the older man and turned to Speers.

'You have seen the siphon,' he said. 'I would like your opinion.' The cave diver rubbed a hand across the line of his jaw.

'Hard to say. From what I could tell the water isn't moving at all. If there is a third cave and the siphon's more than a blind passage it stands to reason the next chamber is on the same level, or higher. If it was lower there'd be some egress point for the water and there'd be a current, even if it was only slight. And the lower cave is vadose, that's certain.'

'What is this vadose?' asked Bouchard annoyed.

'It means the cave is above the waterlogged zone, above the lowest level of the water table. There are two basic forms of cave — vadose and phreatic. A phreatic cave is formed below the water table and is normally part of a subterranean drainage system, dry or wet depending on the season.'

'That's another point,' put in Speers, excitement in his voice. 'This is the dry season here, right? Even if the third cave is phreatic there's a good chance it would be free of water. Christ, I hadn't thought of that!'

'No!' said Bouchard furiously. 'I cannot allow it! We would be throwing away any chance of rescue. At least here we have a known situation. To go into the lower cave and beyond is out of the question; Dr Merrill is injured and the rest of us are in no condition to attempt any such thing. It would be suicidal!'

From the front portion of the cave, well beyond the spill of light cast by the lamp, there was a high-pitched cracking sound like the splintering of some massive bone. It was followed by a thunderous roar as a giant block of limestone thudded down to the floor of the cave from the roof. Irene Bouchard let out a scream and grabbed her father's arm.

'Jesus!' whispered Speers, shaken. 'The place is breaking up!' Tony Grace climbed to his feet, his legs rubbery. He looked over his shoulder into the dim recesses of the cave.

'I don't have to be hit on the head by a bloody great

boulder to know when I'm not wanted,' said the journalist, his voice trembling. 'I say God helps them that help themselves. Let's get the hell out of here while we've still got the chance!'

4

David Penfold worked with the others, scavenging the site for anything that might prove useful, packing food, cooking equipment and warm clothing into the duffel bags that had originally been used to bring supplies down to the cave. The group's rapid, nervous movements cast giant twisting shadows on the walls and ceiling of the cave, hovering around and above them wraithlike, as though waiting eagerly for the survivors to join the shades of their colleagues.

The young archaeologist filled the bags automatically, his mind cold with shock. It seemed to him that his being had been severed into disparate portions and that he now existed on several planes, none in touch with any other. His father was dead, lying fifty feet away, torn and unrecognizable, the last heat from his body draining into the cave floor, and somewhere in his heart David grieved. But it was a distant feeling, a part of him that he could watch objectively, as though his instincts told him that there was no time for the luxury of such pain. Another part of him was logically assembling facts, establishing patterns for survival, a ticking clock that kept him working, tenuously balanced on the edge of panic. At a third and almost unconscious level he was sensing the feelings of the others around him, looking for strengths and weaknesses, wondering who among them would survive the ordeal they were confronted with.

Bouchard sat some distance from the rest, his clothing torn, a film of sweat on his face and a look of confusion and anger in his eyes, as though refusing to believe that the disaster had happened, a man lost without the scaffolding of civilization and normalcy to support him. Irene, his daughter, was helping Mariea Tarvanin and Alice Braden stow supplies, but casting worried glances at her father every few seconds. Tony Grace was scrambling over the wreckage of the platform, his breath coming hard, his movements erratic, using all his will to keep himself from thinking. Speers was concentrating on his diving equipment, stony-faced, hands working lithely, an automaton, reduced to raw animal instinct. Merrill, his back against a crate, eyes closed and lips twisted into a grimace, was lost in the pain of his injury. And Harada — his broad flat face revealing nothing, though his friend lay crushed like David's father — was keeping things moving with calm-voiced instructions, while he packed his own and Takashima's spelunking equipment into knapsacks.

The faded image of a schoolroom, bright with sun from high-flanking windows, came into David's mind and he heard the voice of a teacher, faint and echoing, reciting a poem to the class:

'If you can keep your head when all about you are losing theirs . . . you'll be a Man, my son!'

David paused in mid-motion and closed his eyes. A feeling of nausea clutched at him and he felt as though he was on a racing train, roaring backwards furiously. It was too much to take — the terror of his situation, trapped below the ground, buried alive, was too impossible to comprehend, and at the same time all too real. He forced his eyes open and took a deep breath, wishing hopelessly that it could be all over and knowing that it had just begun.

'Enough,' said Harada. 'There is no more time and we have as much as we can carry.' He opened the metal box containing the extra lamps and began handing them out to the assembled group. Bouchard, seated a few feet away, shook his head.

'I will not go,' he said firmly. Harada lifted his shoulders, his face expressionless.

'Then you will die, Dr Bouchard,' he said simply. David watched as the two men locked eyes. Bouchard's daughter broke the tense silence.

'Papa, please,' she whispered. The grey-haired man turned to her, scowling.

'You agree with this foolishness, then?' he asked. She nodded slowly, not looking him in the eye.

'Yes, Papa, I do,' she said softly. She glanced at David and one hand fluttered, as though wanting to reach out to him. She looked back at Bouchard.

'David has already lost his father. I do not want to lose you.'

The rest of the group began moving towards the rear of the cave, making their way around the ruined platform, led by Speers. David waited with Harada and Irene.

'Doctor, the next tremor could come at any moment,' said Harada. 'We have already waited too long as it is. We must go.' The Frenchman looked over his shoulder and watched the others moving through the wreckage and into the shrouding shadows beyond, then looked at his daughter once more, searchingly, his face a mask of confusion as though he couldn't understand why she was going against him.

'Irene, *ma chère* . . . ' he began, then stopped, his voice trailing away uncertainly.

'I will not leave you, father,' she said, 'But if I stay then you are condemning me to death.' Bouchard climbed wearily to his feet, striking at his trousers, vainly trying to remove the dust from them. He lifted his grime-encrusted hands and stared down at them, shaking his head, then looked up at Harada.

'I will come,' he said. Harada nodded wordlessly and turned away, the hump of the knapsack on his back swaying as he led the way towards the flue leading down to the lower cave. Bouchard and his daughter followed the geologist, Irene's hand on her father's arm. David watched them go, a stab of loneliness thrusting into his heart, wishing that she was touching him, and not the frightened old man who was her father. He turned and looked back along the length of the cave, keeping the beam of his lamp aimed at the floor. He peered into the depths of the crumbling vault, his eyes smarting. He saw nothing except shadowed darkness but his vision was assaulted by a thousand images of his father, turning in his mind's eye like the broken scenes in a kaleidescope. He let out a long shivering breath.

'So long, Pop,' he whispered, and turned away, the tears

falling freely, smiling sadly as he realized that it was the first time he'd called him anything but "father" for as long as he could remember.

One by one they slipped into the narrow mouth of the flue, feet first, pushing duffel bags ahead of them until, at last, David was the only one left in the upper cave. Without a backward glance he thrust his bag into the hole and then followed it, sliding down on his back, his arms tight at his sides, the lamp in his mind shining ahead guiding the way down the narrow, smooth-walled tube. For a single instant David felt as though the tube was the fossil throat of some prehistoric creature, swallowing him, taking him down into its roiling belly, but he blanked the grotesque thought from his mind and kept on, concentrating on the way ahead.

The tremor came when he was slightly more than halfway down the flue and he froze as he felt against his skin the first vibrations from the rock squeezing around him. Faintly, echoing up from the lower cave, he could hear shouting. The vibration began to build, the rock around him twitching as though alive, and he knew that at any second the walls of the flue would contract, crushing him to pulp like an insect swatted by some immense, thoughtless hand, but still he could not move. He felt himself shrinking away from the enclosing walls, trying to get away from the mounting thunder of the quake, but it was impossible and he felt his will dissolving into total panic, a scream of terror welling up from within him. Then the full force of the earthquake struck and the earth heaved around him, the flue rippling like a snaking whiplash, the scream in his mouth stillborn, plucked from him by the infinitely loud and wracking banshee wail of the earth itself. He lay rigidly, the solid rock entombing him suddenly plastic, twisting, impossibly alive. He squeezed his eyes closed, every muscle tensed, screaming at him to move, but he was paralysed with fright, a small voice in his tortured brain telling him that it was going to end, it had to end, it could not go on; but still the earth shook. He felt himself being slammed from one side to the other, the only thing saving him from serious injury being the narrowness of the tunnel. There was a small splintering sound at his side as the glass lens of the light shattered and then the lamp went out.

The horror of the suffocating darkness was followed by something even worse; a soft whispering sound that filtered insidiously through the pounding clangor of the quake. David felt a gentle touch on his neck and shoulders, a caress from the grave that bulged his blinded eyes with fear as he stared sightless at the stone roof inches above his face. The whispering grew and the touch became heavier. He felt a tickling in his ears and then the taste of earth filled his mouth. He squirmed, trying to avoid the steadily rising flood of soil pouring down the flue; the fear that had frozen him giving way to the even more horrifying fear of being choked to death by the earth raining down behind him. He kicked at the duffel-bag ahead of him, cursing it, wishing he could somehow turn and attack it with his hands, his teeth, anything, but there wasn't room enough in the flue to raise his arms, let alone turn to face the open end of the tube.

His head was half buried in the dirt, and he tried to shake it back and forth, but the movement only increased the steady flow, the sound changed now as small rocks fell into the sloping passage, rattling like old bones. Around him David could feel the tremor begin to ease, but he knew that it was too late — the flue was filling and in seconds he would be buried. He opened his mouth to scream and then gagged as it filled with soil. He coughed, choking on the bitter earth, and kicked wildly at the bag, knowing even as he flailed that it was no use. Miraculously it moved and when his feet pushed down again they met empty air. Then there was a blinding flash of light and a voice. Harada.

'*David!*' the voice commanded. 'Heels and elbows! Use your heels and elbows! Pull yourself down!' The voice was drowned as the soil went over his ears and began rising up above his jawline, pouring over his face and into his nostrils. He drummed his feet against the rock, desperately trying to raise his hands to his face but there was no room. The ankle of one boot hooked on a small protrusion below and spasmodically he pulled himself down, freeing himself for an instant, just enough to raise his head and look down along his body, the flooding earth building up behind his neck. Ten feet below he could see the outline of the bag, silhouetted by a ring of light from Harada's lamp. David gritted his teeth and used the light as a beacon, the panic that had overwhelmed him slowly receding. He let the words Harada had spoken fill his mind. Heels and elbows, heels and elbows. Foot by foot he dragged himself down, the weight of the soil on his shoulders a constant reminder of the awful death that waited should he slow down his movements.

A few moments later he felt a firm grip on his ankles and he was pulled, choking and panting, out of the flue and into the lower cave.

5

They stood huddled on the flow-stone pools below the flue opening, shivering with both cold and fear. The tremor had passed, but the awful memory of it remained in their minds vividly, and their close-packed immobility on the tiny dry area provided by the flow-stone was making everyone nervous. They wanted to go, anywhere, as long as it was *now*. Before the second tremor the move to the lower cave had been a matter of choice, but the tongue of earth and stone dribbling down from the mouth of the flue was absolute. There was no way back, and at first glance the dark water of the pool below the mounds of duffel-bags and diving equipment offered no way forward. With the exception of Speers and Harada the flaring light from the lamps revealed expressions of mute shock on every face. The diver on the other hand showed no emotion at all and had barely waited for the tremor to pass before he began strapping on his tanks. He eased himself down from the rock-pools until he was standing on the narrow ledge he had discovered that ran submerged to the siphon, a third of the way around the domed cavern. He turned to Harada, who was still helping David Penfold to clean himself up, and spoke, his dry voice echoing dully from the roof above.

'I'm going to see where the siphon comes out. Get the rest of these bozos on to the ledge here so they're ready when I get back, and make sure the first in line has got a set of spare tanks. It's going to take a while to get everyone and all this

108

gear through and I want to have a supply of air at the other end.'

'And what if the siphon leads nowhere?' asked Bouchard standing with Irene at the top of the wedge of folded rock. The diver shrugged, a sour grin on his face.

'Then we suffocate,' he said. 'There's no air coming down from up top with that tunnel filled and there sure as hell isn't any coming in through the siphon. With eight of us all breathing it'd probably take a day or two before we all dropped.' He turned and waded off slowly, keeping one hand on the cave wall, picking his way carefully along the ledge.

'He is insufferable!' snapped Bouchard, loudly enough for the retreating diver to hear.

'He is also quite correct in what he says,' said Harada quietly. The geologist crouched down beside Alice Braden, who was supporting Daniel Merrill's head in her lap. The trip down the flue had been excruciatingly painful for the conservator and he was almost unconcious. 'How is he?' asked Harada.

'Not very well,' said the heavy-set woman, frowning. 'I think it's more than just his arm. He isn't breathing properly and his lips are going blue. I can't tell if it's because of the cold, or shock, or if he's going cyanotic.'

'Cyanotic?' asked Harada.

'Heart,' she replied. The geologist stood up.

'Do what you can for him,' he murmured. He turned to the rest of the survivors. 'We will do as Mr Speers said. Carry what you can. The lamps are waterproof so do not worry about getting them wet. I will lead off, taking the extra tanks. Dr Bouchard, you and your daughter will follow, then Miss Tarvanin and Mr Grace.' He turned to David. 'Are you all right?' he asked. The archaeologist nodded.

'I'm okay. I still haven't thanked you for . . .'

'Do not bother,' said Harada. 'If you could stay with Dr Merrill until Mr Speers returns, perhaps you could help with him when the time comes.'

'Of course,' said David. Harada nodded briefly, then shouldered his pack. He made his way down to the edge of the pool, lifted a pair of Speers's tanks in his arms, then stepped on to the underwater ledge; the others followed suit until they were strung out behind Harada, waist deep in the freezing water. Speers had already disappeared into the siphon.

Ten minutes later the diver surfaced in a welter of bubbles at the far end of the rock ledge. He looked up and found himself staring at Harada, waiting, the heavy tanks in his arms, the lights of those behind him streaking the dark water with undulating ribbons of gold. Speers spat out the mouthpiece and tipped up his mask, treading water.

'Well?' asked Harada. The diver grinned up at him broadly.

'Air!' he chortled, gloating. 'I didn't stick around to check but it looks like one hell of a big cave back there.'

'Water?' asked Harada. Speers nodded, bringing a hand out of the water to wipe his nose.

'Some. Hard to say how much. Sinter basin's built up around the outlet like a damn; it's just an extension of the pool here. No movement, I didn't check over the side. Ceiling's a good forty feet up though, lots of breathing space.'

'How do we get the others through?' asked Harada.

'No sweat,' said Speers. 'The siphon's only fifty, sixty feet long. I'll take you through on my mouthpiece and we can string a line. The rest of them can do it on one deep breath and pull themselves through. I can ferry the rest of the equipment through later.' Harada nodded. He turned and explained to the others what was going to happen, then placed the air tanks on the ledge at his feet and unstrapped his pack. He brought out a hundred-foot coil of thin nylon normally used for surveying and began unwinding it. He handed one end to Speers and then reached down into the water and knotted the other end around the tanks.

'There is a problem,' he said, standing once again.

'Shoot,' said Speers.

'Dr Merrill. He is close to unconsciousness. He will not be able to make the trip unaided. I have left him with Miss Braden and David Penfold.'

'Get rid of the broad, she won't be any help,' instructed Speers. 'I'll come back for the old man and Penfold. He can use the tanks, 'kay?' Harada nodded.

'Yes.'

'All right, let's get our asses in gear.'

By the time it was David Penfold's turn to make the journey through the siphon the conservator's health had deteriorated even further and without the lightening effect of the water he and Alice Braden would never have been able to bring the now unconscious man to the siphon entrance. As it was both David and Alice were soaked to the skin after dragging him to the end of the ledge. Then Alice slid under the water, her lamp glowing eerily up from below, and David was alone with the ashen-faced man.

Finally Speers surfaced and clambered on to the ledge. He had removed his tanks at the other end of the siphon, travelling back along the survey line holding his breath. He muttered a greeting to David, then removed the line from the fresh set of tanks and attached a regulator and mouthpiece. He jerked the tanks on to his back and strapped them on, leaving the mouthpiece dangling free. He dropped back into the water and nodded up at David.

'Hand him down,' said Speers. 'I'll stick the mouthpiece in. Then get into the water and hold him. You swim much?'

'Enough,' said David. Speers nodded.

'Good. Take a deep breath and you should be able to make it without having to share the air with him.'

Gently David lowered Merrill into the water and Speers took him under the armpits. The diver jammed the mouthpiece between the man's lips. He brought up one hand under Merrill's jaw and pushed it shut, forcing the man's teeth to clamp down on the hard rubber. David watched, frowning; Speers could have been handling a piece of meat for all the care he showed for the injured man, but it was no time to say anything. He dropped into the water, wincing as the freezing water rose to his neck. He treaded water beside Speers.

'I'm going to have to keep one hand under his jaw to keep the mouthpiece in,' said the diver. 'Get in back of him, make a sandwich with him in the middle. Hang on to my arms. When I give you the word take a breath and hold it. I'll take us down. Just hang on, don't do anything, let me do the work, got it?'

'Yes,' said David, his teeth chattering.

'Okay,' said Speers, as David moved into position. 'Now!'

David took a swallowing breath and closed his eyes. A fraction of a second later he felt the water close over his head and they sank into the pool.

David opened his eyes only once during the journey and found that he could see nothing except the back of Merrill's head, the thin hair waving in the water, outlined against the lights clamped beside Speer's mask. The siphon passage seemed endless and David felt the air burning in his lungs as he fought to keep himself from opening his mouth and breathing in water. Just as he was sure he couldn't last a second longer he felt their direction change and they headed up. They rose quickly and as they surfaced David gratefully sucked in a huge sputtering breath. He felt hands reaching down, pulling Merrill up, and then someone grabbed him under the arms and dragged him out of the water. He lay prostrate on the edge of the pool, chest heaving as he filled his aching lungs. Slowly his senses returned and he became vaguely aware of the whispered sounds of people talking; then he heard Alice Braden's voice.

'I'm afraid it's no use, Dr Harada.' David levered himself into a sitting position. A few yards away on the wide rim of the sinter wall he could see a cluster of lights and the silhouetted shapes of kneeling figures. He stood up groggily and made his way along the rim to where the people were grouped. They were gathered around the limp form of Merrill. Harada was bent over him, ear to the man's chest.

'Is he all right?' asked David. Harada looked up and shook his head.

'The man is dead,' said the geologist. 'Miss Braden says a heart attack. It may be that he could not breathe through Mr Speers's mouthpiece.'

'Nothing we could do,' muttered Speers, standing. He shone his light down the gentle slope of the sinter. The rest of the group were resting at its base, leaning on the sodden bags they had carried through the siphon. The diver took a last look at Merrill, then began climbing down the slope, followed by Alice Braden and Tony Grace. David crouched down beside the dead conservator and stared across him at Harada. The geologist's lamp rested on the wall beside the body, throwing Harada's face into sharp relief.

'He didn't die of a heart attack, did he?' asked David. Harada looked down at Merrill's motionless form and shook his head.

'No,' he said softly. 'He drowned. But Mr Speers was right, there was no other way. It was a chance we had to take and it failed. I think he had internal injuries as well. He would not have lived long in any event. He was dying when we were in the second cave.'

'So what do we do?' asked David. Harada looked down the slope of the sinter at the pool of light case by the others' lamps. He looked back at David and lifted his shoulders tiredly.

'With Dr Merrill – nothing. There is no way to bury him. We must keep on.'

'Keep on?' asked David. 'Where?' Harada stood up wearily.

'Come,' he said. 'I will show you.'

He led the way down the sinter wall and on to the smooth flow-stone floor of the cave, his light cutting through darkness. David peered ahead, but the cave was too large to make out its dimensions. Curious, he shone his own light overhead; the beam disappeared into the dark and all he could make out were the huge outlines of immense stalactites high above.

They walked past the exhausted group and continued on, David's feet slipping occasionally on the marble-smooth floor. A hundred yards from the foot of the sinter Harada stopped and shone his light ahead. Finally David could see the far wall of the gigantic, vaulted chamber and something that looked like a narrow ribbon of oil at its base, running away at right angles. Water, flowing coldly, the noise of its passage less than a whisper.

'What is it?' asked David, watching as the beam of Harada's lamp played across the inky surface.

'A river,' said Harada. 'It is the only exit from this cave. Miss Tarvanin has already given it a name.'

'What?' asked David.

'She has called it the Styx,' said the geologist.

PART TWO
THE RIVER

CHAPTER SIX

1

The river moved inexorably downwards as it had for a hundred thousand years and more, searching out its path through the fissures and vaulted chambers of the labyrinthine network deep below the shattered karst landscape of the Yugoslavian plateau.

In the beginning the Styx had been hardly more than a trickle as it made its way between the bedding planes and joints of the massive limestone blocks, but as time passed the water steadily eroded the limestone, gradually increasing the size of the stream and its capacity. Inevitably the young cave system was enlarged in all three dimensions, resulting in a multi-levelled and complex web of channels, tubes and caverns, twisting and turning to follow any weakness in the surrounding rock, carrying the water, like all rivers, to its final destination; the sea, almost three hundred and fifty miles away.

The survivors of the Subrano earthquake had been travelling on the smooth-flowing waters of the Styx for two days, days marked by no rising and falling of the sun, but only by the steady movement of the hands of Izo Harada's chronometer. By the geologist's rough calculation they had travelled almost forty miles beneath the ground in that time. How much actual distance they had travelled relative to their position on the surface was almost impossible to judge because of the countless twists and turns of the serpentine river, but according to Izo's compass they had been travelling in a roughly south-easterly direction. He was concerned about the course they seemed to be taking, although he kept his feelings to himself; there was no sense in worrying the others. He had hoped that the river would move west, seeking sea level at the Adriatic, but instead the Styx appeared determined to follow the gently sloping spine of the interior plateau, taking them towards Albania as the subterranean flow made its way to the Aegean.

Izo knew that if they found no way to the surface within a short time, they were almost certainly doomed to a slow death underground. Sooner or later they would encounter an obstacle which couldn't be surmounted, a sudden sink or a siphon that was beyond their capacity. When that happened they would die, trapped, with no way forward and none back.

So far they had been lucky. For the most part the river was following phreatic tubes, relatively easy to navigate, which were cut long ago when the river's force was much stronger and had filled the passages completely. In the total of twenty hours they had actually spent on the water, they had only twice reached narrowed bottlenecks requiring that they unload the inflatable rafts and carry them to wider areas beyond. Izo had also kept a careful check on the water's velocity and found that it was maintaining a slow steady flow. That at least was encouraging, indicating to him that although the river's path was sinuous, it was fairly level, with no precipitous drops or chutes to navigate. He knew however that such a fall was almost sure to come, and seated in the small lead raft with David Penfold behind him, he kept the strong beam of his lamp pointed ahead and his ears pricked, listening for any change in the sound of the black, slow-moving water.

Izo's lamp was the only illumination to cut through the enfolding, almost suffocating darkness that surrounded them. The other survivors, in rafts strung out behind Izo's moved in darkness to conserve the precious batteries of the spare lamps, relying on the steady cone of light from Izo's lamp, catching sliding glimpses of the deeply-shadowed barriers of rock on either side of them, and the saw-toothed stalactite formations overhead. Occasionally the stream broadened as it crossed the floor of a cavern, but for the most part the survivors were carried along the narrow choking path with less than a foot on either side of each raft.

The positioning of the rafts had been decided on in the siphon cave before the journey began. David Penfold and Izo

Harada rode in the lead raft, and with the exception of a water bottle and Izo's lamp they carried nothing of importance. Behind them, a dozen feet away and secured by a strong tow-line, was the raft holding Irene Bouchard and her father. Their raft, in addition to their personal belongings, carried the group's sleeping gear. The third raft, one of the two large ones that had been salvaged, carried Tony Grace, Mariea Tarvanin and Alice Braden. Their raft carried most of the food supplies and cooking utensils. The fourth raft, tethered on the longest line, was piloted by Frank Speers and held the bulk of the supplies rescued from the earthquake, including all the extra lamps and batteries. Izo hoped that this arrangement would minimize losses in the event of a sudden disaster, assuming that the lead raft would be the first to encounter any problem.

2

David Penfold kept his eyes on the dark silhouette of Izo Harada's back and tried to keep his wire-taut nerves from snapping. His muscles ached from the unrelenting tension and his jaw had frozen into a permanent, hard-bitten frown. After more than fifty hours trapped beneath the ground, he, like everyone else, was walking the fine line between rational thought and wild panic. Every sound was an irritant, while every darkened turn that momentarily hid Harada's lamplight was cause for a split second of horror, wondering for an instant if the light would reappear. Talking was impossible; in anything even close to a normal speaking voice the dark rock walls a few feet away returned broken garbled echoes that turned conversation into chaos. Hours passed with no sound except the wet bubbling whisper of the inky water and thoughts turned inward, blindly seeking solace in memory and finding nothing but the roots of fear.

David had tried to mourn the death of his father, but no feelings came beyond a dull ache in his chest. Seated behind Izo in the raft, nostrils filled with the dank acid tang of the rock, David found himself almost wishing that it was he who had died rather than his father, not out of remorse, or love, but out of envy. His father at least had been spared the living hell of the river. In the first few hours after their escape from the upper cave David had believed in Izo's theory about the river. He had held on to the thought that soon the water would take them to the sunlight again; the thought was an amulet he could fend off the fear with, but its power had soon faded. Each serpent turn in the flow, each reflection off a mineral secretion was reason for hope, and each time the hope was dashed. David no longer believed, he merely survived.

Idly he checked the glowing dial of his watch. It was almost twelve, although whether that was noon or midnight was impossible to tell. By their calculations it was noon, and therefore time for lunch, but his stomach gave no signals. It was something they had all noticed and talked about the day before. Without light, even the artificial day and night they had created for themselves in the upper Subrano cave, the body's timekeeping system began to deteriorate rapidly. Time expanded and contracted almost hallucinogenically, minutes sometimes passing like hours, hours fleeing like seconds. Izo had warned them of the long-term effects that could lead to real hallucinations if some kind of system was not established, a regular schedule to cling to. The day had to be divided into meal times, rest stops, toilet stops and "nightly" camps. By setting up a pattern of events like that Izo hoped to avoid the more severe effects of being trapped below the surface. In his heart David knew that none of it was going to work. It wasn't as though the survivors were taking part in some kind of experiment, or could pretend that they were on a voyage of exploration. They were trapped, and fighting for their lives. All of them, David knew, had only one thought, and it burned in his mind like a white-hot brand: getting out. And that, David knew, was a pipe dream.

He reached forward and tapped Izo lightly on the arm. The geologist turned his head slightly, the lamp on his helmet brushing fingers of light along the slowly passing wall on their left. For a brief instant David saw the scuttling form of a five or six-inch-long cave centipede as it raced into a crack, fleeing the unfamiliar light. David shivered, and wondered how long it would be before they were reduced to eating creatures like that.

'Noon,' he said briefly, shutting the image of the centipede from his mind. Izo nodded.

'We must find a cavern,' whispered the geologist, trying to avoid the confusing echo of normal speech. 'I would like to check the current again as well. I think it is increasing in speed.'

'I'll pass the word,' replied David, glad to have something to do other than stare at Izo's back. He turned and called back into the darkness, knowing that Irene and her father were less than twenty feet away, but unable to see them in the blackness. A few seconds later he faintly heard Irene calling back to the others. David began hauling in on the tether line, bringing their rafts close together, in preparation for stopping. It was tricky enough landing four rafts at the same time without having them separated by ten or fifteen feet of line. As he pulled on the nylon cord tying his and Irene's raft together he heard a faint tearing sound and then the line went slack in his hands.

'Shit!' he hissed.

'What is the problem?' asked Izo in a low voice, keeping his lamp forward.

'It feels like the grommet pulled out of the Bouchard raft,' said David in a whisper.

'Throw her a line,' said Izo urgently. 'There is no doubt, the current is speeding up.'

'I'll need light,' replied David. In acknowledgement Izo turned to face the rear of the small raft. The pool of light from his lamp played over the dark water behind them and then caught the Bouchard raft, suddenly illuminating the drawn figure of Alain Bouchard, huddled in the rear of the raft with a blanket over his shoulders, and his daughter, seated forward. David gestured with the rope in his hand and she nodded, moving right to the edge of the rubber boat. David rose to his knees and flung the length of cord towards the raft. It landed short and he reeled it in again, winding it over his arm.

'Quickly,' murmured Izo, still keeping the light trained on Irene Bouchard. David threw the line again, and Irene leaned out, her fingers almost touching it as it fell to the water once again.

'One more time,' muttered David, hauling in the line. As he wound the nylon cord over his arm he could hear a faint thundering sound beginning to build somewhere in the distance. 'What the hell is that?' he asked.

'A fall of some kind,' said Izo sharply. 'You must hurry.' David nodded and pulled in the last of the line. Holding the coils of line firmly he tossed the rope back towards Irene. Even before it happened he knew the line was going to fall short again, but Irene, in a desperate attempt to catch it, leaned far out over the inflated gunwale of the dingy. The sudden change in weight distribution caused the small, unstable craft to tilt wildly. Irene lurched back wildly, trying to save herself, but it was too late. With a startled cry she flipped over the side of the raft and into the ebony flow of the river, disappearing completely into its frigid depths.

'Irene!' yelled David. Alain Bouchard, horrified at the loss of his daughter, lurched to the side of the raft, causing it to spin, bringing the raft holding Tony Grace and the two other women forward, tangling their lines. Hurriedly Izo played the light on his helmet over the water, trying to locate Irene. Suddenly she appeared on the surface, hair plastered around her face, her mouth gasping for breath. One arm came up and Tony Grace leaned over as the raft swept by, trying to hang on to her. His fingers touched hers and then slipped off. Almost without thought David slipped off his boots and in a single motion dived off the back of the raft into the now rapidly moving river. The air around him was filled with the broken cries of the others echoing off the narrowing walls of the tunnel and the freezing water was a bone-chilling shock. Ignoring the cold and confusion David tried to swim against the current, his eyes scanning back and forth across the slice of water lit by Izo's lamp. Then he saw it, not a hand or face, but a swirl of darkened hair against the even darker water. He lunged across the channel, reaching out and grabbing at it. He pulled and suddenly Irene's face came to the surface, lips blue, eyes rolled back.

'Behind you!' came a garbled cry. Izo. David peered into the darkness, and then, only barely visible in the faint light, was the bulk of Speer's raft. David lifted his free arm, the other cupped around Irene's chin, and the muscular cave diver reached out as the raft swirled by. Speers's hand grasped David's wrist like a vice and began to pull both David and Irene up on to the safety of the large raft.

David felt a bruising pain tear into his back as the raft slammed into the tunnel wall and then Speers had him over the side of the raft, still clinging tenaciously to Irene. With both of them on board Speers ignored David and bent over Irene, tilting her head back quickly, clearing her breathing passages and administering mouth-to-mouth resuscitation. Gagging, David managed to lift himself up and retch over the side of the raft, his eyes barely registering their furious twisting passage down the wildly racing river. Ahead, the bobbing, erratic movements of Izo's lamp threw back only faint light, but it was enough for David to make out the looming rock wall of the tunnel as they careered around a sharp curve, rebounding hard.

'Fend off, damn it!' yelled Speers, looking up from Irene. The cave diver felt around on the floor of the heavily loaded raft and came up with one of the thick aluminium poles used to erect the shelters. He thrust it at David and went back to work on Irene. David grabbed the pole, jabbing hard as they swirled up against the tunnel wall again, pushing them out into the main stream. The sound in the tunnel was deafening, screams and calls for help from the raft ahead lost in the howling din of the rolling water as it pounded down the sloped and steadily narrowing passage. Gritting his teeth against the ear-shattering noise David lashed out again, trying to keep them off the wall, and away from the abrasive rock that could tear the raft to ribbons.

A loud call rose above the shattering roar of the water and David looked up instinctivly. A hundred feet ahead he saw Izo's light suddenly lift up in a smooth curve and then disappear, plunging them into total darkness. Speers had seen the phenomenon too.

'Hydraulic jump!' he roared. 'Hang on!' David had no idea what Speers meant but he automatically did as he was told, fumbling around on the side of the raft until he found the lanyard lines threaded around the gunwales. He grasped them and hung on. Horrified by the sudden and terrifying disappearance of the light ahead, he stared forward, eyes wide, but blind in the all-consuming darkness, the sound of his heart like ragged thunder in his ears. Then the world ended.

The only thing David had experienced which came even close was the sensation of a sudden dropping lift. For a split second there was a feeling of weightlessness as they rose up the curving hump of water, followed by a terrible, nauseating drop as they reached the summit of the jump and slid down the other side. David screamed, the thin sound lost in the hellish roar of the water as they dropped. Then it was over, almost as quickly as it had begun. They reached the floor of the jump and the rushing force of the water spat them forward, spinning wildly, but still intact. Their pace slowed and then there was a dull thump as the bottom of the raft struck something. Dazed, David leaned out with the aluminium pole but it sank into a layer of ooze below them. One way or another they were safe, at least for the moment. And then there was light.

The beam from Izo's lamp washed over them, pausing, and for the first time since he had been dragged aboard by Speers, David saw Irene. She was lying close to the side of the raft, eyes closed, but still breathing. Speers, haggard, his hair slicked down over his face, was bent over her protectively, his hard muscular body heaving as he fought to catch his breath. He bared his teeth at David in a grim smile and the young archaeologist fought down an urge to strike out at the man. He looked like some terrible, predatory animal, looming over Irene. On the other hand, thought David, he had saved both their lives. Then the light was gone, swinging away to check on the others, David supposed. He followed the moving beam with his eyes, grateful for any illumination after the brief, blinding darkness. They seemed to be in a large, high-ceilinged cavern, with the river flowing almost directly through its centre. From what he could see the cave was at least a hundred yards across, and perhaps half that high. The seeking cone of light touched on the point where they had entered the cave and David realized what had happened.

The entrance was high above the floor of the large cavern, a tongue of water surging out of a wide distended mouth in the rock. Limestone secretions had built up over the hundreds and thousands of years the river had been flowing, making a long sloping ramp for the water. The river, flowing faster perhaps after the earthquakes, had formed a hump at the summit of the slide, building up at the lip of the entrance. The "hydraulic jump" Speers had referred to. The jump seemed to have another effect as well — it had tossed out the slime and sediment carried by the water, throwing the ooze up against the sloping banks of the river like some hideous subterranean beach.

'We'd better dry off,' said Speers at last, breaking the silence. 'You and the Bouchard broad are soaked through. You'll catch pneumonia.' The cave diver unclipped a flashlight from his belt and turned to the mound of equipment lashed to the raft, searching for some blankets. David, exhausted, slumped against the side of the small boat and closed his eyes.

3

They managed to find a relatively dry area on one side of the large cavern and quickly set up a temporary camp. Mariea Tarvanin and Alice Braden worked at getting David and Irene warm and dry, covering them with mounds of blankets and sleeping bags and filling them with hot soup cooked on the large, two-burner Primus. At Izo's direction Irene's father and Tony Grace took an inventory of what they had lost on the wild ride over the chute while Izo and Speers went to investigate the next section of the river.

'This is madness,' muttered Alain Bouchard as he helped Tony Grace unroll several sleeping bags which had become waterlogged. 'We will never find a way out of here.' The older man looked around the cave, his drawn, heavily-lined face lit by the flickering light from the primus stove a hundred feet away.

'You're alive, aren't you?' asked Grace lightly. The

journalist kept at his work, going through each bundle of equipment to find out what had been damaged, lost or water-logged. Bouchard sat down heavily on an outcropping of rock.

'A living death,' said Bouchard. 'We should have stayed at the lower cave. Someone would have come for us by now.'

'You don't know that,' said Grace. 'For all you know that lower cave might be full of water by now, with us in it.'

'That would have been better than this,' said Bouchard, waving at their dank, ominous surroundings.

'Speak for yourself,' said the journalist. He began taking the duffel bags back to the point where they had beached the rafts. A moment later he returned to where the archaeologist still sat. He looked down at the old man and shook his head. 'Look,' he said at last. 'You're alive, and Irene is still alive, thanks to David and Speers. Doesn't that mean anything to you? Hope springs eternal in the human breast, and all that? I mean, we do have a chance you know.' Bouchard looked up at the thin, owl-eyed writer and smiled bitterly.

'The proverbial stiff upper lip of the British?' he quipped.

'Bloody right,' nodded Grace. 'You froggies could do with a bit of that now and again, you know.'

'You are trying to provoke me,' said Bouchard, the bitter-ness of his smile gone for a moment. Grace chuckled.

'Absolutely,' he grinned. 'If I make you mad enough it'll make you realize you are still alive.'

'I am too old to be provoked, Monsieur Grace,' said Bouchard.

'Balls,' said Grace. 'You're not too old to help me with some of these bags. I shall start talking about Vichy France or Charles de Gaulle if you don't bend an elbow soon.'

'All right,' said Bouchard, getting to his feet. 'Anything but listening to an Englishman talk about France.'

'That's the spirit,' smiled Grace, and handed Bouchard a duffel bag.

A hundred feet away on the far side of the cave Irene Bouchard and David Penfold sat huddled around the com-forting light and warmth of the hissing stove.

'More soup?' asked Alice Braden, stirring the large pot.

'No thanks,' said David from his nest of blankets. Beside

126

him Irene merely shook her head. Even covered as she was she still shivered occasionally, and her face was pasty and mottled from shock.

'I should get out a pad and do some sketches,' said Mariea Tarvanin. 'I could do it up with oils later and call it "The Drowned Rats". You two really are a sight.'

'If I look as bad as I feel I must look terrible,' said Irene, managing a weak smile. Mariea laughed.

'Touch of lipstick you'd be right as rain,' she grinned. Alice ladled out another bowl of soup and came around the stove to where David sat. She handed him the bowl and spoon but he refused it.

'I don't want any more,' he said. Alice frowned.

'Eat it,' she said firmly. 'Now.' Sighing, David took the bowl and began to eat. She filled a second bowl for Irene and gave it to Mariea who handed it to the pale young woman. Irene took it wordlessly.

'Den mother,' muttered David. Alice smiled primly and stood up, taking the now-empty soup pot down to the river to wash it.

'I think she's terrific,' said Mariea, when Alice was out of earshot. David nodded.

'Me too,' he said. 'Not that I'd ever tell her that. She wouldn't know how to handle it.' David looked around. 'Izo not back yet?' he asked. Mariea shook her head.

'Not yet. He said they were going to walk down a bit.'

'Walk?' asked David. Mariea nodded.

'That's what he said. He looked a bit worried too. One minute the water level is on the rise, the next it's slowing down.'

'I don't get it,' said David frowning.

'Neither does Izo,' replied Mariea. 'That's what's worrying him. But he says there's enough room to walk beside the river as it goes out of the cave.' There was a long silence as they stared into the bright blue flame of the primus stove. David watched the play of shadows over Mariea's strong, attractive features and he felt a tug of longing, remembering the time they had spent together. She looked up and caught his glance and she smiled, almost as though she was reading his mind.

'Peaceful,' she said at last, looking back into the flames.

'That's a funny thing to say,' said Irene, her voice still weak. Mariea shrugged.

'Maybe, but it's true. It's quiet, we're resting, we've come through a bad time. You have to take the moments when you can, no matter where you are.' David suppressed a laugh. Mariea hadn't changed all that much since UCLA. She was an old-fashioned hippie down to her toes. Here they were trapped in a dank tomb God only knew how far underground, and she could still see some good in it. He shook his head and smiled. It amazed him that he could be attracted to a woman like Mariea and to a woman like Irene as well. In almost every way the two women were opposites. He huddled down into his cocoon of blankets and stared into the fire, lost in thought.

Izo Harada and Frank Speers made their way carefully along the narrow ledge above the slime-encrusted bank of the river, working their way slowly downstream. The passageway had begun to narrow within a hundred feet of the cave exit, and now it was less than ten feet across, the ceiling over their heads so low that they were walking in a crouch. The passage was uniformly smooth, a sure sign to both men that the tunnel was normally full of water. Beside and below them the river had slowed to a trickle no more than three feet across and only a few inches deep.

'We're going to have to deflate the boats,' said Speers, a few feet behind Izo. The geologist nodded.

'Yes. Or wait until the flow increases again.'

'How long will that be, though?' said Speers. 'We could wait for weeks and you know it.' Izo nodded again, and stopped, turning his light down to play on the water.

'You are right,' he murmured. 'But it is dangerous.'

'A flash flood?' said Speers.

'Yes,' said Izo. 'This river normally flows at a strong rate. No doubt the earthquake has done something to interrupt the flow. And it is erratic. Only a few hours ago there was enough flow to create that jump we went over.' He reached up over his head and ran his fingers across the smooth, slightly slimy rock above them, then brought his hand under

128

the light. It glistened wetly. It was obvious that the tunnel had been completely flooded in the recent past.

'So, do we wait?' asked Speers stiffly, clearly not liking the idea. Izo shook his head.

'I do not think so,' he said, looking up at the diver. 'As you said, we could wait for a very long time. No, we must keep going.'

'I can't see that crowd back there sitting still for long anyway,' said Speers, gesturing with a hooked thumb back the way they had come. 'Some of them aren't going to last. Bouchard for one.'

'The girl?' asked Izo. Speers shook his head.

'No. The old man. He's cracking up. Claustrophobia maybe, or just panic. He's right on the edge. The girl should be okay if she keeps dry and warm. Neither of them were in the water for long.'

'But you think Dr Bouchard is not doing so well,' said Izo.

'He'll go bananas before very long,' said Speers. 'I can guarantee it. And that's dangerous.'

'I agree,' said Izo. 'But there is nothing we can do.' He stared at Speers, who simply lifted his shoulders.

'No, I guess there isn't,' said the diver, a cold smile on his face.

'We should go on,' said Izo quietly. Speers nodded, and they began creeping forward again. Less than a minute later Izo stopped, so suddenly that Speers ran into him.

'What the hell are you stopping for?' snapped the American angrily.

'Because there is nowhere else to go,' said Izo calmly. He motioned Speers to come up beside him. The diver did so, crawling slowly forward, careful not to get his clothing covered in the muck of the river bank. 'Look,' said Izo, shining his light ahead.

'Jesus!' murmured Speers.

4

It took three hours to portage all their equipment along the almost totally dry tunnel to the point where Izo and Speers had stopped. One by one the survivors cautiously edged forward to have a look, aided by the light from Izo's lamp.

The chasm was roughly circular with a diameter of fifty or sixty feet, its walls cracked, fissured and broken erratically. Above them the walls narrowed quickly, creating a steeply arched ceiling a hundred feet over their heads; below the fall seemed endless, a yawning pit that swallowed the light from Izo's lamp entirely, shrouding the bottom, if there was one, in darkness. The thin trickle which was all that remained of the river was barely enough to wet the stones as it slid over the lip of the enormous hole, but the deeply etched and completely smooth lip where it passed indicated that not long ago the river had roared over the edge of the precipice in a violent torrent, creating a stupendous waterfall.

'We can be glad the flow has stopped,' said Izo, unpacking climbing equipment, aided by Speers. 'Had the river been at full spate we would not have been able to get through the tunnel, and even if we had, the waterfall would have been an impossible obstacle on the climb.'

'Good lord,' muttered Tony Grace, on his hands and knees beside the edge of the chasm. He looked back over his shoulder at the geologist. 'You don't actually mean you intend to climb down this . . . this hell hole?' Izo smiled at the journalist.

'Do you see any alternative?' he asked. Tony peered over the edge again and winced. He edged back from the lip and stood up.

'How deep do you think it is?' he asked. Izo shrugged.

'It is impossible to say. The deepest known cave is a little over 4000 feet. I doubt that this would be any more than that, and probably much less.'

'Why don't you drop a pebble over the side?' asked David Penfold as he worked to bind the now-deflated rafts into tight bundles.

'Already have,' said Speers. 'Couldn't hear a thing.

Doesn't mean much though,' he added gruffly. 'There might be water at the bottom, or mud. I'll bet the hole isn't more than five, maybe six hundred feet.'

'Oh, jolly good,' said Grace. 'You've put my mind completely at rest. I mean after all, what's a mere five hundred feet, or six.' Speers sneered at the British journalist and shook his head, muttering something under his breath.

Half an hour later they were ready. The seven survivors gathered around Izo as he explained their course of action. Bouchard, the elderly archaeologist, squatted on the edge of the group, only barely a part of it, but the others paid close attention.

The geologist quickly outlined the basics of making a rope descent, he and Speers demonstrating how to loop the rope between the legs, around the thigh and back up across the chest. He told them how to pay out the thin nylon cord with one hand while they guided their descent with the other. Izo knew he had only barely covered the subject, but he also knew that too much time spent thinking about the yawning depths of the chasm would be even more harmful than his sketchy description of rope climbing. Using a pair of karabiner clips and two pitons, he hammered an anchor point into the fissured rock of the lip, then threaded one end of the long rope coil through the lozenge-shaped rings.

'Mr Speers will descend first,' said Izo. 'Followed by the ladies, then Dr Bouchard, Mr Grace and Mr Penfold. I will descend last.'

'Why should you go last, when the danger is past?' asked Dr Bouchard stiffly, his voice brittle with fear. Izo Harada sighed briefly.

'Because I will have to reset the rope through the clips. I will be coming down using a different method so that we can retrieve the rope.'

'He's going to do a seat rappel.' said Speers, thrusting his arms into the makeshift knapsack of equipment he would carry down into the chasm. 'And it's a hell of a lot more dangerous than what you'll be doing, and with half as much rope, so why don't you shut up, old man.'

'There is no need to be rude,' said Irene Bouchard, defending her father. Speers grimaced as he fed the coil of rope between his legs and up around his chest.

'Fish or cut bait,' said the cave diver. Then he nodded to Harada, gave a single tug on the anchor rope and let himself over the side, bracing his booted feet on the rock as he "walked" backwards over the edge. A moment later he had disappeared.

One by one the others followed Speers over the side, each one feeling varying levels of bile-throated fear, but each also knowing that there was no alternative. Even Bouchard went down without an argument. Finally it was David Penfold's turn.

According to Speers's echoing instructions from below, there was a wide ledge about three hundred feet down, well within the limits of the rope. David concentrated on that knowledge, forcing himself not to think of the black emptiness at his back. For the first time since the earthquake he was glad to be without light. It was better to have no reference points. He let the universe contract until it was nothing but the thought of the ledge below and the harsh bite of the rock against the soles of his boots.

Three hundred feet. A football field. He shuddered, seeing himself as a small impotent dot on a stadium grid. The rope felt oily beneath his palms and he longed to wipe the sweat that was trickling, stinging, into his eyes.

'Don't think about it,' he whispered to himself. Suddenly, from far below, a light winked on. Speers's lamp. Between his legs he caught a brief glimpse of the others, the size of toy soldiers, then the light winked out. He closed his eyes as the first wave of vertigo swept over him, and he almost let go of the rope as the overwhelming desire to press himself against the rock wall swept over him. He stopped his descent, his fingers clutching the rope like talons, the nylon line biting into the flesh of his leg.

'Relax,' he told himself. 'Irene did it. Mariea did it. Even old Bouchard did it.' Bizarrely a scene from a long-forgotten movie shimmered into his brain, and he could hear the actor's line. 'Feets, don't fail me now!' he said aloud. He bit into his lip until he felt the salt of his own blood, then forced his fingers to open and pay out the line. He began to move again, slowly, fiercely aware of the cramping muscles in his arms and shoulders. There was a blinding spot of pain at the base of his neck and his mouth was alum dry, his tongue a cloying cottonball threatening to choke him. It felt as though he had hung suspended from the rope for an eternity.

And then he was down, with waiting hands helping him away from the rope to the safety of the ledge. He crawled to the protection of the rock wall a few feet away and lay huddled and shaking. He felt hands digging deeply into the fused ropes of muscle in his shoulders.

'You are safe now, chéri.' It was Irene's voice, coming soothingly into his ear.

'Awful,' he managed. The digging fingers softened to a caress.

'I know,' she said. 'I thought I was going to fall. For a time I just wanted to let go of the rope and finish it all.'

'How is your father,' asked David. He could almost feel Irene's smile as she spoke.

'He is my father still,' she said. 'The descent scared him, I think. But he will be okay.'

Another voice came out of the darkness, this time in front of him. Speers.

'You all right, Penfold?' The cave diver snapped on his lamp and David blinked in the sudden rush of light, almost blinding, even though Speers had aimed the lamp at the ground.

'I'm fine,' said David.

'Sure,' said Speers. 'Let me see your hands.'

'What?' asked David, confused.

'Your hands,' repeated Speers. 'Hold them out like I said.' David did as he was told, holding out both hands, which were still frozen in half fists around a phantom rope. Gently Speers peeled back the fingers and then shone his lamp down on the palms. They were scored and bleeding. For the first time David was aware of the burning pain. He stared down at his hands, horrified.

'How . . .?' he muttered.

'You were coming down too fast,' said Speers. 'I could tell by the way the end of the rope was twitching. Grace did the same thing; he's worse than you. Good thing we don't have much farther to go.' He snapped off the lamp. 'Bandage him up,' he said briefly to Irene. There was a movement of air in front of David and then Speers was gone.

'I've got the first-aid kit right here,' said Irene. She came around in front of David and a few moments later she had applied some kind of ointment to his hands and was wrapping them in gauze and tape.

'What did he mean when he said we don't have much farther to go?' asked David, wincing as the gauze touched the flayed tissue of his hands.

'I'm not completely sure I understand,' said Irene's voice out of the darkness. 'But it seems there is something he calls a fill-cone. No more than fifty feet or so below us here.'

'What's a fill-cone?' asked David.

'It is when the roof falls down, I think,' said Irene slowly. 'Pieces of the roof crumble and fall to the bottom sometimes. After a very long time it builds up into a pile. According to Monsieur Speers such a thing exists here, and it is close to our side of this . . . what did he call it, this chimney we are in. We can use it to climb down much more easily, he says,' she added uncertainly. David gave a little coughing laugh.

'What the hell,' he grinned, wishing he could see Irene's face, suddenly wanting to hold her. 'We've been through so much already, what's another bit of rope work.'

'How heroic of you, old man,' said Tony Grace from out of the darkness a few feet away. 'This could almost be a scene out of *The Poseidon Adventure*.'

'Hardly,' answered David, managing a laugh. 'All they had to do was find their way out of a belly-up ship. The way things are going here this river might actually lead us to hell.'

'It already has,' said Mariea Tarvanin. As she spoke there was a sudden gout of light from the edge of the wide ledge as Frank Speers ripped the tab on a magnesium flare. Instantly everyone on the ledge was bathed in the intense white light, their faces glowing and ghostly. David Penfold drank in the scene hungrily, his eyes desperate for something actually to *see* other than the constant blackness that surrounded them like a shroud.

The ledge they stood upon was wide and almost perfectly smooth, as though a massive portion of the chimny wall had simply slid forward seven or eight feet. Once again the rock was worn where the cascading water from above would normally have struck, producing a deep indentation in the ledge half-way along its length. The survivors were strung out along the ledge, most looking over the edge as Speers held the flare aloft. Even taking the harsh light into account David could see that the time since the collapse had taken its toll on all of them. Mariea's face, normally grinning and bright-eyed, was thin-lipped and drawn. Irene, beneath the tangled mass of her hair, looked to be on the verge of illness, her skin almost translucent. The rest seemed to have been equally worn by their ordeal, except for Irene's father. Bouchard was by far the worst. His skin was grey and waxy, the flesh on his face thin and drawn over the bones of his skull until almost every vein and artery was visible. His eyes were sunk deep into their sockets and even in the brilliant light from the flare there was no life in them. It was almost as though what made the old man tick was withdrawing deeper and deeper, sucking what little life there was from his body.

Once again David thought about his own father's quick death in the first collapse, and he wondered how it was affecting Irene to see the life force slowly being drained from her father.

Speers held the flare high for a moment longer, then tossed it into the pit below. With the exception of Bouchard all the survivors went to the edge and watched as the flare tumbled down, sending wild shadows dancing on the furled and shadowed walls of the chimney. The flare struck the fill-cone almost sixty feet below and, peering over, David could see what Irene had described. The cone was a roughly pyramid-shaped pile of debris from the roof of the chimney, far, far above them now. The waterfall from the river had eroded one side of the cone sufficiently to make it collapse further, so that one side of the pile leaned against the wall of the chimney directly below, leading down to the floor like a steep, rough ramp. From what David could see in the flickering light from the dying flare, the actual floor of the chimney was another hundred feet down from the top of the fill-cone.

David tried to spot some kind of exit from the chimney, but he couldn't see it. He knew there had to be one somewhere though, because there was no buildup of water from the river. The flare gave one last sputter, then died, and the darkness rushed in once more. It only lasted for a moment. Izo Harada snapped on his helmet lamp, and they had light once more.

'All right,' he said quietly. 'I have attached a belaying line here. We can proceed to the bottom of the chimney.'

5

An hour later, with all their equipment intact, the group reached the bottom of the chimney. While the others ate a hasty meal and rested, Frank Speers scouted the perimeter of the chimney looking for an exit. With the arduous descent completed everyone with the exception of Bouchard seemed to be in good spirits, all of them clearly elated by their accomplishment. Izo was glad that the group was pleased, but he couldn't share their happiness. As he scooped up the remains of the stew from his plate, his mind went over the implications of their climb down the circular well.

They had dropped at least four hundred feet and according to his compass they were still travelling in roughly the same direction as they had been going before — south-east. If they had been heading west, the descent would have brought them closer to the sea, indicating that they were coming down the sloping side of the Yugoslavian coastal range. If that had been the case, the possibility that the Styx might soon come out into the sun was still there, but with the south-eastern direction almost all chances of that happening had now gone. Izo was almost certain that the Styx belonged to the mysterious classification of underground rivers called sinks — rivers that disappeared into the bowels of the earth, never surfacing, their waters someday climbing to the sun again thousands of miles from their point of origin. By his calculations they had covered close to fifty miles, all of it on a downward path, and now, in a single mile, they had dropped another four hundred feet.

'A penny for your thoughts, Harada-san.' It was Mariea

Tarvanin. Izo hadn't heard her approach. She sat down beside him on a slab of tumbled rock and looked back at the dim light of the Primus stove and the shadowed figures huddled around it. A hundred feet beyond both she and Izo could see the bobbing circle of light from Speers's lamp as he searched for an exit.

'I never sell my thoughts,' said Izo, smiling at the young woman beside him.

'So, give them away,' said Mariea. She fumbled beneath the warm folds of her heavy wool sweater and brought out a crumpled packet of cigarettes. She lit one with a match and sucked greedily at the smoke. Izo shook his head silently, amazed at how different people, especially women, could be. The Tarvanin woman was almost primal, basic, someone who would take with pleasure, and give with equal happiness. The Bouchard girl on the other hand was close, reserved, careful with her emotions. Yin and Yang, he thought to himself. The only way to know either of them would be to take both of them to bed at once.

'Your thoughts,' prompted Mariea again. 'Remember.'

'They are salacious,' he said, smiling. Mariea looked startled.

'You're kidding!' she said. He shook his head.

'No, truly. Salacious and private.'

'I wouldn't have believed it of you,' said Mariea, dragging on the cigarette. 'You don't seem the type somehow. You're more of the zen master kind. Inner peace and the rest of it.'

'Inner peace often includes the joys of love,' said Izo. Mariea looked sceptical.

'I thought that was Tantric Yoga,' she said, grinning.

'You sound as though you have tried them all,' said Izo. Mariea laughed.

'At one time or another,' she said. 'Nothing works, not really.'

'You lack faith,' chided Izo. Mariea laughed again, but softly.

'I lack innocence,' she said. 'I finally came to the conclusion that nothing works because nothing is supposed to work. The world and all of us in it are not supposed to be at peace. It's not part of the game plan. We're all supposed to be as screwed up as possible and die wondering why we had to spend seventy or eighty years finding out absolutely nothing.'

'That is a classic Zen proposition,' said Izo. 'Knowing that you know nothing is the first step to knowledge.'

'And the last. Spare me the enigmas though, o wise one. What I really want to know is, are we going to get out of here?' There was a long silence. The tip of Mariea's cigarette burned brightly in the semi-darkness.

'I am not certain,' said Izo, not wanting to lie, but at the same time not wanting to dash her hopes.

'But it's bad though, isn't it?' she asked. 'I've been watching you. Everyone else was happy as hell to get down that cliff, and all it's done is set you brooding.'

'I did not know I was being so obvious,' said Izo.

'You were to me,' said Mariea. 'Anyway, like I said, it's bad, isn't it?'

'It is not good,' said Izo. 'We are going very deep. The deeper we go, the further we must climb.'

'Rivers don't flow uphill, Izo,' said Mariea. 'Why don't we just stick to the riverbed. It'll come out eventually, won't it?'

'Probably,' said Izo. 'But I am afraid we do not have much time left.'

'Why not?' asked Mariea. 'We've got enough food to last us for a month, light, warm clothes,' she laughed. 'I mean, really, what more could you want if you were trapped a thousand feet underground.'

'A way out,' smiled Izo.

'Like I said, follow the river,' shot back Mariea.

'And if the river goes somewhere we cannot, or simply goes deeper, what then?'

'Then we cross that bridge when we come to it,' said Mariea. She reached out and touched Izo's shoulder gently. 'Cheer up. I mean, it's not as though we have anything else to do.'

'You are kind,' said Izo.

'Not so kind,' smiled Mariea. 'Got to keep the leader happy, you know. I mean without you, who'd get us out?'

'Speers,' said Izo. Mariea nodded, stubbing out her cigarette.

'Which is precisely why I want to keep you happy,' she said. She touched his arm again, stood and made her way down the sloping scree of rocks to the group gathered around the Primus stove. Izo watched her go, the memory of her recent touch strong in his mind. He allowed himself to dwell on the remembrance only briefly, then banished it from his mind, closing his eyes and letting himself drift, willing his consciousness to slip away, taking a few moments' peace before beginning what he was now almost certain was a fruitless search for a way out.

6

The thick cords of muscle in the short man's powerful torso rippled as he swung down the pyramid of rock, his naked toes searching out footholds and the thick fingers of his hands finding places to grasp by touch alone. Without looking down he knew that the others would be where he had left them, clustered together around the weak light of the fire, awaiting his return.

The pounding roar of the waterfall filled his ears, the echo of the giant cataract rebounding from the walls of the huge chimney and sending faint shivers through the rock around him. He smiled to himself, his wide mouth opening revealing his heavy, strong teeth. There had been two hands of his tribe when they began their trek, and now, after all this time, there was still more than one full hand left. Even on the climb down the sheer wall beside the waterfall they had only lost one, and that had been a female, not even old enough to bear children or do any work beyond chewing fat to make skins soft for clothing. A small loss.

He reached the bottom of the fill-cone at last, and turned, his large, dark eyes picking up the faint glow of embers from the fire a hundred yards away, built close to the banks of the river that surged out of the dew of the unseen mist that cloaked the base of the waterfall. He touched his groin to remind himself of his luck and felt a surge of power as his organ swelled. When the others slept he would take the young one, his child by the female who had died when the earth shifted in their home cave. He would have her, and he would keep his luck. They needed nothing more than that, he knew. With it, he could work the miracles needed to release them from their prison, for after all, he was the one who could steal the hearts of animals and place them to lie forever on the walls of his cave. He had the magic, as his father had before him, and his father before that. And he had more. Not just the magic of the colours, he had magic that no one ever dreamed of, so much that sometimes he felt sure that he was indeed a God, the way his tribe believed.

Ignoring the comforting blur of light from the low fire, he skirted the group there and kept to the side of the river, walking close to the edge, his feet sure and strong on the slippery rock, the pads of flesh on heel and toe almost as sensitive as the skin of his hands. He would not fall. He reached the confining wall of the chimney and stopped fully a yard in front of it, even though he couldn't see the vaulting cliff in front of him. He reached out a hand and stepped slightly closer, his fingertips touching the cold rock almost reverently. He moved his hand to his mouth and tasted. A different rock again, by the taste. Softer than the rock above them, less acid on his tongue. A cutting rock, useless for tools, but ideal for the river's purpose.

He fell to his belly, the wet stone against his skin, letting every part of him feel its strength. His organ began to swell again and he almost laughed. He and the river were mated well, for if he was a God as his tribe believed, the river most certainly was a goddess. That something so soft and smooth could cut into cold dead rock was a bigger miracle by far than daubing colour on walls.

But on the other hand, the river could not think. It could be ridden by those who dared, but it could never ride on his back, or on the back of any of his tribe for that matter. The river had strength and power almost beyond belief, but it had no way to use that power except to move.

He levered himself forward on elbows and knees until he reached the water's edge. He waited for a moment, searching the noisy air for omens, then slid his hand over the edge into the bitterly cold water, letting the furious current drag at it.

He could feel his shoulder touching the wall of the chimney as his arm was almost torn from its socket by the rushing strength of the river. Fighting the pull of the current, he brought his arm up until it touched the rock just inside the point where the river headed into its tunnel. He pushed hard, flattening his palm against the tunnel wall, and rose slowly to his knees, bracing himself with his other hand, pressing it against the wall of the chimney. He moved slowly, his hand tracing the smooth interior of the river tunnel. He nodded to himself and began to sing, his voice low and throbbing, its tone matching perfectly the thundering of the river. He asked his question of the river, and received his answer swiftly, a sure knowledge that filled his brain.

There was no air-space. The tunnel was completely filled. He and his tribe, rather than riding the back of the river, would give themselves to her belly. He stood, satisfied by what he had learned, and walked quickly to the dim light of the fire. He would not wait. He would have the girl now, while the others watched him, and then he would take the colours he had managed to bring, and his lamp, and he would leave his mark on the wall of the chimney where the river buried itself. The river would see his mark and know his luck was strong. The river would obey.

7

Izo came awake instantly, his brain still filled with the dream, so clear that it seemed like memory. Speers was standing above him, the light on his helmet tilted up and out of Izo's eyes.

'Sorry to ruin your beauty sleep, Harada, but I found the outlet.'

'A phreatic tunnel?' asked Izo, but it was barely a question. He felt sure of his dream. Speers nodded, his lamp bobbing.

'You got it, dry as a bone except for a few puddles. Nothing on the floor either, just ripples all the way along. When the river's flowing it must go through that sucker like a bullet. We wouldn't have a chance.'

'How long is it?' asked Izo, sitting upright and stretching his neck. Speers shrugged.

'I'm not sure. I only went down it maybe a hundred feet or so. There's a curve in it or something because the light bounces. I didn't want to go too far alone. Want to scout it?' Izo shook his head.

'I see no point. It is our only way. We have no choice.'

'That's what I figured,' said Speers. The diver looked at his watch and frowned. 'Late afternoon,' he muttered. 'Not that it means anything down here. You want to go for it today or camp here?'

'Today,' said Izo emphatically. 'There is no time to lose.' Speers eyed him oddly, then shrugged.

'I'll get the others ready,' said Speers. Izo nodded.

'Dr Bouchard is to be given nothing to carry,' said the geologist. Speers snorted.

'I figured that,' said the diver. 'But just remember, pretty soon we'll probably be carrying him. The old man is dead-weight, and you know it.'

'Tell that to Dr Bouchard. Or to his daughter,' said Izo. Speers frowned, then turned on his heel. Izo stood.

'Speers,' he called. The diver turned.

'Yeah?

'The tunnel. Where is it?'

'There,' said the diver, pointing. 'About fifty yards to the far side of the cone. You have to be looking for it. It's no more than ten, twelve feet across and about the same high.' The diver turned again and headed towards the light of the Primus.

Izo followed the diver's directions and a few moments later he found the dark entrance of the river tunnel. He shone the light of his lamp into the opening and peered down it. Speers was correct in his estimation of the river's usual speed through the pipe. The walls were smooth except for regularly spaced ripples in the rock, indicating that the river normally swept through the narrow tunnel at a phenomenal rate. There was no doubt at all that the tunnel was usually filled.

But checking Speers's facts was only an excuse. Izo stepped back into the chimney and ran his hand up the smooth rock wall, not quite sure what to expect. As in his dream he brought his hand back and tasted it. The musky tang of the rock stayed on his tongue and brought back every detail of the dream. Izo frowned, superstition almost overwhelming curiosity. For a split second he rememebered his feelings the moment he had seen the paintings in the Subrano Cave for the first time. His soul was momentarily filled with dread and forboding and he knew that somehow he was in a place where natural laws were suspended. The Subrano paintings had been lost to man for ages, and here, now, this place and time was even more taboo. Man had no right to be here, lost in the pumping arteries and veins of the earth, following the snaking path of a dead river to some awful destination.

Izo shivered and backed away, shining his lamp on the fluted rock beside the entrance to the tunnel, forcing himself back to reality, telling himself that a dream was a dream and nothing more. Then the beam of his lamp struck a smooth patch of rock and he saw the thing which he both feared and wanted to see. There, its pigment still fresh in the ancient dampness of the cavern, was the scarlet imprint of a hand. A large hand, strong, thick-fingered, wide-palmed. The same imprint he had seen with Tony Grace at the fissure entrance to the artist's cranny in the Subrano Cave. Khan's hand. The hand of the man in his dream.

8

According to Izo's watch it was early evening by the time the exhausted group entered the smooth-walled tunnel that led away from the chimney, each of them, except for Dr Bouchard, heavily weighed down with large bags of equipment. As Izo entered the tunnel he kept his eyes away from the dark spot on the chimney wall which held the imprint of the hand, and mentioned it to no one else. The imprint was a talisman, but Izo had no idea if it was a good or evil omen for them all.

The tunnel went much farther than the hundred feet or so

travelled by Speers, and an hour after leaving the chimney the group was still following the gently undulating tube as it made its way downwards at an almost imperceptible angle. Izo noticed the slight drop however and he became even more depressed. Even if the tube had only run level it would have been better than further movement downward.

They stopped twice to rest, and the second time Bouchard, his voice strident and insistent, demanded that they camp in the tunnel rather than continue on. There was some agreement from the others, but Izo was adamant and they kept moving, their steps becoming slower with each passing minute, and their breathing becoming more laboured. Izo knew that one way or the other they would have to stop soon, but somehow the memory of Khan's hand forced him on.

At a few minutes past seven Speers, in the lead, stopped and turned back to the group.

'Something up ahead!' he called. Izo came forward from his position at the rear of the group. Speers pointed down the tunnel, the light from his lamp reflecting coldly off the smooth rock walls of the conduit.

Fifty yards further on the tube abruptly widened, the illumination from both Izo's and Speers's lamp spreading out and diffusing, giving them a vague and deeply-shadowed glimpse of a cavern beyond. Izo turned back to the others, relief in his voice.

'There is a cave ahead. We can rest soon,' he called. There was a ragged cheer from the rest of the survivors. Suddenly the cheer ended as they felt the deep-throated vibration in the tunnel floor. It was faint at first, little more than a shiver, but then it began to build.

'Boody hell,' murmured Tony Grace, frowning. 'What's that?' The vibration had turned into a distant, booming thunder.

'Oh, my God!' whispered Mariea Tarvanin, clutching at Alice Braden's arm. 'It's another earthquake!'

There was a long silence as each person listened, waiting for the bone-shattering whip-crack of the earth beneath their feet and above their heads. It didn't come, but as each moment passed the thundering sound became louder, resonating in the tunnel until it became unbearable.

'Jesus Christ!' said Frank Speers at last. 'It's no earth-quake! It's the river!'

'*Run!*' commanded Izo. 'Make for the cave ahead!'

The others obeyed instantly, dropping their burdens and running. Speers and Izo stayed behind, each of them word-lessly gathering up as many of the duffel bags as possible and dragging them forward along the tunnel.

'How much time?' asked Speers, panting. Izo shook his head.

'A minute, maybe two. Go!' Ahead of them, the others had disappeared into the cave, the scrambling sounds of their footsteps lost in the now continous roar of the approaching floodwater. Finally Speers and Izo exited the tunnel, their helmet lamps casting long bars of light high to a cathedral vaulted ceiling. Izo swung his head around and the searching beam of his lamp found the others clustered high on a stepped formation of rock, the bright light shining on their fear-filled faces. Izo swung his head again, searching for the river course. He was momentarily startled as the lamplight disappeared into the distance, finally being swallowed up by shadow. The cavern was monstrous — at least equal in size to the Big Room at Carlsbad.

'Grace! Penfold!' roared Speers. 'Get your asses down here and help with this!' The diver's voice echoed and re-echoed among the pillars and stalactites in the giant cavern. Without waiting to see if he was obeyed Speers turned and ran back down the tunnel to salvage more of their equipment. Hastily, Izo began dragging the bags up and out of the shallow bed of the river, handing them to Tony Grace and David Penfold, both of whom had come to help on Speers's command. Together the three men managed to drag everything up to where Bouchard and the women waited. As soon as all was secured Izo raced back down the wide steps of rock and into the river-course again, disappearing into the dark mouth of the tunnel.

David Penfold, his arm protectively around Irene Bou-chard's shoulders, waited anxiously, peering down into the darkness, waiting for Izo's light to reappear.

The thundering grew until it filled the immense room, and now there was something else; a high wind surged into the cavern, blowing at almost hurricane force through the tortured formations of rock around them, setting up an eerie, whistling and moaning counterpoint to the bellowing roar of the approaching water.

'Air pressure!' yelled Tony Grace, a few inches away, his voice rising over the banshee howling. 'The water's probably reached the tunnel mouth, back at the chimney!'

'Then they don't have much time left!' answered David, his eyes desperately searching for any sign of Harada or Speers below them, his heart sinking suddenly at the prospect of trying to continue on without the help of both men.

'They will be killed, David!' said Irene, close beside him.

'There's nothing we can do,' he answered. 'It would be suicide.'

An instant later a small puddle of light appeared, followed almost simultaneously by another. The six people watched as the circles of light grew larger, dancing erratically on the cave floor far below them like some kind of strange alien presence. Then the two men appeared at the tunnel mouth, each one dragging a large bundle. The boats.

David squeezed Irene's arm, then began moving down the steps of rock to the two struggling men below. A few seconds later he was followed by Tony Grace. They reached the river-course and together the four men lifted the heavy bundles up and out of harm's way.

'Don't bother trying to move them too far,' panted Speers. 'Tie 'em around one of the stalagmites. Should be all right.' David looked to Izo for confirmation and the geologist nodded.

'There is no time for anything else,' he said, fighting for breath. 'The water is almost here.' Izo helped David tie the two bundles securely and then all four men stumbled up the rock steps to the others, staggering with fatigue.

They had barely reached the high rock platform where the others waited when the flood reached the cave. The empty mouth of the tunnel was suddenly filled with a frothing torrent that lashed out along the old river-course, overflowing it within seconds, sending swirls of eddying water tearing in and around the rock formations of the cavern floor and completely covering the stalagmites the rubber rafts had been tied to. Within less than a minute the once dry floor of the cavern had been turned into a lake, rippled and torn by rip currents and whirlpools as the surging water searched for release after its confinement. Izo and Speers had made it just in time. Another minute or two in the tunnel and the water would have caught them, killing them instantly. Stunned by the force of the water, and the fate that might have been theirs had they decided to camp in the tunnel, the others watched as the waters thrust towards them.

'You're a lucky man, Izo,' said Tony Grace, watching the seething waters in the glinting light from the geologist's helmet lamp.

'No kidding,' said Mariea, moving down from her perch on a crusted ledge of rock. She went to Izo and unselfconsciously planted a kiss on his cheek. The Japanese turned and smiled at her. 'I'm glad you made it,' she said softly. 'Tony's right, you were very lucky.'

'It wasn't my luck, Mariea,' answered Izo, thinking about Khan's hand. 'It wasn't my luck at all.'

CHAPTER SEVEN

1

'You could almost live here,' said Tony Grace, spooning up the last of his beans. He chewed thoughtfully, gazing up at the ceiling of the huge cavern. The tips of a hundred stalactites were glowing softly in the pale light from the Primus stove, but the ceiling itself was lost in darkness more than a hundred feet above their heads. 'At least you don't get the feeling that the walls are closing in on you.' He took a sip of water from his canteen and sat back against a duffel bag, sighing happily.

'I always knew Limeys were crazy,' said Speers sourly, squatting a dozen feet away, finishing his own meal. 'Who the hell would want to live here?' He gestured toward the rapidly flowing waters of the river The level had gone down and the floor of the cavern was no longer completely submerged, but the river still overflowed its banks.

'I know what he means,' said David Penfold, coming to the defence of the journalist. 'I think if you were down here long enough you might forget there even was a world up there.' He pointed up at the ceiling.

'Not me,' said Speers.

'I hate to agree with our sour companion,' said Mariea Tarvanin. 'But I could certainly use a little bit of sunlight right now. I could never get used to living down here. I don't think anyone could.'

'I saw a film once,' broke in Irene Bouchard, speaking from the edge of the circle where she sat with her father. The old man's eyes were closed and he was breathing heavily. 'It was, how do you call it, a horror film. I forget the name of it, but it was all about a group of people who fall into a cave while mountain-climbing and come upon a whole race of beings beneath the ground.'

'*The Mole People*,' said Tony Grace.

'I beg your pardon?' said Irene.

'*The Mole People*,' repeated Grace. 'That's the name of the film you saw. I'm something of an expert on horror movies. They looked rather like lizards, most of them, except a bunch of rather snobbish high priests. The mountain-climbers get brought before the priests who condemn them to death. It turns out that their form of capital punishment is to be burned to death in a special cave behind a door. It turns out that what's doing the burning is the rays of the noonday sun shining down this incredibly deep pot-hole. The climbers get pushed into the cave and simply hoist themselves up.'

'It's a lot of baloney,' muttered Speers.

'Mole People aside,' commented Mariea, 'I still don't think you could live down here for long.'

'Don't say that,' laughed Tony Grace weakly. 'We may have to.'

'Really though,' went on Mariea. 'I mean, what would you eat? In our case water wouldn't be a problem, but we'd wind up starving to death eventually.'

'Not necessarily,' said Izo, speaking for the first time. 'At first glance a cave may seem like a dead place, but in actual fact there are many living things to be found in caves, even in one as deep as this. I'm sure for instance that if we looked long enough we could find a Proteus.'

'What's a Proteus?' asked Mariea, frowning. 'Sounds weird.'

'A lizard,' said Speers. 'A great big lizard.'

'He is correct,' went on Izo. 'The Proteus is found only in Yugoslavian cave systems, particularly ones with rivers such as this. They are sometimes as much as a foot long – perfectly white, with no eyes. They can live on almost no food at all and some have been known to survive on what few organisms they find in the silt of underground rivers. I would suspect that our river has its fair share of these creatures.'

'You mean we could eat them?' asked Tony Grace. Izo shrugged.

'If necessary,' replied the geologist.

'I saw what looked like a big centipede,' put in David Penfold. Again Izo nodded.

'There are several different kinds which live in caves. What colour was it?'

'I don't really remember,' said David thoughtfully. 'I only saw it in the light for a second. It looked almost red. Is that possible?'

'Yes,' said Izo. 'Several inches long, with very long rear legs?'

'Maybe,' said David. Izo nodded again.

'It is a Brown Centipede. A form of isopod. It kills its prey by injecting a poison with its front claws.'

'Yuck,' said Mariea, curling her lip. 'I could do without those.'

'It is rare to see one so deep within a cave system. They usually hunt much closer to the surface. Perhaps it was escaping the rising water of the river. It is not a swimming creature.'

'You mean there are other things in that water beside the whatchamacallits, the Proteus?' asked Mariea. Frank Speers laughed, the sound coming like a harsh bark in the vast cavern.

'Damn right,' he said. 'I've been swimming in caves like this for more than fifteen years. That water's as thick as soup with all sorts of creepy-crawlies, honey.'

'You're just trying to scare me,' said Mariea. Speers grinned nastily.

'He appears to be succeeding,' said Tony Grace. Alice Braden, tiring of the conversation, began to gather up the cooking utensils.

'I suggest that we abandon this silliness and get some sleep,' she said tersely. Izo held back a laugh. Alice, despite being filthy and bedraggled, still had the prim and proper manners of a schoolteacher. But she was right.

'I agree with Miss Braden,' he said, standing. 'Mr Speers and I will reinflate the rafts, the rest of you should find a place to put your sleeping bags. It has been an exhausting day, but at least we have the river once more. Perhaps we shall find its outlet soon.'

2

In what was becoming a nightly ritual, Tony Grace found himself writing in his notebook an hour later, his sleeping-bag pulled up around his armpits, working with nothing more than the light from his pen. He felt curiously elated as he wrote, as though they were somehow much closer to escaping. He knew it was ridiculous, but he couldn't dismiss the near euphoria.

'Maybe because of our situation I have reached some summit of self-awareness', he wrote. 'I feel as though, for the first time in my life, that I am actually living it. Everything seems to be incredibly clear and meaningful, even the taste of those wretched beans Alice cooked for us a little while ago. My senses of smell, of taste and hearing have become incredibly acute, almost as though the danger we are faced with is some kind of drug.

'I have heard mountain climbers describe danger that way, a feeling of raw life that transcends everything they have ever experienced. God only knows, there has to be some reason why people do dangerous things like racing cars and climbing mountains. Not only once, to gain the experience, but over and over again, recapturing that almost hallucinogenic thrill.

'It even makes you more aware of people, as though each of us was sending out small signals all the time, but it requires the element of fear to make them decipherable. As time passes I can see more good, or at least strength, in Frank Speers than I ever imagined was possible. I still think he is a frightful bore and potentially a very dangerous human being, but he has an almost relaxed association with that feeling of fear. He is totally familiar with it, almost at home with it. Izo is much the same, but his is more of an acceptance, the inscrutable oriental accepting his situation with Buddha-like calm, I suppose.

'Bouchard, I am certain, is dying, one way or the other. He seldom says anything and sleeps at every opportunity. He is a zombie now, and I can see that it is a terrible strain on his daughter, Irene. I can accept Bouchard dying easily enough, but if he infects his daughter with his malaise I will be terribly angry. I suppose I have a crush on her, even though with young Penfold about I haven't got a chance. Oh well. *C'est la vie.* For all Speers's scoffing, I still believe in the other-worldliness of this place. You could live here, Gollum-like, if you had to and if you were willing to accept your circumstances. As Izo suggested, there is food here, and if you wandered along the river you would find enough to eat, I'm sure. Mariea seemed horrified by the thought, which rather amazed me; she of all people should be able to see the possibilites of living in this strange place. This cavern we are in now, for instance, is easily big enough to take St Paul's Cathedral with Piccadilly thrown in for good measure, and even in the weak light we have it is obviously a stupendously beautiful spot.

'But on the other hand, maybe she is right. Or we both are. This is another world, a universe unto itself, but we have no place in it. We can visit, but we cannot stay.

'It must be time for sleep because I'm becoming poetic. I wonder what tomorrow will bring. Sunlight perhaps.'

The journalist clicked his pen and the light went out. Absolute darkness reigned in the cavern, and the only sound was the harsh whispering echo of the river, flowing hard along its banks.

3

David Penfold lay in his sleeping-bag on a smooth area of stone, several "steps" below the place where they had eaten dinner. The rest of the group was scattered about the higher areas above the river. He lay, one arm behind his head, staring blankly up at the unseen teeth of the stalactites high overhead, his other arm held within the warmth of the thermal bag, his fingers touching the comforting length of his flashlight.

For David, the absolute darkness was still the most frightening thing about their situation, although the others seemed to have become used to it to some degree. Or at least no one complained about it. For David the darkness was a terror far more present than claustrophobia or being buried alive. During the dig in the Subrano Cave a carbide lamp had been left on all the time, spreading its comforting light, but here, with battery power at a premium, they spent each night in total darkness, and once again David found himself fighting off the dark demons that had haunted him each night since the beginning of their ordeal.

The horror of the darkness was a subtle one for the young archaeologist. He feared no bogey men or monsters, he feared everything. Without eyes to make logic out of his surroundings the rest of his senses leapt to a heightened state of awareness that left him limp and exhausted with the effort of trying to decipher every small sound within the perpetual night. The faint tumbling sound of a pebble presaged another earthquake, or the bubbling of the water was the beginning of another flood.

He had been that way since childhood, wetting his bed at impossible fears, and it was the childishness of his anxiety that made him furious now. Over and over again he told himself that there was nothing to fear beyond the obvious dangers of their predicament, and that the fact that he was losing precious sleep as he lay in the darkness bathed in a cold sweat was far more dangerous than anything that could possibly be lurking in the blackness beyond his sleeping-bag. Still, he kept his hand on the flashlight, knowing that he would still be holding it when he awakened, like some adult version of the ragged teddy bear he had once clutched.

He stiffened as a small sound came to his ears. He turned his head, vainly trying to locate its source. He heard the sound again, a soft whispering noise. His hand tightened around the flashlight and he pulled it up out of the sleeping-bag, his thumb poised over the switch. He wondered how much of a fool he'd look if he turned it on and woke the others. The sound was constant now, louder, and coming closer, coming towards him. He stared into the pitch blackness, his muscles frozen with fear.

'David?' It was Irene, her voice a low whisper. The sound had been her sneakered feet on the rocks above him. 'David?' she called again, her voice still soft. 'Where are you?'

'Here!' he whispered back harshly. She came forward, following his voice, and a few seconds later David could feel the movement of her body a few feet away. 'Right in front of you,' he instructed Then she was beside him, her hand feeling his chest and shoulders. He pulled her down slightly and they kissed.

'I waited until I was sure my father was asleep,' she said quietly. 'I watched to see where you put your sleeping-bag so that I would know where to go when the lights were out.' She sat back and David could hear her taking off her clothes. A moment later she had squeezed down into the sleeping-bag with him, her flesh cool against his.

'You're cold,' said David, wrapping his arms around her. It was a strange sensation, to hold her in his arms and not be able to see her at all. He began to respond to her closeness and she pressed against him gently.

'I needed you,' she said, one small hand running down the soft hairs of his chest and stomach.

'Not as much as I needed you,' answered David.

4

'Somehow,' said Mariea Tarvanin in a whisper, 'I feel very naked.'

'You are very naked,' said Izo Harada. They had been lying together in his sleeping-bag for almost an hour, ever since she had come to him. Izo hadn't commented on her arrival, nor had she tried to make any explanations although both of them had laughed quietly when a few minutes after her appearance they heard the first sounds of lovemaking coming from the ledge a hundred feet or so away.

'I wonder if they're asleep yet?' said Mariea.

'Probably,' said Izo, a smile in his voice. 'Does it matter?'

'A little bit,' answered Mariea. 'I kind of felt like a bit of a voyeur.'

'But there was nothing to see,' said Izo.

'All right, wise guy, an audeur then. I was embarrassed listening to them.'

'Then you should not have listened,' said Izo.

'It was fairly hard not to,' said Mariea. She could feel Izo shrug beside her.

'You could have chosen not to hear,' he said. 'In Japan, especially in Tokyo, space is so limited that people have developed a sense of personal space and privacy that is absolute.'

'Well, bully for them,' said Mariea. 'I haven't got around to it yet.'

'No,' said Izo, chuckling. 'You are perhaps the most open person I have ever met.'

'Does it bother you?' asked Mariea.

'No,' said Izo after a moment. 'It intrigues me.'

'What? That I'm in your bed?'

'No, not that. You are attracted to me. You know that I am attracted to you. You have done a very natural thing. On the other hand you have been lying with me here for some time and yet we have done nothing but talk. There has been little touching. It is every un-American if I may say so.'

'I wanted to get comfortable with you.'

'And are you comfortable with me now?' asked Izo. It was

Mariea's turn to laugh.

'Don't tell me the Zen master is getting impatient!' she teased.

'No,' he said, smiling in the darkness. 'Merely ready.'

'Oh, really?' said Mariea. Gently, she reached out and let her fingers trail across the muscular and almost hairless ripples of his thigh. She reached the small tightly-curled patch of his pubic hair and then grasped his organ in her hand. 'Jesus!' she whispered. 'I never thought orientals could be so well hung.'

'These things are relative,' he replied. He touched her breast, the tips of his fingers barely brushing her skin. His other hand came up the line of her arm and shoulder to press in at the base of her neck in a soft but insistent movement that brought her mouth to his. They kissed briefly and then she pulled away.

'I didn't think this was going to happen,' she said. 'All the time when we were working on the dig, I'd look at you and think about making love with you, but I kept telling myself that I was being silly and that all I wanted to do was find out what it was like to do it with an oriental. I've never done anything like that. Not even back in the peace and love days. Maybe I'm a closet racist or something.'

'I don't think so,' murmured Izo.

'But why now?' she asked, perplexed.

'Perhaps because of the danger we are in. It makes people more honest with each other.'

'And time,' said Mariea. 'Maybe because we might not have another chance.'

'You are being defeatist,' said Izo.

'We're both talking too much,' said Mariea. 'I can't wait any longer.' They kissed again, and the flow of the kiss became the flow of their bodies. Izo rose above her and she opened beneath him happily, arching to greet him in the blackness, the air rushing out of her lungs as he entered in a long slow motion of exquisite smoothness and then withdrew almost completely in a tantalizing instant. Again and again he repeated the motion, until her fingers dug into the hard muscles of his back. She pushed against him, rising with him, clinging to him, willing him to grind into her as hard as he could, but he kept up the same rhythm. She began to come, again and again in building waves, the intensity of it so strong that she had to bite hard into his shoulder to keep from crying out. Somewhere, in a last sane corner of her mind, she knew that what she was doing was flaunting herself at the death looming before them, but she also knew that if she could feel like this she was still alive, and would fight to stay that way until the last.

5

'I wonder who it is?' said David Penfold, cradling Irene's head in the crook of his shoulder.

'Don't be silly,' she chided. 'It is Mariea, of course, and Izo.'

'Oh come on!' scoffed David. 'Izo?'

'Why not?' asked Irene. She felt David move uncomfortably beside her.

'I don't know . . .' he began, his voice trailing off.

'Is it because you and she used to be together?' asked Irene. David turned in the darkness abruptly.

'What do you mean?' he asked.

'The two of you used to be, umm, close, *n'est-ce pas?*'

'How did you know that?' he asked.

'Well, you said you had gone to school with her, and from the way I have seen you looking at her from time to time I assumed that the two of you had once been lovers.'

'You're not jealous?' asked David unbelievingly.

'Of course not,' said Irene, grinning. 'Why should I be jealous. After all, she is sleeping with Izo, not you. It is you, I think, who is jealous that she would sleep with him.' There was a long silence. Irene settled back into David's shoulder.

'No,' he said at last. 'I'm not jealous. It's just an odd feeling, that's all. Not quite right. I can't explain it.'

'Do not try, *chéri*,' she murmured, her voice heavy with sleep. 'Just be happy for them. There has been little enough happiness for any of us these last few days.

Neither spoke for a few minutes. In the distance the sound

156

of the love-making between Mariea and Izo had softened to silence. David began to relax, comforted by the closeness he felt to Irene, even though he knew that they could not spend the rest of the night together. Suddenly he heard another sound, and not from Mariea and Izo. It was a faint scratching noise almost unheard at first, but slowly getting louder. It seemed familiar to David, but it took him some time to place it. Finally it came to him. Rain. The first drops of rain sounding on the shingles of a roof. He almost expected to feel the touch of wet droplets on his upturned face. Gently he shook Irene's shoulder, nestled closely in his.

'Hey!' he whispereed. She stirred, mumbling. He shook her again as the sounds grew louder. The feeling of rainfall was almost uncanny, even though David knew it couldn't possibly be that. 'Wake up,' he insisted, prodding her.

'*Qu'est-ce qu c'est?*' she muttered, annoyance in her voice.

'Listen!' he hissed.

'I hear nothing,' she said. 'It is the river. The water.'

'Water maybe,' he said, excitement rising in his voice. 'But it's not the river. It sounds like rain.'

'That is absurd,' said Irene.

'Of course it is!' said David. 'But listen!' Irene sat up beside him.

'It is very peculiar,' she said after a moment. The excitement David had felt began to change. He gripped the flashlight again. As the sound around them grew louder it began to shift into something else.

'It is not the sound of rain,' said Irene at last, a note of confusion in her voice. 'It is dry. Like leaves, yes? Dry leaves?'

'That's just as crazy as rain,' said David, the cold fear he had felt before Irene joined him returning. 'There are no goddamn dry leaves down here any more than there is a rainshower.'

The scream split the dark peace of the cave. It was a scream of ultimate horror, the sound of a soul gone mad, sending a snaking shiver down David's spine and bringing the taste of bile to his throat.

The scream came a second time, the sound filled with terrible agony, as though the person was being horribly burned. At almost that instant there were slashes of light coming from all directions as others in the group awoke and shone their lamps in the direction of the sound. Three beams found their target at once, identifying the source of the terrible sound. It was Alice Braden.

The woman's face was twisted into a grotesque rictus of horror as she stood, fifty feet from the place where David and Irene lay, her hands frantically clawing at things which tore at her body.

She was covered from head to toe in hundreds of the foul, red-carapaced centipedes that David had seen clinging to the rock wall of the river earlier that day. The creatures twisted and curled, their half-inch-long stinging claws buried deeply into her flesh, pumping their burning poison into her veins. Even as David and Irene watched, slack-jawed in horror, more of the segmented insects, some of them almost six inches long, skittered up her legs, disappearing into the flannel underclothes the woman wore. The insects covered her as she sank to her knees, flailing her hands in front of her face, trying to pull the creatures away from her eyes and mouth as more and more swarmed over her. One of the large lights snapped on and for the first time David could see the extent of the horror in front of him. There were tens of thousands of the huge insects, swarming up from God only knew where, their clicking claws making the whispering clatter he had mistaken for rain. Half the cavern floor was filled with a seething, moving, twisting mass of the centipedes. Already a searching arm of the swarm was spreading out like some evil stain, cutting the lower part of the cavern off from the upper ledges. Faintly David could hear people's shouting voices but he couldn't move, his eyes remaining riveted on the ravaged form of Alice Braden.

She had almost disappeared beneath the creatures that covered her, and she was completely motionless now, hands dropped to her sides, her face defenceless as half a dozen of the sinuous things slid in between her grimacing lips, entering her mouth, while more flailed and dug at the soft tissues of her eyes. Eventually the weight of the insects on her back and shoulders pushed her forward and she was gone, nothing more than a swollen lump, covered in the lunging, mindless tide of the insects.

Irene tore at his arm, pulling him away from where they had been lying. Dully he turned and looked at her, realizing for the first time that she was screaming at him.

'The river! We must get to the river!' He nodded, grabbing at his clothes, pulling on trousers and a sweater. The cavern was ablaze with light as more and more lamps were turned on, and he almost froze again, watching as the rolling horror of the insect wave split and reformed, moving around obstructions, heading towards them, and towards the others on the higher ledges. Irene pulled at him, directing him towards the river. Speers was already at the bank, throwing what supplies he could into the waiting boats.

'I'll wait thirty seconds, no longer!' he shouted. Stumbling, David and Irene found their way down the steps of flow-stone rock, leaping over a thin line of the creatures that had broken off from the main swarm. The two young people threw themselves into one of the rubber rafts and instantly Speers cast off, pushing with one of the aluminium poles, sending them into the main current of the river.

David turned in the boat and stared back at where they had just been and saw that there was almost nowhere in the cavern not covered by the raging insects. Then, high on the cavern wall, he saw Izo and the others, desperately climbing, looking for some way to escape. Then the boat was swept out of the cavern and into the impenetrable blackness of the river tunnel.

CHAPTER EIGHT

1

'I think we can rest for a moment,' said Izo, his breath coming hard. Behind him Mariea, Bouchard and Tony Grace leaned back against the rough wall of the narrow tunnel. Less than half an hour had passed since their escape from the insect cavern.

Izo had spotted the tunnel opening high on the crusted wall of the cavern when they had first made camp, but had thought little of it. They were following the river then, and any other route was worthless to them. Even now the chances of this tunnel leading them either to the surface or back to the river were almost nonexistent, but it had at least provided them with a way to escape the rolling mass of the hideous insects.

While the others rested, Izo shone his helmet lamp up the gently inclined tunnel. The fissure in the surrounding rock was almost arrow straight, leading up at a gentle angle. The floor of the tunnel was thin, almost sandy. From what Izo could see the tunnel was old and derelict — no water had flowed down its length for centuries; at least they were safe from flooding. Izo turned, flipping the lamp up to shine on the ceiling so as not to blind his companions. Mariea and Tony looked pale and exhausted, but otherwise they were all right. Bouchard on the other hand looked as though he was on the verge of death. His face was grey and covered in a sheen of sweat. His eyes were closed and his chest moved raggedly as he took in breath after breath.

'Breathe more slowly, Dr Bouchard,' he said quietly. 'You are hyperventilating.' The old man paid no attention. Izo gestured to Mariea and she nodded. She pushed past Tony Grace and put her arm around the Frenchman, speaking in whispers, trying to calm him. Eventually his breathing became more regular.

'My daughter,' he said finally, his voice hollow and old.

'She is all right,' said Izo. 'She escaped in the boats.'

'You are lying,' muttered Bouchard. He slid down the rock wall until he was seated, his legs drawn up close to his chest. For a moment Izo had an image of the old man as a dead husk, his juices sucked dry by the hordes of centipedes in the cavern behind him. He shook off the feeling, a shiver running down his spine.

'I am not lying, Dr Bouchard. Irene escaped with David and Speers. I saw them.'

'She was sleeping at my side,' said Bouchard. 'She should have been with me.'

'I think she was with David,' said Mariea, embarrassment

160

in her voice. Without opening his eyes the old man shook his head in denial.

'She would not do that. Irene is a good girl. She has always been a good daughter. She should not have left me there alone with those things. She should have stayed with me.' His voice trailed off raggedly. Mariea realized that the old man cared less about the safety of his daughter than the fact that she had supposedly deserted him. She shook her head sadly and went back to where Izo stood.

'Now what do we do?' she asked.

'Mr Grace,' asked the geologist, 'what is your opinion?' The journalist looked down at the huddled figure of Bouchard and shrugged his shoulders.

'We have no choice, really,' he said wearily. 'Except to take him with us. We can't leave him, can we?' Izo looked at Grace and then at Bouchard.

'No,' he said finally. 'We have no choice. Wake him if you can,' he instructed. 'If not, we will have to carry him.'

Together, Mariea Tarvanin and Tony Grace managed to rouse the old man, and between them, they supported him as they went on along the tunnel. Bouchard's stumbling progress slowed them, and after almost three hours they had covered less than two miles by Izo's rough calculation.

'Will those creatures follow us?' asked Mariea as they stopped again at a slight widening in the tunnel. She watched as Tony Grace slipped the almost comatose Bouchard off his shoulder and dropped to the sandy floor of the rock fissure. Izo dropped into a squat, relaxing. He shook his head.

'I do not think so,' he said. 'To be honest they will spend much time with poor Alice, I think. She will be their focus of attention.'

'God!' said Tony Grace. 'I've never seen anything so awful in my life. They were eating her alive!'

'I think she died quickly,' said Izo. 'They are stinging insects. She would succumb very rapidly, I think.'

'You hope,' said Mariea. 'I think I'll hear her screaming for as long as I live.'

Tony Grace giggled, his laughter on the verge of panic.

'Then you won't hear it for long, will you?' he said. 'We're cut off now. We might as well give it up.'

'Izo?' asked Mariea, desperation creeping into her voice. Izo knew that they were all on the verge of collapse and that it would take little to push them over the edge into panic.

'We are alive,' said Izo, his voice firm. 'We have survived much already. We can survive this.'

'Why?' said Tony Grace bluntly. 'A few hours ago, Christ, an age ago I was thinking how incredible it was to have lived through what we did. But to see her dead like that, killed like that . . . there's no reason, no sense to it.'

'Was there any sense to your life before this happened,' said Izo. The journalist opened his mouth in anger and then shut it abruptly. His lips curled into a bitter smile.

'I don't believe this,' he muttered, the panic draining out of his voice as he spoke. 'I'm stuck in a bloody slit in the rock no wider than a sewer having a philosophical argument with a Japanese geologist. It's madness.'

'It is quite real,' offered Izo. 'And it must be lived with. We are here, and no escape is going to be offered to us that we do not earn. We must keep on.'

'And Bouchard?' queried Grace, staring at the almost unconscious old man. 'How much longer do you think he's going to last?'

'I do not know,' said Izo, letting out a breath in a long sigh. 'He will last as long as he will last. We are not in any position to help him. I do not think there is anything physically wrong with him. He has lost the will to go on. But while he lives, he comes with us. We must continue.' Wearily, the journalist climbed to his feet. He and Mariea grasped Bouchard beneath the arms and pulled him up. With Izo in the lead, his lamps shining on the rock ahead, they moved onward. Grace kept his eyes on Izo's back and the knapsack strapped to it, the knapsack which held everything they had managed to salvage in their headlong flight out of the centipede cavern. As they walked up the still rising floor of the passageway the journalist thought about the contents of the knapsack, and wondered how much food Izo had been able to get. Whatever it was, it was all they had.

Strangely, Mariea's thoughts had drifted into the past, sparked by Tony Grace's comment about the insanity of their plight. She riffled through her memories, trying to piece her life together in a way that would give some kind of meaning to her present. It seemed incredible to her that her entire life could lead to such a horror. She rebelled at the thought that her life would end so terribly and so irrelevantly, and told herself that it would not, could not happen.

Izo maintained a steady pace, his eyes following the contours of the rock as they struggled on, trying to decipher their meaning. Thankfully he had found his compass in the first mad seconds after Alice Braden's scream, so he knew their direction. As far as he could tell, the narrow, high-walled passage was moving almost parallel to the river course – south-east. From the few degrees of inclination he suspected that once upon a time the tunnel they were in had fed from some source high above them, adding a stream to the Styx's flow. He didn't want to raise false hopes among the others, but the continuing slope of the tunnel leading upward held out a faint chance that it would lead to a passage out. It was unlikely that the original opening to the ancient tunnel would still exist, but perhaps it would lead to some other passage-way, or even to the river again.

He fought off emotion as he trudged slowly on, refusing to succumb to the mass of conflicting feelings surging through his mind. He knew that those feelings lay on the perimeter of fear, and fear was something he dare not think about. He thought instead about Mariea, and the time they had spent together. He tried to recapture each individual sensation of her body and his own to it, but each time he thought of those moments he thought about how they had ended, and saw again the seething wave of insects enveloping the body of Alice Braden, thrusting their deadly claws into her flesh, gouging and tearing.

'Enough,' he whispered to himself. 'Empty your mind. Think of Khan. Think of the first man here. Think of the hand.'

Had that strange ancestor been here? he thought. Did he come face to face with another swarm of centipedes? It didn't matter; the strength of the ancient man was here, and Izo let it flow through him, replenish him. He opened himself to the

Neanderthal's being, becoming him.

And Khan lived again within Izo's mind and heart.

2

The Neanderthal sniffed the rock, his guttering fat-lamp held aloft to study the faint striations of the rock. The others stayed within the safety of the large cavern far behind him, but the hole in the wall had intrigued him and he had left the light of the fire, taking the lamp, even though the last remnants of his tribe whimpered as he disappeared into the high, vaulted wall of rock.

The rock was like that of the big cavern, he knew that by its smell, but the air here was different. He sniffed, his large nostrils flaring wide, taking in the cold air, tasting it, examining it.

The air was dead, he decided. It had no ebb and flow as did the air in the main cavern. But his curiosity was aroused, and he continued along the narrow passage, intrigued by the soft sandy floor of the tunnel, its texture so different from the cold, and often slimy rock of the ledges that ran along beside the river. Twice since they had discovered the dark stream he had come close to slipping into the waiting water, both times saved only by the quick magic of his hands.

An hour passed, and the fat in his lamp was almost gone. Khan smiled. It made no difference to him; he didn't need eyes for this place. To prove his magic he placed the lamp gently on the floor of the tunnel and continued without it, thinking about fire, and how necessary it was. He wondered how long they would have lived below the ground like this without the power of his two-stones and the small pieces of wood that were washed down the river and cast up on the banks of the caverns. They would have died of the cold, and the others, perhaps, would have died of fear, scared to move without the comfort of the flickering light to guide their way.

Within moments the faint flame of the fat lamp had been left behind, leaving Khan to travel in absolute darkness. His pace never faltered, however, as he let his feet take him along the floor and his hands gently brush the rock walls on either side. His father had lived like this for one hand of seasons, cut off from light, the power of his eyes robbed from him, and his father had survived, so great was his magic. For Khan, to walk temporarily in darkness was no feat at all. The Neanderthal knew that all the things which had happened were tests of his power, sent to challenge his magic, the magic which had been handed down from his father, and his father before him, and each test gave him more strength. He understood with absolute certainty that he would bring his tribe to the light once more, and the place where they greeted the sun would be better than the home they had left behind.

In the darkness time seemed to pass without meaning, and the Neanderthal had no idea how long he had been walking when suddenly the walls on either side gave way, leaving him with nothing to touch. He stopped, tilting his head back, drawing in breath through his nostrils, his ears tuned to every sound. He grunted softly and listened, the sound returning to him quickly; a cave perhaps, but a small one. He stepped back a few paces, arms outstretched, until once again his seeking fingers touched the rock. Keeping one hand in contact with the cool stone, he followed the perimeter of the cave, discovering quickly that it was little more than a broadening of the fissure he had been travelling along. Turning his face upward once again, he gave a barking cough to the ceiling and listened once more. The sound of his voice came back to him in pieces and he knew that the roof above him was high, perhaps even another shaft such as the one containing the waterfall. Satisfied that he knew the perimeters of the cave, he slipped to the ground and curled himself into a ball, giving in to fatigue. He wished that he had brought his colours with him to mark this place as his own, but he shrugged off the thought easily, for who, including himself, would ever see the markings. A few moments later he was asleep.

3

'We can rest,' said Izo, swinging his light from side to side, examining the small cave. It was less than twenty feet across, but as far as he could tell the fissured ceiling above them went up for at least a hundred feet, perhaps more. The geologist knew that it wasn't really a cave at all, and that the space had been formed by some massive rupturing of two large blocks of stone. He kept his light trained high, wondering just how high the irregular slit went. Gently, Mariea and Tony Grace lowered the stuporous form of Dr Bouchard to the floor of the cave and joined Izo at its centre.

'A way out?' asked Grace, following Izo's gaze. The geologist shook his head.

'I think not,' he answered. 'It is an anomaly.'

'But it might lead to another cave system,' put in Mariea hopefully.

'It is possible,' agreed Izo, still looking up, 'but it is doubtful.'

'Hardly the optimistic one, are you?' said Tony Grace, slumping to the ground, his back against the smooth cave wall. Izo shrugged out of his knapsack and sat down as well. Mariea followed suit. A few feet away Bouchard lay silently, eyes closed, his breath rattling quietly.

'It's like dragging around a bloody corpse,' said Grace.

'Let him alone,' said Mariea. She turned to Izo. 'So what do we do now?'

'Rest for the moment,' said the geologist. 'Then continue on.'

'Why don't we just go back?' asked Grace. 'It might be safe now. Those . . . things, they may have moved on.'

'Perhaps,' said Izo. 'But what if they have not? We would have travelled this distance for nothing. And we do not have enough supplies.'

'How much do we have now?' asked Grace.

'Food enough for two, perhaps three days.'

'And after that?' he asked. Izo shrugged. There was nothing more to be said. After a long silence, Mariea spoke.

'Damned if we do, damned if we don't,' she said softly.

'Anything we do is going to be dicey,' agreed Grace. He stood and paced back and forth across the small floor of the cave. He stopped after a few moments and stared up into the deep shadows of the yawning ceiling. 'Vertigo if we climb, bugs behind us, and God knows what ahead. It really isn't much of a choice, is it?'

'No,' said Izo. 'Not much of a choice.' The journalist lifted his narrow shoulders and his lips moved into a wan smile.

'All right,' he said at last. 'I vote for the unknown. We press on.'

'I second it,' said Mariea. Izo nodded.

'Good,' he said. 'But first we must rest. We will eat when we awaken and then continue.'

'What about him?' asked Mariea, nodding towards Bouchard.

'He's not going anywhere,' muttered Tony Grace. 'Let him be.' The journalist stripped off his heavy sweater, wadding it into a bundle, and settled down on the soft floor of the cave. Izo waited until Mariea had found a place to sleep and then turned off his lamp, plunging the small cave into darkness.

'God!' said Grace out of the blackness. 'What I wouldn't give for breakfast in bed and a hot bath.'

'Shut up,' murmured Mariea. 'You're stealing my fantasy.'

Izo Harada lay in the darkness, his head pillowed on his arm, and listened as the breathing of the others dropped into the heavy slow beat of sleep. He was tired, but even in the total darkness there was no way he could sleep himself. Twice now he had felt Khan's presence and if it hadn't been for the imprint of the ancient man's hand on the rock beside the tunnel mouth he would have thought himself mad. Even with the handprint he questioned himself. He knew that in their present situation hallucination was possible, and if it hadn't been for the constant reminder of his chronometer, he would have lost track of time long before this. He had no feeling for day or night, or even the passage of minutes any more, and the disorentation of time he knew, was one of the first signs of Cavers' Rapture. Being lost beneath the ground the way they were recaptured almost exactly the Lilly experiments with sensory deprivation. First loss of place, then loss of time sense, and eventually, loss of self. Their only salvation lay in the lamp on his helmet and the larger hand-held lamp he'd managed to pick up as they retreated from the insect cavern. Soon though, with all the use he had been giving them, the batteries would die out, and they would have to travel in darkness. He knew that he could survive that way for some time, but he doubted if the others could. Bouchard for instance wouldn't last an hour, while Mariea and Grace would also succumb. The journalist put up a bold front he knew, but Izo had been with him when they had discovered Khan's eyrie in the Subrano Cave, and the geologist knew that Grace was at best an incipient claustrophobe. For a man like that to travel in complete darkness for any length of time would bring on panic; he was showing signs of it already. With Izo's help and support Mariea might last a little longer, but in the end she too would give in.

Not that it mattered, he thought to himself. The batteries would outlast the food, and, what was worse, they had no water. He found himself wondering what Khan would have done, and chided himself for the thought. Khan was dead; the Neanderthal was dust an aeon ago, and couldn't help him, even in dreams. Even to think of him was dangerous, for it meant that he was losing faith in himself.

The geologist turned on his side, and instead of thinking of Khan he forced himself to conjure up the image of his birthplace in his mind, and a vision of his father. He imagined the rich soil of the surrounding farmland, and the smell of juniper wood, burning slowly and filling the air with its almost sacred incense. The smell was so close he felt he could take it into his lungs, and at the same time his ears could faintly hear the soft babbling of the tiny stream that ran by his house, and the wind-chime sound of his mother's laughter.

Finally, he slept, slow tears of memory forming at the corners of his eyes.

It seemed to him that no time had passed when he felt an insistent shaking. He awoke from his dreamless sleep and opened his eyes to the glare of his lamp. From behind the light he heard Tony Grace's voice.

'Wake up, Izo, we've got a problem.'

'What is it?' asked the Japanese, holding a hand up to ward off the bright light that blinded him. Grace flicked it off, leaving him in darkness again.

'It's Bouchard,' said the journalist. 'The bugger's gone.'

CHAPTER NINE

1

The rubber boat sped along the river, borne swiftly forward on the breast of the quickly racing current and kept from colliding with the looming and jagged-edged walls of the tunnel on either side by Frank Speers and his pole. In the rear of the lead raft, David Penfold and Irene Bouchard huddled together, squeezed in among the supplies that Speers had thrown on board in the last moments before casting off. The other rafts, empty, trailed behind, held to the lead raft by their nylon tethers. Every few moments one of them would batter against the sides of the passage, sending a shudder up to the lead boat.

'We'll have to cut them loose,' called Speers from the head of the boat. A lamp lashed precariously to a grommet on the side of the rushing craft threw a wild beam ahead, barely casting enough light to guide Speers as he fought to keep the boat from colliding with the sides of the channel. He dug at the belt around his waist and brandished a diver's knife in the air. 'Come and get this. Cut 'em loose!' he ordered.

As David stood, clutching at one of Speers's air-tanks for support, the tail end raft on the tether snagged a rock overhang, spinning the lead raft in a nauseating half-circle. David was thrown to one side, barely managing to keep himself from being flung over the side. There was a brief tearing sound and the nylon cord parted on the trapped raft setting them free.

169

'One more like that and we're dead meat!' called Speers. 'Come and get the god-damn knife!' David struggled up again and moved forward, his bare feet slipping on the rubberized canvas of the floor. For the first time in the hour since they had escaped from the insect cavern he realized that he was without boots. If they had more walking ahead of them it was going to be rough going. He cast the thought out of his mind and made his way forward. He took the knife from Speers's outstretched hand, then fell to his knees as the river suddenly curved sharply. Grimacing with effort, his face masked with sweat, Speers rammed the aluminium pole into the rock wall, pushing them away from the rows of needle-like calcite deposits threatening to puncture the frail fabric at any moment.

'What about the others?' asked David from the bottom of the raft as the craft straightened again. The air around them was filled with the sound of the rushing water as it tore through the narrow passage, and he almost had to shout to be heard. 'If we find the others, they won't have any room!'

'Screw the others!' yelled Speers. 'Cut the goddamn line before I use that knife to cut your throat!'

David stared up at the shadowed face of the older man, bile rising in his throat. He was filled with fury at the callousness of the man, and at the same time his heart sank with the knowledge that he hadn't the courage to stand up to him.

'Bastard!' he whispered under his breath. He turned, and, still on his knees, crawled back to the rear of the raft. He squeezed in beside Irene and lifted the knife, avoiding the woman's eyes. For a moment, the knife was held poised an inch over the inflated wall of the raft, and he had a brief, but powerful desire to ram the rubber-handled, steel-bladed tool into the rubber.

'And I don't have the guts for that either,' he muttered. He leaned out over the rear of the raft, found the taut lanyard, and in two swift strokes he severed the line. Almost instantly their raft gained speed, and the vague shapes of the rafts behind disappeared quickly from the reflected backlight of Speers's lamp. The single raft and what it contained was their universe now. David slumped down onto the raft beside

Irene, avoiding the searching look in her eyes.

'What of the others?' she asked. 'What will we do when we find my father and the others?'

'Ask Speers,' said David, turning away from her completely. There was nothing more he could say or do. Speers was the authority, the court of last resort. He was nothing more than a passenger. He closed his eyes and leaned his head back against the side of the raft, suddenly filled with an immense weariness. Speers, like David's father, stripped him of strength and adulthood almost without effort, almost as though he had no will of his own. And there, slumped into the back of the raft as it whirled down the swollen underground river, the vision of a terrified and mutilated Alice Braden hot as a branding iron in his mind, David Penfold didn't give a damn.

'Nothing matters now,' he whispered softly, as sleep overcame him.

Irene Bouchard watched as David fell into a troubled sleep beside her. It never ceased to amaze her, seeing the transformation that came to his face as he slept. In a matter of minutes the lines and experience fell from his features and he became a child again. Early in their relationship Irene had found the magic of the metamorphosis a beautiful thing, but now she knew that it signified something unsettling about the young man who was her lover. In many ways, important ways, he was a child. It seemed incredible to her that the sleeping adolescent-featured man at her side was the same man who had been raging within her body only a few hours before, a powerful, thrusting adult male, bringing her orgasm again and again. She wondered now if his power had come from fear, and her own responses aroused from the desperation she felt at their entrapment.

She had seen that duality in his character from their first meeting. It had occurred at the cocktail party thrown by the department, welcoming Dr Penfold to Paris to take up the prestigious archaeology chair. Her father had been furious at the appointment, and it was only the requirements of protocol and Irene's urging that made him attend at all, with her on his arm for support against the boorish American and his

171

vulgar attempts at self-aggrandizement, or at least that was how her father referred to Penfold.

David had been in attendance, almost literally in the shadow of his father as the older man beamed, shook hands and chatted to the faculty wives in his fluid and fluent French. David was clearly ill at ease among the crowd and he sipped at his drink cautiously, his eyes tracking back and forth, watching the party, but taking virtually no part in it. Her first attraction to him had been purely a physical one, a sharp tug that made her stop almost in mid-stride. His handsomeness stopped just short of feminine beauty, and the strange mixture of youth and adult in his expression acted powerfully on her. At first she resisted it, but as the party wore on she found her gaze coming back to him again and again. Eventually their eyes met and the initial tug Irene had felt became an almost desperate desire. Before David she had slept with several men, but none of them had ever aroused the passions that she felt welling up in her that evening.

She managed to break away from her own father and quite blatantly crossed the room and introduced herself to David.

'We have much in common,' she said with a smile, speaking in English.

'For instance?' he answered, smiling sourly, sipping at his drink.

'We are the children of famous men,' answered Irene. 'We struggle in their shadow.'

'That's a little too philosophical for a cocktail party, isn't it?' said David. 'I mean, it's hardly the kind of thing you expect to hear as idle cocktail chatter.'

'You find it hard to understand?' asked Irene, her eyes twinkling. David shook his head and took an ice-cube in his mouth, cracking it with his teeth. He swallowed and grinned.

'Nope,' he said. 'I understand it all right, but I always figured that there was a time and a place for everything. Your line about our parents sounds like something said at an intimate dinner . . . or something.'

'So invite me to dinner and we shall continue the conversation,' said Irene with a smile.

'You're on,' said David, taking her by the elbow and

guiding her through the throngs of people. 'Anything to get the hell out of here.'

He was unfamiliar with Paris, so Irene chose a small and inexpensive restaurant on the Left Bank, within sight of the Seine and the floodlit spires of Notre Dame. They ate under an awning with the cool evening breeze blowing off the water a hundred yards away, and when they were finished they walked along the embankment, David marvelling at the huge barges lined up along the quai and Irene pointing out historic buildings along the way.

They crossed the Pont Neuf at the tip of the Île de Paris and walked back along the Rue de Rivoli past the Tuileries Gardens and the Louvre. By the time they reached the gilt statue of Joan of Arc at Palais Royal, they were holding hands, and as they parted at the Louvre metro station they kissed each other softly.

'I live with my father,' said Irene.

'And I'm in a hotel room with mine,' said David.

'We have time,' said Irene, and she kissed him again. Then she went down the steps into the metro station, her legs weak with the desire to turn and go back to him.

When she reached home she went to her room, undressed and climbed into her bed, her mind dazed with the events of the evening. What had begun as an act of protocol had ended in a burgeoning love affair. She stared up at the ceiling of her bedroom, smiling, confused, and even then, slightly worried by the boyishness she saw so clearly in the man.

The love-making, when it came, was as good as she had expected, but as time passed and she became closer to him, the childishness of his character became more and more a factor in putting distance between them. And now, in the perspective of their situation, she saw that her problem in dealing with David was simply that she had no idea which he was in reality – the man or the child. With her, he acted the man, but threatened by Speers's authority, he became a child. If they ever escaped from here, she thought, as they glided through the darkness, she hoped that David would find the man in himself, and put an end to the child, although she knew that should they survive, her love for him would be a withered thing. She would be his lover now, both for him and selfishly, but if they survived she would end it, for both their sakes.

She opened her eyes, the slowing of the boat bringing her out of her musing half sleep. She sat up slightly, careful not to disturb David, and looked forward. Even as she looked, the beam of light from Speers's lamp picked out a sudden widening of the channel. Within seconds the narrow tunnel had fanned out into a wide, low-ceilinged passage, and then widened again in a smooth sweep as the ceiling rose and the banks receded. A moment later and the beam of light was swallowed up as it skittered over the placid inky surface of an underground lake of immense proportions. She blinked and her eyes automatically went to the roof over them. If it hadn't been for the pale, slightly-illuminated tips of the ranks of stalactites the illusion that they were floating on the surface of some above-ground lake would have been perfect. Even so the lake was beautiful.

'*C'est magnifique!*' she whispered, crouching in the bottom of the raft.

'You say something?' said Speers from ahead. Irene worked her way forward. If Speers was going to talk she wanted it to be in whispers so as not to awaken David. She laughed at herself as she moved up toward Speers; even now she was treating David as though he was a sick child in need of sleep.

'Is is very beautiful, yes?' said Irene, wedging herself in at the bow of the raft, careful not to come too close to the cave diver. He turned to her, his lips pulled back into a taut smile. Irene did her best to smile back, but the filth on the man's body, and the harsh shadow of his face, unshaven since the time of the collapse, was frightening. He looked like an animal.

'Yeah,' said Speers. 'Very pretty.' He eyed her carefully, keeping his smile.

'How far across do you think it is?' asked Irene nervously, wishing now that she had stayed with David in the rear of the raft.

'Impossible to say,' he muttered, staring out across the

water, the beam of the lamp lashed to the side of the boat running ahead of them across the still water without reaching the far side. 'That light's good for a hundred, hundred and fifty yards maybe. Somewhere past that.'

'Will you need help paddling?' she asked. Speers laughed.

'Not going to paddle,' he said. 'The only way to find the exit point is to let us drift. Current's weak, but we're still moving. It'll take a bit of time maybe but I'm not busting my ass rowing around this goddamn place looking for the drain hole when I don't have to. When we get across I'm going to set up camp, eat and get some sleep.' Irene nodded without replying. There was a long silence.

'Do you think we'll find the others?' she asked. Speers looked around, staring at her, his eyes wide in mock amazement.

'I didn't know we were looking,' he said.

'I'm serious,' answered Irene, annoyed by the man's flagrant condescension.

'So am I, doll, so am I,' replied Speers, his voice cold. 'We're following this son of a bitching river until it spills out into the sunshine. It's like paddling across the lake – I'm not doing anything I don't have to, and that includes trying to run down the Jap and your old man.'

'You are heartless,' said Irene, venom in her voice. Speers shrugged and turned back to the lake.

'I may be heartless, but I guarantee, if it was you and me and lover-boy back there who got split off from the river, old Izo would do the same thing. The Jap's no fool – he knows we aren't looking for him. If he can get out, that's terrific, but I'm not risking my life for his. Its a simple matter of survival, sweetheart.'

'Do not call me that,' snapped Irene, the fact that she would probably never see her father again dawning on her for the first time.

'Just trying to be pleasant,' said Speers, his smile broad. Suddenly he pointed forward. Irene followed his finger. 'There you go,' he said. 'Land ho.' He was right. Faintly coming into sight at the edge of the light was a grey multi-ledged flow-stone bank. At one time or another the levels of the lake had fluctuated, each time leaving a smooth plane of rock deposit to mark its passing. There was more than enough room to pull up the raft and make some sort of camp.

Speers reached up and flicked on his helmet lamp. He swung his head around, and quickly found the dark oval slit that marked the river outlet. He grunted to himself, nodding. He rummaged around beside him and came up with the small collapsible paddle that was used with the raft. He dug into the back water, pulling them in slow jerking lunges towards the shore.

'You cook,' he said, as they neared the shore. 'There's food in the top duffel bag, and the spare Primus is lying around loose somewhere. When we land you can wake up lover-boy and get him to help you.' There was no question in the harsh man's voice — he was giving an order, and he expected it to be obeyed. A moment later the bottom of the raft scraped on an unseen ledge just below the surface and they came to a sliding stop. They had landed.

2

Frank Speers sat cross-legged in front of the gently hissing Primus stove, his eyes fixed on the two sleeping figures a few feet away. Penfold and the woman slept close together, back to front, gaining what warmth they could. Even fully clothed, complete with a bulky sweater, the woman was attractive. Speers watched the rise and fall of her breasts and felt the fabric of his jeans draw tight. It wasn't the first time he'd been aroused by her either. He snorted to himself and swallowed another mouthful of coffee made with the bitter, mineral-laden water of the river and the scarce remnants of a jar of instant.

'Long time now,' he said to himself in a whisper, keeping his eyes on Irene. In fact it was so long ago, he couldn't remember the last time he'd had a woman without paying for it.

It hadn't always been that way. Growing up in the Umatilla

area of Florida's heartland women had been easy to come by, and just as easy to lose. He could remember the first one clearly enough, even though her name had long since faded from his memory. She'd been dark, with maybe a little Indian in her, the daughter of one of the migrant pickers that came and went during the picking season when the oranges were ripe. He'd taken her in the night, almost under her father's nose, nestling her down on the warm soil only a few feet away from the shack where the rest of her family stayed during the harvest. God only knew why she'd done it with him. Maybe she'd expected him to pay her, or treat her family better, or maybe she'd done it simply because he'd shown an interest.

His problem was that he'd never wanted to settle down, and there didn't seem to be any percentage in women doing it unless there was that chance they might hook you, and he'd never lied to anyone about that. The thought of marriage and children was enough to make him run like hell. He didn't want the hardship and boredom he'd seen his own mother and father endure on their small orchard farm, beating their brains out each year just to get by.

The diving hadn't helped his getting along with women either. It tended to make for something less than romantic conversation when he described his job, even when he embellished it with stories of things he'd found while checking sewer blockages, and there wasn't a hell of a lot interesting you could say about chipping rust and shit off the pylons of offshore drill rigs.

Eventually he'd just stopped trying with women. There were plenty of them to be had in Miami and Orlando and just about anywhere else he worked, and in the end he found a solution to the question of women which was more than satisfactory; he paid for exactly what he got, and there was nothing left when it was over except the taste of stale liquor on his breath and an easing of the tensions in his crotch, for a little while at least.

At twenty dollars a week for the last ten years, he figured he'd spent about ten thousand dollars on women. A lot of money sure, but it was still a hell of a lot less than being married would have cost him.

But it was different now. Here. He swigged the rest of the coffee and put the cup down gently on the ground. He stared at Irene, feeling the hot pump of blood through his veins. The memory of the sounds he had heard in the darkness of the insect cave came back to him. He'd listened to her short gasping breaths and the slap of flesh, and then the sharp moans from her and it had almost driven him crazy. The Tarvanin woman had been getting her ashes hauled as well, with the Jap no less, and it infuriated him. He was a man too, and he was damned if he was going to die down in this slimy hell hole without having one last piece of ass. He let his eyes linger on the inner crease of fabric at Irene's hip. If she'd take lover boy, she could take him as well.

He stood, his face set firm and hard with resolve. He padded over to where the two young people slept and touched her shoulder. She stirred but didn't waken. He remembered a trick a buddy had taught him in the navy. The guy said he'd learned it from a commando or something. Speers placed his hand over Irene's ear, pressing gently, changing the air pressure against her ear drum fractionally. Her eyes snapped open instantly and she stared up at Speers. He put a finger to his lips and motioned her to get up.

'What do you want?' she asked suspiciously, her voice low.

'You,' said Speers, his mouth spread into the familiar death's-head grin that seemed to be his trademark.

'You are insane,' said Irene. 'Go away.'

'Bullshit,' said Speers. 'You and me are going to get it on, and I don't care what you, or what lover-boy thinks about it. I've been wanting you from the beginning, and now I'm going to have you.'

'That is rape,' said Irene, raising her voice. Beside her David Penfold began to stir.

'No, it's not,' said Speers, extending his hand to her. 'Down here there's no such thing as rape. There's only conquest. The strong takes from the weak, and I think even you're smart enough to know that lover-boy there isn't any fountain of strength or whatever you want to call it.' He snapped his fingers noisily. 'Come on. I've got a blanket roll.'

'What the hell is going on?' asked David Penfold, awakening. He sat up, blinking in the dim light from the Primus.

'I'm taking your woman, lover-boy,' said Speers. He grabbed Irene by the wrist and started dragging her to her feet.

'This is crazy!' said David. He struggled upright. 'Irene, what the hell is this?' Irene managed to shake loose from Speers. She stumbled to her feet and backed away from both men.

'Speers wants to rape me,' said Irene, her voice shaking. Instinctively she wrapped her arms across her chest.

'Forget it, Speers,' said David, his voice dark with anger. He reached to his belt and pulled out the diver's knife Speers had given him to cut the line holding the other rafts. He held the knife out threateningly, its oiled blade glistening in the blue light of the stove.

'You're kidding!' laughed Speers. He walked slowly around David, edging towards Irene. David leapt between them, still holding the knife outstretched.

'You're going to kill me?' asked Speers. 'You kill me and you think you'll ever get out of here alive? You, lover-boy, leading your lady love by the hand. Without me you don't go anywhere, and without her I don't take you, get the picture.'

'I'll manage,' snapped David. Behind him he could hear Irene's rapid breathing.

'And if we hit something like another tunnel filled with water, one we have to use *my* tanks to get through? What do you know about Scuba, lover-boy?'

'I'll learn,' said David. Speers laughed again.

'You won't learn, you'll die, lover-boy, and the lady with you. Both of you are going to die for her honour?'

David felt a hand on his shoulder. He turned slightly and saw Irene beside him.

'He is right, David,' she said wearily. 'Without him we will never make it. And we would always wonder if he was going to abandon us. It is a small enough price to pay.'

'You can't be serious!' he sputtered. 'You're going to . . . to . . . screw with that bastard?' She nodded.

'There is no other way. If he wants it, I will give it,' she said. She stared at Speers, her eyes cold as death, then turned back to David. 'This is not real, David. None of this is real. We are living a nightmare, and Speers is part of that nightmare. And it is my decision, not yours. If there is any hurt, it is my hurt, not yours, do you understand me, David?'

'I must be going out of my mind!' moaned David, looking from Irene to Speers and back again. 'You're about to sleep with someone else and you're acting as though you don't even care!'

'I don't,' she said briefly. 'I cannot afford to.' She stepped around the hissing Primus and joined Speers. The rough-faced diver grinned across the sputtering light.

'Why don't you just toss that knife over here, lover-boy?' he said softly. 'You still having that in your hand might, well, you know, put me a bit off my stride.'

For a single instant David tensed, his muscles willing him to leap across the small, gently flaming stove and drive the knife deep into the arrogant, smiling bastard's chest. Irene's voice, calm and even, stopped him.

'Give him the knife, David. Give him the knife and then go away for a little while.'

Eyes wide, still not believing what was going on, David dropped the knife and backed slowly away, stumbling over the lava-like waves of rock that made up the stone ledges of the lake-shore. Speers waited until David had gone back twenty-five or thirty feet and then, still watching him, the diver bent low, his face thrown into terrible relief by the flames, and turned off the stove. Darkness collapsed around him and David fell to his knees on the hard rock, pounding his fists until they bled, raging silently at his cowardice. He raised his hands to his ears, trying to block out the whispering echo of the diver's barking laugh in the distance, and failed. There, on his knees, staring into the velvet blackness, his body shook with his hatred for Frank Speers, and even more, his hatred for himself.

CHAPTER TEN

1

'The question is, which way did he go, forward or back,' said Tony Grace. Izo Harada shone the beam of his hand-held lamp around the small cave, looking for some trace of the old man's movements. The soft, dust-like clay of the way they had come wasn't repeated in the passageway ahead. Izo guessed that the sediment in the lower passage had been washed down from an ancient pothole, now closed, in the ceiling above them, while the upper passage was bare rock. The lower passage was marred by their own footsteps, so there was no way to tell which way Bouchard had gone.

'I'll give you odds he went ahead,' said Mariea Tarvanin, peering up the angular passage leading out of the cave. 'He might be crazy, but I don't think he'd risk going back to the big cave. He saw those bugs too.'

'But why on earth did he go anywhere at all?' asked Grace, pursing his lips thoughtfully. 'He looked about dead when we arrived. I wouldn't have given him credit for suddenly haring off like that.'

'People do desperate things under stress,' said Izo. He put the lamp down on the ground and shrugged into the knapsack. 'It is possible that he awoke and panicked.'

'I know that feeling,' muttered the lanky journalist. 'I've wanted to cut and run more than once in the past little while. You have this great whacking voice inside your head screaming at you to get out, get out.'

'You too?' grinned Mariea. 'Not only do you steal my bathtime fantasies but you hear the same crazy voices.'

'Perhaps we should get married,' said Grace. Mariea threw a quick look in Izo's direction, then turned back to Grace.

'Sorry,' she said. 'I'm taken for the duration.' The journa-

181

list smiled back at her.

'A mere joke,' he said dryly. 'I'd already gathered that your heart pined for another.'

'A truly gallant knight,' said Mariea, laughing. She turned back to Izo. 'So, which way?' she asked. Izo was shining the light down the upper passageway. It was as narrow as the one they had entered the cave through, but while the lower tunnel had been smooth and almost perfectly oval, the upper route was spiked and uneven, with boulders in jagged shapes tumbled on the floor, making walking difficult. In geological terms the passageway had gone "rotten", its walls and ceiling so ancient that they were in a state of collapse. Eventually the tunnel would disappear, sealed by falling rock from above.

'Ahead,' said Izo finally. 'And hope that he has gone this way. Without food or water he will not be able to get very far, especially in his condition.' The geologist stepped into the narrow tunnel, the light splaying out ahead of him. Mariea went after him, followed by Tony Grace.

After an hour they still had found no trace of the missing archaeologist.

'I don't believe it,' said Tony Grace, flopping down on a large rock to rest, his breath coming hard. 'That old man must be half goat to have got this far. And in the dark as well.'

'Not in the dark,' said Izo. 'He took my helmet and the lamp.'

'Bully,' said the journalist, a surprised look on his face. 'Then the old sot wasn't completely crazy after all.'

'Apparently not,' said Izo.

'Let's get going,' said Mariea tensely. 'This place gives me the creeps.'

'More than any other place we've been in the past few days?' asked Grace.

'It's so dead,' she said slowly, looking around. The walls of the tunnel were only an arm's length away, while the roof above them was cracked and broken, large, gaping shadows showing where pieces had collapsed. 'I get the feeling the whole place is going to cave in on us any minute.'

'Little of this fall is recent,' said Izo, trying to calm her fears. 'I don't think you have anything to fear. The chances of being here when part of the roof comes down are very slim.'

'Umm,' said Tony. 'I did an article on that kind of thing once. It's rather like flying. Your chances of being in an air crash for instance are well over a million to one.'

'Tell that to the people who just happen to be the "one" in your statistic,' answered Mariea. 'Anyway, odds or not, let's get going.'

'All right,' said Izo. 'We will continue.' They began moving ahead again.

'On the other hand,' said Tony Grace, bringing up the rear, 'we did happen to be in that cave when there was an earthquake. I wonder what the odds were of that happening?'

'Shut up, Tony,' said Mariea, clambering over yet another chunk of rock in the passageway.

2

According to Izo's watch they had been travelling through the broken-roofed passage for almost three hours when it suddenly changed. Coming over a mound of rubble that almost completely blocked their way they found that the tunnel abruptly fell, forming an obliquely-angled hole that led into the darkness beyond. The hole was no more than two feet wide and to the untrained eyes of Mariea Tarvanin and Tony Grace it seemed impassable. It was here that they found the first sign of Dr Bouchard — a smear of blood left on a sharp rock outcropping adjacent to the hole.

'So where the hell is he?' asked Tony Grace, squatting in front of the hole in the tunnel floor. 'He certainly didn't go down *that*.'

'He must have,' said Mariea, looking at the small aperture. 'Though God knows how he did it.'

'The technique is called reptation,' said Izo, shining his lamp down into the cavity. 'Although I doubt that Dr Bouchard was thinking in technical terms. It means to crawl like a reptile.' The geologist reached out and dabbed the small patch of blood with his finger. 'He may have become trapped part way through and struggled,' he said.

'Are we going to follow him?' asked Mariea. Izo nodded.

'Once again, we have little choice,' he said. 'It looks small, I know, but I have traversed much smaller, I assure you, Mariea.'

'Marvellous,' said Tony. 'That's fine for you, but what about me? If I got stuck in there I'd go stark raving mad.'

'Look at your shoulders,' said Izo, smiling. 'They are much narrower than mine, and the shoulders are the widest part of the body. If I can get through, so can you. Unhappily we have no rope to bind us together.'

'Why would we need rope?' asked Mariea.

'It may be a pot,' said Izo. 'In which case it could become a vertical fall without any warning.'

'For vertical fall I gather we can read straight down?' said Tony Grace.

'Perhaps,' said Izo. 'At any rate I shall go down it feet first, just in case. Would you hold the lamp?' He handed the light to the journalist and took off the knapsack. – 'Shine the light directly into the hole as I go down. When I give you the word, pass me the knapsack, and then send Mariea after me. Give her the lamp. Follow when you hear my order.'

The geologist slowly backed down the hole, wriggling slightly to pass his shoulders through the narrow space. A moment later his voice echoed up to the other two.

'The angle is very shallow,' he called. 'Much like the passage to the lower cave at Subrano! Mariea should come down head first. Push the knapsack in front of you as you come!'

'Off you go, dear,' said Tony, patting Mariea on the shoulder. She smiled at him sourly.

'If I didn't like you so much I'd kick your ass around the block,' she said.

'It's my British sense of humour,' he grinned back. 'It's far too sophisticated for you colonial types.' He gave her a little push towards the hole. 'Go on, m'lady, your Samurai is calling, and I'll be right behind you, never fear.'

Mariea fell to her knees, pushed the knapsack down the hole and then followed it, the lamp in her hand casting an eerie glow that filtered back up into the upper passage. It receded quickly as she moved downward. Tony Grace took a last look around the ruined passage and grimaced.

'Just when I was getting used to it,' he muttered under his breath. Then, gritting his teeth against the rising flood of claustrophobia that threatened to engulf him, he went head-first down the hole, scrabbling with his hands as he moved, trying to keep the faint glow of Mariea's lamp in sight.

For Tony Grace the crawl through the "squeeze" seemed endless, but less than a minute actually passed between his entrance into the hole and his exit. He pushed himself out of the downside entrance, following the glow of Maria's lamp, and stood finally, to find himself in a long cavern, less than six feet high, so that he could not stand up right. Maria and Izo crouched together, looking down the length of the large, basement like room, the lamp shining across a dry floor, its surface cracked in irregular rectangles, reminding him of pictures he'd seen of parched desert areas. It was obvious that once upon a time the floor of the cave had been mud.

'Thank God that's . . .' he began, rubbing at the aching muscles in his arms.

'Quiet!' snapped Mariea, and pointed. Then Tony saw what they were looking at.

There, at the far end of the cave, covered in filth, his hair in a tangled mass and his eyes glowing fiercely in the light from the lamp Izo now held, was Dr Alain Bouchard. One sleeve of his sweater was hanging loose and Tony Grace could see a large area of what appeared to be blood. The elderly man crouched on a small mound of rock close to a shadowed area that looked as though it might be the cavern exit. Izo's helmet lay at the man's feet, its light casting a dim glow on the cave floor.

Suddenly Bouchard began to scream, a wild babble of French that echoed insanely from the low roof and angular walls of the cave.

'What's he saying?' asked Mariea. Tony Grace, the only one of the three who spoke French, listened, trying to decipher the crazed sentences.

'He's warning us away,' he said at last. 'He says we're

agents of the devil, sent to take him down to Hades. Something like that. He's gone right off his nut.'

'So what do we do?' asked Mariea, apprehensively, looking down the cave at the man.

'Go to him,' said Izo, watching Bouchard carefully. 'Go to him slowly and try to calm him.'

'Right,' muttered Tony Grace. 'And who's going to play psychiatrist, may I ask?'

'You can speak French,' said Mariea.

'Marvellous,' said the journalist. 'I can tell him when the next train for Lyon leaves the station. Izo's the philosopher, let him handle it. Bouchard doesn't need conversation, he needs a tranquillizer.'

The elderly archaeologist began to scream at them again, backing up until he was against the wall of the cave. Even from where they stood the others could see the spittle forming at the man's mouth, dripping down over his chin.

'Lovely,' whispered Tony Grace. 'Now he's drooling.'

'Forget that,' said Mariea. 'What's he saying, for Christ's sake!' Tony listened again, his brow furrowing as he tried to make sense of the man's ramblings.

'I think he's afraid to go on,' said the journalist. 'He keeps talking about fire and brimstone. He really does think he's on his way to hell.'

'He may not be far off the mark, either,' said Mariea, sniffing. 'Do you smell that, Izo?' The geologist tested the air and frowned. Tony Grace followed suit.

'Sulphur?' asked the journalist.

'Yes,' said the geologist finally.

'And it's hotter, too, or is that just my fertile imagination?' said Tony Grace. Sweat was beginning to form on his brow, and not because of his recent exertions in the "squeeze". 'What the hell is it, Izo?'

'I'm not certain,' said the geologist, 'but I think the source of both the smell and the rising heat come from that tunnel just beyond Dr Bouchard. It may be a hot spring.'

'Water?' asked Grace.

'Mineral water, and hot,' said Izo. 'Probably unfit to drink.'

'I haven't had anything liquid since the big cave,' said the journalist, licking his lips. 'I'd drink anything right now, Satan's brew or not.'

'We have to deal with Bouchard first,' reminded Mariea. Izo nodded.

'I will try and calm him,' said the Japanese softly. In a half-crouch he began making his way across the floor of the cave, his feet sinking deeply into the ancient dried mud as it gave beneath his weight. For a moment Bouchard continued his high-pitched harangue, but stopped when he saw Izo approaching. The wild-eyed man picked up the helmet lamp and brandished it at the geologist, edging towards the irregularly-shaped exit from the cave.

'He's going to bolt,' whispered Tony Grace to Mariea. They watched as Izo stopped halfway across the cave floor and began to speak softly in Japanese, the gentle cadence of the words stopping Bouchard. The old man listened for a few moments and then began to laugh, the sound spewing out of his mouth in spitting jerks. Izo took another step forward and Bouchard thrust the helmet out again, swinging it back and forth like a weapon. He began to screech at Izo furiously.

'Now what?' asked Mariea.

'He thinks Izo is the devil now,' said Grace. 'He's calling on the holy trinity to come to his aid.' Izo began moving ahead again, and then Bouchard began scrabbling across the mud floor, crab-like, his back still to the wall.

'He's off!' said Tony. Izo pushed forward, his feet dragging in the deep material on the floor. He lunged at Bouchard and missed. The old man leapt into the dark mouth of the cave exit and was gone. Mariea and Tony came after Izo rapidly, joining him at the broad fissure in the cave wall. All of them were covered in dust pushed up from the cave floor.

'Now what?' asked Tony.

'We follow him, quickly,' said Izo. He took the lamp from Mariea and headed into the tunnel.

The floor of the opening headed downward at an angle, forcing the trio into a stumbling run to keep from falling as they chased after Bouchard. The walls came together rapidly until they were no wider than a man's shoulders, the rough, deeply-cracked rock encrusted with thin, razor-edged crystals of calcite that tore at their clothing. Above them, the roof lowered until it was low enough to make them duck, and still the passage descended.

Without warning the floor dropped away beneath Izo's feet and he fell back, his fall cushioned by the knapsack. He began to slide downward, unable to brake because of the sharp layers of calcite that would have flayed his hands to the bone. Instead he tried to dig his boots into the hard rock floor, but it helped only fractionally. If the angle of descent became any steeper he would fall headlong, the others after him. From ahead the smell of the sulphur became stronger and Izo had a quick horrifying image of the tube he was sliding down emptying directly into a steaming fumarole in the earth, a deep pit of water, heated to boiling by the white-hot magma below the earth's crust.

An instant later he reached the bottom of the precipitous passage, wincing with pain as Mariea Tarvanin's booted feet struck him in the small of the back. Both of them struggled out of the way just as Tony Grace came rocketing down the last few feet of the slope. Izo climbed to his feet and pointed the lamp outward into the cave they had fallen into; as the light broke over the chamber he knew that his fears of falling into a fumarole had not been groundless.

The chamber was at least as large as the one in which they had encountered the centipedes; a long, roughly triangular cavern stretching out beyond the limits of Izo's lamp, the central hall draped and filigreed with hundreds of stalactites and gigantic columns encrusted with calcite and sulphur deposits. Scattered between the huge columns across the undulating floor of the chamber were dozens of rising plumes of steam, some coming from what seemed to be pools of water, others venting from bubbling cauldrons of fuming mud. The entire cavern was filled with a steady roaring hiss as the steam rose, filling the air with the thick stench of sulphur, and coating the walls and ceiling with crystalline deposits that glistened like jewels as Izo swung the lamp to and fro, searching for Bouchard.

'Can you see him?' asked Mariea, trying to wipe some of

the dust and grime from her face.

'There!' said Izo, finally picking off the lone figure of the archaeologist.

'My God!' whispered Tony, his voice barely audible above the sounds of the escaping steam. 'He's going to kill himself!'

Somehow, with nothing but the fading beam of Izo's helmet lamp to guide him, Bouchard had made his way into the centre of the cavern, scaling a pile of rubble fallen from the roof of the chamber a millenium ago. From where they stood, still high on the sloping rear wall of the cave, the three could see that Bouchard was completely surrounded by vast pools of steaming mud and water, his only way forward being across a narrow ledge running low between two of the circular pits. Unless he came back to join them.

'He'll never make it across that,' said Mariea.

'We have to make him come back this way,' said Izo, training the light on Bouchard.

'I don't think so,' said Tony Grace. 'He's on the move again.' The journalist was right. Bouchard had been standing still until then, waiting on the pile of ancient limestone. Now he was going down it, headed for the ledge between the pools.

Without stopping to explain, Izo headed forward at a loping run, cutting down the slope to the floor of the cavern, then threading his way between the columns and pools, racing towards the pile of rubble. Mariea and Tony followed a few seconds behind, slipping on the slimy surface of the rock which was perpetually drenched by the steam filling the air of the cave.

Bouchard was halfway across the ledge when they reached the top of the rubble pile. Izo had thrown off the knapsack and was slowly moving down the far slope of the pile.

'Bouchard!' he called. 'Stand still!' The geologist's voice rang with authority. It was enough to stop the panic-stricken archaeologist. The old man paused midway across the ledge at a point where it began to narrow until it was less than a foot across. To the left was a pool of mud at least thirty feet across, its surface grunting with large bubbles as sulphurous gasses from somewhere in the bowels of the earth rose to the surface. To the right was a slightly smaller pool of dark water, its

189

surface cut with wisps of steam, the edges of the pool rimmed with a dozen different mineral deposits. Izo made it to the base of the rubble pile and began to walk carefully along the ledge. Tony Grace began slipping down the pile towards the two men, but Mariea grasped him by the wrist and pulled him back.

'Let him do it alone,' she said.

Slowly, Izo made his way across the ledge until he was less than ten feet from Bouchard. The old man's arms, legs and hands were a mass of deep gouges and Izo knew that Bouchard had taken the climb down the last tunnel hard. As Harada approached, the terrified Bouchard cringed, edging farther along the ledge. Izo stopped.

'Bouchard,' he said. 'Come to me!'

'You are the devil!' screamed the old man, backing up. 'I have sinned but I have made my confession! You cannot take me!'

'I am not the devil,' said Izo firmly, his voice echoing strongly from the towers and galleries of the giant cave. 'I am your friend!'

'You lie!' screamed Bouchard. 'You lied to all of us. You have led us into hell!'

'Bouchard!' commanded Izo. 'You will die if you go any further! Come to me! Now! Before it is too late.'

Painfully, the old man raised his arm and began to cross himself, mumbling the ancient invocation. With each word he took another step backward, feet sliding on the slippery surface of the rock.

'*In nomine Patris, et Filii, et Spiritus Sancti . . .*'

'Bouchard!' cried out Izo. But it was too late. The old man slid on the rock, his feet skating on the treacherous surface of the ledge. For a moment he hung suspended over the pool of fuming mud, and then he dropped, a huge gout of the brown sulphurous ooze flying up, splattering on to the ledge and Izo. The geologist rushed forward and dropped on to his hands and knees at the point where Bouchard had fallen. The old man flailed in the thick mud, screaming horribly as the superheated muck seared his flesh. Izo tore off his heavy sweater and flung one end of it toward the sinking man, but it was hopeless, Bouchard was beyond help. From their vantage point on the mound Mariea Tarvanin and Tony Grace watched as the old man was sucked downward, almost as though he was being pulled deeper by some terrible unseen creature who dwelt in the suppurating ooze. He was still screaming as the mud rose to his chin, his arms striking the boiling surface of the pool, and then he was gone, the mud covering his tortured face, leaving nothing but two arms above the surface, the hands opening and closing spasmodically in a hideous parody of a farewell gesture. Then the arms slid beneath the surface and there was nothing.

Izo rose to his knees and stared down into the grotesquely bubbling pool. He stayed like that for a long moment, then dragged his sweater back and stood slowly. He turned and looked back at the two people on the mound and from where she stood Mariea was sure that she could see something die in her friend's eyes.

'Come on,' she said to Grace quietly. And together they climbed down the sloping pile of limestone rubble towards Izo and the horrible place where Alain Bouchard had died.

CHAPTER ELEVEN

1

The raft moved sluggishly along the slow-moving river, the speed of its current cut in half by the immense reservoir of water in the lake far behind them. Without the standard of Izo Harada's chronometer there was nothing to mark the passage of time as they meandered along, but as far as David Penfold could tell, at least twelve hours had passed since the obscene confrontation between himself and Speers. In all that time he had said nothing to either the cave diver or Irene Bouchard.

Even though he knew that her decision to let Speers have her was based on logic, he still could not come to terms with the terrible jealousy he felt, or the overwhelming sense of inadequacy that accompanied it. He felt somehow that he had failed her, that he should have defended her better, even though he knew that any such defence, even if it had been successful, would have been worse than useless. Without Speers they were completely helpless, and both of them knew it.

Thankfully Speers had not used his power to bait the young archaeologist; he had simply used Irene and returned her without saying anything, although there was the tacit understanding that should he want her again, he would take her just as informally.

Their places in the raft were as before, with David and Irene in the rear and Speers in the bow with the lamp; the only difference was the space between David and Irene. Before they had sat close together, now Irene sat as far as she could from David and the few times their eyes met she looked away quickly.

For Irene Bouchard, the experience with Speers had been devastating. The act itself had been mercifully brief, but its aftermath had left Irene in a state of utter confusion. At first she tried to slough the event off, marking it down to the extreme situation they were in, but her mind would not let it rest. She had been used, not horribly or violently, but simply used, as casually as someone would use a piece of tissue. Speers had made no attempt to excite her, or interest her in his prowess. He had simply lubricated himself with spittle, entered her and ejaculated, treating her neither with tenderness nor anger. He had withdrawn from her and then, half an hour later, he had requested that she take him in her mouth. She did so, and once again he orgasmed. A few minutes later he had fallen asleep, wrapped in his bedroll. She had taken one of the small flashlights from Speers's cache and gone in search of David, finding him huddled less than fifty feet from where she had left him. He awakened when she turned on the stove to create some warmth, but he had not approached even though she knew that he was awake. He had not spoken to her, nor she to him, so they were left alone with their thoughts.

At first Irene had wanted to comfort David, and tell him that the sex with Speers meant nothing and changed nothing between them, but even as the thought formed in her mind she saw its hypocrisy. The sex had changed things; not so much because it was a mark of infidelity but simply because of his intolerance of it. For the first time in her life, there, a thousand feet below the surface of the earth, Irene knew what it was to be a woman in a world of men. Speers had used her casually, as though she was less than human, and David's jealous reaction made it clear to her that no matter how he might protest, the basis of his feeling for her centred around the zone between her thighs.

She suddenly understood that womanhood was timeless, and that except in very superficial ways nothing had changed since Mariea Tarvanin's Khan, the Neanderthal artist from Subrano, had walked the earth. In fact, in a major sense, things had become worse. In Khan's day there were taboos about menstruating women, or pregnant women, leaving them at least with some kind of mystery and power. Now even that was gone.

As she sat hunched in front of the meagre warmth from the Primus she wondered if she would become pregnant. She had not brought her diaphragm with her, knowing that it would tempt her to sleep with David if the chance arose, and dreading her father's discovery of it. She tried to calculate when her last period had been and gave it up; there was no way she could be sure of dates. And if she was pregnant she would have no idea who the father was — David or Frank Speers.

She dozed fitfully in front of the stove, the same thoughts going around and around in her head, and the next day, on the river once again, she found herself still thinking about it. Both the man in the front of the small raft and the man beside her had robbed her of herself and the only real conclusion she came to was that they were equally guilty of rape.

As they moved steadily along the winding, rough-walled channel she let the word come into her mind again and again. Rape. She tried to make it force her to anger, but all she felt was a strange, floating feeling that somehow she had become liberated by the whole thing. She smiled to herself, and realized that her best revenge would simply be to survive.

2

The unmarked hours passed slowly on the river, the harsh and dim-lit limestone landscape on either side of them always changing, but seldom very different. The river twisted and turned, following faults in the massive slabs of rock, sometimes seeming to turn back on itself, but inevitably moving onward into the darkness that was barely breached by the searching light commanded by Speers at the head of the boat. Now and again David picked off small tunnels running off on one side or the other but neither Speers nor Irene paid them any heed. From time to time as well, the tunnel walls narrowed or widened, but for the most part they maintained a width of about thirty feet, the ragged dripping ceiling above them seldom less than twenty feet away.

Finally, after what seemed to be an age, Speers slid the small raft to the edge of the tunnel. They approached a wide ledge cut into the rock, creating a platform forty or fifty feet in length, jutting out over the sluggish water.

'We'll camp here,' said Speers. He hopped out of the raft, carrying a line with him, snagging the small craft's tether to a rock outcrop, tying it down expertly. Wordlessly, Irene clambered out of the raft, moving as far away from Speers as she could. 'Hand up the supplies,' ordered Speers. David did as he was told, lugging the heavy duffel bags, now musky with the odour of mildew and incipient rot, then lifting them up to Speers. The diver piled the bags carefully on the ledge, then offered a hand to David. Ignoring it, the young archaeologist boosted himself up onto the ledge. Speers shrugged and set about the task of unpacking the stove and some food.

On Speers's orders Irene cooked the meal, and the three survivors ate silently. Several times Speers tried to start a conversation, but neither David nor Irene made any attempt to respond. Finally the diver gave up. He unpacked his bedroll and after turning the Primus light down to a dull glow, he turned away from the other two and settled down to sleep. The relief in Irene's face as the hard-faced man turned away from the light was so intense that David almost felt it as a physical force. She had obviously been bracing herself for another sexual episode with the man. David waited until he heard the deep harsh sound of Speers's snoring breath before he moved across the ledge to where Irene sat huddled. He sat beside her for a long moment, not speaking. Finally, he reached out and touched her shoulder gently, his eyes questioning. She looked up at him, taking her eyes away from the cool light of the Primus, and smiled weakly.

'Are you all right?' asked David, his voice a whisper. Irene nodded.

'Of course I'm all right, David,' she answered. 'I'm not bleeding, am I?'

'No, but . . .' David didn't know how to pursue the subject. Irene sighed deeply.

'Look David, he, that man, has had my body, do you understand? He has taken me under duress when I was not willing, that is all. I have lost nothing of myself. I have lost no dignity, nor self-respect, or any of the other things that your damsels in distress are supposed to feel. I feel only disgust, David, and some anger that I am not a man.'

'Look . . .' began David again, 'I'm sorry.'

'For what?' asked Irene sharply. 'That he has had sex with me? That he has used my body?'

'I'm sorry that it happened,' said David lamely. 'Speers is a pig.'

'He is a man,' said Irene. 'And he took what he wanted, like all men.'

'Like me?' asked David. Irene shrugged.

'I do not think you are much different than he is, *chéri*,' she said. 'You see me as nothing more than a female body. As something to enjoy yourself with. I do not think you see me as a human being, David, any more than he does. You are more polite, yes, and you have more taste and education, but you and he are men, and see women the same way.'

'I don't think you understand me very well,' said David,

anger rising in his voice, 'if you think that I'd do something like he did to you.'

'If you had the need and the opportunity I think you would,' she said in reply. 'When we made love together I could feel the tension in you, draining out. I was some kind of release for you, that is all.'

'And I didn't provide anything like that for you?' asked David hotly. 'You've never used me that way?'

'Perhaps I have,' she said. 'It does not matter any more, David. I think what we had together is gone now. I care about nothing but myself and my survival. Do you understand that, David.'

'I love you,' said David simply. Irene smiled.

'I do not think so, David. And if you do, it is a love which I do not want any more. No, please go. I want to sleep.'

David stood up and looked down at her, a wave of anger bursting over him. He turned abruptly and stared at the sleeping form of Speers, a dozen yards away.

'You want me to kill him, is that it?' asked David. 'I'm supposed to defend your goddamn honour like some kind of knight in shining armour? Is that the kind of thing your old man taught you. Chivalry and chauvinism? Is that what you want?' he hissed.

'I want nothing from you,' she said, looking up at him, her large eyes dark with fatigue. 'From you or anyone else. If you kill him, it will be for yourself, David, not for my honour.'

David looked down at her, his mind whirling, desperately trying to come up with something that could be said, to salvage what there had been between them, but nothing came. He shook his head slowly and walked away, moving to the far end of the ledge, close to where the boat was moored. He stared down at the inky water, barely visible a few feet below him in the pale light reflected off the walls of the tunnel by the Primus. He let his hand reach out and grasp the cold, slippery length of the nylon line, fondling it as a cold ache formed in the pit of his stomach and tears welled up in his eyes.

It had happened to him endlessly, he thought to himself. Something good would happen to him, and then it would be taken away. As though his life was a long, taunting school-yard game. He shook his head, feeling the warmth of his tears flowing down his grime-covered cheeks. Self-pity. That's what his father would call it. But his father was dead, so it would be Irene who would tell him that he was feeling sorry for himself. But that was gone as well, so there was nobody to taunt him except himself.

He kept his fingers on the nylon cord, and stared down into the slowly moving water. Maybe she was right. Maybe it didn't matter anymore. They were as good as dead, and already buried. What they were now was not alive. They were shades, acting out a mockery of life in a hideous under-ground limbo. Mariea had named the river well, because it was definitely carrying them to Hades. Mariea. Gone now with all the others. He ran his other hand through the tangled mat of his hair. Christ! More than a dozen people had gone down into the Subrano Cave, and now there were only three left alive. He turned his head, looking back along the ledge. He could see the dark shape of Speers and beyond that he could see Irene, now settled for sleep herself. He looked down again at the rope in his hand. It would only take a few seconds and he could be gone. He could sit back in the boat, with Speers's lamp to guide him, and glide off to eternity. Or better still, why take the boat? All he had to do was let himself down into the cold water and be carried away, to become food for the swarming life that inhabited the dark currents. Or would he die? Maybe he would survive, a Gollum on the Styx, his flesh paling with the passing years, feasting on the sludge and slime, the raw meat of blind fish and the albino Proteus. Doomed to an existence of constantly ruined hope as he searched endlessly for an exit that didn't exist.

David shivered in the cool air of the cavern, the image of himself as a creature from a nightmare making bile rise in the back of his throat, filling his nostrils with an acid burning.

No, he didn't have the guts for suicide. He would do as he was told. He would bow to authority, the way he always had. His father, his teachers, his lovers, and Speers. He laughed quietly to himself as a tune came into his head.

'*We're off to see the Wizard, the wonderful Wizard of Oz,*

197

because, because, because, because, because . . . ' Maybe
that was it he thought. Maybe it wasn't the Styx at all. Maybe
it was the yellow brick road, and he was some latter-day lion,
off to get some courage. He turned away from the river,
retrieved his bedroll and, thinking of Judy Garland, he tried
to sleep.

3

Frank Speers woke from the nightmare, beads of sweat on his
forehead and his jaws aching from the harsh grating of his
clenched teeth. His father had been whipping him, the long
belt slicing down with that God-awful whistling sound he
remembered so well, the brass buckle cutting into the flesh of
his back and his buttocks, leaving scars he still carried.

Speers looked over his shoulder, past the dim light from
the Primus. Both Penfold and the woman seemed to be
asleep. He sat up quietly, using the back of his hand to wipe
away the sweat from his forehead. The dreams he had were a
curse he carried and he went in constant fear that someone
would find out the horrors he lived in the night. Jesus!
Sometimes it was enough almost to make him wet his sheets
like a kid. The worst was when he woke up crying. The
dreams were weakness, and weakness was something he
couldn't stand in others, and loathed in himself.

He padded across the damp rock to the Primus, gently
turning the knob and increasing the light, pushing back the
shadows of the ledge. He poured a measure of water from one
of the canteens into a small pot, threw in the final instant
coffee crystals and set the pot on the stove. He squatted
down, staring into the hissing flames, waiting for the mixture
to heat.

He wondered how long it was going to go on. From the
first moment of the collapse he had measured his life in
passing minutes, taking nothing for granted. He grimaced.
His whole life had been like that, really. He'd never been able
to count on much, if anything. Except himself. As he

squatted he lifted his arms, feeling the play of muscles across his chest. At forty he still had a better body than Penfold, or any of the others except the Jap, and he was gone now. His body had been the only thing he cared about for as long as he could remember.

He shook his head, a sour smile on his face. After the dreams he always went through the same ritual, the checklist of his life, making sure he was still the best. He supposed that it could have been different. When he was a kid the teachers had said he was smart, but his old man had never cared about that. His old man had only cared about the Groves.

'The Groves,' he whispered. The phrase brought back a thousand unbidden memories. He remembered seeing the book about skin-diving in the school library. He'd stared at the pictures of the cool water and the almost magical figures of the divers who made the sea their home. He'd taken the book out of the library and brought it home to show his father, but the old bastard had laughed and thrown the book across the room.

'Who needs a skin-diver in the Groves?' he'd boomed, laughing at Speers until tears ran down his face. He'd kept up a constant string of jokes about swimming around the orange trees, taking jabs at his son whenever he could, asking the boy if he'd like a spear-gun for Christmas so he could bring down more oranges than he could by hand. Finally Speers had forgotten about the book, tucking the memory of the pictures away in his soul until some future time.

It came sooner than he'd thought. His father had died and within a couple of years the Groves had become too much for his mother to manage and they'd been sold. Frank Speers and his mother moved to a small town outside of Orlando. He quit school and hit the road, earning his living up and down the length of the State, supporting himself on the boom of the middle and late fifties. He'd done everything from heavy construction to working on the offshore rigs in the Gulf, but he never really forgot the diving book. He took lessons whenever he could, and eventually, soon after his twentieth birthday, he'd received his certificate. He went home to his mother, staying long enough to borrow a thousand dollars from her. He'd bought enough basic equipment to get him started and he'd never looked back, working as a free-lance diver for whoever was hiring. Eventually he established a solid reputation in the business as the kind of man who'd do work that no one else would — the dirty jobs and the dangerous ones. It was a reputation that suited him just fine. No one bothered him, and the pay was good.

Loneliness was something that never bothered him; in fact he cherished it. He had no time for women, except those he paid for, and he didn't care for the company of men except when he was drinking. He exuded a toughness that kept most people at bay, and he preferred it that way.

Once he'd come close to loving someone, a woman he'd met while on a job in Switzerland, surveying a series of flooded caves for a German group who wanted to turn them into a tourist attraction. The woman had been one of the executives' secretaries and for a while Speers was willing to change his mind about living alone. It hadn't worked though, and when the tourist trap deal fell through, she'd gone back to Frankfurt with her boss. He'd gone on a drinking binge for a week after that, and later he thought of it as a narrow escape.

The coffee began steaming in the small pot and Speers removed it, turning down the flame of the Primus. He held the pot by its handle and blew on the coffee, cooling it. He took a hesitant sip, his eyes still on the steady flames of the stove.

He had his philosophy, he thought to himself, and it was a good one. He wanted nothing out of life, and was willing to give nothing. He simply wanted to live out his years, that was all. He looked around the confines of the river tunnel, watching as the shadows cast by the light from the stove flickered across the rutted, saw-toothed ceiling. He grunted softly to himself. It didn't look like he had many years left. By his estimation they had food enough for about two weeks on pretty good rations. He glanced at the sleeping forms of Irene and David Penfold. The food would last a hell of a lot longer if it was just him. He took a deep drink from the cup, then wiped his lips, enjoying the burning feeling as the hot liquid trickled down his throat.

Not that it mattered, he assured himself. They weren't going to last any two weeks. Two days was more like it, and that was if they were very lucky. The fluctuation of the river was indication enough that they were in trouble. Much as he hated to admit it, Speers knew that Harada was right. They had already been victimized by one sudden flooding, and judging by the slow current of the river now, it seemed likely that they were going to be in for another one. This time, he thought, they might not be so lucky.

He finished off the coffee and turned down the stove until its flame was barely visible, letting the shadows flow in until he sat alone in a tiny circle of the harsh blue light. He looked out into the darkness, wondering if he should wake up the woman again. It might help him sleep. He shrugged the idea off. Once was enough. She'd let him do anything he wanted to her, but there had been no life in her at all. She was no better than a whore, and he'd use her only when he really had to. He stood up, hugging himself against the cold air of the cavern, and went back to his bedroll.

CHAPTER TWELVE

1

There were a dozen apparent exits from the steaming cave in which Alain Bouchard had died, but at least half of those were all but completely filled with mud while most of the others were too small to be any use to a human being. There were only two possible choices; one was a downward-sloping passage that was barely more than a slit in the rock, a crack between two large rock formations. The floor of the fissure was split and wet, evidence that water flowed down it regularly. The other passage was much larger, a low, oval tunnel which, if they chose it, would force them to walk stooped over.

'Time to spin the wheel of fortune again,' said Tony Grace, raising his voice over the hissing roar of the boiling cauldrons of mud and steam in the giant cave.

'I'm for the big tunnel.'

'That's because you don't like the little slit,' said Mariea. The two exits were within a few feet of each other along the rear wall of the cavern. Izo stood and watched as a trickle of muddy water slowly made its way down the floor of the fissure tunnel.

'There is more chance if we take the narrow way,' he said at last. 'The larger tunnel is more convenient certainly, but it is dry, and from what I can tell it has been dry for some time.'

'That's fine by me,' muttered Tony. 'I've been wet for long enough.'

'Oh shut up,' said Mariea gently.

'If our object is to find the river again, then we must follow the water caves,' finished Izo.

'I still don't see the point of trying to make it to the river again,' said Tony, his voice serious now. 'We don't have any boats and you said yourself a long time ago that we couldn't survive in that water swimming.'

'We can only hope that we find the river again ahead of the others,' said Izo. There was little conviction in his voice.

'How the hell are we going to know if we're ahead or behind,' said Mariea, frowning. 'It's not like anyone's going to be leaving a trail of breadcrumbs or anything.'

'We have no choice,' said Izo. 'The only certain exit from this system of caves lies with the river.' The geologist frowned. 'We can only hope.'

'That's hardly a scientific approach,' said Tony Grace. He shrugged good-naturedly. 'But who needs science? If you say the narrow route, then that's the way we shall go.'

'Well,' said Mariea, smiling. 'At least you don't take much convincing.' The bony journalist grinned back at her and shrugged again.

'I'm hardly in a position to argue with Izo, now am I?' he answered. 'My best strategy so far has consisted of trouser-

202

wetting panic.' He shook his head. 'No. I'll back our oriental friend to the end. Lead on, Izo!'

Izo shone the beam of his lamp into the crack and led the way out of the steaming cave. Within a few moments the sound had disappeared behind them. Almost instantly Tony Grace regretted his easy acceptance of the fissure route. The clammy, slightly greasy walls of the passage were only inches from his narrow shoulders. If he deviated at all from the exact centre of the floor he brushed up against the rock, each touch telling him just how enclosed he was. He tried to keep his eyes fixed on the bobbing light from Izo's lamp a few feet ahead, but still the sweat began to form all over his body as the fear grew within him. After an hour of it every nerve in his body was screaming for some release from the rapidly building claustrophobic horror that was threatening to overtake him at any moment. More than once the words began to form in his throat, requests for Izo to speed up, or for Mariea to keep her distance behind him and not tread on his heels, but he knew that the words would come out as screams instead, so he gritted his teeth and kept on.

As they progressed small streams of water joined the tiny trickle on the floor, the water seemingly coming from nowhere, emanating from minute cracks in the walls and the ceiling somewhere lost above their heads. Two hours after leaving the steaming cave and the water was up to their knees, moving in a steadily strengthening current.

'Jesus!' muttered Mariea from behind him. 'What the hell do we do if this gets any deeper.'

'Swim, of course,' said Tony harshly, the small joke spoken almost explosively.

'Funny fellow,' answered Mariea, and they slogged on. The water was freezing cold and soon Tony had lost almost all sensation in his legs. He wondered how long they could keep it up in the frigid water, and even more important, how long it would be before his nerves snapped entirely. Vainly he tried to call up other images, familiar memories from his past, but none of it did any good. Almost as though she could read his mind Mariea spoke from behind him.

'Try reciting the multiplication tables,' she said. 'It helps.'
Tony nodded and did as she suggested, letting his mind fill
with the ingrained ritual of numbers, repeating them over
and over in his head until the formation of the words lost all
meaning. He lifted each leg automatically, and when his arms
or hips touched the hideously close walls of the fissure he
spoke the numbers out loud, as though they could act like
some sort of incantation to keep the steadily shrinking
universe of slimy rock at bay. Soon he had lost all track of
time and place, and he bumped into Izo heavily before he
realized that the geologist had stopped.

'For God's sake, don't stop!' hissed the journalist. The
walls seem to be squeezing in on him and it felt as though his
heart would tear out of his chest.

'Quiet!' commanded Izo in a whisper. Grace did as he was
told, his own ears straining to catch the sound which had
stopped the geologist. He heard nothing but the blood
pounding in his veins and the harsh rasp of his own breathing.

'What is it?' asked Mariea Tarvanin from behind him.

'An echo,' said Izo at last.

'I don't understand,' said Tony Grace. He knew that if
they had to stand in the hideously narrow crevasse for much
longer he was going to scream.

'There must be a widening ahead, a cave perhaps.'

'Then for heaven's sake lets get to it!' said the journalist.

Izo began moving again, with Grace close on his heels.
Within a few yards the floor of the crevasse began to drop
abruptly, the cold water pushing hard against the backs of
their legs. They were forced to reach out and grab at the slimy
walls to keep from being pushed over by the speeding flow.
As they progressed down the canted slope the walls began to
narrow as well. At first Tony Grace thought it was his imagination, but he soon realized that his worst fears were coming
true — the walls really were closing in on him. Within
minutes the crevasse was no longer wide enough to walk face
on, and they were forced to turn and shuffle sideways, their
faces to the wall less than six inches away. As the passage
narrowed the water naturally rose, until they were moving

through the crack with the cold fluid frothing up around their armpits. Izo refused to be hurried though, and felt his way slowly, making sure that the floor was still solid below them. A sudden dip or pothole could throw them off balance, and in the narrow confines of the crack a fall could be fatal.

'Oh God! How much farther?' moaned Tony Grace, slipping forward, his teeth chattering. Izo, his arm cramping from the effort of keeping the lamp up out of the water, shook his head.

'Not much more,' he gasped, the water now coming up to his chin. 'Keep moving!' Tony kept pressing forward, his fear of sliding under the rushing water overshadowing the terror of the minute fissure they were moving along. He turned his head slightly, checking on Mariea. She was right behind him, her head tilted back to keep her mouth out of the water. Her arms were stretched above her head, her clutching fingers trying to find grips on the slippery rock walls.

'Need any help?' spluttered the journalist. He remembered suddenly that Mariea was a good four or five inches shorter than either he or Izo, so the water level would reach higher on her. Wild-eyed, the artist shook her head, her hair plastered around her oval face. Even in the dim light Tony could see that her lips had turned blue with the cold.

'Just . . . keep on,' she managed, the water flooding into her mouth, almost choking her. She spat it out and motioned Tony to keep going. He did so, trying to keep up with Izo.

Suddenly the light disappeared and for a terrible moment Tony thought that the geologist had slipped and fallen into the rushing torrent. Then the light reappeared, pointing back at them. The sound of the water seemed to have multiplied a thousand per cent, and then, almost as if by magic, the journalist took a stumbling step forward and found himself freed from the confines of the crack. He was standing in an open cave, the water from the fissure roaring out of the cavern wall as though from a broken conduit. Spluttering and shaking her head like a spaniel, Mariea appeared out of the spurting crack. All three were soaked through and shivering in the cold air of the cave.

'Strip,' ordered Izo. He began unpacking the sodden

knapsack.

'I beg your pardon?' asked Tony Grace.

'Get out of your clothes,' repeated the geologist without looking up. 'If you stay in them you will succumb to hypothermia. In our present condition it would be fatal.' He pulled the contents of the knapsack out on the slightly-tilted floor of the cave, keeping the supplies out of the rebounding spray from the torrent. Tony and Mariea began to take off their clothes, looking about the new cave as they did so.

It was a strange, almost dead-looking place, unlike any of the caverns or passageways they had been in before. It was quite small compared to the gigantic cavern where they had been attacked by the insects, but it was still roomy, approximately the size of a large two-storey house. The glare of Izo's lamp picked out the crumbled, rotten-looking roof of the cave, and the walls, once rough-edged and hard, had the same deteriorated appearance. A deeply marked shadow on the far side of the cave turned out to be a deep, steep-walled pool partially filled with water, while forty feet away the stream that gushed out of the crevasse raced along a deeply-etched fissure in the floor to disappear at last into the far wall. Both Mariea and Tony quickly realized that there was no exit from the cave, or at least none that they could see.

Izo eventually found what he had been searching for, a small box containing the white, brick-like blocks of solid fuel for the Primus. He forced his numbed fingers to open the pocket of his climbing jacket and brough out a small plastic vial of waterproof matches. He set one of the fuel bricks on the floor, tugged open the waterproof matches and after two or three times, managed to get the block glowing. It began radiating heat instantly. When he was sure that it was going Izo stripped off his own clothes, and, naked, the three people clustered around the tiny pocket of warmth.

'How long will that last?' asked Tony, nodding at the glowing fuel brick.

'An hour or more, I think,' said Izo. 'Long enough for our clothing to dry.' They had arranged their clothes on several boulders Izo and Tony had rolled close to the fire.

'What's the point of having dry clothes?' asked Mariea

dully. 'I mean, it's not as though we've got anywhere to go.'

'She's right, Izo,' said Tony. 'You've got us out of some bad spots so far but I rather think this is the end of the line. There's simply no way out.'

'That would appear to be the case,' agreed Izo.

'So what do we do?' asked Mariea, 'Just sit here and die?'

'No,' murmured the geologist. 'We sit here and think.'

2

'I still think the entire idea is outrageous,' said Tony Grace. Their clothes had dried and, using three small stones and a second block of fuel, Izo Harada was heating up a tin of stew from the knapsack.

'We're really not in a position to choose, are we now, Tony old bean?' said Mariea lightly, looking hungrily down at the bubbling tin balanced precariously on its tripod of rocks.

'It won't work,' said the journalist. 'Will it?'

Izo laughed. 'The principle is sound,' he said, stirring the contents of the wide-mouthed tin with a tin-opener. 'However, I am a geologist, not a hydrologist or an engineer.'

'I'm not worried about it working so much as worried about how long it will last,' said Mariea. 'Come on, Izo, that stew's got to be ready.'

'We use the lid for a spoon. Three lidfuls and then pass it on?' said Tony.

'Agreed,' said Izo. He handed the bent lid of the stew tin to Mariea.

'The plan,' she said through a mouthful of the hot mixture. 'Like I was saying, how long will it last?'

'It's impossible to say,' answered Izo. 'We can build the cofferdam successfully, I think. There is enough rock here. We can divert the stream, or a good deal of it, into the pool. Eventually though the pool will fill and the water will try and force its way past the cofferdam. Even if the cofferdam holds the water level will eventually rise above it. If the rate continues as it is now I would give it two or three hours perhaps.'

'Is that enough time?' asked Tony, taking the makeshift spoon from Mariea. Once more Izo lifted his shoulders.

'Enough time for what?' asked Izo. 'It is three hours more than we would not have. We may find high ground, or another chamber, or another exit route. It is impossible to say.'

'In other words all the work could be for nothing,' said Tony.

'Quit badgering him,' said Mariea. 'You treat him as though he's responsible for us. He's not our father, for Christ's sake.'

'Wouldn't my mother faint dead away if he was?' said Tony. He laughed and reached out to clap Izo on the shoulder. 'She's right, Izo. I'm sorry. I'm not one of these people who acts well in a crisis. Courage is not my strong point.'

'I would argue that,' smiled the geologist. 'You have claustrophobia, yet still you proceed. You are very scared, yet still you proceed. You laugh, you make jokes. You live. That is courage.'

'Not really,' grinned Mariea. 'It's just that Tony's very adaptable. He's actually getting used to it down here.'

'Umm,' said Tony, grimacing. 'That's what you think. Anyway, Izo, when do we get to work on this damn dam, as it were?'

'As soon as I have had my turn with the spoon,' said Izo.

When they had finished eating the three survivors set about creating the cofferdam which Izo had described. The effect the geologist hoped to create was a short-term draining of the exit passage. From what Izo could tell after a brief inspection of the spot where the water left the cave, they were faced with another very small passage, much like the one which had led them to Alain Bouchard. Gushing and foaming, the water leapt down the sharply-angled hole, filling it completely. Without draining there would be no room to breathe in the tunnel.

They began shifting rocks from the far side of the cave by the pit-pool, lugging them to the stream's exit point. Slowly but surely Izo began to build up an angled wall across the main current, steadily deflecting more and more water across the cave floor. At first he didn't bother chinking any of the cracks in the wall, trying to keep too much pressure off the newly-created breakwater, but as the wall grew, Tony and Mariea began finding smaller stones to plug the holes, until almost the complete force of the stream had been deflected away from the exit and now poured in a steady sheet across the cave floor, splashing noisily into the steep-sided pool.

'Bloody marvellous!' said Tony Grace, standing up weakly, surveying their work. 'The thing actually does the job!'

'Well don't stand there admiring it, for God's sake!' breathed Mariea. 'The longer we wait, the more water is going to fill up in the pool.'

'We should be on our way,' agreed Izo. 'Stepping around the two-foot-high wall of rock they had created, he shone the powerful beam of his lamp down the newly revealed hole. It was no more than eighteen inches across, the walls thick with the slimy residue of the actinomycetes bacteria. In his years as a caver, Izo had moved through smaller "squeezes", but he knew that this one would push his two friends to the limits of their endurance, especially Tony. If ever there had been a place designed to terrorize a claustrophobe, it was this squeeze. He would be completely surrounded by the rock, feeling its touch everywhere on his body, the odour of the slime-covered stone pressed tight to his nostrils. There would be almost no room to manoeuvre, and any progress would have to be made by minute wrigglings and small motions of the toes of their boots. Izo took a long worried breath and then exhaled slowly. If there were any problems at all he knew that Tony Grace would panic, and to panic in a narrow trap like the one they were faced with would be fatal, both for him and the person behind.

'Not very big, is it?' said the journalist, looking over Izo's shoulder. The geologist turned and looked up at his friend.

'It is big enough,' he said slowly, 'if you keep your head.'

'I'll do my best,' said Tony, his mouth suddenly dry. The small hole looked like some horrible reptilian mouth waiting to suck him down.

'I shall go first,' said Izo. 'Mariea will follow. Tony will come last.'

'Good idea,' said Tony nodding. Mariea looked confused.

'What do you mean?' she asked. Izo started to speak but Tony answered for him.

'Izo would be diplomatic,' explained the journalist. 'But he wants me to go last in case I come apart at the seams, if you see what I mean.' He smiled at Mariea brightly, but there was fear in his eyes. 'If I panic he doesn't want you behind me, plugged up as it were,' he continued, his voice cracking slightly.

'Don't be silly,' scoffed Mariea, looking Tony squarely in the eye. 'You haven't come this far to freak out now, have you?' The journalist shrugged.

'We're about to find out,' he muttered. With a final nod, Izo slid into the hole, going head first, his arms extended in front of him. Seconds later his boots disappeared and Tony and Mariea were alone in the cave. A few feet away the water pounded heavily against the roughly-built cofferdam.

'I hope that thing holds,' muttered Tony. Mariea reached out and grasped the journalist's wrist.

'It will, and so will you,' she said firmly.

'I really could marry you,' said Tony, smiling at her in the darkness. 'Too bad you and Izo are . . . involved.'

'Oh, shut up,' said Mariea, pushing him gently towards the waiting hole. 'If we get out of this alive I'll marry both of you. Quit making up excuses.'

'Izo wants me to go last,' protested Tony.

'For once Izo is wrong,' said Mariea. 'Now get down the hole. I'll be right behind you.'

The journalist did as he was told, slithering down into the tiny wound in the ground head first, his arms extended, following the weak gout of light reflected back from Izo's lamp. Immediately the terror was upon him again, a hundred times worse than it had been in the fissure passage. His face was pressed into the musty slime of the rock, and he could feel it pressing against his back and his thighs. He was completely enclosed, with less than an inch of leeway on either side. The only way he could move was by digging in the toes of his boots, pushing himself forward inch by inch. He heard Mariea's movements behind him and felt his stomach heave. With Izo in front and Mariea behind there was no escape. He felt a series of racking shudders consume his body and he pushed forward, scrabbling vainly at the walls of his prison, trying to get some purchase with his fingers. He could see Izo's light ahead, diffused by the geologist's own body, and he moved desperately towards it, his body somehow twisting so that he was on his side. His breath began to come in short, sharp gasps, the ragged sound harsh in his own ears. Suddenly, horrifyingly, he felt his ankles catch on something behind him and a bubbling screech escaped from his mouth.

'Relax!' It was Mariea's voice. For an instant the panic lifted and he realized that it was her hands on his ankles. 'It's all right!' The journalist shook free, all rational thought gone, logic replaced by a blanketing terror. He pushed hard, his feet smashing back into Mariea's outstretched arms. He rushed forward, a new sound coming to him, the sound of rushing water, the sound of the cofferdam crumbling behind them in the dark cave they had left, and the roaring sledgehammer of water that was coming towards them, to drown him, trapped in their sewerhole tomb.

'Izo!' screamed Mariea, warning the geologist.

Thankfully the sinuous passage had been worn smooth by the constant flow of water through it over time, so there was nothing to snag at the journalist's clothing. Even so, he battered himself badly as he surged ahead, his fingernails tearing on the unforgiving rock, his shoulders and legs bruising as he hurled himself forward by main force, caring only to be out of the choking, killing hole.

Mariea tried to keep up, pushing ahead on her elbows, thrusting back with her toes, but Tony was well out of reach. She dreaded the thought of him reaching Izo and trying to force his way past the geologist. Her fears about a confrontation between the two men vanished, replaced by a more present terror. The horrifying sounds that had been part of Tony's nightmare now became a reality; from far behind she could hear a heavy crumbling noise, and she knew that the cofferdam was breaking up under the pounding force of the water behind it. She screamed, freezing momentarily as she felt a gentle feather touch creep up her leg, and visions of the swarming wave of insects that had drowned Alice Braden reared in her mind. She shook her leg, vomit rising to burn in her throat as she felt another touch and then another.

There was nothing she could do as more and more of the creatures seemed to slide under her clothes, the icy touch of their legs reaching to her soul, her arms trapped ahead of her, unable to tear them away. One of them touched at her chest and throat, burrowing between her breasts, and involuntarily she looked down, knowing what she would see.

There were no insects — instead, barely visible in the last threads of light reflected down the impossibly narrow tube, there was a dark line of fluid, so slow-moving that at first she thought she had cut herself somehow and what she was seeing was blood. Then she realized what it was — water, the first trickle from the stream trapped behind the dam. Tony Grace's panic was forgotten, and she began to scramble ahead, fired now by her own vision of a choking sudden death.

Tony Grace was almost within reach of the light from Izo's lamp. His wide, terror-filled eyes made out the dark silhouette of the geologist's boots only a few feet ahead. Mindlessly, his whole being screaming with the awareness of the millions of tons of rock surrounding him, he reached out with clawing fingers, trying to attach himself to the slowly-moving figure ahead. He had to pass him, to get out, to be able to stand. Faintly, on the edge of consciousness he was aware of the movements behind him, and not recognizing the scratching pursuit of Mariea as she scrambled forward, he lunged, striking the side of his head against the tunnel wall as he blindly struggled to grab Izo's feet. Blood began to ooze out of the long gash above his eye and finally his fingers found the heel of Izo's boot.

'Let me past!' he screamed. Izo shook his leg, vainly trying to break the hysterical man's grip, but Grace was suddenly all over him, swarming up over his neck, squeezing himself against the ceiling of the tunnel, crushing the breath from

Izo's lungs. The geologist lost his grip on the lamp and reached back, trying to push the wildly flailing journalist away.

'I've got to get past!' screamed Grace. His hands found Izo's hair and he gripped it, levering the geologist's head back and heaving himself forward at the same time; trying to squeeze over Izo, although any rational person would have seen that it was impossible. The lamp had slipped down the incline of the tunnel, striking the rock wall at a sharp bend, the beam shortened into a tiny intense circle of light ten or fifteen feet away. The light seemed to taunt Izo as he fought to break free of the lunatic hold Grace had on his hair. The geologist managed to get one elbow under himself and with a heave he arched his back, smashing Grace into the ceiling of the tunnel. The journalist's grip loosened for an instant and Izo rammed back with his legs, kicking hard. Grace screamed, in pain rather than panic this time. He fell back and Izo was free. Knowing that his only salvation lay in keeping away from the terrified man Izo dragged himself forward as quickly as he could. He reached the lamp and took a precious second to look back over his shoulder; shining the lamp behind him.

Grace lay doubled up in the tunnel behind him, his thrashing figure sharply outlined in the light. He seemed to be caught on some small protrusion in the tunnel wall, and in the high-powered beam of the lamp Izo could see the blood that covered the crazed man's face. The journalist managed to free himself and jerked forward, his face taut with pain, his eyes blinking away the steady flow of blood that poured down from the wound on his forehead and temple.

'Bastard!' he croaked. 'I'll get you, bastard!'

'Then do it!' urged Izo. He knew that if Grace could focus on the anger he felt then his panic would be dissipated. 'Come and get me!' he taunted. He straightened as best he could and with the lamp in his grip he pushed ahead. From behind he could hear Grace scrambling after him.

'Your fault!' bellowed Grace, his voice echoing. 'We'd be dead by now! We'd be safe and dead! Your fault!' The man's breath was coming in huge sobs as though the air was being torn from his body. Izo paid no attention, keeping his mind on the task at hand. He pushed with elbows and toes, elbows and toes, keeping up a steady rhythm.

The water struck like a battering ram, and except for the tickling trickle felt by Mariea there was no warning. It was a solid thing, filling the tunnel completely, pushing a cluster of tumbled boulders in its maw. Even before she was fully aware of what was happening one of the rocks smacked into the back of Mariea's head and she lost consciousness. Instantly she was swept into the thundering body of the flood, her limp form banging into the walls and roof, thrown forward like a log in a mill race.

Had the tunnel been older and its walls more jagged the three survivors would have undoubtedly become snagged, drowning in the violent surge of the suddenly released torrent. As it was the three figures were flushed down the smooth conduit, ejected finally into a dark-walled chamber of unseen dimensions. Somehow, Izo's light had come through the mad rush down the tunnel unscathed and Tony Grace, coughing and vomiting water, managed to haul the unconscious forms of Izo Harada and Mariea Tarvanin up out of the still powerful flow of the stream. Then, his panic consumed and forgotten in his exhaustion, he too collapsed beside the roaring water.

Mariea was the first to awaken, her head pounding. She sat up, groaning, bracing herself against a large tumbled boulder beside her. The flood of water in the stream had died to an innocent meandering freshet, the soft sound of the flowing water setting up a tinkling whisper in the cavern. Groggily Mariea looked around. The lamp had fallen from Tony Grace's hand and lay beside his still form, the lantern on its side, throwing a long beam of light across the rock-strewn, uneven floor of the cave. Mariea climbed to her feet and moved unsteadily across to Tony. At first she thought he was dead, but then she saw the slow steady rhythm of his chest and she breathed a sigh of relief. After examining him briefly she moved past him to where she could see the huddled form of Izo Harada. As she approached, the geologist groaned, the low sound echoing strangely in the cavern. She went to him quickly as he struggled to sit up, cradling his head and supporting him with her arm at his back. He opened his eyes, breaking the crust of blood that had streamed down from a deep cut just above his eyebrow.

'Tony?' he asked, his voice thick.

'He's okay. A few cuts and bruises, but he's all right I think. He's sleeping, or out cold.'

'We should wake him,' muttered Izo blearily. 'He might have a concussion.'

'Think about yourself for a minute,' cautioned Mariea. 'You don't seem to be in such hot shape yourself.'

'I am all right. A headache, no more.' He took a deep breath and then let it out slowly. 'Have you looked for the lamp?' he asked.

'I didn't have to,' answered Mariea, her brows furrowing. 'It's right beside Tony. Over there,' she pointed with her free hand. There was a long silence.

'And the lamp is on at this time?' asked Izo slowly.

'Of course it's on, how else could you see . . .' Suddenly aware, Mariea's voice trailed off.

'That is the point, of course,' said Izo, his voice emotionless. 'I cannot. It would seem that I am blind.'

CHAPTER THIRTEEN

1

For several hours Frank Speers had been carefully gauging the speed of the current on the Styx, and by his calculations the rate had increased by almost fifty per cent over that time. There was no apparent increase in the amount of water flowing down the river, so he presumed that the slope of the river-bed had changed abruptly and they were heading down at a much steeper angle. He had more to worry about; he had also noticed that the ceiling over their heads had begun to smooth. Where there had been stalactites and dripstone deposits before, there was nothing to be seen but a smooth, and from the looks of it, slimy curved surface, with no trace of any kind of formation.

'Weird,' he muttered finally. David Penfold, seated in the rear of the raft, heard Speers's voice and, almost against his will, replied. He had been living with his own thoughts, silently, for the entire day.

'What is?' he asked. Speers, glad himself of someone to talk to, explained. David smiled coldly.

'Bet you wish Izo was around to explain,' he said. Speers shrugged.

'I can do without the Jap,' he said, a trace of anger in his voice. 'I don't need him to tell me what's what.'

'So tell me,' said David, almost taunting. 'Tell both of us.' He glanced at Irene, but she was paying no attention to the exchange between the two men.

'If I didn't know better I'd say this was a phreatic tunnel,' said Speers, turning the lamp up to the ceiling, twenty feet above them.

'You mean normally full of water?' asked David, becoming interested in the problem in spite of himself. Speers nodded.

'Yeah. I mean, that's what you'd think if you had a tunnel with no deposits of any kind — like this. But it doesn't make any sense.'

'Why couldn't it have been phreatic, then changed. Maybe just because of the earthquake or something,' said David. Speers shook his head.

'I thought of that,' he said, still looking up. 'But it doesn't fit. If this had been a water-filled tunnel up until a little while ago, then there'd be no formations at all, but a couple of miles back there were stalactites all over the place, remember?' David thought for a moment, then realized Speers was right. Up until an hour or so before, the roof had been a maze of the sword-like shapes dangling above them.

'Well,' said David finally. 'It's got to mean something.'

'Sure,' said Speers sourly. 'And I've even figured out what it does mean, though that doesn't make any sense either.'

'Explain,' asked David.

'If there's no deposits on the ceiling, that means the ceiling is covered by water most of the time, or at least long enough so that no stalactites can get going. On the other hand, this place doesn't show any of the signs of being a phreatic tunnel, other than that.'

'So?' asked David. Speers grimaced.

'So it means that sometimes this tunnel is filled with water, but only from a point about two miles back. That's what doesn't make any sense. There was nothing special about that point, no extra water coming in, no new streams joining the main flow, not even any dry tunnels that I could see. It's crazy.'

There's got to be an explanation,' said David. 'On the other hand it may not be important.' Speers laughed, a low ugly sound.

'Don't kid yourself,' he said. 'Down here, anything like that is important.

They continued on in silence, broken only by the occasional burbling sound as Speers fended off with the aluminium pole. Then all three of the people in the raft heard the new sound — a terribly familiar whisper in the distance.

'Hear it?' asked David. Speers nodded.

'What is it?' asked Irene, speaking for the first time in hours, sudden fear coming to her eyes. 'I've heard that before!'

'You betcha, sweetheart,' said Speers, peering forward, sweeping the light ahead. 'It's a waterfall. Like that hydraulic jump we went over. Bigger though. A lot bigger.'

'How far?' asked David. Speers shrugged.

'Quite a way. Weird too.'

'What?' asked David.

'It sounds a lot bigger, but the water's not going any faster. I don't get any of this at all.'

'I see what you mean,' said David. 'If it's a bigger waterfall than that jump we went over, how can there be half as much water?'

'Less than half,' said Speers. 'Look at this.' He dug the pole into the water, pointing it straight down, then pulled it up again. 'The pole is five feet long. I hit bottom, rock bottom, not just mud, before my wrist goes under the water. On top of everything else, it's getting shallower.'

'It's crazy,' said David, looking over the side.

'Crazy, but it's good for us,' said Speers. 'As far as I can tell the current's just about constant now, and the bottom's less than five feet down. We can get out and wade. We're not going to be swept over any falls or anything like that.' He turned to Irene and tried to give her a reassuring smile. She responded blankly. Speers scowled. 'I'm trying to make you feel a bit better, for Christ's sake,' he said. 'You were looking frightened. The least you could do is give me a bit of a smile.'

'Compassion from you, Monsieur Speers?' said Irene, her voice low. '*Merde* for your compassion.'

'What does that mean?' asked Speers.

'Shit,' said David noncommitally. Speers gave Irene a long penetrating glance, then turned away, looking forward again.

'Come up here and give me a hand,' he said to David, without turning around. David did as he was told, working his way forward around the supplies until he was squatting beside Speers, his weight pushing down the thin floor of the raft. The cave diver handed David the light, then began stripping off his clothing.

'What the hell are you doing?' asked David, watching as the lean, muscular man undressed. In less than a minute the diver was naked. David found himself staring at Speers's groin, imagining the man's now flaccid organ hard, thrusting in and out of Irene. His heart began to pound and a white heat formed behind his eyes. Desperately he buried the feeling and looked away, swallowing his anger.

'I'm going over the side,' replied Speers at last. He rummaged around in the hummock of supplies in the centre of the raft. 'Glad I've still got this,' he said grinning, holding up the dark shape of his wet-suit. With a speed borne of long habit Speers slipped expertly into the rubber suit. Unlike a standard diving-suit his equipment had been specially designed for subterranean diving and came equipped with felt-lined, tight-fitting boots and insulated gloves. While he was undressing and then climbing into the suit the raft had

218

drifted on its own. The sound of the falls had increased tenfold and the muted thunder was ominous, no matter what Speers felt about its potential for danger.

Speers strapped a set of multiple flashlights to the brackets on either side of his mask, flicking them on. He ordered David to turn off the large lamp, and then slipped over the side, taking the aluminium pole with him. He kept one hand on the raft, treading water, feeling for the bottom with the pole again. After a moment he nodded to himself and let his feet touch the bottom. He was now guiding the raft, feeling ahead with the pole to make sure that he wasn't about to step into an unseen pothole. He turned and looked up at David who now sat in the front of the raft. David blinked in the sudden wash of light from the compact twin flashlights on either side of Speers's mask.

'I'm going to take it real slow,' said Speers. 'If it looks like the water speed is picking up I'm going to give you the word to jump over the side and hold the raft back. When I say jump, do it. Got it?'

'Yes,' said David.

'Right,' nodded Speers. 'I'm going to be looking for a ledge, or somewhere we can tie up. If you see anything I miss, let me know.'

'Okay,' answered David. Speers turned away again and continued forward, up to his armpits in the water. The sound of the falls ahead was now deafening. David turned, glancing back at the dim figure of Irene, crouched in the rear of the raft. She seemed very small, tucked in beside the large mound of supplies. Her hair was plastered around her face and her clothes were torn and filthy. David grinned and waved back at her, realizing that he probably looked even worse. Irene made no answering signal. Frowning, David turned again to the front of the raft, keeping his eyes on Speers. He squinted, wondering if he was seeing right. It seemed as though Speers was moving to even shallower water. He was three feet in front of the raft, hanging on to the front lanyard, but where a moment ago he had been up to his armpits the water now only came halfway up his chest.

'It's getting shallower!' called David, shouting above the

219

roar of the falls somewhere ahead. Speers nodded.

'And faster too!' he called back. 'Bit of a rip current here! Get ready to come on in!'

'Right!' answered David, suddenly feeling flushed with elation. For the first time in days he felt as though he could be useful.

'Watch your feet!' ordered Speers. 'The bottom's getting all broken up!'

The water was now clearly much shallower. Speers was walking waist high. The increased speed of the water was obvious as well. Speers was now right up against the front of the raft, holding it back against the current, the water foaming angrily around him.

'In!' yelled Speers, struggling with the raft. David didn't hesitate. He climbed over the side immediately, hanging on to the lanyard. As the icy water seeped rapidly through his clothes he shivered involuntarily, then clenched his teeth against the biting cold. He ignored the feeling and grabbed at the lanyard hauling back to keep the raft from being swept away. David slipped, losing his footing as he dropped into a pothole. He went under and came up sputtering, now soaked to the skin.

'You all right?' called Speers. David bobbed his head.

'Okay,' he managed. He could feel his hands going numb on the slippery nylon of the lanyard and he wondered how much longer he was going to be able to endure the freezing water.

'There!' yelled Speers, pointing ahead. David shook his head, trying to get the water out of his eyes, and peered forward, following the wide beam of Speers's light. A hundred yards ahead he saw a line of white froth raised by the sudden tossing of the water. Beyond the line of foam there was nothing. The light disappeared, swallowed by the velvet darkness. Speers swept the lights to either wall. On the left there was a narrow ridge, looking no more than five or six feet wide. It rose like a narrow ramp, up the side of the tunnel, shearing back into the wall just as it reached the ceiling.

'Hold her here!' commanded Speers, turning to David, who stood struggling on the other side of the raft.

'I've got to get something!' David nodded and Speers let go of the lanyard and lunged over the side of the raft. The added weight and the fact that Speers was no longer helping to hold back his side put a terrible strain on David as the lanyard bit into the flesh of his hands, already scored and tender from the long slide down the rope three days before. Although it was less than two minutes, it seemed like an age before Speers dropped back into the water and took up the strain. David looked across at the man. He seemed to have something like a bandolier over his shoulder, and he was carrying one of Izo's climbing hammers in his free hand.

'Going to moor us!' explained the diver, raising the hammer in the air. The raft had slipped forward another fifty yards and each time Speers's lights veered out over the thin line of cresting foam David could see just how large the chasm in front of them was. Even at this close range the reach of the light was just barely enough to find its way to the other side. He pulled his eyes away from the looming hole that was coming closer with each passing second and turned his attention to Speers.

'Go left!' ordered the diver. Instead of simply going with the current, Speers was pulling the raft to the left, out of the main stream, making towards the steeply-angled ledge thirty feet away. David tugged at the lanyard, trying to help in the manoeuvre, biting back a moan of pain as the thin cord bit even more deeply into his injured hands. 'Almost there!' called Speers. 'Get around to the front and hold her steady!' David did as he was told, struggling against the increasingly powerful current, feeling the unseen forces below him in the water tugging at his legs. He remembered a story his father had once told him about a friend of his who had been holidaying in Nova Scotia. The man had been only knee-deep in the water, but a sudden rip tide had come up, swept him off his feet and carried him out into the open sea before he could do anything about it. The man had drowned.

A few feet away, Speers was manhandling a long

length of rope from one of the spare climbing kits, threading it through the lanyard several times until it was secured at half a dozen different points. Then he took the hammer, shifted slightly until he was facing the rock wall a yard away, and began hammering a crampon into a small fissure in the ledge. He worked quickly, securing the crampon, then passing a larger karabiner clip through it, and finally threading the rope through the clip and tying it off. He waved to David who dropped the lanyard gratefully. The raft swung around hard, thudding against the wall of the tunnel, but it stayed where it was. Speers boosted himself up on to the ledge and gratefully David slogged across to the raft and pulled himself into it.

'End of the line,' called Speers from the ledge.

'Want a hand?' asked David turning to Irene, who was still sitting in the same position. She shook her head.

'I can do it myself,' she said. She looked up at him and frowned. 'You'd better get out of those wet things or you'll catch pneumonia.' David nodded, then climbed up out of the raft and on to the ledge. He was struck by a sudden feeling of exhaustion that was almost like a blow. His body seemed to be on the verge of shutting down. David shook the tiredness off. He still had to get out of his clothes and eat before he could rest.

'Come and take a look at this!' called Speers, his voice echoing above the fury of the waterfall. He had climbed all the way up the steep ledge, and was crouching at the edge, his lights flashing back from the mouth of the tunnel. David clambered up the canted ledge carefully; even though the slab of rock was relatively wide it was made treacherous by the spray thrown up from the waterfall below. David went the last few feet on his hands and knees, hugging the protective rock wall. Speers shifted slightly, giving him room. Speers unclipped one of the sets of twin lights from his headgear and pointed them straight down.

'What the hell . . . ?' muttered David. He found himself staring down a steep-walled shaft at least two hundred feet across, but instead of the yawning depths he had expected it seemed no more than twenty or thirty feet deep. The bottom was covered in water, the waterfall outlet of their tunnel churning up the pool into a foaming maelstrom.

'That was my first impression, too,' grinned Speers, his mouth no more than six inches from David's ear. The diver fanned the beam of the flashlights around the base of the pool slowly. David frowned.

'I don't get it,' he said loudly. 'There's no outlet tunnel.'

'Sure there is,' replied Speers. 'Look up here.' He trained the beams high up on the far side of the cauldron-shaped hole. Almost fifty feet above their own level was a wide pear-shaped opening in the rock.

'Are you crazy?' asked David. Speers shook his head.

'Took me a minute to figure it out.' He shone the light down to the pool again, searching the shining surface until he locked the beam in to a small rock protrusion jutting out a foot or so above the water. 'Keep your eye on that chunk of rock for a minute. Won't take long.' Mystified, David watched the rock, wiping cold spray out of his eyes every few seconds. Finally, annoyed, and chilled to the bone, he turned to Speers.

'Look,' he started, 'I've had enough of the games. Why don't you . . .'

'Check the rock,' commanded Speers. David turned back and stared down into the hole, his eyes following the beams from Speers's flashlights.

'You moved the light,' said David. He checked carefully, but the rock had disappeared.

'Nope,' said Speers, his mouth pulled into a wide grin. 'It's under water.'

'You mean the level's rising?' asked David. Speers nodded.

'It's a resurgence cave,' he said. 'There's one or two of them around. There's a place in France . . . Generest or something like that. It rises a foot a minute through fifty feet, stands still for a couple of minutes, then takes almost an hour to go back to its original level. Regular as clockwork. They think its got something to do with a series of reservoirs that drain through siphons of varying diameters and positions.'

'You mean like the lake we went through?' asked David.

'Right. And it explains why there weren't any stalactites for the last couple of miles of this tunnel. That outlet is a good fifty feet up. The pool must fill from a stronger stream down there, fills up to this point, floods the tunnel all the way back until the level of the water in this tunnel is equal to the level of the outlet tunnel up there. I guess that completes the cycle — too much water drains out of the upper passage, so the level starts falling again.'

'I think you lost me back a bit,' said David.

'Water seeks its own level. That just about covers it,' said Speers. 'The point is, the waters going to come up the side of the shaft until all we have to do is float out on it. Then we ride it up to the outlet tunnel and we're away.'

'It's still kind of fuzzy,' admitted David. 'But I'll take your word for it.' Speers shook his head.

'Jesus! You're the one with the college education. Just imagine that you're going through one of the locks in the Panama Canal. That should give you an idea.'

'So what do we do now?' asked David.

'Wait,' said Speers.

2

As the water slowly crept up the steep walls of the cauldron, David stripped and dried his clothes, keeping his naked body as close as possible to the comforting heat of the Primus. Silently, Irene made some food — yet another meal of canned stew and dried biscuits — while Speers maintained his station on the high edge of the rock ledge, keeping track of the climbing water level.

When the food was ready he made his way down the steep ledge and retrieved his clothes from the raft. He changed quickly, then squatted down in front of the Primus, warming his hands over the steaming pot of stew. Irene, her face expressionless, served out three tin plates full of the glutinous food, then moved away from the stove.

'I've been doing a count,' said Speers, speaking around a mouthful of food. He crammed half a biscuit into his mouth as well, washing it down with a swig of water from one of the canteens. 'It's coming up about a foot every two and a half minutes. We've only got about half an hour to wait until it's level with the tunnel here.'

'And according to you, we just float up to the other tunnel, right?' asked David.

Speers nodded, chewing off another piece of biscuit. He took the remains of the hard-tack and dipped it into his plate of stew to soften it.

'That's it,' he said. He looked past the stove to where Irene sat, eating slowly, her eyes on the quickly flowing water.

'What's eating her?' asked Speers, nodding in her direction. David frowned.

'You,' he said shortly. 'Me. Men in general.'

'Oh,' said Speers. He went back to his food. David kept his eyes on Irene, trying to fathom what was going on in her head. She had said almost nothing for the whole day and the few times he caught her looking at him, her eyes had been full of anger. David sighed. Not that he blamed her. She had been totally betrayed – by Speers, who had used her, and by himself, who had done nothing to help. The weak and the strong, he thought to himself. Equally bad. The worst of it was, he found his own anger towards Speers fading, replaced by a slow and grudging respect. In their present situation the fact that the diver had slept with Irene was of neglible importance. Snatches of lectures from long ago swam into his mind: *Droit de seigneur, territorial imperative, tribal dominant* – take your pick, he thought.

The survivors of the insect cave had become a tribal unit, with Speers at its head. As such he ruled totally, and the only way to change that would be to kill him. Irene, as a human being, was worthless to the unit, providing no essential service, so in fact her only value to the unit was as a sex object. They had gone back to Khan's time, and in those days, muscle was virtually all that counted. He shook his head, wondering what the Kate Millets and Betty Friedans of the world would do in their situation. In the civilized world 'survival of the fittest' had become anathema over the years, but the Styx was about as far as you could get from the civilized world.

'Reality strikes,' he said to himself softly. Speers looked up questioningly.

'What?' he asked. David shook his head and smiled.

'Nothing,' he answered. 'Just thinking to myself.' Speers laughed.

'That's your problem. You think too much. Just gets you into trouble.'

'And the fact that you don't think keeps you out of it?' asked David. Speers laughed and shook his head. He dished himself up some more stew and took another biscuit.

'No, I guess not,' he said. 'But I bet I didn't get as screwed up about things as you do.'

'It's not worth arguing about,' said David, suddenly overcome by a sweeping tiredness. It seemed to him as though every muscle in his body was aching, and all he really wanted to do was sleep, even though he knew it was impossible. He yawned. 'We're just not the same kind of person,' he said finally.

'I guess not,' said Speers. He looked up at David, his spoon half way between his plate and his mouth. 'I'll tell you this much though — I never would have bet on you getting this far. I had you pegged as a pretty weak link.'

'I suppose I should take that as a compliment,' said David. Out of the corner of his eye he could see Irene watching them talking. Speers shrugged at his comment.

226

'Take it any way you want,' he said. 'It's just a fact.' The diver finished his food and dropped the dish onto the smooth rock of the ledge with a clatter. The implication was clear; it was Irene's job to pick it up and wash it off. He wiped his mouth with the sleeve of his navy sweater and stood up. He looked down at David. 'You should get dressed. We'll have to push off pretty soon.'

'Okay,' answered David.

David dressed and then wordlessly helped Irene wash off the dishes and repack the Primus. He thought about trying to speak to her, but the cold, almost lifeless expression on her face warned him off. As they put the supplies back on the raft David noticed that the sound of the waterfall was becoming quieter and quieter with each passing moment as the water rose. Speers came back from his vantage point at the top of the ledge.

'Almost level,' he said. 'Let's get on board.' They climbed into the raft and waited, Speers keeping his flashlight pointed at the water close to the mouth of the tunnel. 'Any second now,' he said. The line of foam had all but disappeared. At the last moment Speers unclipped the karabiner from the crampon he had hammered into the rock, then pushed hard with the aluminium pole. They moved towards the mouth of the tunnel. David bit his lip, trying to remember that they were not heading over a precipice like the one that had existed at the mouth of the tunnel only an hour before. Speers gave a final push with the pole, fighting the newly-formed reversing current that was trying to sweep them back into the passage, and then they were out, floating freely on the quickly rising pool of water.

'Just like an elevator,' grinned Speers, looking at David. The diver bent down and unfastened the Velcro strips holding the raft's two collapsible paddles. He took them both out and handed one to David. Speers demonstrated the technique of telescoping the handle and David followed suit.

'Now what?' asked the young archaeologist.

'We paddle across to the other side. Get us right under

the exit tunnel.' David dipped the lightweight metal scoop into the water on his side of the raft while Speers paddled on the other. Within a minute they had crossed the bubbling swirling pool of water and had reached the other side. 'Use your paddle,' said Speers. 'Keep us up against the wall.' David nodded. The diver reached down into the raft and came up with the large lantern they had been using to light their way down the river. He switched off the twin sets of flashlights he still wore and turned on the lantern, removing his headgear at the same time. He flashed the big light back across the pool, sweeping the beam around until he found the tunnel mouth. Water from the main pool was flooding back into the tunnel in a thick bulging stream that rose halfway up the opening. David shivered as he watched; there was something almost obscene about it, as though the tunnel mouth was some valve in an immense heart, and the river was its life blood, pumping heavily back and forth. David kept paddling lightly, keeping the raft up against the smooth rock wall of the slowly filling pit.

'How much longer?' he asked. Speers shone the light up towards the opening above them, visible now as a deep oval shadow in the rock. To David's untrained eye they didn't seem to have made much progress.

'Can't say,' replied Speers. 'It's going to take a while for that tunnel we came out of to fill up. That's what's slowing us down. We'll just have to ride it out.'

In the end, although they had no watch to time it by, the climb up the cauldron took almost two hours longer. Both David and Speers watched anxiously, Speers checking with the lamp every few moments, but Irene, in the back of the raft, seemed totally uninterested in their progress, and in the second hour she closed her eyes and slept, or at least appeared to be asleep.

'Okay,' said Speers, as they came up level with the opening. 'Fend off a little.'

'I don't get it,' said David.

'Just do it. I'll explain later,' snapped Speers, watching the mouth of the new tunnel. David did as he was

228

ordered, pushing them away from the opening, back out into the main pool.

'Got to give the stream bed a chance to fill up,' said Speers finally, as they stood off the tunnel mouth by a dozen yards. 'We'd be grounded otherwise.' The diver focused the lamp upwards, the beam striking the roof of the cauldron a hundred feet or more above their heads.

'What's the matter?' asked David, sensing Speers's anxiety.

'I was just wondering how high the water was going to get,' he said, his voice worried. 'If it goes up above the cave mouth we don't have a chance.'

'Do we have a choice?' asked David.

'No, I guess not,' said Speers. He shone the light back on the entrance to the tunnel. The water was streaming in heavily, foaming slightly at each corner, the current so strong that David was having a hard time keeping them out in the main pool. 'Let her go!' commanded Speers. David lifted his paddle out of the water and immediately they were swept forward towards the tunnel. Speers grabbed the aluminium pole, preparing to keep them from jarring against the walls of the tunnel. An instant later they were inside the tunnel, speeding down the newly formed stream. In the reflected light from the lamp, which now faced directly forward, wedged into the bows of the raft, David could see countless rock formations on the ceiling less than a dozen feet above their heads.

'Check the roof!' he called to Speers, relieved. The diver looked up for a brief instant, then turned and nodded happily to David. With formations like that on the roof the tunnel was definitely not phreatic, so it seemed that they had been spared a quick death by drowning.

They moved quickly along the rocky passage, carried on the strong current created by the waters thrusting out of the cauldron pool behind them. The passage was almost perfectly straight and from what Speers could tell, it was falling at quite a sharp angle. If this theory was correct, the upper stream they were travelling on would join the main flow of the river at the point where the upper stream reached the same level. As they continued downward the diver felt a rush of elation, even though he knew their chances of escaping were still slim. They had surmounted one more obstacle, and for now, that was all that counted.

His optimism was short-lived. Less than an hour passed before both he and David Penfold began to notice a lessening in the current and a definite fall in the water level. Both men could see the damp marks on the sides of the tunnel which showed the previous high water point.

'Shit!' spat out Speers. 'It's falling!'

'What happened?' asked David.

'The pool is starting to empty back there,' he muttered angrily. 'The water's draining out.'

'How much farther to the main river?' asked David. Speers banged his pole into the rock wall a few feet away.

'How the hell do I know?' he snarled. 'You ask stupid questions, lover-boy. Why don't you just shut up, all right?' David felt a flush of anger at his use of the nickname. He turned and looked back at Irene, but she was still sleeping, huddled against the pile of supplies in the centre of the raft. He swallowed his anger silently.

They continued on, augmenting the failing current with their paddles, trying to get as far as they could before the stream died completely. As the current disappeared they came out of the narrow tunnel into a wide, low-roofed cavern, its ceiling worn and flat. At first David thought it was normally under water, but then he noticed that the rock was old and dry, cracked in a million places, its surface a different colour from the rock around it. Ahead of them was a small lake formed on the floor of the cavern, and beyond that, visible through a broad fissure, was the surging water of the main stream. Both Speers and David let out whoops of joy.

'We made it!' yelled Speers, his voice echoing tinnily from the low ceiling. The diver trained his light directly on the opening on the far side of the cavern, the beam dancing over the surface of the broad stream beyond.

'Saved by the bell,' said David, grinning. He turned to Irene. She had her eyes open and was staring forward. 'We made it!' he said to her. She looked at him and nodded without speaking.

'Damn!' breathed Speers happily. 'I sure would have hated to carry all this stuff too far.' He peered forward. 'It looks like there's some kind of dry bank area beside the main stream. Once we get across this lake here we can call it a day. I'm whipped.'

They began to paddle across the flat surface of the lake. With each stroke David noticed that the blade was coming up covered in a red clay material. Speers had noticed too. He dropped his paddle and poked down with his aluminium pole.

'Some kind of sand bottom,' he said. 'Must be off the capstone up there. He pointed up at the roof above him. There was a jolt and the raft ground to a stop.

'What the hell?' muttered Speers. He dug in with his pole a second time. David looked over the side. Even in the semi-darkness he could see that the water was only two or three inches deep.

'We'll have to get out and wade,' said Speers, his features twisted unpleasantly. 'Get some of the weight off.' He looked pointedly at Irene. 'We all get out.'

'Well,' said David, trying to inject a note of humour. 'This will be my second soaking of the day.' Nobody laughed. Speers got up and slid over the side. A few seconds later David followed. The raft immediately lifted and David was pleased to find that the sandy ooze on the bottom was only an inch or two deep. It looked as though he wasn't going to get soaked after all.

'Out,' said Speers coldly, jerking a crooked finger at Irene. 'We need more freeboard.' David was about to protest that they didn't have to make her get out when he realized that once again Speers was right. Even as they waited for her to clamber over the side of the raft the water level had sunk lower. With David and Speers pulling on the looped lanyard at front and Irene pushing from behind, they began to move across the shallow lake towards the broad V-shaped opening that beckoned a hundred feet away.

'No sweat,' breathed Speers, tugging on the line. 'Couple more minutes and we'll be across. There's enough time.'

David nodded and kept tugging on his side.

Suddenly the bottom fell out from under him and he dropped up to his neck, his grip on the lanyard the only thing that kept him from going under completely. Beside him Speers had apparently fallen into the same hole. He heard a scream and looked back over his shoulder, trying to pull himself up out of the water by boosting himself on the side of the raft. The scream had come from Irene. When both he and Speers had dropped the boat had lurched forward, throwing her into the water out of reach of the raft. The scream came again. David tried to work his way around the side of the raft, moving to the rear, and it was then that he realized he was not up to his neck in water. Every movement he made was an incredible effort, his legs refusing to pull up out of the soft clinging ooze that had trapped them.

'Speers!' there was no answer. He could here Irene struggling, but the lamp in the boat was pointing forward, and the rear of the small craft was in darkness.

'David! Save me!' Irene's scream filled the low-ceilinged cavern with a terrible echo. David worked furiously, trying to shift himself back. He moved along the side of the raft, but he knew he was going too slowly. Irene's screams had turned into desparate groaning sounds and he could hear her hands beating on the surface of the water as she tried to keep afloat.

David finally reached the back of the raft, and clinging on he scanned the dark surface of the water. He spotted her no more than ten or fifteen feet away and without thinking, he cast himself off from the side of the boat, the gluey bottom of the treacherous lake tugging at his legs, sucking him down.

'Hang on!' he called. He threw himself forward, his chest striking the now almost waterless surface. The muck began to pull at him with slightly less force as he spread his body weight over a large area. Somehow he managed to move a yard closer to Irene, but it wasn't enough. She was panicking, thrashing around, letting gravity and the subsurface ooze pull her inexorably down.

Suddenly the surface of the lake was bathed in light and David found himself staring into Irene's terrified face. Her shoulders were under now and only one arm was visible, beating weakly at the surface.

'Penfold!' roared Speers from behind him. David tore his eyes away from Irene and looked back over his shoulder, the ooze drawing him down another inch as he did so. The diver, covered almost completely in the red muck, was standing in the rear of the raft, chest heaving, a coil of rope in his hands. As David watched, Speers threw the coil, the strong, yellow cord snaking out over the surface of the lake towards him. The end of the coil landed less than a foot away from David's outstretched arm. He heaved, and his fingers locked around the lifeline. He turned again, the rope in his hand, and lunged out, desperately trying to reach Irene. There was little left of her above the surface — the top of her head, and a single clutching hand.

David pumped his legs in a hideous, slow motion parody of a running man, hurling himself towards her, his eyes riveted on the slowly opening and closing fingers of the single hand. Then, with less than a yard between them, the hand slid beneath the surface and she was gone.

'No!' screamed David, the sound torn from deep within him. In a final superhuman effort he pushed himself forward yet again, and dug down with his free hand. For a single moment he felt the touch of her hair in his fingers, and then it slid out of his clawing grip.

He barely felt the firm tug of the rope as Speers hauled him back to the raft. When the diver had brought him close enough he leaned over and grabbed David under the arms, lifting him bodily out of the bog-like lake.

'No more,' whispered David, his throat choked with tears as he lay propped against Speers in the rear of the raft. 'No more.' The diver reached out and put his arm around David's quaking shoulders and looked back across the featureless glistening lake that had swallowed Irene. He could feel the sweeping loneliness that was consuming David, and it was a loneliness he knew well. He gritted his teeth against the tears he felt and turned away, knowing that this was not the place or time for grief.

PART THREE
THE DEVIL'S
STAIRCASE

CHAPTER FOURTEEN

1

'We must take stock of our position,' said Izo, his back against a large slab of rock. His eyes were open, but Mariea and Tony Grace could see that they were still sightless, the eyes sunk deep into their sockets below the deep gash in his forehead. 'You have emptied the knapsack?' Tony nodded and then, realizing his error, he spoke.

'Yes,' he said. 'Right here.'

'Tell me what we have, exactly,' said Izo. The journalist looked down at the meagre pile spread out on the rock floor of the cave. It wasn't much.

'Five tins of food,' he enumerated. 'Three stew, two baked beans. Nine solid fuel pellets. Two containers of waterproof matches. One lantern. One spare battery. One coil of rope . . .'

'How long is the coil?' asked Izo, interrupting. Tony picked up the small skein.

'About fifty feet. That yellow nylon stuff.'

'All right, go on.'

'A dozen or so of those clips you used.'

'Karabiners,' said Izo nodding.

'Right,' said Tony. 'And the same number of the little spikes. A rock hammer . . . the kind with a pick on the other end. Three magnesium flares.'

'Go on,' urged Izo. Tony glanced at Mariea and grimaced. She shrugged her shoulders helplessly.

'That's it,' said Tony. There was a long silence. Finally Izo spoke, his voice firm.

'All right,' he said nodding. 'We know our limitations.'

'Too right!' breathed Tony despairingly.

'It is better to have something than nothing at all,' replied Izo. 'Things could be considerably worse.'

'How?' asked Tony. 'I almost killed all of us, and you're blind. How bad do you want it.'

'You didn't kill anybody, Tony,' said Izo. 'The cofferdam burst. If anything I am to blame.'

'Thanks for the vote of confidence,' said Tony, 'but you know perfectly well it was me. I panicked.'

'It is in the past,' said Izo. 'It can neither help nor hinder us in the present.'

'How the hell can you be so bloody forgiving!' said Tony, his voice catching in his throat. 'Why doesn't somebody take a swing at me or something?'

'It would serve no purpose,' said Izo evenly. 'I am not being forgiving, I am merely being a realist.'

'Izo's right,' said Mariea, repacking the knapsack. 'Self-recrimination isn't going to do anyone any good.'

'We must keep on,' said Izo. 'Now, since I cannot see, you must describe this place to me. Tell me everything you see.'

Tony Grace picked up the lantern and swung it slowly around the perimiter of the small cave, describing it as he moved the light.

'It's no more than a big room, actually. Approximately fifty feet per side. The ceiling is about twenty feet above us and it's . . . umm, rotten I suppose would be the best word.'

'Pieces broken out, fractured?' asked Izo.

'Yes, exactly,' said Tony. 'The floor's covered with big blocks and slabs of rock. From the roof I suppose. The stream runs a little off centre down the middle of the cave.'

'Leading where?' asked Izo, concentrating, trying to build an image up in his mind.

'There's a big crack in the far wall of the cave,' said Tony. He paused, trying to gauge its size. 'It runs right up to the ceiling. About five feet wide at the base, perhaps treble that up top. Anything more?'

'Does the stream fill the entire floor of the crack?' asked Izo.

'Wait a tick. I'll go take a look,' said Tony. He threaded his way across the littered floor of the cave, taking the lantern with him.

'Are you going to be all right?' asked Mariea, bending over Izo, a hand on his shoulder. He covered her hand with his own and smiled.

'I think so. The blindness is almost certainly temporary. It is not such a handicap in the darkness anyway.'

'Quit being so goddamn brave,' said Mariea, squeezing with her hand. 'I can't stand it.'

'I will do my best to be cowardly,' grinned Izo. A few moments later Tony Grace returned.

'It's no more than a trickle now. Maybe an inch deep on the floor of the exit. The way the water has been coming and going you'd think we were living in a block of flats with people taking baths all the time.'

'It is understandable,' said Izo. 'The earthquake almost certainly opened up new routes for the water to take. As they fill and find new ways of movement the flow will change erratically.'

'In other words, this cave could fill up with water in the next hour,' said Tony.

'It is possible, although unlikely,' said Izo. 'We must do our best to make our way where there is ample room to move out of any new currents.'

'Keep to the high ground?' said Mariea. Izo nodded.

'Yes,' he said.

'And if there is no high ground?' asked Tony.

'We just had that conversation,' said Mariea scowling. 'Let's quit going around in circles and get a move on.'

'I agree,' said Izo, rising to his feet shakily. Mariea steadied him, but he gently removed her hand. 'It is not necessary,' he said. 'I suggest that we use that coil of line to rope us together. Tony in front, myself in the centre and Mariea in the rear.'

'You want me to lead?' asked Tony, unbelieving. Izo nodded.

'Who else?' said the geologist, smiling. 'You are the man of words; you can describe things to me as we go along and I will

239

give what advice I can.'

'And if I make a mistake?' asked the journalist. 'What then?'

'We die,' put in Mariea coldly. 'So don't make any mistakes. Simple.'

'I hate working under pressure,' sighed Tony, shaking his head. Mariea and Izo both laughed.

'You'll learn to love it,' cooed Mariea.

Roped together they made their way out of the cave, edging through the crack which carried the trickling remnants of the torrent that had almost drowned them. Within a few minutes it became clear that they were not travelling through a simple cave system. As Tony described the scene, swinging the big lantern back and forth over the rock-strewn passage, Izo realized that the caves were not caves at all, but rather sections of a large tunnel that had once carried the full flow of a mighty river – perhaps a major tributary of the Styx. Every fifty or a hundred feet they would come upon a new chamber, and would have to either make their way through narrow fissures or clamber over mounds of rubbled stone.

The various chambers had been created along the joint lines of major blocks of limestone, and over time, and with the absence of water running through the tunnel, falls had occurred. Tony Grace's description was an apt one; it was, he said, rather like going through the watertight chambers of a big ocean liner. The only problem of course, was that these chambers were in no way waterproof, and if there was a major flood behind them they would not be able to escape. The sides of the tunnel were piled here and there with rubble, but there were no piles high enough to save them from anything but a minor influx of water. Even without Izo's handicap, movement would have been difficult, but having to point out each boulder and stone, guiding the sightless man at every step, made their progress almost unbearably slow. After three hours they had gone less than a mile.

'This is crazy,' said Mariea under her breath as they took a rest break. Ahead of them was yet another mass of broken rock barring their path. The ground at their feet was scattered with pieces of limestone varying in size from pebble-like scree to boulders to immense blocks as big as automobiles. It was almost as though the passage had been intentionally made as an obstacle course.

'Perhaps you should leave me here,' said Izo calmly.

'Don't be silly,' said Mariea. 'We wouldn't be going any faster without you.'

'That is not true,' said Izo.

'It doesn't matter whether it's true or not,' said Tony Grace, climbing to his feet again. 'We are not leaving you behind. No more discussion.' And they continued on. As they walked Izo tried as best he could to find his own way, working with his sense of hearing, measuring off echoes, and also trying to decipher their situation by the angle at which they were climbing, but none of it was much help. He relied almost totally on Tony's voice ahead of him, and Mariea's supporting hands behind. He knew that if his blindness didn't lift soon, he was going to become a dangerous burden to his friends.

They began climbing another mound of rubble, and as they reached its summit Izo could feel a slackening in the rope as Tony came to a sudden halt. Izo stopped immediately, not wanting to bump into him, and waited.

'Good Lord!' breathed the journalist.

'What is it?' asked Izo.

The strong beam of the lantern was barely sufficient to give more than slight definition to the incredible sight that lay ahead of them, and their slow and interrupted movement hadn't prepared Tony for the vastness below.

Twenty feet down the rubble pile the tunnel suddenly smoothed, with almost no fallen boulders to bar their way. The ceiling, before no more than forty or fifty feet above them, now leapt upwards in an incredible vault, curving into a gigantic dome at least four times that high.

'It's like a giant's cathedral,' whispered Tony, almost at a loss for words. The roof of the cavern stretched away into the distance, not sloping down to the floor for at least two thousand feet. Tony tried to envisage the monstrous flow of water that must have flowed along the incredible vaulted passage; a behemoth; a thundering, roaring, raging thing in the bowels of the earth. In the distance, almost at the limit of the lantern's beam, the light flickered across a wide stream of water, moving diagonally across the cave.

'There's a river,' said Tony.

'Which way does it flow?' asked Izo quickly.

'Across the cave, not along it,' said Tony. Izo dug into his now tattered jeans and pulled out his compass. He reached forward blindly, fumbling it into Tony's hand.

'By the compass,' he said. 'Which way?' Tony took the small device and held it steady in his palm, waiting for the needle to stop its swinging motion. He knew as well as Izo that the magnetic needle could be wildly inaccurate this far underground, but he said nothing.

'East,' he said at last. 'East-south-east,' he added correcting himself as the needle fluctuated slightly. 'Why is it so important?'

'The flow is considerable?' asked Izo.

'Yes,' agreed Tony.

'I know what you're thinking,' said Mariea, who had joined them atop the rubble pile. She stared out across the vast underground plain to the dark thread of water. 'You think we've found the Styx again.'

2

'Well, what do we do, wait, or go on?' asked Mariea. They sat on a broad, sloping intrusion of rock some fifty feet away from the smoothly-flowing river. 'Or does it make any difference.'

'You mean about the others?' asked Tony. She nodded. The journalist lifted his shoulders wearily, edging a little closer to the dully-glowing flames of the three Primus fuel pellets they had ignited. 'The chances are good that they have already been past,' he said. 'I checked where the river exits —

'there's a wide edge along one side; easy enough to walk along, for the moment at any rate.'

'They may have left some sign if they stopped here,' said Izo, staring sightlessly at the river. 'You have found nothing?'

'Nope,' answered Mariea. She began hacking the top off one of the tins of stew, smashing at it with the pick end of the rock hammer. 'No garbage or anything like that. They may not have camped here at all. If they've been through, that is.'

'Who the bloody hell are we trying to kid!' burst out Tony, anger in his voice. 'We don't even know if this is the same damn river! For all we know they could be a hundred miles away from here and going in a completely different direction. It's not as though this hell-hole came with a road map.'

'You must use reason,' interjected Izo. 'This is a major river flowing in the same direction as the one we were travelling on before. We climbed for a considerable time when we left the cave of the insects, and then we went even further downward. The chances of this being the original river are very good. You must not give up hope.'

The journalist picked up a small flat chip of stone from the floor of the cave and skipped it into the river. He scowled, his face drawn and grey in the flickering light.

'I'm tired of hoping,' said Grace. 'God! I've even lost track of how long we've been trapped down here.'

'You're still alive,' said Mariea crisply, taking a final whack at the tin. She peeled back the lid and slid the opened container in beside the fuel pellets. 'And the only alternative to hope is giving up. If you want to stick around here, go ahead, it'll just mean more food for me and Izo.'

'We are all under a great deal of stress,' said Izo, turning toward the sound of his friends' voices.

'Quite the understatement,' said Grace, flicking another stone into the water.

'We must keep our strength,' went on the geologist. 'We should eat and then get some rest. The river cannot go on forever, Tony. We will find a way out.'

'Will you put that in writing?' grimaced the journalist.

'Shut up and eat,' said Mariea. 'And then we'll sleep. Izo is right.'

Izo Harada sat in his sightless dark, listening to the even breathing of his sleeping friends. He could feel the warmth of the fuel pellet fire on his cheek and in the distance he could hear the rustling passage of the river as it flowed through the cave. He had insisted that Tony describe the cavern and the river in minute detail, so as he sat he was able to conjure up an image of it around him, letting himself pretend that the lantern was out and that, rather than visualizing, he was remembering. He pushed back the fears that fought for control of his mind, and by strength of will held back the wrenching terror of his blindness.

He stood up carefully, making as little noise as he could, and followed the sound of the water until he stood at the edge of the river. He could almost taste the water, and it gave out its own chill, competing with the ever-present coldness of the caves. He knelt, feeling forward with his hands until he reached the very edge. Tony had told him that the river had cut a deep trench through the cave, flowing a good six of seven feet below the level of the floor. He bent down, listening intently, as though the water could talk to him, tell him how much farther they had to go.

He sat back, thinking about his past, and the past of his people. There had been a time when a man in his position, blind and a burden to his colleagues, would have thrown himself into the water, sacrificing himself in an honourable death. But would it serve a purpose now, he wondered. He moved away from the edge and crossed his legs beneath him, assuming the classic lotus pose, hands upon his bent knees. He breathed deeply, willing his senses to recede, searching in his heart and soul for some kind of truth to guide him.

At the flickering edge of vision in some inner eye a figure moved, familiar and close. It was at once impossible and real, a joining of thought across an unimaginable gulf of time and civilization, a melding of purpose that could bridge any chasm. Once more, in vision or hallucination, oracle, or by some force so strong within that he remained forever in the very stone, Khan lived again.

3

The last remnants of his tribe were clustered around the tiny fire, made with the final lump of animal fat they had. There was no food now, and the small one cried all the time. It would die soon, and at least then there would be food for the others. He himself would not touch the flesh of his own kind, but the others were under no such taboo. It did not matter to him — he knew somehow that he would live the longest, come what may.

It would be their final camp, he knew. It was the only way. Without light and food they were as good as dead anyway. When they had slept he would guide them out of this giant place, and they would walk until they fell, or found the light at last.

And the light would be soon. It was more than a feeling, it was a knowledge deep within him, bred of a thousand clues, most of which he did not understand, but only knew intuitively. The movement in the air was stronger, and there seemed to be an eagerness in the water flow as it made its way across the cave and exited through the gashed hole that seemed so clearly to be the image of the place between a woman's legs. It would birth them again, into the light of day, and he would be victorious, a true leader of his tribe.

Or at least what was left of it. Four now, three women and the child. Soon the child would be gone, and there would only be the women. It didn't matter. He smiled, watching the small group from his place beyond the light. He would lie with them all, and they would make him a new tribe. There would be others in the place where they came up out of the ground as well. Life would be good. His magic would not desert him; rather it would carry him up from the ground to sit on a hilltop and see the sun again.

His people, the women, had no faith. They spent all their time huddled together, their tears staining their cheeks, afraid of the darkness and the cold, terrified that they had been eaten by the earth. He had tried to tell them, almost as a story, that if they were eaten then that was good, for it meant they would be released, just as food was eaten and released in any one of them. It was a simple thing.

He stood, restless, and went to stand by the river again, a thing he had done many times now. He had a strange feeling in his belly that they must hurry if they were to find the light, and he felt as well that the light would trick him, and make him work his magic strongly, a final proof of his power. He breathed deeply, one large hand caressing the thick hairs across his chest and taut stomach. He had no fear of such tests. He was the son of his father, the greatest maker of magic in his tribe. His father had been able to tease fire out of wood. He would be able to bring himself from the bowels of the earth into the light. He had travelled with his people into the kingdom of the afterlife and the place of spirits, and he had survived. He would live again and tell the story to all who would listen.

He gave a deep powerful growl, warning his people that the time was near. His ears pricked, summoned by a phantom wind, and from somewhere he was sure he could hear the faint whistle of a bird in flight. Omen after omen, telling him to make haste. He turned, his deep set, powerful eyes scanning behind him in the weak light from the fire. The immense cavern seemed to stretch to infinity, but he knew its dimensions, for only that day they had travelled the length of it. His nose twitched, and he felt an itching in his palms. Every muscle in his powerful body spoke to him, urging him to move, and do so quickly. He shook his head, clearing it of thought. There was no time to dream any more, it was time to act. He turned, and at a run, moved towards the fire, calling out his orders urgently.

Izo opened his eyes and it was only after a few moments that he realized he could see again; not well, but at least he could distinguish light and dark. He felt a surge of wild elation, and almost called out in his joy, but he stopped himself. He unravelled himself from the lotus, his muscles aching. It felt as though he had been in the position for hours. He held out his hand in front of him, and faintly, like vague grey shadows, he could make out the outlines of his fingers. Gently he reached up and touched the gash in his forehead. It was sore, but the swelling seemed to have gone down somewhat. He wondered if the swelling might not have caused his blindness. It didn't matter — for he could see again!

He stood, blinking, looking down at the water, then turned. There was only the faintest light from the last of the fuel pellets, but it was enough. He crossed the floor of the cave and sat down by the fire. On the far side of it he could make out the huddled forms of Mariea and Tony. He wanted to wake them and tell them about his sight, but he let them sleep; there would be time enough later.

He frowned, remembering his dream of Khan, and wondered if it was a dream at all. He wondered if his subconscious was using the image of the Neanderthal as some sort of mechanism to keep him hopeful, or whether it was a sign that he was going mad. All he knew was the man's reality. He could almost smell him, as though he stood no more than a few feet away, and Izo's still bleary eyes automatically scanned the floor of the cave around him for signs of the fire made by Khan's people. He turned, on instinct, exactly as Khan had done, and stared down the length of the cavern, trying to focus on the distant wall or rubble half a mile away. It was no use; he could see no more than Khan and knew no more about why the vision bothered him than the Neanderthal did. But it was there, a disturbing lurch in his guts that refused to be denied. Logically there was nothing to fear, but acting on his instinct, and following Khan's suit, he woke the others.

Both Tony and Mariea were ecstatic at the news that Izo's sight was returning but, on the other hand, they were both exhausted. Neither of the two seemed to have profited by their sleep.

247

'We're still saddled with the same question,' said Mariea, brows furrowed. Each time she moved her head it seemed to give her pain. 'Do we stay and wait for the others to come cruising by, or do we go on?'

'I think we should go on,' said Izo. 'I have a bad feeling about this place.'

'Not being too scientific,' said Tony. Izo smiled, turning toward the lank writer.

'No. An intuition,' he said. He could make out Tony's features now, even though they were still blurred. It seemed as though his sight was going to return fully.

'I know what you mean,' said Mariea. 'It's just too big. Makes me feel really . . . I don't know, useless. Like I was all alone in the Houston Astrodome or something.'

'Well, whatever it is, its given me an absolute corker of a headache,' muttered Tony.

'You too?' asked Mariea. 'I thought I was going to die when Izo woke me up. Hammer and tongs.'

'You both have headaches?' aked Izo, suddenly very alert. They both nodded.

'A bad one,' said Tony.

'Right,' said Mariea.

Izo bent down and inspected the spot where Tony had lit the solid fuel pellets to give them some warmth. He motioned to Tony and the tall man squatted down beside him.

'I cannot see well enough,' said the geologist, urgency in his voice. 'But you must tell me quickly — have the pellets gone out, or have they been consumed.' Tony picked up one of the white oblongs. A third of it crumbled at his touch, but the rest remained solid.

'It looks like it just went out,' said Tony. He turned to Izo questioningly. 'Does that mean something to you?' Izo nodded.

'Hypoxia,' he said. 'You are both tired, headaches. Soon your eyesight will become blurred.'

'Hypoxia?' asked Grace. 'That's lack of oxygen.'

'Correct,' said Izo. 'We must leave the cavern immediately. Gather up what is left of those fuel pellets.'

'I don't get it,' said Mariea, frowning. 'How can their be a lack of oxygen? This place is full of air.'

'It may well be,' said Izo, taking the woman by the arm and leading her quickly down to the river. 'But not at this level. 'We have been breathing a large concentration of carbon-dioxide. I was at the river and perhaps received less than either of you because I was in the airstream leading out of the cave. Had I been with you up here none of us might have awakened.'

Pausing only to gather up the last of their meagre belongings Tony Grace followed Izo and Mariea down to the river. They began moving quickly towards the dark oval tunnel mouth which marked the exit from the gigantic cavern.

'I still don't understand quite,' said Tony Grace, walking behind Mariea and Izo. 'How could the cave become filled with carbon-dioxide?'

'It is a common feature of cave systems with poor circulation of air,' said Izo without turning. They entered the tunnel and began picking their way along the narrow ledge which ran along beside the dark ribbon of the river a dozen feet below. 'There is a cave in Germany where the concentration of carbon-dioxide is almost ninety per cent.'

'And we never would have known a thing,' said Grace, amazed. 'We go through absolute hell and wind up being almost killed by something we couldn't see.'

Izo, now back in his position at the head of the group, shone the weakening beam of the lantern ahead. It had been in constant use for at least two days and he knew the heavy-duty battery wouldn't last much longer. Izo's sight was returning more and more with each passing minute, and as his vision came back the thought of being without the light of the lantern began to consume him. He quickened his pace, driven on by the failing light and the strange optimism of his vision of Khan. Although it defied all logic he felt sure that the last stage of their journey was close at hand and his gradually strengthening eyes peered forward, searching along the pale beam of light.

Any fears Izo might have had about a sudden flood surging

down the tunnel were quickly dispelled. It was clear from the passage's geography that the water had been flowing at a fairly constant rate for centuries. Thick masses of 'soda-straw' calcite formations hung down from the roof of the tunnel, the thin, milky tubes of calcite hanging down to within two or three feet of their heads. The calcite tubes were another indication that there was little or no air circulation in the cave behind them, since the delicate rods could only form in an almost motionless atmosphere. The river itself had etched deeply into the soft limestone floor of the tunnel, so that within a few minutes the trio of survivors were at least thirty or forty feet above the water. The ledge they were travelling on was broad and well defined, with almost nothing to cause them difficulties except the occasional boulder in their path.

Less than an hour passed before the ledge began to slope downward along the tunnel wall, moving towards the river. The way became increasingly steep to the point where Izo and the other two were forced to hang on to the slippery surface of the tunnel wall for support. Then the tunnel itself began to narrow quickly, forcing the peaceful flow of the water up until it almost topped the ledge itself.

'What's going on?' asked Tony Grace. Ahead of him, outlined in the light from the lantern, Izo shrugged.

'There is an intrusion of some kind of rock. It appears to be travertine from what I can make out. It is much harder than the limestone. It is squeezing the river, to put it simply.' As he walked Izo kept his eyes on the ground before him, choosing each step with care. The closer the ledge came to the water the more slippery it became. He urged the others to walk carefully as well.

'Is it going to get any narrower?' asked Mariea.

Before Izo could answer, the question was answered for him. With the freezing waters of the river lapping at their feet the tunnel abruptly ended and they were in the open again.

Tony came out of the tunnel to find Izo and Mariea transfixed where they stood. In the middle distance, a thousand feet away beside a gigantic pool of inky water, sat David Penfold and Frank Speers around the welcome warmth of the

Primus stove. With shouts of unrestrained joy that echoed wildly upwards, Mariea and Tony Grace raced across the flat, featureless expanse of the cave floor to their colleagues.

Izo stayed behind, the beam of the lantern shining upward.

Even though its weak light could only penetrate part way up the striated and folded rock wall beside him, Izo knew with a sinking sensation in his heart that one way or the other, their long journey along the River Styx was almost at an end. He flicked off the lantern to conserve what was left of the battery and slowly went down to join the others.

CHAPTER FIFTEEN

1

The five remaining members of the Subrano archaeological expedition sat closely around the heat and light of the small stove, each lost in his or her own thoughts. Their pleasure at meeting again had faded and now, with their meal completed, fatigue was slowly but surely claiming them, one by one.

Izo, his sight now fully returned, sat slightly apart from the others, his mind methodically going over their options. After the first flush of pleasure at being reunited, Frank Speers had taken the geologist aside and with the information the diver had given him, combined with the evidence of his own eyes, Izo had a reasonably clear idea of their situation.

His first assessment of the cavern had been depressing enough; Izo had recognized the formation as a major volcanic chimney with the pool as its only exit. Then Speers had lit a magnesium flare and the true dimensions of their predicament were revealed.

The chimney was of mammoth proportions, larger by far than anything Izo had ever seen, either in person or in photographs. It rose, straight up for at least a thousand feet — the limit of vision given them by the flare. In the brief, intense glare of the magnesium torch Izo had taken in the incredible sight. The sheer walls were cracked and marred by the passage of time, but nowhere that he could see were there any major ledges or points where they could rest. The barren floor of the cavern was evidence enough that little or nothing had fallen from either the walls or the unseen roof of the chimney for aeons. Standing at the bottom of the awesome pit was like being placed in the basement of a gigantic skyscraper and looking up the empty lift-shaft. To climb it would be almost an impossibility.

But there were no other exits. Speers and Penfold had been camped in the chimney for what they thought was at least a full day and a night, and in that time they had been able to find no break in the walls. Both men had done a slow walk of the entire perimeter and both had come up empty-handed.

'And the river?' Izo had asked. Speers had taken him down to the pool. The pool was in fact almost large enough to warrant being called a lake. It was at least four hundred feet across, the water level coming to within a foot of the stone floor of the cavern. At first glance it seemed utterly calm except for a small area where the river flowed into it, but Speers had shown Izo otherwise. Using a spent match to demonstrate, the diver had lowered himself beside the edge of the pool, telling Izo to do the same. As gently as possible he had reached down, delicately placing the small sliver of wood on the apparently calm surface of the water. For a brief moment the matchstick stayed where it was, held by the surface tension of the water. Then, almost faster than the eye could see, it had vanished, sucked downwards with unbelievable force.

'It's a huge siphon,' said Speers. 'The entire flow of the river ends up here, then gets sucked down into the foot of this chimney. I'm willing to bet it gets blown out an old volcanic vent, and not far from here either — look!' He had taken Izo around to the opposite side of the huge basin of dark water, squatting down again at a point directly opposite where he had done his conjuring trick with the disappearing match. 'There,' said Speers triumphantly, pointing. Izo followed the direction of his finger. Deep within the pool, at least twenty feet down, was a faint shimmering glint.

'What is it?' asked Izo. Speers grinned.

'Light, my friend, that's what it is. That spot of light is the way out of here. The way outside.'

'I do not mean to dampen your enthusiasm,' said Izo carefully. 'But I think it could be many things. A reflection perhaps. Light from your stove reflecting somehow off a mica outcropping.' Speers shook his head, still grinning.

'No way,' he said, almost gloating. 'I've checked it out in complete darkness, with Penfold. We've both seen it in the pitch darkness, no stove, lamps, matches or anything. It's still there.'

'Then why have you waited?' asked Izo. Speers winked at him.

'Smart, aren't you? What? You think I don't have the guts to dive into that?' The diver gestured at the dark pool.

'I only asked why you had not already done it,' said Izo softly.

'I'm not a complete turkey, Harada. You know as well as I do why I stuck around. I wanted to see if there was any difference in the light between one time and another. Day and night.'

'And is there?' asked Izo. He winced as a wave of pain slashed into his brain. He ignored it, knowing that the wound in his forehead would be giving him headaches for days to come.

'It never completely fades, but there is definite change,' said Speers, his voice serious. 'I figure it never disappears because of moonlight, reflected starlight, that kind of thing. Down there it's a total absence of light; on the surface it never gets absolutely dark.'

'It could be some form of bioluminescence,' argued Izo. 'Glow worms, luminescent fungi or bacteria in a cavern further on. It might fluctuate due to temperature changes in the water. Any number of things would cause the light levels

253

to shift.'

'It's the outside, Harada,' stated Speers, his voice filled with an iron-willed desire. 'I know it's the outside.'

'And David, what does he think?' asked Izo. Speers shrugged.

'He's willing to go along with it. He's not convinced, but he knows there's no other way out of here.' The diver gestured widely. 'Look at this place! We're at the bottom of the biggest goddamned well in the universe. You actually think we're going to *climb* out of here?'

'It would be difficult,' admitted Izo. 'But it might be better than chasing after your phantom light.'

'Phantom, my ass,' snapped Speers. 'You can see it as well as I can. It's real, Harada. And it's the only way out.'

'How do you propose to do it?' asked Izo. Speers smiled.

'I've got a single tank and regulator left,' he said. 'I figure there's about twenty minutes of air in the tank. That's enough for me and one other person going buddy on the mouthpiece to get out of here. There's enough food for at least a couple of weeks for the rest. They can wait while we go for help.'

'Why two people?' asked Izo. 'Why not dive by yourself?'

'It's never smart to dive by yourself,' said the harsh-featured man. 'If one of us gets hung up on a rock, or caught somehow, the other can help him out. Just makes good sense.'

'Or you could be condemning the other person to a terrible death,' said Izo. Speers shrugged.

'That's up to the other person,' said Speers. 'I'm not forcing anyone to go with me.'

'Who did you want to accompany you?' asked Izo. 'Have you thought about that yet?' Speers nodded.

'Yeah,' he said, looking at the geologist coolly. 'I figured before it was going to be Penfold, of course. I didn't have much choice. But with you here . . . well, I don't know. The spot's open if you want it.' He waited for the older man's reply. Izo smiled and shook his head.

'No,' he said. 'I thank you for the offer, but I think it

would be unwise to leave the others here without someone who had some experience with caves.'

'Suit yourself,' said Speers, and the conversation had ended. The question of who would accompany Speers still had not been resolved, and the diver had said nothing about it at dinner with the others. He had made it clear that he would make the attempt the following day.

Izo waited until the rest of the group had given in to sleep before he rose from his place by the waning heat of the Primus. He picked up the flashlight from the mound of supplies that Speers and David Penfold had managed to salvage then walked across the barren, almost perfectly smooth floor of the immense pit, stopping beside the pool. He flicked off the flashlight and peered into the depths of the somnolent water. Speers's light was still there, a dull glow lost in the gloomy darkness of the deceptively still-looking water. Izo cheched his chronometer. If it could still be trusted it was nów almost two o'clock in the morning, and yet the light still glowed. Izo shook his head, trying to reach some decision. He sat back on his haunches, his fingers lightly touching the dressing Mariea Tarvanin had placed on his wound. The pain was still there, and the headaches came and went, but it was nothing he couldn't bear.

He stared into the water again. What would Khan have done? He thought to himself. What *had* Khan done. There was no evidence of the Neanderthal in the cavern, so if he and his tribe had reached this place, how had they left it? The thought that perhaps the group had never arrived at the immense chimney never crossed Izo's mind. He *knew* that Khan had come this far. It was as though he and the ancient man were brothers, locked together over time.

To Izo it was not a matter of belief, it was a matter of fact. Khan had come this way forty of fifty thousand years before. He had stood where Izo now stood, and he had asked the same questions in his mind. And somehow, he had found an answer. The pool, or the horrifying, dizzying heights of the chimney? Had there been a light in the pool then, glowing, tempting? Had Khan believed in the pool as the way, or the chimney? How had he decided?

Izo stood, stumbling slightly, a wave of dizziness over-coming him for a fleeting moment. If Khan and his people had gone into the pool and drowned their bones would long since have disappeared. If they had climbed the chimney to some distant exit, then there would be no sign either. It was an impossible choice.

The worried man slowly worked his way back along the river-bed to the point where the water gushed out of the narrow crevice in the sheer walled chimney. He climbed up the ancient flow-stone deposit left by the rushing water over the millenia until he stood beside the entrance, the water only a dozen feet away. He looked back down the slope and across the giant expanse of the chimney floor.

Khan had stood there. He had stood, and seen the same things in the dim light of a campfire burned by his people, much like the distant glow of the Primus. Khan had seen the small reflections of his fire on the surface of the lagoon-sized pool of black water, and he had stared up into the impossible reaches of the chimney. But what had he seen, and what had he done.

Without conscious thought, his heart pounding in his chest, Izo turned around, lifting the flashlight and flicking it on. Instantly a small puddle of yellow light glowed on the rock wall. He played the light carefully back and forth, examining every inch of the smooth surface without any clear knowledge of why he was doing it except a tugging, itching knowledge of Khan, an intuitive bond from one man to another. And then he saw it; the legacy that Khan had left behind, a sign bright and alive as though it had been placed upon the unforgiving rock only hours before. Four small drawings that told the story of Khan's last moments here, and the recording of his thoughts, the process of his mind as clear as speech. Slowly, almost reverently, Izo Harada approached the rock wall, the flashlight still marking the spot. He reached out and touched the stone, tears welling up in his eyes. A shiver ran down his spine and for a moment the pain behind his eyes lifted. He turned, looking over his shoulder, almost expecting to see the short muscular figure of the artist behind him, but there was nothing. Izo took a last look at the drawings, then turned away, running down the flow-stone slope to the distant light of the stove.

2

'But how on earth did you know?' asked Tony Grace. Hours had passed since Izo's discovery. He had awakened David Penfold first and the archaeologist had concurred with him. Now the entire group was clustered around the small drawings on the wall.

'It seemed likely,' said Izo, trying to make logic of his feelings for Khan. 'He was an artist, and if he had come to this place I felt sure he would have left some mark.'

'It's spooky,' said Mariea, staring at the delicate lines. 'Do you really think it's a clue to the way out of here?'

'It's bullshit,' said Frank Speers. 'And I've had enough of it. I'm going to get my gear ready.' The others ignored the diver as he turned away and went back down to the camp.

'I think it must be almost like a notebook,' answered David. 'The man had seen something, and he tried to work it out graphically. It was the logical thing for him to do. The first two drawings work out the idea of things being smaller the farther you are from them. The tree remains static, giving you a fixed point, while the man becomes smaller in relation to it.' David swung the beam of the flashlight slightly, lighting the other two drawings. 'The second set seems to refer to the chimney here. A small man standing in a circle while there is a half moon circle far above him. The second drawing shows the same man standing in a much larger half moon.'

'The meaning is quite clear, I think,' said Izo. 'Khan saw a small gleam of light, far up the chimney. He managed to work out the idea of perspective, and came to the conclusion that in reality the light was much larger – a way out. The idea was then to climb to the larger "half moon" as David calls it.'

'Don't you think that perhaps *you* are the one jumping to that conclusion?' asked Tony Grace somewhat sceptically. 'For instance, that half moon might be just that – his idea of the moon. Some kind of religious talisman perhaps, or maybe even just wishful thinking.'

'Perhaps,' said Izo nodding, 'but I prefer to give him more credit. This is the way out.'

'I find it hard to believe,' said the journalist, shaking his head. 'I've been a science reporter too long to put my faith in something scrawled on a rock wall a couple of dozen millenia ago. It's too much of a risk – you can *see* the light in the pool.'

'You must make the choice,' said Izo. 'There is science, the technology of Mr Speers and his air tank. And there is this. A message left by someone who perhaps might be your ancestor.'

'There is also my own bloody fear,' said the writer, expelling a long breath. 'You know what happened when I panicked before. If I did it up on this rock wall I could kill everyone. I'd freeze.'

'Or you could split the difference,' said Mariea, smiling. 'We'll go up, Speers can go down, and you can wait here.'

'Too right!' laughed Tony Grace weakly. 'And what if both of you are wrong? I'd prefer a quick death to waiting around alone down here. Thank you very much indeed, but I'm leaving with everyone else.'

'With Speers?' asked Izo. The journalist nodded.

'If he'll have me,' he said. 'I'm sorry, Izo, but I just can't make myself believe in your ancient fellow here.'

'It is a hard choice,' agreed the geologist. 'For all of us.'

'So let's quit procrastinating and do it!' said Mariea.

3

In the end, it took very little time to prepare for their departure; neither group intended carrying anything at all in the way of supplies since they both were pinning their hopes on escaping, either from the chimney, dubbed The Devil's Staircase by Mariea Tarvanin, or through the siphon. In the case of Izo's group, made up of himself, David and Mariea, the climb would take hours. Speers and Tony Grace on the other hand expected to be free of their subterranean prison within minutes of dropping into the pool.

'Well,' said Tony Grace, his voice filled with emotion. 'This is the last farewell, I suppose.' He stood with Frank Speers on the edge of the pool. Speers had given the thin man his wet-suit to wear, while the diver himself wore nothing but a pair of cut-off jeans. Speers had the air tank strapped to his back and he had tethered himself to the journalist with a length of nylon cord. Speers, wearing the only mask, would lead Tony, sharing the mouthpiece as they went.

'I wish you well,' said Izo. He took Tony's outstretched hand and shook it firmly. 'I hope you are right,' he added, turning to Speers. The diver grinned and slid the mask down over his face. He gestured to Tony Grace who turned, putting his back to the pool.

'I'm always doing things arse backwards,' he said, grinning nervously. On impulse Mariea stepped forward and kissed the man squarely on the mouth, and even in the harsh light from the lanterns they could all see the journalist's cheeks become inflamed. David Penfold gave the two men the thumbs up and then Speers flicked on the twin set of flashlights on either side of the mask. He gave a brief wave, nodded to Tony Grace, then stepped backwards off the lip of the pool. There was a huge splash and then the two men were gone, sucked down by the surging current hidden just below the surface. There was a brief flash from Speers's lights below the surface and then that was gone as well. Izo, David

259

and Mariea were alone. They turned away from the pool silently and went back to the still burning Primus.

There was virtually no proper equipment for them except a single climbing belt and its tools. Izo and David had gone through all of the supplies on the raft and had found nothing that might be of use on the climb except two more coils of rope, giving them less than two hundred feet of line altogether. For the most part the climb would have to be made without tethers or safety lines, and once they had begun there would be no turning back.

The flickering light from the Primus cast long shadows in a slow dance across Izo as he strapped on the climbing belt and picked up the coils of rope. He checked his watch, then looked at his two friends.

'There is little that I can say,' he murmured, smiling. 'Except that we are undoubtedly better equipped than Khan and his people were when they made this climb. I am sure he had no rope at all, or rock hammers, or pitons. I am not saying that it will be easy, just that it has been done before, so that we should not think that what we are attempting is impossible.'

'You really are convinced Khan climbed this?' asked Mariea, staring up into the darkness. Izo nodded.

'Yes, I am convinced. And I am convinced that he succeeded.'

'Well, as long as you're in the lead again,' said David. 'Just tell us what to do.'

'It will not be for me to say,' said the geologist. 'You will have to make many judgements on your own as we go. Technically, this is what is referred to as a free climb. Handholds, footgrips and jams will appear and you must take advantage of each one as it comes.'

'What's a jam?' asked David. Izo demonstrated, holding up one hand.

'A jam is a crack in the rock, narrower at the bottom than it is at the top. It is too wide to grip with your fingers, but you can insert your hand flat, then fold it into a fist. The friction will hold you in place.'

'It sounds painful,' said Mariea, frowning.

'It could well save your life,' said Izo. 'I will climb first, followed by Mariea, then David. I will attempt to climb to the limit of a pitch, a full length of the rope. When I have climbed that far I will hammer in a piton, attach a karabiner, and belay the rope. When that is done the second person can climb, using the rope for extra grip, and as a safety line. By that time I will have moved up to the second pitch, taking the other coil of rope. I will attach it with a piton and karabiner as well. When David reaches the top of the first pitch it will be his job to unfasten the first line and pass it up to Mariea, who will be waiting with me at the top of the second pitch. In that way we will travel in roughly two hundred foot sections. At the end of each two hundred foot unit I will try to find as good a position as possible to rest. Is that clear to you both?' Mariea and David nodded.

'A little confusing,' said Mariea, 'but I guess I'll get the hang of it.'

'I think you will,' said Izo. 'It sounds difficult but like any climbing this is mostly a matter of common sense.'

'And luck,' put in David. He glanced up at the imposing curbed slab of rock several hundred feet away, and barely visible in the meagre light from the stove. 'What about lamps?' he asked.

'A good point,' said Izo. 'We will leave one of the large lamps on, with its beam pointing upward, and I shall carry another. Each one of us will also carry a flashlight.'

'Why the lamp at the bottom?' asked Mariea nervously. 'Frankly I'd rather not know what was underneath me.'

'We will need it to find grips,' said Izo. 'And if you do not want to see what is below you . . .'

'Sure,' she interrupted wryly. 'Don't look down.'

'Exactly,' grinned Izo. 'Now, shall we begin?'

4

Even in the damp cold of the underground chamber the sweat was running freely down David Penfold's face. He had been climbing for three hours, and to him it seemed like an eternity. Above him, echoing faintly, he could hear the faint tapping of Izo's hammer as yet another piton was set into place. David's chest heaved against the rock as he drew in another shaking breath. His hand crept out, the fingers bleeding and sore, searching for yet another minuscule crack. His other hand gripped the thin lifeline tightly. His eyes peered at the rock inches from his face as his leg shifted, his foot digging into another tiny break in the stone. They had long since left the glare of the light on the cave floor behind, and except for the brief periods when Izo reached the top of a pitch and shone his light downwards, he had been working almost blindly.

Only once had he looked down. The light, so bright and glaring when they began to climb, had turned into a pinprick, and the giant pool had shrunk to the size of a glittering silver dollar. Vomit had risen in his throat and a wave of vertigo had almost swept him off the wall of stone, but he had crushed his cheek against the cold rock, squeezing his eyes tightly shut until the terrible feeling passed. He had been close to the top of the ninth pitch, roughly eight hundred feet up. That had been an hour ago, and he had completed four more pitches since then. Each time the thought of his being more than a thousand feet up with nothing keeping him there but a single strand of rope and the strength of his own hands came into his mind, he banished it, concentrating desperately on the rock in front of him, letting his mind fill with the touch and smell of it. Since the beginning of the climb they had rested only twice, crammed on to faint ledges in the stone, not talking, each lost in his own fear, each step bringing them closer to the unseen summit, and further from the yawning pit below, spawning ground of recurring visions in which each one saw himself falling in a slow terrible cart-wheel of arms and legs, screams of horror echoing until the terrible impact at the bottom.

David sensed that he was coming to the end of the pitch and looked up, expecting to see Mariea's boots above him somewhere, but there was nothing. Frowning, he continued to climb, sure that he was right about the distance he had come. Then, almost magically, the rock in front of him disappeared and he found himself staring at the grinning figures of Izo and Mariea. David grabbed at their outstretched hands and boosted himself up over the edge, sprawling on to the hard rock floor. He lay there for a moment, gasping, then rolled over and sat up.

'Funny,' he said, still breathing hard. 'You might have told me you found a place to rest.'

'We didn't want to get you excited,' said Mariea, still grinning from ear to ear. 'I almost killed Izo when I got up and found him sitting here. But he said that you make mistakes when you think you've hit the top and the last thing we want is a fall.'

'What do you mean the top?' said David. 'This isn't the summit.'

'There is no summit, David,' said Izo. 'This is a volcanic flue, not a main channel to the core. And what we are sitting in now is a vent.'

'But what did Khan see?' asked David, still not quite believing it. Izo lifted his shoulders tiredly, his face in the lantern pale and lined with pain.

'Perhaps he saw light from this vent, or another higher up,' said the geologist. 'But the fact that there is a vent like this means that we will eventually find our way.'

'You mean this might lead to the outside?' said David, stunned. Izo nodded.

'Perhaps,' he said. 'There is a chance at least. 'And if not this one, then another.'

'Then let's go!' said David, climbing to his feet, his exhaustion suddenly gone. Izo stood up much more slowly, leaning on Mariea for support. 'Are you okay? asked David.

Izo nodded briefly.

'Only tired,' he said with a weak smile. 'I am not as young as the two of you, and I must admit to my head aching from this wound.' He lifted a hand to the stained bandage over his eyes.

'Why don't we rest for a while,' suggested Mariea.

'I agree,' said David, his voice concerned. Izo waved the objections away.

'No. We will go on,' he ordered. 'You go ahead, David, and I will lean on Mariea . . .' He handed David the large lantern, waving him forward. David nodded and went ahead, shining the beam along the smooth, slightly curved surface of the rock. The walking was easy, the floor of the tunnel smooth and even. The passage moved upwards at quite a steep angle, and then, after they had been walking for ten or fifteen minutes, it suddenly flattened out, following some route ordained a million years before when white hot lava had poured through the almost perfectly circular tube.

At first David thought it was light reflecting back from the lantern in his hand, but suddenly he realized that there was another source of light ahead of them. He touched the switch on the lantern for a moment, dousing the light, and then he was sure. He turned on the lantern again and began to run.

'*Izo, Mariea, it's sunlight!*' he yelled. Beneath his feet the smooth hardened lava gave way to a thick loamy soil. Then he reached the mouth of the volcanic vent, turned by the ages into a cave in its own right. He stood, transfixed, staring. He didn't even notice when Mariea joined him.

There, setting on a horizon David thought he would never see again, was the gigantic brazen disc of the sun, casting a copper glow into the clear, dusk bowl of the sky. Below them meadows rolled down in gently undulating hills, the deep light of the setting sun turning everything to gold. A breeze began to blow, fanning David's face lightly as he turned his head, drinking in the scene around him, a vast panorama of land and sky that reduced the twisting dark passages behind them to nothing. He saw a skittering shape in the sky, a small black dot that transformed itself into the wildly gyrating shape of a swallow, and tears welled in his eyes. He turned, to find Mariea at his side, and without a word or thought, he gently took her hand.

'My God!' whispered David, looking out across the rolling hills. In the far distance he could see the faint blue line of the ocean. 'This is the most beautiful thing I've ever seen.'

'Where's Izo?' asked Mariea. They turned and found the geologist on his knees, bent over, examining something on the packed earth floor of the cave. They tore themselves away from the scene at the mouth of the grotto and joined him.

'What is it?' asked Mariea, squatting down beside the geologist.

'See for yourself,' said Izo, sitting back. David looked down and saw what his friend had been examining.

There, embedded in the rich earth of the cave, and only partially revealed after five hundred centuries of erosion by wind and rain, was the skull of a man, its earth-filled eye sockets staring outwards at the dying sun. A small ridge of bone ran from front to back along the saggital crest, like a soldier's helmet. The brows were large, but not protruding, and the visible portion of the jaw was strong and powerful.

The sun had fallen even farther towards the horizon, the almost horizontal rays now pouring into the cave, bathing the skull with light that turned the ancient bone to gold, a shimmering, almost unreal thing on the floor of the cavern. The three survivors stared down at the last remains of the man who had led them out of the darkness.

'Khan,' whispered David. 'They must have buried him here.' He reached out and gently touched the forehead of the skull. The bone was warm, heated by the sun. 'I wish I knew what they had really called you,' he said.

'It doesn't matter,' said Izo, standing. 'You believed in him, and no man could ask for more than that.'

'I wish . . .' began Mariea, tears falling freely from her eyes. 'I wish he could come with us.'

'Let him be,' said Izo. Then the three turned and left the cave, walking in the world again.

*   *   *

Deep below the earth, unseen except by the single fading eye of the lamp on the cold and soundless floor of the chimney, an object rose for a moment in the dark pool. A diver's mask. Then it was swallowed up and the surface of the pool was calm once more.

FICTION

GENERAL

☐ Chains	Justin Adams	£1.25
☐ Secrets	F. Lee Bailey	£1.25
☐ Skyship	John Brosnan	£1.65
☐ The Free Fishers	John Buchan	£1.50
☐ Huntingtower	John Buchan	£1.50
☐ Midwinter	John Buchan	£1.25
☐ A Prince of the Captivity	John Buchan	£1.25
☐ The Eve of St Venus	Anthony Burgess	£1.10
☐ Nothing Like the Sun	Anthony Burgess	£1.50
☐ The Memoirs of Maria Brown	John Cleland	£1.25
☐ The Last Liberator	John Clive	£1.25
☐ Wyndward Fury	Norman Daniels	£1.50
☐ Ladies in Waiting	Gwen Davis	£1.50
☐ The Money Wolves	Paul Erikson	£1.50
☐ Rich Little Poor Girl	Terence Feely	£1.50
☐ Fever Pitch	Betty Ferm	£1.50
☐ The Bride of Lowther Fell	Margaret Forster	£1.75
☐ Forced Feedings	Maxine Herman	£1.50
☐ Savannah Blue	William Harrison	£1.50
☐ Duncton Wood	William Horwood	£1.95
☐ Dingley Falls	Michael Malone	£1.95
☐ Gossip	Marc Olden	£1.25
☐ Buccaneer	Dudley Pope	£1.50
☐ An Inch of Fortune	Simon Raven	£1.25
☐ The Dream Makers	John Sherlock	£1.50
☐ The Reichling Affair	Jack Stoneley	£1.75
☐ Eclipse	Margaret Tabor	£1.35
☐ Pillars of the Establishment	Alexander Thynn	£1.50
☐ Cat Stories	Stella Whitelaw	£1.10

WESTERN — BLADE SERIES by Matt Chisholm

☐ No. 5 The Colorado Virgins	85p
☐ No. 6 The Mexican Proposition	85p
☐ No. 7 The Arizona Climax	85p
☐ No. 8 The Nevada Mustang	85p
☐ No. 9 The Montana Deadlock	95p
☐ No. 10 The Cheyenne Trap	95p
☐ No. 11 The Navaho Trail	95p
☐ No. 12 The Last Act	95p

WESTERN — McALLISTER SERIES by Matt Chisholm

☐ McAllister and the Spanish Gold	95p
☐ McAllister on the Commanche Crossing	95p
☐ McAllister Never Surrenders	95p
☐ McAllister and the Cheyenne Trap	95p

SCIENCE FICTION

☐ Times Without Number	John Brunner	£1.10
☐ The Dancers of Arun	Elizabeth A. Lynn	£1.50
☐ Watchtower	Elizabeth A. Lynn	£1.10

WAR

☐ The Andersen Assault	Peter Leslie	£1.25
☐ Killers under a Cruel Sky	Peter Leslie	£1.25
☐ The Serbian Triangle	Peter Saunders	£1.10
☐ Jenny's War	Jack Stoneley	£1.25

FICTION

GENERAL

☐ The Free Fishers	John Buchan	£1.50
☐ Huntingtower	John Buchan	£1.50
☐ Midwinter	John Buchan	£1.25
☐ A Prince of the Captivity	John Buchan	£1.25
☐ The Eve of St Venus	Anthony Burgess	£1.10
☐ Nothing Like the Sun	Anthony Burgess	£1.50
☐ The Memoirs of Maria Brown	John Cleland	£1.25
☐ A Man	Oriana Fallaci	£1.95
☐ Savannah Blue	William Harrison	£1.50
☐ Duncton Wood	William Horwood	£1.95
☐ The Good Listener	Pamela Hansford Johnson	£1.50
☐ The Honours Board	Pamela Hansford Johnson	£1.50
☐ Buccaneer	Dudley Pope	£1.50
☐ An Inch of Fortune	Simon Raven	£1.25

HAMLYN WHODUNNITS

☐ Some Die Eloquent	Catherine Aird	£1.25
☐ The Case of the Abominable Snowman	Nicholas Blake	£1.10
☐ The Widow's Cruise	Nicholas Blake	£1.25
☐ The Worm of Death	Nicholas Blake	95p
☐ Thou Shell of Death	Nicholas Blake	£1.25
☐ Tour de Force	Christianna Brand	£1.10
☐ King and Joker	Peter Dickinson	£1.25
☐ A Lonely Place to Die	Wessel Ebersohn	£1.10
☐ Gold From Gemini	Jonathan Gash	£1.10
☐ The Grail Tree	Jonathan Gash	£1.25
☐ The Judas Pair	Jonathan Gash	95p
☐ Spend Game	Jonathan Gash	£1.25
☐ Blood and Judgment	Michael Gilbert	£1.10
☐ Close Quarters	Michael Gilbert	£1.10
☐ The Etruscan Net	Michael Gilbert	£1.25
☐ Hare Sitting Up	Michael Innes	£1.10
☐ Silence Observed	Michael Innes	£1.25
☐ The Weight of the Evidence	Michael Innes	£1.10
☐ There Came Both Mist and Snow	Michael Innes	95p
☐ The Howard Hughes Affair	Stuart Kaminsky	£1.10
☐ Inspector Ghote Draws a Line	H. R. F. Keating	£1.10
☐ Inspector Ghote Plays a Joker	H. R. F. Keating	£1.25
☐ The Murder of the Maharajah	H. R. F. Keating	£1.25
☐ The Perfect Murder	H. R. F. Keating	£1.10
☐ A Fine and Private Place	Ellery Queen	£1.25
☐ The French Powder Mystery	Ellery Queen	£1.25
☐ The Siamese Twin Mystery	Ellery Queen	95p
☐ The Spanish Cape Mystery	Ellery Queen	£1.10

NON-FICTION

GENERAL
☐ The Chinese Mafia	Fenton Bresler	£1.50
☐ The Piracy Business	Barbara Conway	£1.50
☐ Strange Deaths	John Dunning	£1.35
☐ Shocktrauma	John Franklin & Alan Doelp	£1.50
☐ The War Machine	James Avery Joyce	£1.50

BIOGRAPHY/AUTOBIOGRAPHY
☐ All You Needed Was Love	John Blake	£1.50
☐ Clues to the Unknown	Robert Cracknell	£1.50
☐ William Wordsworth	Hunter Davies	£1.95
☐ The Famlly Story	Lord Denning	£1.95
☐ The Borgias	Harry Edgington	£1.50
☐ Rachman	Shirley Green	£1.50
☐ Nancy Astor	John Grigg	£2.95
☐ Monty:The Making of a General 1887-1942	Nigel Hamilton	£4.95
☐ The Windsors in Exile	Michael Pye	£1.50
☐ 50 Years with Mountbatten	Charles Smith	£1.25
☐ Maria Callas	Arianna Stassinopoulos	£1.75
☐ Swanson on Swanson	Gloria Swanson	£2.50

HEALTH/SELF-HELP
☐ The Hamlyn Family First Aid Book	Dr Robert Andrew	£1.50
☐ Girl!	Brandenburger & Curry	£1.25
☐ The Good Health Guide for Women	Cooke & Dworkin	£2.95
☐ The Babysitter Book	Curry & Cunningham	£1.25
☐ Living Together	Dyer & Berlins	£1.50
☑ The Pick of Woman's Own Diets	Jo Foley	95p
☐ Coping With Redundancy	Fred Kemp	£1.50
☐ Cystitis: A Complete Self-help Guide	Angela Kilmartin	£1.00
☐ Fit for Life	Donald Norfolk	£1.35
☐ The Stress Factor	Donald Norfolk	£1.25
☐ Fat is a Feminist Issue	Susie Orbach	£1.25
☐ Fat is a Feminist Issue II	Susie Orbach	£3.50
☐ Living With Your New Baby	Rakowitz & Rubin	£1.50
☐ Related to Sex	Claire Rayner	£1.50
☐ Natural Sex	Mary Shivanandan	£1.25
☐ Woman's Own Birth Control	Dr Michael Smith	£1.25
☐ Overcoming Depression	Dr Andrew Stanway	£1.50
☐ Health Shock	Martin Weitz	£1.75

POCKET HEALTH GUIDES
☐ Depression and Anxiety	Dr Arthur Graham	85p
☐ Diabetes	Dr Alex D. G. Gunn	85p
☐ Heart Trouble	Dr Simon Joseph	85p
☐ High Blood Pressure	Dr James Knapton	85p
☐ The Menopause	Studd & Thom	85p
☐ Children's Illnesses	Dr Luke Zander	85p

TRAVEL
☐ The Complete Traveller	Joan Bakewell	£1.95
☐ Time Out London Shopping Guide	Lindsey Bareham	£1.50
☐ A Walk Around the Lakes	Hunter Davies	£1.75
☐ Britain By Train	Patrick Goldring	£1.75
☐ England By Bus	Elizabeth Gundrey	£1.25
☐ Staying Off the Beaten Track	Elizabeth Gundrey	£2.95
☐ Britain at Your Feet	Wickers & Pedersen	£1.75

HUMOUR
☐ Don't Quote Me	Atyeo & Green	£1.00
☐ Ireland Strikes Back!	Seamus B. Gorrah	85p
☐ Pun Fun	Paul Jennings	95p
☐ 1001 Logical Laws	John Peers	95p
☐ The Devil's Bedside Book	Leonard Rossiter	85p

FICTION

CRIME/ADVENTURE/SUSPENSE

☐ The Killing In The Market	John Ball with Bevan Smith	£1.00
☐ In the Heat of the Night	John Ball	£1.00
☐ Johnny Get Your Gun	John Ball	£1.00
☐ The Cool Cottontail	John Ball	£1.00
☐ The Megawind Cancellation	Bernard Boucher	£1.25
☐ Tunnel	Hal Friedman	£1.35
☐ Tagget	Irving A. Greenfield	£1.25
☐ Don't be no Hero	Leonard Harris	£1.25
☐ The Blunderer	Patricia Highsmith	£1.25
☐ A Game for the Living	Patricia Highsmith	£1.25
☐ Those Who Walk Away	Patricia Highsmith	£1.25
☐ The Tremor of Forgery	Patricia Highsmith	£1.25
☐ The Two Faces of January	Patricia Highsmith	£1.25
☐ Labyrinth	Eric Mackenzie-Lamb	£1.25
☐ The Hunted	Elmore Leonard	£1.25
☐ The Traitor Machine	Max Marquis	£1.25
☐ The Triad Imperative	Dwight Martin	£1.50
☐ Confess, Fletch	Gregory Mcdonald	90p
☐ Fletch	Gregory Mcdonald	90p
☐ Fletch's Fortune	Gregory Mcdonald	£1.25
☐ Flynn	Gregory Mcdonald	95p
☐ All the Queen's Men	Guiy de Montfort	£1.25
☐ Pandora Man	Newcomb & Schaefer	£1.25
☐ Skyfire	Thomas Page	£1.50
☐ The Last Prisoner	James Robson	£1.50
☐ The Croesus Conspiracy	Ben Stein	£1.25
☐ Deadline in Jakarta	Ian Stewart	£1.25
☐ The Seizing of Singapore	Ian Stewart	£1.00
☐ The Earhart Betrayal	James Stewart Thayer	£1.50

HISTORICAL ROMANCE/ROMANCE/SAGA

☐ Hawksmoor	Aileen Armitage	£1.75
☐ Pipistrelle	Aileen Armitage	£1.25
☐ Blaze of Passion	Stephanie Blake	£1.25
☐ Daughter of Destiny	Stephanie Blake	£1.50
☐ Flowers of Fire	Stephanie Blake	£1.50
☐ So Wicked My Desire	Stephanie Blake	£1.50
☐ Unholy Desires	Stephanie Blake	£1.50
☐ Wicked is My Flesh	Stephanie Blake	£1.50
☐ Lovers and Dancers	Michael Feeney Callan	£1.50

NAME ....

ADDRESS ....

....

Write to Hamlyn Paperbacks Cash Sales, PO Box 11, Falmouth, Cornwall TR10 9EN.

Please indicate order and enclose remittance to the value of the cover price plus:

U.K.: Please allow 45p for the first book plus 20p for the second book and 14p for each additional book ordered, to a maximum charge of £1.63.

B.F.P.O. & EIRE: Please allow 45p for the first book plus 20p for the second book and 14p per copy for the next 7 books, thereafter 8p per book.

OVERSEAS: Please allow 75p for the first book and 21p per copy for each additional book.

Whilst every effort is made to keep prices low it is sometimes necessary to increase cover prices and also postage and packing rates at short notice. Hamlyn Paperbacks reserve the right to show new retail prices on covers which may differ from those previously advertised in the text or elsewhere.